DON'T BEND

PRAIRIE COVE ONE

E. S. LOUIS

ISBN: 978-0-578-46526-5

Don't Bend was first published in 2018 by Mill City Press under the title **Prairie Cove I: Don't Bend**. This *revised edition* (**Don't Bend**) has been re-edited by the author.

ACKNOWLEDGMENTS

To my wife, Lee Pierce,
the Artist who my mother said adores me, who filled my life
with opportunities beyond my wildest dreams.

DEDICATION

I dedicate this first book in the "Prairie Cove" series to the
noble women and men who are professional law enforcers
who put body, mind, and soul at "policing" and who understand
the difference between "Community Policing" and "Soldiering."

CHAPTER 1

Welcome to the Realm of Saha

"Bravo-Tango-Two to Dispatcher."

"Dispatcher...go ahead BT-2."

"We're on foot...in pursuit of a Puerto Rican male...wearing a blue jacket...east on Harrison Street...inside Fairview Park parking lot...headed towards golf course and Veteran's Parkway... wanted for holding up Harrison Liquors this morning...looks like...he's making a run for the Veteran's Parkway area near Bascomb Boulevard Day Care building."

"BT-4. We see them coming in our direction on Bascomb. Suspect is a black male wearing a light...baby blue jacket, making for the Bascomb School yard. Belay that transmission. Suspect just entered the front yard of a white house, mid-block, going into the backyard."

Bang! Bang!

"Prairie Cove Operations: 2245 hours: October 4, 1973."

"BT-4. Shots fired... Shots "Bravo-903-Alpha to dispatcher""

"Dispatcher. Go ahead 903.

"I'm Adam Robert, arrived on-scene."

"Roger that, 903"

"Well. What have we got here," asked the B903A, Sgt. Mike

1

Gisby, looking at Hampton who, by far, is the most ominous presence at the scene, a few inches taller than his partner Big Daddy Wright.

"It ain't our shooting, Sarge. You might want to talk to those two over there," offered P.O. Hampton.

"Torio, DiSalvo; I see a body. Talk to me. Where's his weapon," asked Sgt. Gisby.

"We haven't found it yet, Sarge," answered DiSalvo.

"What kind of shit...? B903A to dispatcher," said Sgt. Gisby into his Walkie-Talkie.

"Yeah, go ahead 903."

"Can you switch over to admin channel?"

"As we speak, Sarge."

After Sgt. Gisby switched over, "B903 to dispatcher."

"Go ahead 903."

"Can you assign me a couple of available service units or a two-man unit, along with the wagon, tech support and EMTs to my shooting scene here? Also, dispatcher, we're gonna need a lighting truck."

The dispatcher complied with the request, and a search of the area was conducted with each officer using their flashlight along with the lighting truck sweeping the whole area over the course of one-hour. By this time Homicide and a reporter from the town's one newspaper also arrived at the shooting scene which was taped off with yellow "Police" tape.

"Which one of you two miscreants was the shooter," asked Sgt, Gisby as Wright and Hampton continued combing the immediate area with the other officers.

"Sarge, I think... I think I was," mumbled Torio.

"You 'think'," asked Gisby. "Whatchu got; shit for brains or something? We've got a fucking dead man who was laying up in here; with fucking newspaper reporters sniffing all around edging to break the tape, and the best you two bimbos can come up with is a 'think'? FBI's gonna have fun fucking you two in the ass and sending youse up the Wazoo. Then this poor guy's family's gonna have orgasms suing the living fuck out of one or both of you two maggots, the department and the entire City of Prairie Cove. All I can say is, somebody better come up with more than a 'think' before we leave here, or asses are gonna fry. Francis, keep those reporters back from my crime scene; and I want a report from every swinging dick that comes beyond my tape."

Eventually, one of the cops inside the tape did come up with a .380 automatic pistol "found" some ninety minutes later underneath a car still parked at the curb, right across the street from where the "suspect's" body was originally found.

Back in Time

Now let's go back in time from this shooting scene for a while to January 1946 in the United States where two "black" girls had the great good fortune to be born and raised by wise, resourceful, and loving parents in the scraggly Texas panhandle region. The parents, Austin and Mary Alice Hampton, had the deep love and good sense to stick together like velcro. They did everything they could to properly raise their big-mouth, narrow-minded fourteen and fifteen-year-old daughters into adulthood without either of them losing their virginity in wedlock.

The girls, named Queenesther "Queenie" and Mayethel "May-May" Hampton, were born only about ten months apart when Austin and Mary Alice were newly-wed teenagers. As a matter of fact, Austin said "I do" at the point of Mary Alice's father Dallas Davis' double barreled shotgun just two days before that first\eldest girl Queenie was born.

Ever since that very day, Austin swore he would have married Mary Alice without the imposition of her father's shotgun. Yet and still, Mary Alice's abdomen was swollen up so big that initially the Humane Society of Texas wanted to prosecute Austin for the commission of an Aggravated Sexual Rape. About nine months earlier, Mary Alice bum-rushed poor Austin and had her way with the naïve and terribly shy eighteen-year-old Austin the

3

day after her eighteenth birthday. So, the charge of Rape never was even a factor here.

Austin got off being tried and convicted, because the Texas high court found that, "The Humane Society of Texas lacks standing to bring forth any charges against either one of the parties. Nigras are considered the same as livestock; and the size of their heifer's bellies ain't none of law-abiding white folks' business, no-how. We cain't be bothered with other folks' kids. We cain't even rustle up enough cowboys to drive these longhorn calves. Besides," the high court further declared, "big roebuckin' nigras are the backbone of Texas society. Try gittin' a longhorn to pick peas and cotton. It won't work. The poor sombitch ain't got no hands!! Besides, you start interfering with these big, long-shanking black bastards, next thang you know, they'll all be over here a-groveling and a-groping after our precious white womens...knocking all of the walls out of all the sweet white pussy. If one of us go to mount one of our busted-up white wenches, it'll be like sticking your pecker into a sink hole with an echo. You'll wind up swearing before God All Mighty that you're gittin' sucked in, all the way to hell. Y'all gwone home now. Mind your own business; and leave them nigras to figure their mess out for their own selves. Case dismissed."

Yet, and still, when you get right down to it, a pregnancy can do a big number on a pretty girl's body. Especially if that self-same young mama is about to birth a child sired by a great big six-foot-six inch tall galoot the likes of Austin Erasmus Hampton. A big sasquatching roebuck like that can easily turn "eye candy" into an eye sore. Yet barefoot, coming in at pretty-near five-feet-ten, Mary Alice Hampton wasn't nobody's Shorty-Arty, either. She put something on that big ole boy's ass! He thought he had the U.S.D.A. burrowing beef, but she served his ass up like breakfast pork chops.

Of course, back in the mid-1940s, medical science wasn't advanced enough to tell a couple if they were birthing a boy, or a girl, or a tumor. All the Davis family knew was that poor Mary Alice girl was liable to get busted up by delivering something mighty big, coming in at anywheres well over a couple of feet long to Heaven-only-knows how big. All throughout the rest of her life, Mary Alice would constantly remind her own two daughters of the hours she spent in labor, bearing both of them; screaming and cussing out Austin and the midwife; hollering and hollering things like, "Bitch, I don't care if you have to cut my damned head off; just git this mothuhfuckuh out of my ass!"

And if that didn't beat all, that last-born Hampton gal, that fast-assed May-May, carried her fat ass up to Prairie Cove, Illinois, and out-did her older sister Queenie by being Mary Alice's first daughter to become a mama; an unwed mama at that. And if that didn't beat all, young May-May Hampton spat out worrisome-assed twin girls. She named them Maimee and Maggie Lee Hampton, in their granddaddy Austin's last name. Their own daddy Willie Pickens out-ran Austin's shotgun.

Of course this was before "black" women started going gaga in child birth and naming their kids with first names that sounded like those weird new prescription drugs the doctors gave them to bear the kids. With their minds numb with that prescription dope, those poor moms had to be reading the medicine boxes to come up with names sounding like Ubiquinol, Thorazine and Coco-Quinine for their newborn kids. But Austin and Mary Alice didn't play that mess. May-May had already made a mess of her life by dropping drawers too soon. So they were determined that she wasn't gonna make a mess of these new baby's lives by hanging one of them weird sounding names on them.

Yeah, boy. That May-May Hampton may have been a kind of slow thinker, but she was one fast young heifer on the draw...or should I say out of the drawers.

To Queenie, her sister May-May's giving birth to those twins was worse than having to go through a total hysterectomy. Having her younger sister jump past her into womanhood by pre-emptively activating her womb, was the supreme slap-in-the-face. This act alone guaranteed and certified that May-May was by Texas state law, a "grown-assed woman"; and "cherry-assed Queenie" was still nothing but an "unliberated child."

Adulthood

May-May never ceased rubbing the facts into Queenie's face that to her, Queenie was still a child along with May-May's twins. May-May constantly said things like, "Child, I am free, black, and grown; and the mama of twins. Bitch, unless you can make it into Jet or Ebony magazine for having triplets, you can't be no more woman than that."

And those twins? By the year 1946, when they were about five years old, it was plain to see that they were destined to grow up to be worse than the two-headed hound that guards the gates of hell. According to their mother May-May, they could do no wrong. No matter if they both hauled off and slapped the living stew out of you, you weren't supposed to put your hands on them. You were expected to tell May-May about it, and she would "deal" with them. Yeah. Right.

Now, all throughout this mess, May-May's mama Mary Alice, being a stay-at-home housewife and mama, had to bear witness to all of this crap. Finally, one day in total exasperation, while she and Austin were alone, poor Mary Alice broke down crying, "Aw, Austin, I am so thankful to the Lord that May-May finally raised up off of her big trifling ass, and decided to go back up north to Prairie Cove, Illinois with them worsome-assed twins. Why did we go and let that child spend that summer vacation up there. If we had kept her ass at home down here with her sister, she wouldn't have gotten pregnant. I can't be bothered with baby-sitting no worsome-assed kids!"

"I hear you talking, baby. But after all is said and done, she's damned lucky that a sucker like Levi Mabry came along and pulled her and the girls back up there to PC," said Austin. "I don't care what nobody says, he's a good nigguh; a bigger man than me. Ain't no way in hell I could put up with any more of that racket and aggravating bullshit. That gal and them damned twins is more than any one person can deal with. Say a prayer for old Levi. He's gonna need it. Hell, at 62-years-of-age, before them three get through with his rheumatoid arthritic old ass, he's liable to wind-up sitting on a stool; hugging hisself; a-rocking back and forth, banging his old bald head up against the wall; mumbling to himself in a corner; all cockeyed, blowing spit bubbles."

"Now Austin, he's a grown-assed man. He's the one who went panting after her young ass. That's his fault," added Mary Alice.

"I hope to shout," answered Austin.

"He knew how to draw up his own mouth and say 'no.' You didn't have to go over there after him, and poke that shotgun upside his head. He came a-crawling his old ass up to you, whining and begging for your pardon and permission for May-May's hand," replied Mary Alice. "Of course he was lying like a gap-toothed 'gator, talking about how that gal 'took unfair advantage' of him. Even if he was laying up on his rusty old ass, he got it up to do the do. Know what I'm saying?"

"Aw, I hear you talking, baby. But nowadays, every time I come around him, he be mumbling, 'Pussy is a trap! Pussy is a trap.' I don't know if he's talking to me or the wall."

"I don't recollect ever hearing him say that," said Mary Alice. "But, it don't matter. Like I said before, he came a-sniffing and begged for it! Now he's working with them young men as a gandy dancer back out there on the railroad; busting his ass laying tracks and ties, trying to provide for that ungrateful heifer May-May and them greedy-assed twins. Poor old man's gone all week; but he damned sure turns his pockets inside-out and leaves the money at home with May-May, true-to-form, each and every Friday night."

"And gits a break from their aggravating asses four other nights out of the week. What a price to pay for freedom. Irregardless, he's man enough to go to work and pay for what he wants. Even a jackass deserves some credit for pulling the wagon without the crack of the whip," said Austin.

"Aw Austin, we need to stop making fun of them. He must really love her and them babies."

"Yeah, but they ain't his! And he keeps mumbling the same thing to hisself. If pussy is such a trap, why does he keep bringing all of his money back to it each and every weekend?"

"That's what a natural man is supposed to do when it gets good to him; praise the Lord, go to work; do the job; git the paycheck; and bring the 'bacon' home to 'mama,'" said Mary Alice.

"Ah-HA-Haaaaa! That'll plug-up a shotgun," said Austin.

Heaven's Priorities Supercede Ours

Like said before, Austin and Mary Alice Hampton raised their girls on that small patch of parched panhandle, prairie land that they leased from a landlord in Booney, Texas. But regardless of how hard they worked that soil and loved their daughters, their efforts just didn't seem to be enough to make a positive impression on their debt to that cut-throat landlord; to the Hampton family's financial status; or to their eldest daughter Queenie's determination to maintain her virginity.

No matter how those money-grubbing "black" preachers tried to explain it, Heaven never really had any regard for Judeo-Christian societal customs, norms, family planning, scheduling or intentions for their kids. Heaven seems to always have its own priorities and desires for all creatures to mainly "be fruitful and multiply"; even if it kills them. Maybe that's why a lot of folks are ravaged by torrents of hormones, mostly during our earlier years when we're young, dumb, and full of "it"; just like Austin and Mary Alice, and their two daughters Queenie and May-May.

In regard to the Hampton sisters, this hormonal phenomenon manifested once again. But it was brought on, this time, by Queenie's seeming determination to catch up with her younger, trash-talking sister May-May's attainment of adulthood, by getting rid of her own virginity as soon as possible.

"You know, your sister plans to be down here next weekend," Mary Alice informed Queenie.

"So—!"

"So, you're gonna be busy tending her kids. I keep telling y'all, I paid my dues: I cain't be bothered with no worsome-assed kids."

"MaDear, May-May is still a child herself; and younger than I am. What kind of fool do I look like? She can keep an eye on her own kids," retorted Queenie.

"The poor girl dropped two babies in one shot. She's finally coming home to visit us. Cain't you give your sister a break?"

"Aw, MaDear. How come you're, all of a sudden, feeling obligated to promote her ass," asked Queenie.

"Ain't nobody feeling no obligation to promote a damn thing," declared Mary Alice. "I'm just saying; I'm trying to get the members of my family to co-operate and support each other."

"Which means, you're just trying to cultivate more grandbabies for you and MyDaddy."

"Never mind grandbabies. I'm just trying to promote all of my babies into taking on the responsibilities of being grown-assed women like they're always claiming. Since your sister May-May moved up there to P'Cove, me and your daddy got a break, and wound up with one less mouth to feed. And seeing how big your ass is growing, you alone are about to eat us out of house and home: be throwing down more and more chow each and every day. It's just about time for your ass to git grown for real, and you get up and get the hell out of here, too."

"Aw, I get it. MaDear's turning into a nookie bookie, instigating on the side lines, just to save money."

"Nawl. 'MaDear' is just speaking the truth of life. Me and your daddy ain't getting any younger. It's gittin' time for all of you 'grown-assed women' to work together and tend to your own responsibilities."

"Thanks MaDear. Where am I going to find a man of my own kind out here in the middle of nowhere? Guess I may as well back my behind up under a mule," said Queenie.

"Where you hike up your behind is your prerogative. Maybe you can be nice to your sister, and go back with her up to PC and hike your 'grown-ass' up there in Illinois. They got more nigguh mens up there than you can shake your fat ass at. That's got to be why they named that town Prairie Cove; with all them long-strokin' sombitches in one place, they ain't got enough bedrooms. So, nigguhs be humping all out in the prairie in them coves along the Mississippi and Illinois Rivers."

"I can see right now that nothing I say is gonna make any sense to you. You're on a tear. And I'mo take me a walk. Bye-bye," said Queenie.

"That's your best bet, 'cause I'm about one second off of slapping the red piss out of me some smart-ass 'grown-ass.'"

And with that, Queenie stomped right out of the house, letting the spring-loaded screen door slam shut with a bang. She wisely kept stomping her way over the next ridge, because she knew that as nice and mild-mannered as Mary Alice Hampton was, Mary Alice was liable to blow up like a raging, dog-faced baboon when responding to sassmouth from one of her overbearing, obnoxious, bodacious daughters.

The Face-off

Two days later, Queenie's sister May-May and her twins finally arrived from PC.

"Y'all go on out there in the yard and play. And watch out for them damned gila monsters and rattlesnakes. I cain't be sucking no poison outta y'all's asses," shouted May-May to the girls. "Now. How's my virgin-assed, no-humping, childless, big sister been doing," May-May asked as she spun around to face Queenie and look her dead into the eyes. "You been staying out of trouble or gittin' you some?"

"Cain't you say 'hello', before showing your big ugly ass," asked Queenie.

"I just call a spade a spade you ignorant, grunting heifer," replied May-May.

"Keep running your mouth, I'mo be grunting upside your bitch-assed head with that spade MyDaddy's got out there on the back porch."

"MaDear always says that in a clench, when trying to fend for yourself, don't be fucking around with peoples, and you shouldn't pick up nothing you cain't eat. Bitch, I'll be using that spade to bury your sorry ass," retorted May-May."

"You crocodile-mouth heifer; if you even thought you could pull that shit off, you would apologize to me," said Queenie.

"Y'all hush!! I don't care how grown you both think you are. I'm still the bigger woman 'round both of you. Anybody be whuppin' ass, or wielding spades up in here, it's gonna be me," insisted Mary Alice.

Obviously amongst the Hampton women, pregnancy was the trump card defining the real moment of womanhood. Even Austin butted in, "Shoot. Even a monkey can have a period. To be a real woman, you've got to be somebody's mama. I'm just saying."

"And I'm just saying, men folks should keep their two cents to themselves when women folks are quantifying and qualifying each other. It's bad enough with men trying to be like us; dress like us; and try to make us to look like a skinny, pancake-assed boy. Now you guileless sombitches are trying to define us," stressed Mary Alice. "Next thing you know, y'all be getting married and trying to conceive kids up in your nasty asseholes. That's when women will have to take your dumb asses out back of the coal shed and put you out of your misery."

"Now, Mary; that's enough, now. Sometimes you go too far. It's bad enough we mens have to succumb to the power of pussy, and your daddys' shotguns. Now you're talking about arming women to regulate men. Next thang you know, you females will be making babies outta spit, without a man and swearing God is a woman."

"So—" blurted out all three Hampton females in unison.

CHAPTER 2

Tex-Mex

Mary Alice always warned Austin Hampton, "Baby, I love and respect our daughters, but if either one of them was to get wounded in the head, there wouldn't be no blood seeping out. All that would flow down their faces would be a steady stream of tiny dicks. Between Queenie's raging hormones and determination to have sexual intercourse, both of us and God Almighty in Heaven know it's just a matter of time before some poor-assed cowboy down here gets rustled by her overbearing, obnoxious insistence upon having her way."

"Shoot. It seems like it was only yesterday I was stressing out from losing our youngest baby, May-May, to unwed motherhood. Now, I know damn well, from the same signs, that I am assuredly facing absolute disregard and disgrace in another dose. These girls are about to drive me insane from trying to ride shotgun over their horny asses…especially this oldest and biggest one," moaned Austin. "But at least I've got one thing working in my favor: there ain't no other negro men within 100 miles of our homestead. All that's out there on that scrub-assed prairie is tumbleweeds, rattlesnakes, wild hogs and a sprinkling of cockeyed, half-breed crackers and dipped-shit Mexican males. And those kinds of fellows are only interested in humping chickens, and stump-jumping longhorn cattle...don't make no difference if it's a bull or a heifer. It don't make no never-mind to them dumb sombitches; just so long as it ain't no colored wench."

"Humph. So you say," muttered Mary Alice under her breath.

Austin was further confident that, "None of them crackers has got balls enough to try to wallow with a big ole collard green eating, gooch-eyed, nappy-headed colored gal who has B-B shots and quinine knots on the back of her neck for a hairline."

But, as time passed, little did Austin know that Queenie Hampton was becoming more dead-set on jumping on whatever would hold still. So it may as well have been whatever kind of male who would come along. Bless her heart, she earnestly didn't know no better. That poor, ignorant woman-child grew more and more frustrated with just playing with herself. Afterwards, she always used to moan and groan, "I-have-my-needs!"

Well, anyway, she finally caught sight of her first victim; one of those "white" and "brown" hybrids, locally called a Tex-Mex... a real ridge-running, stump-jumping, chicken-humper from some sod-house out on the prairie. Truth be told, the dog-eyed sombitch spotted her first with his one silver-blue eyeball and other brown eyeball. On this day, around high noon, he was out riding on the range, minding his own business, on his old sway-backed mule named Otha, when he spotted Queenie's big brown ass; all alone, down at the creek; scrubbing the clothes she wore on the rocks.

Tex-Mex Recon

There she stood in perfect, buck-naked splendor. As big as this woman was, she looked as though she didn't have an ounce of fat on her. With itty-bitty titties and great thick thighs, at five-feet-eleven inches tall and weighing about one-hundred-seventy-five pounds, she had a washboard abdomen, with an exquisitely curvaceous, pear-shaped body like some kind of an elite athletic, high-hurdling, half-horse, female centaur. Her body was so breath-takingly beautiful that that poor cockeyed Tex-Mex boy slid down off his jackass; dropped straight down to his knees; and sat back on his haunches, at the same time, kind of like that stubborn mule did as though he said, "Aw, fuck this shit!" and he got fed-up with that dumb-assed boy yanking on his reins, jostling around on his sore back.

That half-breed, melanated fool-boy and his honery jackass both just sat there on the side of the ridge, one dumbfounded and the other exhausted, squatting on their haunches with their dicks dug into the dirt...the Tex-Mex had a hole in the crouch of his britches. That jackass started to bare his teeth, just a-braying, "Haw. Haw. Hee-Hawww!"

Queenie's face may not have been that fancy, but her finely chiseled body could make a dead man's "Johnson" stand at full erection, breaking through the ground all the way from six feet under. Now, that's the power of pussy, partner. Queenie knew this, and started to strutting and profiling like the cock-of-the-rock in a ditty-bop parade. When she caught sight of that ugly-assed boy gawking at her, she didn't even have the decency to bother to cover herself up. She just stopped and stood there with her hands on her hips; feet apart at shoulder width; and her legs kind of hyper-extending, bowed back a bit at the knees in a power-pose; flexing her haunches and quads: with them itty-bitty titties pointing straight at that old dumb-assed boy. If it wasn't for that mule, that fool would have been lost.

He finally snapped out of his stupor, and tried his damnedest to crawl over and cower behind a bramble bush while trying to hide his thing, and shut that ignorant animal up from making all of that racket like he was some kind of tornado siren.

"Who dat? Who dat? What you lookin' at boy? Cain't a woman have no privacy," feigned Queenie.

"I...duh... I... Uh-ruh," was all he could get out of his mouth. He sounded like he had a mouth full of marbles with a wad of cotton stuck in his throat.

Queenie rapidly sauntered up the ridge to him, and snatched the jackass' reins from his hands. With one powerful pull of the snaffle bit to the roof of the ass' mouth, she yanked the beast up off his rump and onto its four feet. She then led old Otha over another few yards and tied him to an adjacent scrub tree. Still staring at the boy, Queenie mimicked him saying, "'Duh-h-h. Uh-ruh-h.' Are you supposed to be talking to me or mocking the damned jackass? Or maybe something's wrong with your mouth and you're just tongue-tied? ... Well? Are you just gonna stay stoopin' back there on your ass, like you're trying to take a dump; looking more stupid than this fool mule of yourn?"

He was realizing the universal power of nature; but she was just beginning to realize the raw physical power of her body on a man for the first time in her life. She was getting more cock-sure, brazen, smug, horny, and conceited by the minute. She right away sensed his lack of self-confidence as a further sign of her total domination of the situation. She slowly reached up and started caressing her small breasts, and rubbing her hairy belly and powerful thighs. Yes, her pubic hairs were thick and nappy, covering not only her vaginal area, but also her thighs and buttocks. All she needed was some hoofs, and you'd swear she was a hybrid horse...a centaur, for real. Her nostrils flaring, she cooed, "Um-hmm. Boy, look at you. You keep staring at me, one of your old cockeyes is gonna pop right out of they socket."

"Now, loo-looka here gal. I ain't bothering nobody. I'm m-m-minding my own business. You cain't be telling me what to do with my eyes. I ain't loo-loo-looking for no trouble, now."

"Then, what's that poking out of your pants from 'tween your legs; a kick-stand or a crank-shaft?"

"Looka here, now gal. I reckon if a naked woman snatches a man's mule from him and ties the sombitch up to a tree, and be hanging something out there all up in the poor man's face...long's I ain't touching nothing or nobody, you cain't be telling me what to do with my eyes! Go'on now girl. Ain't nobody bothering you."

Recon Compromise

By this time, the sassy Queenie was standing right over him with her nappy loins only inches away from his face. "Boy, ain't nobody studying you or your damn eyes. Judging by what's poking out from between your legs, you got something bodacious on your mind. Yeah, you're thinking you're the man; man enough to work this! Well, here it is Mister; looking dead at you, all up in your face. Whatchu gonna do? Keep sitting there on your haunches: whining like a bleeding bitch or be the man you're yearning to be?"

Although he was about ten years older than her, she was about five inches taller and around fifty-five pounds heavier than him. He was so paralyzed and submissive, he was like a whimpering baby in her hands, afraid she was going to drop him.

Recon Surrender and Capture

"Boy, what's your name anyways?"

"Sh-Sh-Choate."

"What?"

"B-B-Buddy Choate. Spelt with a capital 'C-h' that sounds like 'S-h.'"

"There you go again with that childish-assed stuttering. What the fuck's wrong with you any ways, nigguh; You the product of some kind of in-breeding or something? You're so weak and dufous, you act like a suckling pig."

"Why I got to be a pig. You come fucking with me. I was minding my own business...wasn't bothering you. How'd you like it if I hauled off and called you a dumb..."

"Yeah. Go ahead. Say it, and I swear before God and all the stars above, I'll knock all of the rest of your teeth down your throat. Whatchu think your name Choate means, fool? A choate is a baby pig."

"Be that as it may. Yet and still, if you just haul off and try to slap me just on general principles, I'mo try my damnedest to knock all your teeth out, too," vowed Choate.

"You see that ridge over yonder?"

"So?..."

"My daddy is just on the other side of it. Whatchu think Austin Hampton gon' do when he hears me a-hollerin', and comes a-running over that ridge with his shotgun and sees your lil' hybrid ass laying pipe up his favorite daughter's naked ass?"

Saving Face

And just like that, she thrusted her camel toe right into his nose, nudging his head back so far that he was resting on both shoulder blades while she squatted down over him. With his nose jammed shut, he was forced to breathe through his mouth. He commenced to bucking, kicking, and whimpering, "Aw, my Lord, sweet Jesus. Will Rogers. Ef-Dee-Aura. I swear; and I do declare. Lord, take me to the water. I do believe I'm 'bout to be baptized!! Aw, help me. Lord, please help me; somebody please..."

And with that, she started to grinding her hips and humping real hard on his face: only this time she was on all fours, ramming his head back down into the Johnson grass. Even a blind man could see that by this time, she was a humping maniac; a merciless savage. She now knew full well that she had total absolute power over him.

Although he was a few years older than her, she was about five inches taller and around fifty pounds heavier than him. Still grinding her hips into his face, she reached back clenching his erection so hard, his eyes straightened up and looked like they were about to explode in his head. He was so stunned and submissive, he was like a whimpering baby in her hands, begging for a diaper change.

That overbearing, obnoxious, smug and conceited gal spun around backwards on his face and was all over him like a monkey on a football; pawing, gripping, nuzzling, squeezing, rubbing, kissing, licking, sucking, squirting and humping in erratic spasms. "Um-hmm. Yeah. Mothuhfuckuh, you mines! Jest keep a-laying there like a bump on a log, and I'mo set your lil' narrow ass on fire; hump you 'til your mothuhfuckin' nose bleeds. Send your little sawed-off ass crawling back home to your mammy, draped over your mule like a Indian blanket, sucking one thumb in your mouth and with the other one up your ASS! You like my pussy? Like my pussy??"

"Yeah! Yeah!! Yeah-Yeah!!! OKAY – OKAY!" screamed the poor boy.

This time, while in transition, without even losing a beat, she snatched his raggedy trousers to his ankles, and dragged her crotch from his face to his scrotum in one stroke. She was really rough with him. At the hookup, she was all humpbacked, gripping every inch of that poor helpless young man: first rimming his dickhead around her labia major, then inside and deeper around her labia minor, and then sinking it in, grinding him down to the A-bone.

In a high pitched falsetto, Buddy started screaming, "Oh-My-God. I'm gonna cum! I'm gonna CUM!!" But her strokes got to be too long and his little wee-wee popped out. She was still humping the air, squirting, grunting and squealing like a spastic wart hog separated from its sow in the midst of full-blown coitus.

"Boy, if you don't hurry up and git that little stump back in there, I'mo be whupping your little ass like you my redheaded stepchild. What's your problem anyways?"

In one last act of desperation, Choate called out to Otha, "Yhaa-a, boy. Here, Otha." When the jackass refused to respond, Choate commenced to whimpering again, "Aw, Dear Lord. Help me! Please, please help me Lord Jesus... Oral Roberts... Roy

Rogers... Will Rogers. I swear, and I do declare, y'all git my dick outta this gumbo, and my nuts outta this sand, I swear before God and all the stars of Heaven that I'll never fool around with another black assed female as long as I live. Y'all git me outta here, and I'll do what you will."

Disarmed

Never-the-less, Buddy always maintained a certain small amount of pride. He presented himself more like a true cowboy, with Otha as his imaginary horse; always mumbling to himself, like he truly believed it, "Once a man starts something, I reckon he ought to finish it."

By now, Queenesther was nuzzling her nose all up into his scrotum. And he was starting to huff and puff again like a steam locomotive. He got kind of nervous, based on his lack of experience with human female sex. "Uh-uhm! Uh-uhm! If the good Lord meant for us to carry on this way, he'd have made your nose into a quinnie," he said as he sat up and pulled back from the frustrated Queenie.

"Aw, you wants to play grab-ass? Queenie's got a quinnie for your little monkey dick. Yeah, sugar. It's kind of wet..." started Queenie.

"Gad damn!! You cummin' all over my dick. Yeah, girl. All this ass; bring it back home to daddy," said Choate.

All of a sudden, he was twitching and blinking again, and collapsed all spastic, and whining when she bucked him off her. Savagely, she reached out and grabbed him by his dirty sun-bleached hair and said, "That's all you got cowboy? Aw, nawl, suckuh. You cain't be wimping out on me like this. I was waiting on the big bang like my sister said."

"If your sister's ass is as big and powerful as yourn, there's another broke-back sombitch leaning on his knuckles out here somewheres. I know a man ain't supposed to cry, but gaddamn; I ain't no stone Buddha or a big strapping roebuck like your people. Give a poor midget, Tex-Mex chicano a break. At least be patient, and break my lil' ass in slow. There's supposed to be a method to every kind of madness."

It was pitiful how that poor boy started to begging and whining again as she buried his face into her crotch, he started whaling, "Aw, my sweet Lord. Jesus, help me. Help me somebody please. I cain't breathe… I cain't breathe!! Sons of the Confederacy, Gene Autry, Santa Ana. Make this big bovine fuck-monster let me go. Lord, I don't want to die out here like this. She won't let me catch my breath. I cain't breathe. I cain't breathe."

She mocked him as she shoved him down; locked his head between her massive quads by crossing her ankles; and commenced to grinding in his face again, "'Once a fella starts something, I reckon he ought to finish it,' one way or another, mothuhfuckuh."

"Bitch! Gimme a chance. Gimme a chance. I cain't learn nothing if I'm dead!"

This kind of wrestling and grab-ass went back and forth for a little while longer until he caught his breath. Old Buddy finally broke loose of her scissors-like grip; hitched up his britches; untied and mounted Otha; and commenced to trying to high-tail it off into the horizon. But due to the pronounced sway in Otha's back, and his persistent hard-on, the mules' dick was once again plowing the dirt. So Choate had to dismount and run along beside the poor sombitch to get up some speed.

Just before their two asses made it to the crest of the next hill, Queenie, still lying there on her side, yelled, "See you tomorrow; same time; same place. Better drink some milk and eat some spinach, 'cause your little narrow ass is gonna need it. If you be late, I'mo ride your jackass' ass off into town with you roped and running behind, and me telling every honkey and chicano I see that you been all up inside me…every which-away but loose."

"Yeah. And then, I'll just stand there and watch them string your ignorant black ass up from a second floor railing. If it ain't no crime to hang a nigger, it for damn sure ain't no crime for a Tex-Mex half-breed to git some nigger pussy. Only ones be mad is your mammy and your pappy. Adios, Amiga. See you soon. Ha-Haaa." And with that, Choate and Otha disappeared over the crest of the hill, both kicking up rocks and a cloud of dust.

Queenie washed out her ass; finished with washing her clothes, and headed on back to her daddy's little shack with its dirt floors.

CHAPTER 3

An Accounting

"Where you been, gal?" asked Austin. "Your mama's been worried stiff."

"Aw MyDaddy, I was just down at the creek taking a bath and washing my clothes."

"Half the day into the sunset, just to wash your ass and a few measly-assed clothes? Whatchu comin' down with; arthritis or rheumatism or something?"

"No sir. After that, I waited around and let myself dry off and…and rewashed the clothes some more just to git out some…"

"Alright, alright. Save it for your mama," said Austin. Just because Queenie was acting like a fool, didn't necessarily mean that her daddy was genetically encoded to be one, also. Austin stopped asking questions and started paying more attention to her comings and goings: like noticing that creepy Choate boy hanging around the ridge near the Hampton spread one time too many. Since his jackass Otha contracted a serious urinary tract infection behind his genitalia always dragging in the dirt, Choate had to walk by the Hampton spread a few times until the infection went away. Queenie's threat scared the boy so bad, he felt obligated to follow her orders and show up precisely when and where she told him.

An old proverb holds that when some people live in hell so long, they come to think of it as a rose garden. Even though Buddy Choate was a little Shorty-Arty, he was all Queenie had for her "needs." Queenie grew to look forward to meeting up with him; and being more and more amazed at how fast he could nail her sweet spot. And even though she was a senseless brute in the beginning who deliberately tried to bang up his body and mind, he still longed to be with her more and more as she settled down to grind it out in unison with him.

But, Choate failed to realize that experienced cock-blockers, especially fathers with more than one exquisitely built, hot-blooded daughter, manifest certain traits of paranoia relative to their daughters' suitors' dicks having no conscience. Nevertheless, Austin did well at hiding his suspicions by never asking anymore questions or uttering even a mumbling word about noticing that pussy-whipped hybrid boy and the dufous daughter's comings and goings. He was letting things pan out: giving them enough rope to hang themselves.

Who's the Fool

Buddy Choate was a full-grown man at twenty-seven years of age; and Queenie was a full-blown young woman at only sixteen years of age. Nevertheless, she got into Choate's head; and they started becoming more and more habituated toward each other as each day went by. The more he came back around her, the more demanding she became; and the more blind and foolish they both became. He, also, started getting so used to her that he began to demand to be with the willful young woman. He just didn't want anyone else to know about his business, and thereby stifle his chances of being inside her.

Choate got to be so beside himself that he started behaving as though he was addicted to her; not even having the common sense to know when to moderate himself or stop. Once she realized that she had made him this stupid, she knew she had the power over him. So, at this point, there were two fools...a female dominatrix and her male sapsucker. Neither one of them had the power of a responsible adult to get ahold of themselves and be more discreet about their rendevous.

Since the Alamo, the only thing appreciated about cross-breeding in Texas was mating donkeys and horses...to make cheap jackasses for dirt poor racist "cowboys." Things started looking like young Queenie and Choate were kind of sticking their necks out to make asses out of old Judge Roy Bean's interpretation of Texas law, and the very reason those thieving pirates fought and died stealing that dinky little Alamo from its rightful owners, the Mexicans.

Austin had enough sense to know that as much as he loved and cared for his daughters, he couldn't sit on top of them twenty-four hours a day; especially when the oldest daughter Queenie was acting stupid, in heat, and hell-bent on being the brood mare for and by humping anything that would hold still for her. Poor Austin Hampton wound up having to bend his back scratching a living out of that blanched Texas prairie soil to feed his poor family. He just believed that if he'd be good, the sweet Lord Jesus would take the matter into His hands and make a way for the Hamptons.

Well, it appears that sweet Lord Jesus did in fact take the matter into his hands. Folks around the Texas panhandle in those days believed that following Jesus represented Heaven's only Way. Men believed to be wise realized that getting horny was Heaven's main way of making humans carry out Heaven's will "to be fruitful and multiply." And people of all ages and eras all know that Heaven, once again, doesn't give any more of a damn about a father's plans for his precious daughter than It does for a bitch trying to raise her last puppy. Obviously, we humans are as expendable as straw dogs.

So when Queenie's belly began to rise, similar to how her

younger sister's belly had risen before hers, Austin forgot about Jesus; and decided to step up to the plate; and take the matter into his own hands. He grabbed poor Queenie by both shoulders and shook the whole truth out of her...well, some of the truth. She didn't admit to her father that she really, really liked that gooch-eyed hybrid boy. Austin would have commenced to choking and slapping her like a Sasquatch strangling an organ grinder's pet monkey.

Even when the ignorant girl's belly was really all swolled-up, that greedy, selfish, hybridized fool Choate wouldn't layoff tapping that black ass. As a matter of fact, he was hitting it so hard, fast, and constantly that on one summer night Austin sat bolt upright from a flat-out supine position in his bed, swearing to Mary Alice that he had just heard wild hogs rooting and squealing just over the ridge. He let off a couple rounds of buck shot in the air. Unbeknownst to him, those shots scared that old nasty boy so bad, he ran off and left his old dirty, funky britches and Otha. Naturally Otha commenced to hee-hawing his ass off; and Austin came investigating the spot just after Queenie ran back toward the house.

When Austin found those nasty old jeans, he cut Otha loose and caught sight of the swollen Queenie just disappearing around the bend, heading for the back door of the house. When he got back to the back stoop with the jeans, he handed them to Mary Alice saying, "I don't know. I reckon you better handle this one. I'm about to go loco on somebody's ass."

Although Austin never caught clear sight of that creep, the next few nights Austin laid low in the scrub brush waiting in Queenie's place for the dufous boy's return. Finally, on around the fourth night, the Choate fellow came skulking back, whispering in a soft falsetto voice,"Queenie? O-oooh, Queenie. Is my sweet piece of nigger meat ready for some more basting? Where you is, Sugar?"

Suddenly, Choate felt the bones in his neck popping as numbness overtook his body and his hearing began to fade; the last thing he heard was a voice in basso profundo saying, "HERE I IS, SUGAR. Now, hush your mouth and git some shut-eye."

On second thought, Choate couldn't have known what happened: he never made a peep or even a grunt. The snatch and pop of his neck was lightning fast like the strike of a king cobra and the death-roll of a crocodile combined. All in the same instant, Austin wrenched poor Choate's neck a second time in the same fashion that gangs of southern Caucasian males did when they cornered and lynched a lone "negro" male. Only here, there was no rope, no tree, and nobody pulling on his ankles to stretch his neck until the numbness and deafness took over. Just Austin snapping and popping Choate's neck with a death grip and simultaneous wrenching of his whole body as though he was a pair of wet Levi's 504 denim jeans being shaken out before they had a chance to dry all shrunken up.

Disposal

At six-foot-six inches in height Austin, during his baseball-playing days, was a well-respected catcher in the Negro Leagues of professional baseball. His ability to block base runners headed from third base for home plate was legendary. Not only could he receive the full force of the runner's body, stop him dead in his tracks and tag him out before he reached home plate; but when occasionally covering third base, he could follow through and throw the baseball to first or second base or home plate in the same motion, so hard, fast and accurate that the poor team mate catching his pitch would often scream from the sting of catching the pitch.

So, in the hands of Austin Hampton, Buddy Choate never suffered any sort of pain, giving him reason to scream.

After doing his deed, Austin hefted and roped-down the boy's lifeless corpse over Otha's back; led the ass over the ridge and about two miles out, away from the area of the Hampton homestead, into the lone prairie to where he had already dug a deep grave on the previous nights. It was in a desolate area frequented only by denisons like coyotes, buzzards, Gila monsters, and rattlesnakes. Otha seemed to know instinctively not to give this big Hampton fellow any grief. So, when Austin gave his ass a hand signal to stop, the ass damned-near made a screeching sound when he halted. He just stood there frozen like a bronze statue of Andrew Jackson's ass, not batting an eyelid; not flinching a muscle; not even breathing too hard. So it was just a matter of lifting the scrawny corpse up off of Otha's back and dumping it into the grave along with the saddle, blanket, reins, halter and martingale. Otha stood stark still, all bug-eyed and after a few moments, starting to quiver, almost like he thought his honery ass was next up to go into that deep hole. But once Austin laid down the shotgun, it was short shrift before the grave was covered.

He then turned to old Otha who right off began to shit, fart, and piss while standing in place, quivering like the Chicago hawk was blowing straight up his behind like a winter gale breeze blowing off of frozen Lake Michigan. Austin couldn't help but laugh out loud and tell the mule, "Simmer down, now son. Simmer down. Ain't nobody gonna do nothing to you, except...smack you cross your honery ass. Yhaa. Yha-a-a-a. Git the hell outta here!!"

If Secretariat had come running up to him at full Triple Crown speed, Otha would have been kicking rocks back in his face from a standing start. Aw, that sombitching jackass was high-tailing it and hauling ass faster than he had ever dreamed of running in his whole life. As he reached the top of the second ridge about two-hundred yards out, he stopped all of a sudden, and spun around bucking and kicking, and snorting; facing the howling Austin Hampton who by then was all doubled over in spasms of laughter. That smart ass drew back his lips, bared his teeth in a shit-eating grin; just a-screaming at the top of his lungs, "H-E-E--H-A-W. HEE-HAW!!!!"

Austin respectfully told him, "Go ahead on, boy. Go on. You're free, now. Happy trails to you."

Otha dipped his head, reared up on his hind legs like the Lone

Ranger's white horse Silver, bucking, snorting and kicking, and galloped off hee-hawing at full speed; ever so often bucking and kicking at the air in the moonlight.

People often talk about the cow that jumped over the moon. But on that full Harvest moon night, out on the lone Texas prairie, Austin Hampton could have sworn he saw a jackass jump over the moon…from the top of a ridge. No one could have told that poor man that he didn't see old Otha jump so high, he could have kissed the sky. Now that's some faith, hope and freedom for your ass.

Choate's Obituary

Seeing how Buddy Choate didn't seem to be too talkative about his private affair with Queenie Hampton, he never did any bragging about his "sweet piece of nigger meat." For a half-breed Tex-Mex boy in white supremacist Texas caste system, that would bring on a form of degradation among the dirt poor redneck and Tex-Mex women that was "lower than whale shit." And that was the grade of pretty near every cracker in the panhandle. Besides that, none of the "whites," "Indians" or Mexicans in the whole area of the lonesome prairie seemed to give two hoots about that nasty little gap-tooth boy, anyways. They had their own problems.

Buddy Choate was about as useful as titties on a longhorn bull. As it turned out, the few inhuman Caucasians who resided out there in that panhandle region who knew of him, never had anything to do with him. They never even missed him or the sound of his harmonica. He was considered an embarrassment and a detriment to the automatic assumption of supremacy that most redneck Texas males and wannabee Caucasoid Mexican males tried to project. As a matter of fact, most of these beings were about ready to lynch Choate for sniffing around after their gals, too. They kind of wished he would disappear anyway.

All said and done, nobody missed the shiftless Buddy Choate but that simple minded fool Queenie Hampton. And her daddy Austin made damned sure to put the fear of God in her ass, and told her to "Have a Coke and a smile, and shut the fuck up!" And anyway, around this time in 1946, the "white" folks were too busy thinking about further robbing, and double-crossing their new "niggers," the "Japs." This was like the second coming of the Oklahoma land rush where on the day of the rush, the first miscreant who reached the land and drove the stake would be given that land as his property. Only, some of the thieves "jumped the gun": went out the night before, and drove in their stakes into the ground sooner than the others. That's how the lying, hypocrites got the name Oklahoma Sooners. Wonder if they will ever give the property back or pay for it when they awaken to the truth that the real, original "Indians" included amongst their chieftains and fellow tribesmen the folks "white people" had been calling "African Americans," "Blacks," "Negroes," "Coloreds" and "niggers." These folks were already here in the Americas long before a "white man" or European even knew the hemisphere existed.

After all was said and done, it looks like those new Japanese "niggers" acted stupid, too; started turning their other cheek; and leaving it all in Jesus' hands the same way those dumb-assed "black niggers" did. This is a big part of what gave those lying, thieving, inhuman "whites" the eternal right to continue to spread their fake religion, laws, constitutions, snake oil, mule grease, and treaties to continue justifying their stealing other folk's land. Next thing you know, they'll be looking to swindle Otha and the cow that jumped over the moon: claiming "One step for man. One giant leap for mankind."

Pretty soon, we'll all be bamboozled into fighting World War III, still "defending" the trespasses of the United States billionaires by sending another generation of naïve American kids into other people's countries on suicide missions and wild goose chases against their citizens who will be called "terrorists" in their own land.

Rest in peace Buddy Choate. At least you died seeking pleasure, instead of stealing some other fool's treasure. We hope Austin planted your rancid ass deep enough in the ground so that the critters can't find you and scratch your ass up.

CHAPTER 4

Planning the Great Escape

Austin Hampton was by no means a wealthy man, but he faired pretty well in his teenage years playing catcher in the professional Negro Baseball League. He was in no way a flashy person or one of those fancy zoo suit-wearing types of young melanated hipsters. Neither was he pre-occupied with hanging out in juke joints, and lying up with his next piece of tail. Austin kept his head level; his hands in the soil; and his pecker in his pants. He thus kept enough of his baseball-playing money in his own stash to take care of himself and his eventual family. That's how he was able to lease the spread in Booney, Texas for little money. The homestead soil was too depleted for any sort of serious cultivation, so the dumb landlord leased it to the Hamptons who were his first tenants in over thirty years. That Texas prairie was the most lonesome place in Tornado Alley.

Being a frugal man, one of the few conveniences he allowed his family in the mid-forties was a telephone. He purchased one of the types that you see on the TV shows like "Lassie" and "Roy Rogers" that came in a wooden box; hung on the kitchen wall near the back door, with the mouthpiece affixed to it, and the earpiece strung from a cord.

31

No sooner than he got back to the house after burying Buddy Choate that night, Austin made his way to his wife Mary Alice to speak to her about calling her sister Anne Lee and his cousin Percival "Percy" Jarvis, a police sergeant up in Prairie Cove, Illinois.

Mary Alice's sister Annie Lee, who was Percy's wife, had always tried to convince Mary Alice and Austin to move up north to PC with their girls. That way Austin could join the police force with his cousin Percy. But now that Percy had been promoted, he was living well off of the police sergeant's pay. "I realize that we all come from down that way, but the lone prairie-ee ain't no place for lone Negroes to be," Annie Lee often teased the Hamptons.

And with Queenie's pregnancy meaning there would soon be one more mouth to feed down there in the Texas panhandle region, it began to make more sense to Mary Alice to talk to her husband Austin about making that move up to Prairie Cove. That night, before she could barely get into the explanation to her husband for the move, Austin was grinning and bucking like that jackass Otha had carried on when he was cut loose. Big old Austin kept chanting like a little boy, "Let's go. Let's go. Let's go." So Mary Alice repeated to Annie Lee how Austin behaved and what he kept saying. And when Annie Lee told her husband Percy the good news, Percy called his cousin Austin right back, bragging all over the phone. "Shoot, man. We can drive from up here in PC to down there in Booney in just a little over half a day. It ain't like folks is still driving Twenty Mule Team Borax conestoga wagons across virgin prairie land. A few hundred miles in a car on the super highway ain't nothing but an extended Sunday drive. When do you think y'all might be ready to go?"

"As fast as y'all can git down here," shouted Austin.

"Well, you know, considering how I've got this paid police detail to do, I've got one more day of work left, Annie Lee and me can be there in Booney the day after tomorrow, sometime in the evening... Saturday evening."

"Well, we'll be skipping out kind of early on the lease; but that's our prerogative, 'cause the lease is all paid up through next month. And we ain't got nothing else worth bringing but some pots and pans, our few clothes, some fried chicken, potato salad and banana pudding. Now mind you, I'm talking about some real banana pudding: the kind you make from scratch and bake: none of that ready-mixed chemical concoction from a box they be selling to y'all up there in PC. No wonder so many peoples up there be dying from that sugar diabetes and gout; dragging their asses around on their knuckles, and going blind."

"Well, hell! If you really wants to make a man grin like a monkey eating shit out of a light socket, then whup up a batch of that good ole Texas Bobby-Q, and bring it along too," suggested Percy.

"Ain't enough time. You know how colored folks don't like eating nobody's bloody red meat. Beef Brisket, done right, takes damn near a day in and out of the wrapper. Hell, if I ever served your black ass some bloody read meat, I'd die of shame seeing you puking up your guts and shitting all over yourself," said Austin. "Tell you what, though; we don't have to be down here in Texas for us to make you a batch of Texas Bar-B-Q. Soon's y'all hurry up and come get us the hell outta here, you'll be eating so much Texas-style Bar-B-Q beef, pork and chicken, right off your own back porch in sombitching Prairie Cove, that you'll be shitting that stuff outta your ears and nose from now on 'til the day you die. Now, what else you want...some champagne?"

"Awl, hell nawl! That weak-assed stuff tastes like panther piss laced with smack water and black strap molasses," moaned Percy. "Now, on the real side, old man Artis Garfield just brung me back a gallon jug of that Mud... Mississippi Mud from down 'round Bobo, Mississippi: corn liquor so smooth, you'll be cockeyed before you know what hit you," said Percy.

"Yeah. Like what happened to old Uncle Ernie," said Austin. "After guzzling down a few double-hookers of that shit, that old suckuh's eyes shut down on him. He damn near cried himself a river. Woke up one morning, two weeks later, and saw a cardinal sitting on the window sill beside his bed. He swore it was a miracle. To the day he died, he couldn't end a sentence without saying 'Praise the Lord; PTL.' Couldn't take two steps without toting that blue Masonic Bible, tucked up under his arm; with them red suspenders over his shoulders."

"That's all 'cause his greedy old ass got too happy suckin' that hooch," warned Percy. "You've got to sit back, settle down, and respect that shit. Sip it slow, and savor it, and it'll respect you for a while...git you to feeling all warm and cozy, and slap the living cowboy shit outta your happy ass."

"Ha-Ha-a-aaa. Boy, you ain't got no kind of sense, talking about your own peoples like that," teased Austin.

"See y'all Saturday evening; and by Sunday afternoon, we'll all be back up here in sweet home PC: and you and me be sitting out back on the porch: take out our teeth, and get cockeyed," said Percy.

"Ha-Ha-a-a-aaa," shouted Austin. "We'll be ready, willing and waiting. Remember how to get here?"

"Yeah; like I remembered how to get our asses the hell out of there back in 1936. Don't forget, we all grew up down there, way back when. Now, here it is 1946, and that still ain't no place for a working man to be. Them damned penny pinching peckerwoods want to work the hell out of a nigguh, and pay him off in peanuts. Up here, they got more good paying jobs than they've got men. They don't care if you're a holy rolling, ham-boning, buck-dancing nigguh or a Buddha-hugging, slant-eyed gook. A man can get fired from one shop and walk over across the street and get hired in another, all in the same day. They need people to make and lay these railroad tracks, bricks, sewer pipes and each and every goddamned thing else it takes to setup a hustling, bustling town. You may as well come git it while the gittin' is good. We'll be bringing y'all home on Saturday. That's all there is to it," swore Percy.

Now, Back to the Future

As was expected, by the fall of 1974, twelve months after Officer Torio took Mr. Otis Briscoe's life, the two "black" cops, P.O. Booker T. Hampton and P.O. Craig Wright, were never summonsed to give testimony in the "manslaughter" "trial" of P.O. Joseph Torio shooting Mr. Briscoe.

Torio opted for a jury-waived trial, where the judge makes the finding of guilty or not guilty.

The general feeling of the "judge" was similar to that of the police union and the rank and file of the PCPD; "support your local police" whether they are shown on tape shooting a "Black" man in the back of the head. Torio and DiSalvo were completely exhonerated and allowed to return to duty.

By the end of 1974, the civil complaint was filed. The Briscoe family settled out of court with the City and its police department by moving mother Briscoe and the rest of her family from the crowded project apartments, and relocating them into more spacious public townhouses out in the PC suburbs; and left them with a pittance after the two-faced racist attorneys gouged out their share of the settlement and the Briscoes paid the taxes.

Booker's "Sambo" partner Craig "Big Daddy" Wright bent to the pressure by selling out, speaking in Torio's favor, and being "meritoriously" promoted to the rank of Detective. But Booker scared the hell out of the department rank and file and Joey Torio; telling Torio in no uncertain terms, "Mothuhfuckuh, where ever you go, always be looking over your shoulder, because 'The Phantom Negro' will be watching you."

P.O Booker T. Hampton was unofficially labeled a renegade cop by the white police union, and black-balled from promotions and choice assignments for eleven years until a new police administration was brought in by a newly elected progressive mayor who instituted law enforcement reform.

Torio and DiSalvo were slowly re-inserted back into the patrol division and the melanated communities, because the "white" ones wouldn't tolerate their kind of "shit."

Now, Once Again, Back to the Past

True to form, that Saturday evening in June of 1946, Percy and Annie Lee Jarvis arrived and drove through the one-block long downtown section of Booney, Texas, and to about seven miles out on the other side of the town to the Hampton spread. They loaded up Austin, Mary Alice, and pregnant-as-all-hell Queenie, and drove the old Pontiac sedan back around the Booney town limits, out the state highway toward Prairie Cove, Illinois.

That hot Southwest summer sun was no problem, because it had started to set as they pulled off on their journey north. There were no "colored" toilets along the way back to Illinois, especially in places like Texas, Arkansas and around the boot heel of Missouri near the Illinois and Kentucky borders where the Ohio River meets the Mississippi River. So they stopped a few times, with the last stop in southern Illinois, to get some gasoline and relieve themselves behind some bushes. Luckily no cracker cops or peeping toms came along sniffing for money. The cops would have been called and the men would most likely have been robbed in the name of the "public ordinance" against dew-dewing in the woods while not being a bear, as sanctioned by some outlaw, illiterate "Justice of the Peace," with his paws out, looking for his cut of the innocent people's money.

It's a shame how un-American those "fellow Americans" were, back in those days and even today. It was like they were working in league with the Russian Communists and Nazi Germans. And at the same time, they expected everyone to pledge allegiance to the American Flag with them, while they wore their sheets and hailed their Confederate and Nazi flags. What a paradox; or maybe the U.S. is just that dumb?

Never-the-less, they kept the car rolling by Percy and Austin taking turns at the wheel. The two big men didn't want the women to drive, because if the crooked cops stopped the car, they most likely would have arrested the driver to justify the robbery, rape, etc. So Percy and Austin kept the car rolling along in relays like the old pony express. Just after sunrise the following day, they arrived safely in Prairie Cove on a pleasant, sunny Sunday. And true to form, Percy and Austin finally wound up sitting on the back porch smoking Texas Style Bar-B-Q spare ribs, beef brisquet, while sipping Mississippi Mud. But they both were so tired from the long drive that no sooner than they finished one glass of the homemade liquor, they both fell asleep.

The ladies were understanding enough to finish smoking the ribs and brisquet, and leave both of their tired men sitting where they fell asleep, all night. "I knew it. I knew it. Austin knows full well he cain't hold no liquor. Especially no dad-gum Moon Shine; with me trying to lug his big ass inside. Look at the poor baby laying back there drooling all on hisself. It's a wonder he ain't pissed on hisself, to boot," declared Mary Alice.

"Don't go counting your chickens before they hatch. Like Percy said, that Mud works in mysterious ways; and I didn't git the chance to put on Percy's rubber diaper or bib," giggled Annie Lee.

Adjustment

When Austin woke up the next morning and saw a cardinal sitting on the banister about fifteen feet away, he blurted out, "Lord, have mercy on my soul!"

Percy's eyes opened up just as Austin uttered the first word. He sat bolt-upright exclaiming, "What...what kind of shit?..."

"Aw, Percy. See there? You scared the little redbird away. Did you see it? Did you see it?"

"Nawl, fool. I wasn't the one who scared the damned thing off.

Only thing red I see is your blood-shot eyes. Come on, let's get cleaned up; we've got to get you down to the employment office and get you hooked up to a job. Never mind a sombitching early red bird on the bannister, the early "black" bird in the employment line gets the best job. I'll see you out front in fifteen minutes."

Austin was just grateful to escape the jurisdiction of the little back-country, Texas panhandle town; and avoid a possible lynching for killing that dim-wittedTex-Mex boy Buddy Choate. Being in Prairie Cove was like having a thousand pound weight taken off of his head. Now, all he had to face was getting a job, and watching his last foolish daughter swell up and give birth. Here he was, the thirty-seven year old father of two daughters under eighteen years of age, about to make him a grandfather a third or possible fourth time. "Lord, please don't let this be another set of twins," he moaned while shaving.

"We just deal with one day and one thing at a time. The Lord will make a way," vowed Mary Alice watching her husband while she ironed his work clothes.

"Yeah. And while we be busting our asses one day at a time, the Lord is dropping two babies at a time on nigguhs; all behind a dumb peckerheaded boy gitting some thrills on some dumb Hampton boodey. When the Lord said turn the other cheek, my daughters took Him literally, thinking He meant that after they dropped their drawers and turned one ass-cheek, they had a Heavenly duty to turn the other cheek of their boodey. Yeah. I get it: two sets of cheeks turning and churning, and two sets of twins falling out of the sky by a fool-assed stork. These sombitching twos are gonna be busting our asses; and we ain't even allowed to comment on this play," claimed Austin.

"Austin if you don't watch your mouth, you're gonna cause a giant hole to open up in the ground and suck us both to hell."

"After all that time and shit we put up with down there in Booney, ain't nobody scared of no devil. Ain't neither one of them, Jesus or the devil, on my side as much as you. I'm sick of these stupid-assed white people and their bullshit laws, history, patriotism, pharmaceuticals and religion. All the lying sombitches are doing is mollifying dumb nigguhs so crackers can hog all the money for themselves."

"Now Austin, I ain't no more asking you to stand for their mess than I expect one of them to be putting up with ours. I'm just trying to say to you that just because you got away with wringing one no-good sombitch's neck, ain't no reason for you to think of trying to wipe out every other white person you see. You're so busy pointing one finger at them while you've still got three fingers on the same fist pointing back at you. Now, tell me who's most likely to have the forked tongue and two faces?"

"Whatchu talking 'bout, Mary Alice?"

"You know full well what I'm talkin' about. You need to get a-hold of yourself and check you out. The white world ain't about to change the way you expect it to overnight. We've just got to stick, adhere, join and follow every move of these thieving bastards. Keep your mouth shut; take care of business; and take over. And right now, all you need to do is go to work; do your job; git your pay check; and bring the sombitch home to me each and every pay day. I'll be home busting these two so-called 'women's' asses about their no-count men and their worsome-assed kids. No matter what, white folks always gonna be racist, and circle the wagons around their kind when the shit hits the fan. We've just got to leave the sombitches alone; band together, and put something on their asses like we're doing in baseball, basketball, football, and boxing, and on and on…three times better to stay ahead of them, and git out from under their feet. Now git your big ass up out of here, and go make us some money to buy us our own home."

"Yes, dear," said Austin as he finished buttoning his shirt. And when Percy came back downstairs, they both headed off to find Austin a job.

CHAPTER 5

Batter Up

Percy first took Austin down to the brick yard where he was immediately hired as a clay mixer and mold setter. That evening, Percy had Austin out on the front porch explaining to him how much to produce so that he could work in harmony with the other workers. "I heard you were fast. But always try to remember that the pace you set at first is the pace that white man is always gonna expect you to out-do. I would lay back a bit. Don't do so much too quick, Cuz."

"Gotcha." Just then, Austin spotted a young man come out on the front porch of the small house set back in the rear of the other house across the street from the Jarvises. The young man noticed Percy and Austin on their porch and started to walk down his driveway over to them. He appeared to be in his mid-to-late-twenties; kind of short in height at about five-feet-six inches tall, one-hundred forty-five pounds in weight, bow-legged and pigeon-toed, with a peanut shaped bald head that had a slight dip in the middle.

"Evening Mr. Jarvis. Hope you been doing fine."

"Aw, we git by, Lester B. We gits by. Lester B, I'd like you to meet my cousin Austin Hampton, here. Austin, this my lonesome-assed, cross-the-street neighbor Lester B. Johnson."

"Pleased to meet you Lester B," said Austin.

"Austin Hampton? Catcher for the Naptown ABCs," asked Lester B.

"For a while anyway, 'til my left achilles tendon got spiked and all shredded up."

"Well I'll be blessed. You never know who's related to who, or who in the world you gonna meet. Pleased and honored to meet you, Mr. Hampton."

"Pleased and honored to meet you too, sir," said Austin as he extended his over-sized right hand which swallowed Lester B's medium-sized right hand like it was a baby's hand. "Just call me Austin. Everybody calls me Austin."

"Please keep a-calling me Lester B. I'm just plain ole Lester B to all of the folks 'round here."

"Lester B, you know May-May. Well Austin here is May-May's daddy. He and the rest of his family just moved up here from back home in Texas. They're gonna be staying with us for a while until they get on their feet," said Percy.

"Well, welcome to PC and the neighborhood, Austin. With that old paint factory over there across the railroad tracks and all these dag-gone trains rumbling through here, it may not be nothing very fancy, but we got some good people here. The Jarvises helped me settle in, too. Next thing I knew, I was up on my feet, renting Miss Russell's old garage over there, and making me a little home."

"Yeah, Austin, Lester B. converted that ugly little, broken-down ole garage into a right neat and comfy little home. And I do mean to say, give this young man a hammer and some nails, and he'll do everything with wood except cook it. Aw, he knows how to lay some wood, now. He knows his stuff," said Percy.

"Well, at this point, I'd be proud to take Cousin Percy's out-house and convert it into a place to stay, too," cracked Austin.

"Yeah, well you keep wishing in one hand and shitting in the other. Then tell me which one gets full first," said Percy. "We don't have no stinking out-house. We've got fresh running water, hot and cold, all hooked up by Lester B to the city fresh water and sewer lines."

All three men broke out in belly-busting laughter; hardly noticing young May-May and her obviously pregnant older sister Queenie amble out of the front door into their presence. Percy cleared his throat in a warning signal causing the other two men to straighten themselves up and act like they had some sense. Lester B's eyes and mouth lit up in a smile of amazement and obvious deep appreciation upon seeing the majestic Queenie looking down on him.

Austin and Percy, upon noticing Lester B's sudden interest, smiled to each other. "Lester B, this is my very single niece, Ms. Queenesther "Queenie" Hampton; Austin's eldest daughter, and of course you already know her worsome younger sister May-May."

"P-p-pleased to meet you Ms. Queenie. P-p-pleased to meet you...and it's always good seeing you, too, May-May," stammered Lester B who all the while kept his eyes only on Queenie; dumbfounded as if he had been slapped upside his head by her daddy's Louisville Slugger baseball bat.

"Man, you look like you are having a mini stroke. Are you okay? Ain't nobody that good looking that you got to act like the rest of us don't matter. You folks today get bent out of shape by everything," teased May-May.

After a pregnant moment of silence and throat-clearing by Percy and Austin, Queenie softly said, "Uncle Percy and MyDaddy, Auntie Annie and MaDear said for y'all to come on in and eat."

"Tell your Auntie and your Mama we'll be there directly, baby," said Austin.

As the two girls walked back into the house, Lester B's eyes were still focused on the obviously pregnant Queenie. Even with the baby bump, she still was a head-turner. But Lester B didn't seem to care one way or the other; pregnant or not. May-May was right; he was really starting to look foolish. One would think the poor man had first met Cleopatra or Nefertiti or somebody. Heaven was certainly having its way on this day.

"Oh-h-h, Lester-r-r. Earth is calling Lester B. Come in Mr. Johnson," teased Percy.

"Huh? Aw. Yeah, yeah. Uh-ruh, what was we saying?"

"We were talking about how your mouth be all gapped open, and you be drooling all over yourself like you done lost your rabid-assed mind. Acting like you're coming down with dengue fever or something. That gal ain't no more thinking about no twenty-something-year-old man than the moon is thinking about a dumb dog down here howling up at it," said Percy.

"Yeah, but a gal that swolled-up with no man better be glad to get some attention from any sombitch howling about stepping up to her wagon and pulling it for her. A man's gonna be a man, and a wise woman will pull him on up to her, when the man is giving her the eye," quickly interjected Austin. "Ain't no sin for a man to like what he sees: especially if the older, more knowledgeable man is willing to step up to the wagon and just start to pulling. By the time a man is deep in his twenties, he has a pretty good idea of what's good for his ass. Besides, I'm tired of riding shotgun over pussy. As you can see, I dropped my guard again, and another sombitch sneaked pass me. I'm gittin' too old for this shit. I welcome all seekers to take my place, and correct my ineptness."

"Yeah. Now that both of them damned shotgun barrels is bent backwards, pointing directly at your big head," teased Percy.

"You've been watching too many of them damned cartoons and 'The Three Stooges.' But, I submit: you've got a point there, Cuz. How about we invite this young fellow... I mean man to dinner? Don't seem fair that we leave the good man standing out here all alone on the porch while the rest of us goes inside to feed our faces," said Austin. "Lester B, soon's you commence to barking like you mean it, I guarantee you the woman in the moon is gonna hear you up there. Just in case she be sleeping, I'mo be howling and pitching a bitch in the background for you."

"Aw, most definitely, Lester B, you've got to come sit with our family for dinner. You already have the gal's daddy batting for you. You might as well run the bases," said Percy.

"Much obliged, Brother Percy. You and Ms. Annie brought me this far; I might as well have confidence in myself; up my game and try to play ball like the big-leaguers," said Lester B while looking over at Austin.

Percy and Austin followed Lester B into the house smiling like two commandos escorting their prize prisoner into interrogation. The women had already seated themselves with Queenie sitting at one end of the dinner table. As Percy and Austin seated themselves, this left the only open seat being the chair at the other end of the table across from Queenie. Because everyone was staring at him, Lester B seemed rather shy and reserved at first. He just couldn't stop grinning and glancing at Queenie. And she couldn't stop grinning and batting her eyes in response to his intense interest in her.

Everyone, including the three other women, immediately noticed Lester B and Queenie appreciating each other. Mary Alice looked across the table winking and blinking to her sister Annie Lee: and Austin and Percy smirked and knodded to each other. May-May kept nudging her bare foot into her sister's bare foot, underneath the table cloth.

Queenie, uncharacteristically, was actually very shy at first. She kept bowing her head, staring at her plate with her hands folded in her lap. Normally rather overbearing and somewhat obnoxious, she now just sat there at the table as though she was actually confused. After all, she never had decent courtship before, while growing up out on that lone Texas prairie. Of course everyone present at the table knew this except Lester B.

"So, Lester B, I'm quite impressed that such a young man as you can make such a beautiful home for himself out of an ordinary garage. You, already, have achieved more than my wildest dream," confessed Austin.

"Well sir…"

"Please call me Austin; same way I'm calling you Lester B. I ain't nobody special neither, and we're all grown folks here," declared Austin.

"Well… Austin, you are someone special to me. Someday I

hope to attain my wildest dream, which you already have achieved."

"Now what in the world could that be? Seeing how we ain't even got a pot to piss in, and are still mooching off of the goodness and graciousness of our family."

"Well 'that' is the word 'we.' It ain't no fun just living in that old garage alone, with me mooching off of the goodness and graciousness of y'all's family. Like my mama used to say, 'Why keep seeing that the grass is greener in your neighbor's back yard, when you have acres and acres of diamonds in your own?'"

Austin thought for a moment, then said, "Hell, if I had a diamond, I'd have a house like yours."

"And with all due respect, if I had a diamond, it would be a family like yours," said Lester B.

"Aw, look-a-there. So that's how you got all that you have. You don't hold back no horses or mince no words. Smart man. Smart man. Every man should have a son-in-law like you to add a bright side to life. Especially if they have one pregnant teenaged daughter, and another one the mother of my four-year-old twin grandkids; and nothing for a son-in-law," said Austin.

"Mr. Hampton, I'd be proud to oblige you," answered Lester B.

"With what?" asked Percy.

"Percy, you ain't stupid, and neither is Austin," said Mary Alice.

"It's the man Lester B that I'm worried about. Any man subject to taking a liking to this swolled-up, crocodile-mouth heifer has got to have some problems with his brain or either he's cockeyed from drinking that raunchy Mississippi Mud," said Annie Lee.

"Whoa, Nelly. Don't y'all think we're getting a little bit ahead of ourselves? We needs to hear what Ms. Queenesther has to say on this matter," replied her sister May-May.

After a moment, "Well, whatever I think about this game, don't y'all think I ought to be saying it in private with the man who's supposed to be stepping up to the plate or hitchin' up to the wagon" asked Queenie. "This ain't no South Carolina slave auction, you know. This is 1946; not 1846. Y'all are supposed to be inviting the man over here to serve him dinner. But now, instead, you're trying to serve me up to him."

"Amen to that, sister," said May-May.

"Yeah. This whole team of jackasses needs to be reined in. Suckuhs are gittin' all out of hand up in here. The food's starting to get cold. Can we please get to eating," asked Annie Lee.

And with that, the meal was blessed; plates and silverware started clinking and clacking; and lips started sipping and smacking to some good old fresh squeezed lemonade, shredded beets sautéed in butter, garlic and black pepper; beet greens stir-fried with purple cabbage and mushrooms; potato salad; fried catfish and hot water cornbread.

A while later, just as everyone finished the main course of the dinner, a generous slice of Percy's deep dish, big ugly apple pie was served to all with a large dollop of homemade vanilla ice cream that Percy had churned, himself.

Finally, after everyone finished their desert, Percy and Annie Lee led them to sit in the front room of the little shotgun house, where they offered hard cider and whiskey to settle things down after dinner. Of course Queenie wasn't about to imbibe for obvious reasons; and neither was under-aged May-May about to be offered anything alcoholic.

Unlike the other shotgun houses at the end of Blake Street by the railroad tracks, Percy had built a nice cozy, stone fireplace onto the Jarvis' house. They all sat in a semi-circle around the fireplace with Austin and Mary Alice sitting in big comfortable armchairs to the right. May-May, Annie Lee and Percy all sat on the 3-seater sofa facing the fireplace. And Lester B and Queenie sat on the 2-seater love seat to the left of the fireplace, facing Austin and Mary Alice.

Queenie was still grinning and gushing all over herself, nervously side-glancing at her sister May-May who was sitting to her right, holding and squeezing her hand reassuring her. Queenie was acting much like she had when she first saw Lester B standing out front; quiet, pensive, and dufous.

After Percy had finally served those of legal age their preferences, he returned to his seat just as Austin finished sipping some of his drink and cleared his throat exclaiming, "Yes Lord. This Old Crow's got a kick to it just like that Old Grand Dad."

"Irregardless, you don't mix nothing with this shit, either; not even no ice. If you do, it won't wait 'til the next day to bust yo' big head wide-open," warned Percy. "You just sip this shit a little bit at a time, real slow, and ease it back down your throat with respect…like you do with that Mississippi Mud."

"Shoot, man. Now you're scaring the living hell out of me. What you put in this shit; nitro-glycerin and hydro-chloric acid or something," asked Austin. "You act like you're scared of everything you got to drink in your own house: like this place is a goddamn bomb factory or something."

"Like I said, you best respect this shit. If you suck this up too fast, you're gonna wake up like Dorothy with the Munchkins in the Land of Oz," warned Percy. "And while we're on the subject of taking things slow and with respect, Lester B, I've got to say, you're a good nigguh. You seem to take your time with everything you do and you do it right. You've always been respectful to Annie Lee and me. Now with Austin; you got to watch out for him and his invisible shotgun. He's always smiling and cordial, but he will bust a sucker up side his head and shoot him in his ass behind these two big ole ugly gals of hissun'."

"And who are you supposed to be; Lester B's daddy?" asked Austin.

"May as well be. Somebody's got to recognize and speak up for him around here. Out of respect for his daddy, I'm more like his Godfather. He's always been there for me and Annie Lee. I'm still Queenie's uncle. But come to think of it, we all should be here for these young peoples. I don't care if you're up here in Illinois or down south in lonesome Texas; it ain't fair for colored peoples nowhere out here in this world now-a-days," said Percy.

"Yeah. And considering how my niece's belly is all swolled up, her daddy with his no-count shotgun was sleeping on the job.

Percy, go on and do what you do. Your big galoot cousin here needs some back-up," declared Annie Lee.

"Mr. and Mrs. Jarvis, and Mr. and Mrs. Hampton, with all due respect, I ain't scared and I can speak for myself," said Lester B.

"You better git started now son, because this big collard green eating heifer's liable to jump up any minute and bowl your young ass over. When you step up to this plate, you better be bold and confident, and knock a grand slam home run. You're stepping up in the big leagues now, son," warned Annie Lee. "This gal plays smash-mouth ball just like her daddy."

That's when both Queenie and May-May let out bursts of squeals of laughter and giggles.

"Y'all behave, now. Can't you see grown folks is taking care of serious business," asked Annie Lee.

"Annie Lee, you need to lighten up. Can't you see every woman here is a mother, except you? Our daddy or Uncle Dewey didn't need no shotgun to intimidate Austin or Percy," said Mary Alice. "These are my daughters, and I'll be the one to decide when they're grown."

"Baby sister, we can easily go outside and settle this shit right now," offered Annie Lee.

"Y'all hush. It's on you Lester B. Speak now or forever hold your peace, because once these women get to yapping and scrapping, you ain't getting a word in edge-wise," warned Percy.

"Mr. and Mrs. Hampton, Queenie and May-May, I just want to say that just like when I first met Mr. and Mrs. Jarvis, I took a liking to all of y'all the very moment I first met you today. It's true Queenie, I do think you are about the finest woman I have ever met in my life. I don't have no problem with you being with child by another man. Since he ain't stepping up to the plate, all I'm asking for is a chance, with your parents' blessing along with your sister and your Auntie's and Uncle's acceptance. I would like to start by visiting you and getting to know you. Mr. Hampton, I know you told me to call you by your first name, but this is official. I'm asking for your overall permission to court Queenie."

"In consideration of Queenesther's condition today, Austin, you're a damned fool to tell this man 'nawl,'" warned Percy.

"You think I don't know that? And if I do wind up being that stupid, you can take my shotgun, haul my ass out back of the coal shed, and blow the back of my head out if I even look like I'm about to draw my mouth up to say no. As of this moment, I am permanently retired from riding shotgun over anything. Lester B, seeing how you feel man enough to wrangle with this woman, go ahead-on and knock yourself out. Miss 'grown-assed' woman, what you got to say? This man ain't exactly too ugly neither. He's free, black and grown; got a home of his own and a craft to boot," said Austin.

"MyDaddy, I ain't got nothing to say in front of all y'all. This ain't no King Arthur's court where men just pawn a woman off like she's a whole hog or side of beef. Y'all gave Lester B permission; now it's up to me to see what the man's gonna do," declared the shy, yet stern Queenie.

But if history stood for anything, Queenie was anything but shy. She was a battle-tested dominatrix trying, for the moment, to pass herself off as a temporary wimp.

"Since when have you never had anything to say in front of everybody. Either you is, or either you ain't. And you ain't shy neither, you two-faced heifer. Go on and tell the man for sure, instead of leaving him dangling like he's a whole hog or a side of beef hanging off the wall with a hook up his ass," shouted Annie Lee.

"MaDear, please tell Auntie to leave me alone. I don't need no nookie bookie. This is my life," pleaded Queenie. "Lester B, I ain't making no promises, especially in front of all of these nosey old folks of mine. I know I might be pregnant and stuff, but any man want to be right by me, has got to be right by my baby. I don't owe nobody nothing, so I ain't obligated to take no mess. I ain't out to just be nobody's girlfriend, neither. I can do bad by myself. Just because they're presenting you don't mean I'm obligated to accept you. If you ain't right, don't come acting like they're trying to tell you to act."

"Now, that's what they call a cockeyed point of view. She layed up there, bared her ass and humped one sombitch. Now she's sitting up in here all swolled up, demanding righteousness from the next one," said Annie Lee. "Next thing you know, she'll be shouting 'Praise the Lord', 'Glory Halleluiah', trying to act like some rabid-assed, hypocrite, born-again, christian virgin."

"Like I said before, all I'm asking for is a chance to get to know you; to be your friend. If you wind up not appreciating what you see, I can respect that, and leave you be," answered Lester B.

"Well. Ain't nobody else been trying to take a swing. Looks like you're the man up," confessed Queenie.

"Well now, it looks like we've got us a probationary, big league, booger-bear hookup here," scoffed May-May. "Only time will tell if the lil' nigguh can hang in here with the pitches."

And the whole group fell out whooping, howling, and laughing. Even stone-faced Queenie broke out in a sunshine smile and longing glance at Lester B. But he wasn't smiling so readily since May-May called him a "lil' nigguh."

Reminiscing

Later on that autumn evening in 1946, while alone in their room, Austin asked Mary Alice, "Baby, where in the world did I go wrong? No matter how hard I've tried, I have failed to get my daughters to the reception before the conception. Babies are popping out of their asses two at a time, with the real daddies nowhere in sight. What's wrong with me?"

"Austin, ain't none of this mess your fault or mine. We're only human. And as parents, we can only do so much in raising a child before their environment gits a-hold of them, and perverts their minds against their parents' teachings. We conceived these girls; birthed and raised them to be good people. And the next

thing you know, the ungrateful young devils found a way to do
what the hell they wanted to do, and make themselves 'grown-
assed' women before their time. Aw, they thought about what we
said, alright. They kept their drawers on their hips and their faces
in their books. But, true to form, they thought out-of-the box.
They must have been taking dick up both drawer legs. Now,
they're left holding the bag; and the men, behaving like boys,
have gone off elsewhere to play. You couldn't sit on them girls
twenty-four hours a day; seven days a week; three-hundred
sixty-five days of the year. You ain't no damned Superman. It
was just a matter of time before they found a way to out-slick
themselves. It only takes a second. You'd have been called
everything from a 'cock-blocker' to a 'jealous old fool' for trying
to save their ungrateful asses from their fate. 'MaDear and
MyDaddy' can't save 'grown-assed' daughters from their fate
when the stupid girls are determined to bend the rules in order to
get their way. Part of being grown involves a person becoming
so wise and strong that they don't have to bend to the 'norm' or
go with the 'style' of the environment in order to satisfy their
'needs.'"

"Yeah. You got a point there, baby. When it comes to riding
shotgun over pussy, we're damned if we do, and damned if we
don't. But, irregardless, I still hurt in my heart. Ain't much
choice for a youngun carrying somebody else's baby, and ain't
even married to the cunthound sombitch."

"Austin Hampton, you're a good man. And this place called
'Earth' ain't meant to be no kind of Heaven alone. It's part hell,
too. So, no matter how much good you do, there's always gonna
be some more trouble around it. Matter of fact, it always seems
that just where you think you've found the most Heaven, there's
bound to be the most hell. So, if you find yourself starting to be
mad or sad, just scratch your ass, and git glad. Just like you
cain't git mad at that dog for licking his balls, we cain't get mad
at the bitches for licking their asses. We've just got to keep on
pulling and pushing our own wagon as a team for the rest of our
lives; doing the very best we can; accepting our new roles as

grandma and grandpa, until our days on this earth are over. That's all we can do, Austin. That is all we can do," said Mary Alice.

"My mama and daddy was right. I found me one dad-gum good woman when I met and married you, Mary Alice. MaDear always warned me that if I ever broke your heart, she would come back and haunt me to the grave."

"Yeah, and if your ass ever gets so happy that you do break my heart, MaDear can rest assured, I'mo be the one to dig a deep hole and dump your big ass in your grave. Then MaDear Hampton can save her energy, take her own time, and start right off to kicking your ass for all Eternity."

"Ha-ha-a-a-a! Now, that's what they meant by that old saying 'love you to death'," laughed Austin.

"Yeah. Well, there are certain times when you don't bend your will or the rules. If you don't bend your back, another sucker can't sit on you" said Mary Alice.

CHAPTER 6

Queenie's Turn to be a Woman

As time passed, Lester B and Queenie grew closer together, and closer to the time for her to give birth to her baby. Just as Austin warned, it was not easy for a pregnant, unwed, "colored" teenager to get help in bearing a child in those days in downstate Illinois or hardly any place else in the U.S. Other than family, Queenie had no visible means of support or insurance; no responsible husband or father of the child. Even the one "black" medical facility in PC turned her away for pre-natal care.

Lester B saw this time as an opportunity to really win Queenie's heart. In early autumn of 1946, he took Queenie over to the Missouri side of the Mississippi river to the Infirmary at St. David's Hospital where the nuns referred Queenie to the midwife Miss Arzella King who had just moved up to Prairie Cove from Shreveport, Louisiana. No sooner than Miss King got settled into her apartment, she took Queenie under her care. "Yeah, big mommy. You 'bout ready to spit that baby out. I can tell by the way it's laying back in your hips, this one gonna be a great big old boy." And that was right around the time when Queenie started experiencing back pains and breathing problems after the dog days of August.

Mary Alice and May-May, also, started hanging by Queenie's side throughout her experience, with Annie Lee, also, filling in occasionally. Finally, around October 3, Queenie started experiencing the violent movement of her baby. Mary Alice sent Lester B to pick up Miss King. They both arrived back at the Jarvis house in a matter of minutes. Lester B was sent out of the bedroom while Mary Alice, Annie Lee, and May-May stayed in the room with Queenesther and Miss King. Austin and Percy were still at work, and away, and the twins were in school.

"Shi-i-i-i-it! Aw-aw, MaDear, I cain't take no more of this pain," moaned Queenie.

"I can already see the crown of the baby's head. Ain't no need for you to be losing yours," encouraged Miss King. "At this stage, it's best I don't give you anything. It could cause trouble now."

"Bitch, I don't care if you have to cut my fucking head off. Just git this mothuhfuckuh out of my ass," screamed Queenie.

"Um-hmm. Yeah, baby. I bet you'll think twice the next time before dropping drawers, and gapping your thighs for another black snake," teased Annie Lee from the foot of the bed.

"Judging from the color of the crown of this baby's head and it's red straight hair, it definitely wasn't no 'black snake' that did this deed this time," assured Miss King.

"Don't make no difference. A snake is a snake regardless of its color. A black snake will bite you just as fast as a white snake," declared Mary Alice.

"Either way, she'll never forget how this big-headed bastard's gonna bust out of her ass tonight," assured Annie Lee. "A woman can run faster with her skirts up..."

"Than a man can with his pants down. Auntie Annie, cain't you see my ass is about to be ripped wide open? I don't need another one of your old maid tongue lashings," yelled Queenie.

"Ha-haaa! Go 'head on Reverend Sugar Mama. Preach to me. Tell Auntie all about it. Don't make no difference if it's a boy or a girl coming out. One little head with no face goes in; and a big headed sombitch with a monkey face comes busting out of your ass, with both of y'all screaming like James Brown blowing blue flames outta his ass hole. E-E-E-OW!!!," shouted Annie Lee.

"Aw MaDear, please git your aggravating-assed sister off my case. I cain't be bothered with this bitch and her bullshit. I got enough pain in my ass as it is."

"Now Annie Lee, let's don't keep picking at her. She's about to pay her dues," said Mary Alice.

"Yeah; in spades. The crocodile-mouth heifer laid her dumb ass up there and let some sweet-talking sombitch squirt his jism all up in her black ass. Old rancid-assed Loosey Goosey's about to lay one hell of a golden egg directly," teased Annie Lee.

"You midget bitch, I swear 'fore God, Auntie or no Auntie, soons I bear this child, I'mo be whupping yo' lil' narrow ass," bellowed Queenie in a deep baritone voice.

"Oh yeah? You think that big headed lil' monkey-mouth bastard is busting your big bull moose ass now? Wait 'til I git one of my feet up in there. Your breath is gonna be smelling like sole and shoe leather before I'm through with you, you foolish young whelp" said Annie Lee.

"Never mind her, Precious. Push, push. Let loose all that anger you've got inside to push your baby out into this world. Bring him home to you now mama. Hot diggity-dog. Here he comes. Well, well and well. Annie Lee was right. We got us a big headed, bouncing baby boy," declared Mary Alice, "Be careful. I cain't tell his dick from his umbilical cord."

Seconds later, after busting his way into the world, 'Bighead' finally broke out in a solo scream of his own. It was a big baby boy indeed with a big head like Queenies 'golden egg' at over fifteen pounds, twenty-four inches long, and golden hewed skin; a head full of long, curly red hair. One eye was silver blue, and the other eye was brown. Even though Austin and Queenie remained silent on the subject, it was plain enough for a blind man to see that other than his mama, no one very melanated or Negroid was involved in this baby's conception.

The Name

Queenie named her baby Booker T., after the most respected and revered mulatto of his time; Hampton Institute professor and Tuskegee Institute founder Dr. Booker Taliafero Washington. Queenie didn't dare give her new baby his daddy's last name of Choate, because, well, as we all know, that would send up flags all the way back to Texas, leading the Texas Rangers to her father Austin Hampton. So she proudly gave little Booker T her father Austin's surname, Hampton, just like her; her mother Mary Alice and sister May-May, and the twins.

By getting pregnant out of wedlock, Queenesther knew she had done herself, little Booker, and her family a dishonor back in 1946. After she spent all of those months in dependency and those hours in labor, she apologized for being so vulgar, rude and inconsiderate to Auntie Annie, Miss King, her mother Mary Alice, and all of the others not present, who had tried to comfort and encourage her through the gestation and birthing process. And once her mother Mary Alice and Auntie Annie Lee laid eyes on baby Booker, the two women commenced to playfully argue over whose baby Booker T was going to be.

"I deliberately tried to make you mad at me, because a woman needs somebody else to scream at when she's going through labor," conceded Annie Lee as she turned to Queenie while holding little Booker T. "I may never be able to give birth to babies of my own, but like the old folks say, 'you don't need to drink the whole ocean to know the water is salty.'"

"Auntie Annie, you need to stop. You know you was speaking Gospel from the heart, calling a spade a spade. But that's all right. My baby is here now. We all got to move on...gots to git-to-gittin'," said Queenie.

"Yeah. Long as your ass don't git-to-gittin' too happy and knocked up again anytime soon. I ain't gittin' paid to be running no sombitching foster home up in here. And there ain't no social security in pussy. You gittin' my drift," asked grandma Mary Alice.

"Yes, ma'am," said new mama Queenie. "But, MaDear. If you say so, the state will pay you to be his foster mother: the suckers will pay you big 'til he's eighteen."

"I cain't be bothered with no worsome-assed kids. You drop the drawers: you change the diapers seek the checks."

If You Have Your Own Place, You Never Wear Out Your Welcome

The Hamptons stayed in Prairie Cove, Illinois with Annie Lee and Percy for just over a year, before they were able to save enough money to purchase an abandoned two story apartment building and a used electric company pickup truck for cash in full. Austin and Mary Alice settled in the apartment on the second floor of the storefront brick building at the corner of Page and Upton Streets, a fairly busy intersection. Austin continued pulling shifts baking bricks over at the PC brickyard. With the occasional help of Percy, their wives and the girls, the Hamptons were able to put the building together inside of a year. After restoring the building, Austin leased the two retail spaces on the first floor as a Chinese takeout restaurant and laundry, with the Hampton's three bedroom apartment on the second floor just a few blocks around the corner and down the next street over from Annie Lee and Percy's house.

By this time Queenie had fallen into a deeper relationship with Lester B. As usual, she remained true to her hard-headed, self-serving way of thinking, and took advantage of the chance to move into the former garage Lester B had converted into a one bedroom home where she could satisfy her "needs." Lester B had always worked construction and was a solid provider. But his easy manner changed somewhat as time moved on. He became less tolerant and more assertive, and determined to have the relationship proceed with him being the supreme arbiter of their union.

Mary Alice even asked Queenie, "Don't you feel that Lester B is a bit too flippant with you, and too strict on Booker T?"

And Queenie's lie was, "Aw, naw, MaDear. Lester B is just doing his best to make us a happy home. If it wasn't for him, me and Booker would still be living up under y'all, gittin' on your last nerves."

In actuality, Booker was living under a more hellish regime than his mother Queenie, while staying in Lester B's house. Lester B's frustration and impatience with the little boy was becoming more and more obvious. The bottom line was that Booker T was not Lester B's child. If Queenie was away from the house, and Booker so much as made any kind of sound, vocal or otherwise, Lester B would come down on him in a barrage of yelling and cursing that was finally transitioned into the physical realm.

"I swear, if I find out that mothuhfuckuh is whupping on that boy, I'mo pop him with my snubby and have Austin whupping on his ass. No wonder Lester B don't like the boy. He's not Lester B's child. If a man truly loves a woman, he's gonna love the child, too. Y'all are a package, and should be married. If he cain't stand the heat, he needs to git his little evil ass outta the kitchen."

"MaDear, marriage ain't necessary nowadays. Besides, I just ain't ready to go that deep with nobody."

"Well, the sombitch is going deep enough up in your ass and upside your baby's head. Ask me, that sucker shouldn't be getting nothing for free."

"Aw MaDear, he ain't gittin' no more freebies than I'm gittin'."

"Well then, you both need to be paying some dues by making some kind of commitment to one another. And you better start thinking about what Booker T is getting. He deserves more than just man-handling and whuppings. He needs a daddy of his own, too. That way your daddy can start being more of a grand daddy.

But yet and still, your smart ass had to go jump the gun ahead of time and start humping that old cockeyed, redheaded, half-assed cracker sombitch back in Booney. Now, your daddy ain't got nothing to fight for, except his little, hybrid grandson. If you would just git up off of your needy ass, you and Booker could move into your own place. Austin's been digging out that basement and setting up the frame for a nice little two bedroom apartment down there. You ought to be talking to your daddy. God blesses the child who has her own, you know."

"Yeah, well I already know the rest of that tune. I'm a grown-assed woman," blurted Queenie in self-defense.

"Yeah, and a crocodile-mouth, 'grown-assed woman' can still get the red piss smacked out of her by her mama. Bitch, you don't never git so high and mighty and grown that you can talk shit to your mama. There's more in being grown than getting to hump who in the hell you want to without consideration of what you're gonna be putting you, your child and the rest of your family's asses through. All you so-called young adults today are concerned with is having your own place for the satisfaction of your own sexual needs. You worked yourself up into a fever and dropped drawers for that no-good, monkey-assed Tex-Mex moron. Now you've turned to humping this little bow-legged, baboon-assed nigguh. Yeah fool: ain't nobody playing stupid for your ass. Austin will soon be kicking his ass; and I don't want to have to do the same to yours. You made this child, now step up to the plate and start being more of his mama. Am I getting through to you?"

"But, MaDear. All I want to say is, all of y'all, and Auntie Annie and Uncle Percy was the ones pushing Lester B all up in my face."

"Never mind that shit. You're the one who stepped up to the plate and felt the need to take your swing, too. Now own up to the umpire's call. Am I getting through to your dumb ass?"

"Yes, ma'am."

"I didn't raise no punk-assed bitches; and I, for damn sure, ain't about to be one. Now, do what you do, and straighten out this mess. Don't let me have to come down there and start to popping that lil' sawed-off Napoleon sombitch in his little narrow ass."

"Yes, ma'am."

CHAPTER 7

Lester B Finally Shows His Ass

Lester B seemed to love working construction. In his whole life, he never felt as much bliss as he felt when he constructed or rebuilt a building. It wasn't heavy construction like building skyscrapers or bridges over the Mississippi River. The heaviest part was mainly hauling dirt with the dump truck he had rebuilt, and doing small construction jobs like converting Mrs. Mattie Russell's old garage into a pretty decent little cottage. His equipment was mainly an old Mack dump truck pulling a flatbed loaded up with his old reconditioned bulldozer.

Lester did things like gut the garage; frame the inside walls; string electrical wiring; lay down a concrete floor; run plumbing and insulation under the sheet rock and floor for passive heat; plow out and lay the concrete driveway; planting a lawn around it. Besides, this all provided the widow Russell with another guaranteed source of income other than her small pittance of a pension and social security check from her deceased husband Rayfield.

It was now 1950, just over three years, since Queenie and her little boy Booker T. Hampton moved into the Russell's garage/converted home with Lester B. Johnson. Little Booker had just turned four years old, and Queenie was satisfied with being Lester B's common-law wife. But, little Booker was also a little booger who was really starting to get on Lester B's last nerve. Lester always complained that things would be better if Booker would just "shut the hell up" and give a working man some "space and peace." Lester saw that Queenie wouldn't empathize with him, so his only alternative was to stop off at Roscoe's Lounge after work; have a few beers; listen to the radio news over the hub-bub of lying and bragging macho fellow self-employed "construction workers"; and then go home by seven o'clock that evening.

On this evening, Lester B had a couple of shots of whiskey on top of four bottles of beer before finally driving his truck home. He pulled up in front of the newly converted house; got out of his dump truck; fumbled through his keys; staggered across the newly laid driveway; unlocked the front door of the house; and walked into the living room. As he passed through the front door, he could hear Queenie back in the kitchen moving pots and pans.

As usual, four-year-old Booker T was whining for attention. Only this time, he was yelling, "Mommy. I want some milk!! I want some milk!"

Lester B sucked his teeth and sat down in frustration in the living room chair with his elbows on his knees and his head in his hands.

Queenie stuck her head into the living room from the kitchen saying, "Aw. I thought I heard somebody come in the front door. Can't you say hello or something? What's wrong with you? Why you looking so long-faced and stupid?"

Booker T seemed to sense Lester B drawing more of his mother's attention, and increased his whining to screaming. At that point Lester B lost control and shouted, "I cain't take no more of this shit!"

"'Shit'? Whatchu mean 'shit'? Man, I bust my ass like you do; cleaning this house; cooking your food; and babysitting my son," said Queenie.

"You're supposed to clean and cook, and do whatever else to maintain this place. And that damned kid ain't none of my fault," insisted Lester.

"Fault? What do you mean 'fault', sucker?"

"Bitch, cain't you discipline the little bastard and shut him the fuck up?"

"Did you say 'bitch'? Do I look like your mama?"

"Hell naw," yelled Lester B as he stood up.

"Then why are you calling me her name?"

Lester B jumped up off of the sofa, stepped forward; clenched his fists at his sides as he stood up to his full five-foot-six inch height. He slowly continued his approach toward Queenesther, stopping almost face to breast with her, looking up to her, deliberately saying, "I bust my ass to provide for your ungrateful black ass and some other mothuhfuckuh's whining little puss-colored, mix-matched eyed bastard; and all you give me is this shit?"

Lester B apparently forgot that this was Austin and Mary Alice's daughter Queenesther. She was also vicious May-May's big sister. Slowly and even more deliberately, Queenie snapped back at him, between clenched teeth, "Ain't nobody here scared of your little sawed-off, runt ass. Just 'cause you cain't hold your liquor, and come crawling in here with your breath smelling like wild wolf pussy, you think you're The Man and I got to be your 'bitch'? Booker T cain't help being born out of wedlock. It ain't none of his fault that he was born to me this way. But even a dog deserves some respect." As she eased back a couple steps closer to the dish rack, she snarled, "You want to see a bitch, you need to take your little funky ass back home to your mama what spoiled you!"

Just as she rested her right hand on the counter, Lester B commenced to raising his right hand as if to go upside her head. In that split second, her hand came up with the ice pick from the dish rack, and she deftly drove the implement through the palm of Lester B's right hand.

As he let out a blood-curdling scream, he bit her on right

hand and she bellowed, "Mothuhfuckuh, I will kill you. My own daddy never raised his hand at me. Who in the hell do you think you are?"

As he let go and backed off in pain and terror, she crept forward toward him, recoiled for another stab. Lester B was forced back into the small space between the refrigerator and the sink, earnestly pleading, "Queenie please, please. Baby please. Slap me; kick me; punch me back. But baby please don't stab me with that thing no more. I realize I was wrong; a dumb mothuhfuckuh. Baby, if you let me go this time, I swear I'll make it up to you. I swear 'fore God I won't never, ever raise my hand at you no more. Please don't hurt me no more."

"Your best bet is to back your little midget ass on out of here, now. You ever come near me again, I swear I'll poke your fucking eyes out." She grabbed Booker T by the hand, who all the while was holding onto her right leg, and walked through the living room and out of the front door, warning Lester B, "I'll be back with MyDaddy for our stuff. I don't want nothing of yours. If you know what's good for your ass, you best high-tail it out of here 'fore we gits back." From there, she went right up onto Mrs. Russell's back porch, banging on her back door.

As Mattie Russell peered out of the curtain, she opened the back door saying, "What's going on, baby girl. Why y'all crying so?"

"Aw, Miss Mattie. Can I please use your phone to call my parents?"

"No problem, Sugar. Y'all come on in here. What you gonna do with that bloody ice pick?" As Queenie tucked it into her apron pocket, Mattie further said, "Y'all come on in here before the nosey neighbors start peeping out the windows, trying to stick their noses into your business. The phone's just over there by the 'frigerator. Help yourself, sugar. Boy, git your little mannish behind over here and give Miss Mattie some sugar."

"Thanks Miss Mattie," said Queenie. After a few moments, Queenie spoke into the phone, "Hello? MaDear? Yes, ma'am, it's me, MaDear. Can y'all come git us? We just need a place to stay 'til I gits on my feet. I'll tell you when you get here." Just as Queenie hung up the phone, she heard the sound of Lester B's truck engine start up and start to ease on down the street and out of the neighborhood.

Extraction

Mary Alice arrived at the house a few minutes later. Although she was calm, she was still very serious; cordial and appreciative to Mattie Russell. She reassuringly walked the crying Booker and his mother to the pickup truck. No sooner than they were seated inside, Mary Alice started inquiring about what was going on between Queenie and Lester B. She didn't bother to pry too deeply into the situation other than to say, "Well, well and well. Judging from how your eyes is all red, that suckuh must of tried to haul off and knock the living stew out of you. You don't have to say a word. I can see by how your eyes ain't wet, and you got a hold of yourself, you must have went to work on him. Is he still in one piece?"

"All but what I did to his hand."

"Wait a minute. Is that a bite mark on your right forearm? You must've put a serious whuppin' on that little nigguh's ass, because real men don't bite a woman...unless they panic while getting a serious booger-bitch beat-down. You must've gone baboon on his ass...scared the living shit out of the poor boy."

"Ain't none of this blood mine. I only stabbed his hand through with this ice pick. He tried to hide, bite and begged for mercy like a bleeding little punk."

"Ha-ha-a-a-a-a. That's my baby! I didn't raise no punk-bitches. I'm proud of you Queenesther. And I sure hope the Booker Man saw it all, so he won't grow up wanting to, or even think about, putting his hands on a woman. But now, if a bitch puts her hands on him, he's got the eternal right to whup her ass like she's a man. If a man's gonna insist on being a 'man', a woman's got to always be a woman...they each gotta respect each other. Your daddy didn't beat my ass or y'all's asses, so better not no other mothuhfuckuh dare to try to touch you in that way neither. Aw, I haven't forgotten how he had to shake the truth outta you always running off behind that ridge out back of the house with that no-good half-breed. But, that's when he turned you over to me to lay hands upside your head. And I didn't even touch you then."

"Is MyDaddy home yet?"

"Oh, yeah: he's there. When's the last time you saw me driving this old piece of truck?"

"When the eye doctor put that stuff in his eyes, and you had to drive him home 'cause he couldn't see."

"Well, you know he ain't sick now. And he, for damned sure, ain't stupid. He kind of figured y'all was due to have a lover's blowout. He bet me a long time ago that all you seem to like is men smaller than you, mo-fo-better to have the upper hand in an ass-whuppin' contest."

"More for better to whup ass, if push-comes-to-shove," said Queenie. "Besides; us women are better suited for critical thinking in crucial situations."

"Ha-ha-a-a-a-a. Listen at you: talking like the Grand Master Booger Bitch of the Universe."

"Just like my mama."

"Women cain't be weak...especially when they're smaller like me and my sister Annie Lee. That's why God made things like ice picks; hatchets and bricks in hand bags; irons, and cast iron skillets; and itty-bitty gut-guns we can carry in our special secret places. But, you and May-May got your daddy in you. That's how come you two heifers come out so big and mean. Men are gonna always be in for a big surprise when they go to raise their hands around you two. And you smart as a whip, too. Always keeping you a lil' nigguh."

"Aw, MaDear. Let's please forget about that fool. Maybe it's a good time to get a few things out of his house without MyDaddy getting all involved."

"Involved? Let that little stump-daddy bring his narrow ass back here anytime soon. I'll show him some 'involved' as in re-volved, evolved into a revolver. Raise his little monkey hands at one of my babies. He must be out of his natural mind."

"Aw, MaDear. Naw you didn't. How'd MyDaddy let you leave the house with your snub-nosed baby brother that has the two last names Smith and Wesson?"

"Like I said. God made mysterious things we can hide in our secret special places. It's not healthy for women to always be thinking weak. A smart woman has always got to be ready above and beyond the call of duty. Do things like keep a pot of scalding hot water on the stove. And if the sucker really goes for bad, love him to sleep, tuck him in bed and sew his ass up in the sheets. Never know when a sombitch will get mad; try to man-up, and commence to slappin' a sorry bitch upside her head. Never be weak; three-hundred sixty-five days of the year; seven days a week; twenty-four hours a day…never-be-weak. Always have that ace in the hole, ready for his macho bullshit. I don't care if it's with a gun, a pair of scissors, an ice pick or whatever: the wild mothuhfuckuh has got to be trained and tamed."

CHAPTER 8

Single Motherhood

After a few trips back and forth to the house, Queenie and Mary Alice finally packed the remainder of Queenie and little Booker's few items of clothing and other necessities into the back of the pickup truck, and headed for the Hampton Building.

When they arrived at the location, and finally brought all of their items down into the basement apartment, they found Austin upstairs, just sitting in his easy chair, smoking his pipe and grunting derisively a few times while listening to the women talk.

Booker, upon seeing his grandfather, ran toward him, diving into his lap and outstretched arms. All Austin could say was, "There my boy. There my boy. Hold still here, while I bite me some of this big belly." Booker T. squealed with joy. In contrast to the abuse he had to endure with Lester B's protocol, Grampa Austin was the man he wanted to be like when he grew up.

A few weeks after Mary Alice got Queenie and Booker settled into their basement apartment, Austin's mother Sage Hampton moved in with Austin and Mary Alice. In spite of being declared legally blind from diabetes, Sage eventually managed to master getting around the apartment by feeling her way around so well that she could make most of her way without feeling for the walls or furniture.

Sage loved to cook, and kept the old coal stove burning in the kitchen all day long, through the dead of winter, as well as throughout the dog days of summer. She always kept something to eat on the kitchen counter; especially on Sundays, when she would keep a bowl of lip-smacking, finger-licking-good, southern-fried chicken on the kitchen counter top near the stove.

But the highlight of her day was her telling stories to little Booker T. He was about one-hundred eighty days from going on five years old by now, and he would sit in total absorption and fascination with Sage frequently telling the same story over and over again. His was an inquisitive and imaginative mind that was hungry for information and the chance to logically deduce the outcomes of various situations. He loved to hang around Sage who picked up on his tendencies and encouraged his questions as an opportunity to induce him into reaching his own conclusions. When he couldn't come up with the right answer, she would inspire him with more of the right questions. His imagination soared by listening to her stories, advice and warnings which were often scarier than his watching movies of the Werewolf, Frankenstein and Dracula showing at the Deluxe Movie Theatre or listening to The Shadow on the radio. "The Shadow knows. Moo-oo-ah-ah-ah!" Regardless, his was a mystical, magical world while sitting at the kitchen table, up in a chair on his knees, by the window, absorbing endless stories between Sage and the radio.

Because Austin was such a hard-working provider and investor, Mary Alice Hampton never had to seek any employment. For a few hours each day, she would give Sage a little time to take a break from Booker T's incessant questioning. That's when Sage would allow herself her one vice; two fingers of Gordon's gin in a short glass with a teaspoon of sugar. When reminded by Austin of the doctor's advice about her diabetic condition, she would always answer, "If I had a little dog who could piss gin, I would tie his little ass to the head of my bed and suck his little dick 'til we both fell dead." That would definitely make the doctor agree to leave her be.

As even a fool could see, Sage was very colorful in expressing herself. Maybe this was how little Booker T developed such a colorful imagination. Grown-ups would often warn each other in pig latin, "When the little nigguh asks you a question, don't be half-stepping in giving him the answer. Leaving him to draw his own conclusion about 'birds and bees' will scare the living shit out of you."

Even though Mary Alice was very well provided for by Austin, she wasn't too thrilled about the idea of continuing to support either of her two "grown-assed" daughters with weekly allowances. One day she finally insisted, "Queenie, if you're old enough to have 'needs', conceive and bear a child, and you keep talking-the-talk about how your ass is so grown, at some point in time, don't you think you ought to be walking-the-walk? I mean, especially when kids are getting old enough to start school pretty soon,their single mamas are free to go get a single job. I'll keep watching my grand baby and drop him off at Booker T. Washington Grade School; and sometimes pick him up at 4:30 in the afternoon, but you've got to go take your big grown ass to work someplace. I don't care if it's washing dishes in the Chinese restaurant downstairs or scrubbing 'nicotine' stains out of people's drawers next door in the Chinese laundry. Come to think of it, old man Feng's got a spot open in his laundry, and another spot open in his restaurant. You need to git down there and talk to him."

"Aw MaDear, I can't be bothered with washing other people's drawers. What am I gonna be looking like trying to wash something out of what's been all up in a gook's ass? Give me a break."

"I'mo give you a break alright; more like a broken jaw if you don't hurry up and git your trifling ass down there, and make him take that 'Now Hiring' sign down out of his front window."

So, Queenie's first job turned out to be working upstairs for Mr. Feng, on the street level from where she was living. It turned out to be a blessing to be working that close to home with a choice of two locations; in the restaurant sometimes, and in the laundry at other times.

"Chinese ain't like them supremist snobs from other countries. They don't cheat you out of your pay; but they sure make a nigguh bust her own ass working for each and every penny," Queenie would often declare.

Better job setups just didn't exist for a female melanated high school drop-out in those days. The Feng family was very considerate of their landlords the Hamptons. Nevertheless, this was a favorable setup for Queenie, because even though her mother Mary Alice demanded that she go to work in the building, Mary Alice and Sage doted over Booker T upstairs. This eventually turned him into an attention freak who believed all women were born to be very, very nurturing and very, very attentive toward him.

Booker's Bonding

Booker T became so attached to Mary Alice that she couldn't sit down without him sitting on her lap. Even when she eventually came down with the "sugar" diabetes, she would be injecting her insulin with a hypodermic needle in one thigh while he was still sitting on her other thigh. It got so that people started swearing that Booker's feet never touched the ground until his first day of school.

And let's not forget Sage. Booker would make her tell so many stories that she would go hoarse. This was really her excuse to sip some more of her "special elixir." "Lord have mercy on my soul. This child gon' wear me out into a deaf mute," she would exclaim.

By the time he started school, those two women had spoiled him so much, he didn't know what to do with himself. It got so he didn't know who was his mama. On his first day of school, when Queenie reached down to take his hand, he snatched it away saying, "Whatchu doing? I'm a big boy, now: and you ain't my mama, no how."

When Queenie looked over at Mary Alice, Mary said, "That's your baby. I'll be downstairs, out on the sidewalk waiting for y'all.

As Queenie pulled him along behind her, he commenced to screaming like a wild bobcat. Standing close by, Sage whispered to her, "You better start busting that ass now, while he's little. Else, when he gits big, he's gonna be like a four-hundred pound gorilla, feeling entitled not only to sassmouth you, but to be showing-off on you...in public."

With one hand, in one fell-swoop, Queenie whacked him on his behind, saying, "Straighten up here, now. Goddammit, I'm in charge from here on out. And-yes-I-am-your-mama," smacking his behind emphatically with each word.

"Don't do it with anger. Lay it down with conviction: just enough to get your point across," Sage whispered.

Booker T shot Sage a look like a CIA agent who had just discovered his handler was a KGB counter-spy. Queenie caught it, smacking his behind again, saying, "You-got-something-else-to-say-Mr. Buster Brown?"

"No ma'am. No ma'am. Okay, okay, Mama Queenie, I'll be good," he pleaded.

"Well, I don't hear you saying nothing about you being sorry," said Queenie.

"That's enough Mama. Even I can see you've made your point," whispered Sage.

"Yeah. But you didn't see how this little monster cut you up with his eyes."

"I'm sorry, Mommy. I'm sorry Great Gramma Sage," said Booker T. "Y'all give me one more chance, I swear I'll be good." He learned this trick watching Maggie Lee and Maimee getting whippings. "Can I go to the bathroom?"

"Yes. Go ahead. But hurry up. We can't be late."

Love at First Sight

Booker T experienced his first deep crush; on his first grade teacher, Miss Helen Kennedy at Booker T. Washington Grade School in Prairie Cove. There was no such thing as kindergarten in PC back in 1951, so Booker started the first grade when he was still only five years old...almost six. He was so appreciative of Miss Helen Kennedy's nurturing and attentive style of teaching that he made the best grades in her class...hand's up and down. Both of his hands were always raised and waving, even before the woman could draw up her mouth to finish asking the first question. So, the other kids in the class began to say, "What's the use? She's only gonna call on him." Sage would tell him each morning, "Stay focused."

It was like he had ESP and could anticipate Miss Kennedy's thoughts. He was so entuned to her, it was almost like he would breathe when she would breathe. The boy would do anything to hog that poor young woman's attention from the other kids in the classroom.

But, what mesmerized Booker even more was the sight of her legs. Oh, sure; there were other women. He would watch his mother Queenie's friends while she was pressing their hair: like the neighbor Miss Louise Robinson while she sat on the floor in front of Queenie, showing an ample portion of thigh. But, she had to be very careful not to draw up her knees, or she would find one of Booker's miniature cars zooming under her dress as though her thighs were the entrance to his imaginary underground parking garage. He would even make the screeching sound of the tires turning on the cement floors, "Er-er-er-er!"

Every time Queenie threatened him, Louise would speak up for him, saying things like, "Aw, girl. He ain't no problem. Let the child have his play."

"Girl, you don't know who you're calling a child. Before long, this mannish-assed lil' nigguh will be humping on your leg.

His Johnson gits so hard, he can't even feel me giving him a whupping," swore Queenie in pig-latin. "He just be standing there like a cigar store Indian; not even batting an eyelid. If he don't lighten-up, I'mo have to git him fixed during summer vacation."

"Ha-haaa! Queenie, you ought to be ashamed of yourself. Don't you hurt this baby. He don't know no better. He's just raring to be a man before his time."

If she only knew that she and Helen Kennedy were to be Booker T's proto-type standards for every female he would ever meet during the rest of his life. If a woman's thighs weren't thick, she was just another one of the boys.

Disciplining Booker T

By now, Booker's life circle pretty much included school and Grandma Mary Alice's apartment. He was getting so much nurturing and attention from the women that he temporarily lost consciousness of the men like Grampa Austin Hampton and Uncle Percy Jarvis.

At school, he was gently prodded to excel in his studies by his teacher Ms. Kennedy. Once, she took a day off and was replaced that one day by a substitute teacher. Booker suffered so much that day that the school called Queenie to take off from work and come and get him.

Auntie Annie Lee would visit her sister Mary Alice every day; which pretty much covered her own life circle. On the day that Booker feigned being sick, Annie Lee feigned being angry with him by chasing him around the apartment with a fly swatter until he would dive under Mary Alice's bed giggling, calling his Auntie Annie names like "stupid," "Ugly Lady," etc.

Theirs seemed to be a love-hate relationship from its inception. Most often, Mary Alice would move the bed and hold him by the ankles, bottoms up, for Auntie Annie Lee to pretend to give him a spanking. But, this one time, Grandma Mary Alice warmed his behind for faking sickness, and skipping school. Yet and still, Booker was thrilled by every minute of his grandma's and Auntie's intense attention. He relished being pursued by them and having them challenge his speed and wits.

Then, to round out this rousing day, there were the evenings after dinner; at the dinner table where the radio was perched. Between the regular serials like "The Phantom," "Fibber Magee & Molly," and "The Shadow," there were Sage's homespun stories. This boy's mind never rested. His vivid imagination was piqued constantly.

CHAPTER 9

Nothing Stays the Same

Mary Alice's legs progressively began feeling numb with her feet feeling like she was stepping on needles and pins; all from the diabetes. As time passed, this developed into serious neuropathy where she started losing all feeling in her limbs. When the signs of gangrene started to appear, first a toe, then one leg was amputated. Then the other leg began to bother her.

Right around that time, Sage had a massive heart attack: and Mary Alice wound up having a massive stroke. Both were hospitalized. But, Sage couldn't recover, and eventually passed away. She was laid to rest back home in Arkansas where her people held her funeral.

Two days after getting back from Arkansas, Austin Hampton lost his life while working in the brickyard. While guiding the operator of the crane that was moving a pallet of bricks, he was accidently crushed by a forklift moving another load of bricks. The family knew this would be too much for little Booker to bear, so they went back into that "birds and bees" kind of protocol, and told him that Grandpa Austin and Great Gramma Sage had just gone away for a while. He accepted this.

But, facing the truth of this kind of reality was just too much for Mary Alice's feeble heart to bear. Austin was more than her "husband." They were a unit like "The Cisco Kid and Pancho." Outside of work, wherever you saw one, you would most likely see the other. But, Heaven was merciful to Mary Alice. On the same night of Austin's demise, his beloved Mary Alice joined him in his Journey to the Other Side. They were so young; only forty-five years old, each.

At the funeral, Austin's coffin was closed. But, Booker T refused to go up for the last look at his Grandma Mary Alice, and pay his respects. He threw a grand-mal fit right in the aisle of the Galilee Missionary Baptist Church while waiting in the reviewing line. He could just barely see his grandmother's face showing up above the opened lid of her coffin.

"Naw, naw y'all. I see Gramma's face trying to hide up there in that thang," he screamed at the top of his lungs. He earnestly believed that Mary Alice was trying to hide while Queenie and Aunt May-May were trying to drag him up to her so she could give him a whipping with the fly swatter. He threw such a fit that Queenie and May-May had to drag him outside of the church.

When Queenie threatened to give him a spanking, he screamed, "You put your black hands on me, my gramma's gonna git up outta that thang, and slap the red piss outta both y'all!!"

May-May and Queenie both burst out horse-laughing at the serious little Booker T's language. To which Queenie replied, "Little boy, once again, I-am-your-mama. That lady up there in that casket is your grand mama...my mama. If you keep showing your behind, she's just gonna lay there, and keep ignoring you while I whup your mannish little ass. So, you may as well git it into your hard head that your ass is all mines, now. Give me any more lip, so-help-me-God, I'mo skin you alive; throw you in that damned casket with your grandma; bury you with her, and make another boy just like you that's even bigger and better than you are. Now straighten your little worsome ass up here, and act like you got some sense."

"Y'all gonna make me go up there to see her," seriously asked Booker.

"Do you want to go up there to see her?"

"No, ma'am."

"Then go on back in there; sit your ass down with Auntie Annie and Uncle Percy."

"Yes, ma'am. Queenie?"

"Naw. From now on, I'm 'Mama.' You got a problem with that?"

"No, ma'am... Mama," he replied.

"Good job Mama Queenie. You The Woman, now," said May-May.

"Next time you go to light into his ass, remember to save some for me," teased Mattie Russell coming up the walkway.

"And me, too," said Auntie Annie Lee from the doorway of the church, as Booker T, with an impish grin, ran back inside the church with the twins.

Daddy's Home

Mary Alice and Austin Hampton's youngest daughter Mayethel "May-May" Hampton was now 26 years old, re-united, and finally married to the natural father of her twins; another "hard working" railroad man named Willie Pickens. The only difference was his being of a younger age than old Levi Mabry.

Yeah. Old Levi Mabry finally kicked the bucket, and made his passage, too. May-May woke up that morning and decided to tend to her "needs." That last time, old Levi came and kept on going. Yeah, she did a double clutch and hit him with her turbo-thruster. It was like poor Levi just locked in freeze-frame, whimpering like an itty-bitty kitty-cat yearning for a saucer full of milk. Even though his heart stopped beating, his hips kept humping and pumping in a spastic post-mortum autonomic humping motion. Finally, after a horrendous herky-jerky cream-pie, his muscles short-cicuited. May-May tried slapping him a few times, but he wouldn't come back. Mind you, a May-May slap comes with a flash of lightning, too.

Like May-May's daddy Austin always said, old Levi was "a good nigguh." He put his body and soul into the notion, but his heart was just too weak to hang with the motion. He died in a piece, and may his soul rest in peace. Amen.

Learning Life's Lessons

During the mid-1950s, Prairie Cove was rife with hustle and bustle, and opportunity. Older "black" folks from surrounding towns say that in its heyday, small town PC was, also, the home of many of the metropolitan area's wealthy "white" elite. Yet, even though the "whites" tried like hell to hog-it-all for their own kind, the descendants of the "black" people still maintained what property they acquired; and had the good sense to earn, borrow and spend their money within their own tight-knit family and community.

By the time he was eight-years-old, Booker T. Hampton not only came to realize that he was despised and feared by both "blacks" and "whites" for the color of his features, but he also derived a strong sense of security in being named and looking like a lot of other strong-minded and successful self-reliant people.

Due to this, young Booker T. Hampton had a tough row to hoe. Just as the original Booker T. espoused the principles of Industry, Thrift, Intelligence and Property, young Booker T had no choice but to live by these principles early-on in his life. With that name, and having been raised along with his older female cousins, he had to resort to thinking and doing things much like that wildebeest calf born on the Serengeti Plain in Africa.

Those girls did everything to him except cook him. If they were beating him up one minute, they were loving him up the next. Females in the Hampton clan didn't think they were weaker than men. For his own survival, Booker T had to learn how to out-think females, and figure out how to schmooze them at the same time: these females were so merciless and insensitive in how they handled him.

His main drawback was his hot temper and big mouth. He had to learn to also follow the principles of another great melanated "African-American" male like Whitney Young who stressed the principles of "Keep your mouth shut: take care of business; and take over." At such a young age, this was a formidable task for young Booker T and any other youngsters his age.

But, by being Queenie's only child, raised within the Hampton clan, he had to learn life's lessons much sooner than a newborn wildebeest calf trying out his new skinny legs on the Serengeti Plain. And indeed he did catch-on to problems and solutions very fast.

By Queenie, being so young, she had no way of raising Booker on her own in those early days. So Booker's Aunts, Uncle, grandparents, and cousins took turns pulling him in. And at nine years of age, he continued to play them all like a virtuoso violinist plays his Stradivarius instrument. From day one, he was earnestly nestling his face into all of these female's bosoms. The little bastard realizing that he was the only male in his generation of the family, wormed his way so deep into these nurturing women's hearts that he had them all fighting amongst themselves just for the right to hug him.

When she was twenty-seven years old, Queenie became a gospel singer, singing bass with the Spirits of Harmony gospel quintet; and moved Booker with the group to a hell-hole "negro-popping town" called Hallville, the next state over to the east, called Indiana. So, during these years, when the Hallville school semesters were over, Queenie would send Booker back to Prairie Cove to spend the summers with her sister, his Aunt May-May and her twin daughters Maggie Lee and Maimee. What was worse, they were around five years older than Booker, and each one could fight like a demon with an iron staff. They showed him no mercy; and treated him like he was a cross between Cindarella and their pet monkey.

May-May always made sure that when Queenie left any monetary consideration for Booker's well-being, the twins would get the major portion first. This is normal behavior expected of any mother, but not to the point of making little Booker wait until her girls had taken their Saturday night baths, then leaving him to bathe in their dirty, scummy, brown bath water. Most children his age were probably too ignorant to complain, but very early on, little Booker didn't stand for this. He would just wash up his "hot spots" in the men's room of the gas station down the street. He would just rough up two paper towels; wet and soap them up, and then he was good to go.

Boy, Git Yo' Head Outta That Bed!!

The woeful wail of the old factory whistle across the railroad tracks from Aunt May-May's little three-room shack hardly created a stir from her and her twin girls. They had grown immune to the sounds of the trains and the steam whistles, having lived in the shotgun shack beside the railroad tracks for so long. But, not so for their guest, young cousin Booker T, who at nine years of age was kind of tall.

"Woo-woo-woo-woo-oo-oo-oo."

At first, it sounded like the factory whistle off in the distance. But then as it got louder and louder, there was the terrible roaring, hissing, rumble, chug-chug, and vibration in the very ground itself. It sounded and felt like a tornado coming through.

"What the... Aw, naw. I done pee'ed... Wait a minute. My front ain't wet...just my side is wet," Booker T muttered to himself. "Aw, shoot! No fair!!! I'm sick of this, man. This ain't no fair. Just because I'm the youngest, why I always got to be the sucker...always stuck sleeping beside this fool at the foot of the bed? She pisses on me so much, I smell like her big old funky butt.

Piss-ass, trifling, black heifer! No wonder they always make me sleep on the same end of the bed with her. Better not say nothing though, 'cause this fool can fight like she's crazy. I feel like turning into a werewolf, and biting her in her ugly face while she's sleeping, drooling on herself. Aw, heck man! If Aunt May-May cain't train this trifling heifer, who am I?"

CHAPTER 10

Hope

But, in spite of the inconvenience, Booker instantly knew he had to get up and be outside in a hurry, because he could hear the distinctive sound of Aunt May-May's next door neighbor, Hope Newcomb, hitching up Cecil, his honery old jackass to his junk wagon. Hope didn't waste no time doing what he had to do. Each and every day, he always said, "The early bird gits the worm. You gots to decide if'n you wants to stay on the porch hongry, whimpering and whining all day like a lazy slacker puppy or do you wants to run with the hounds, make your own money, and buy your own grub. You gots to pull yo' head up outta yo' ass, boy. Be on the ball. Hustle…git-to-gittin'. I don't care if you is sick and starvin'. If you don't work and git your own, you for damned sure ain't gittin' none of mines."

In pissy pants and bare feet, within minutes Booker was running up to the old man. Hope, after hitching up Cecil to the wagon, boosted Booker upon the wagon seat, climbed up on his side and said, "Yhaaa, git up there old mule." And they were starting off in the dark on another day's junking journey, riding into the sunrise.

Twins Caught Off-guard

A while later, Maimee got up; squatted on the slop jar, making so much noise that it caused her twin sister Maggie Lee to wake up saying, "Dag, girl. You make more noise than a draft horse pissing and farting out in the street."

"Shoot, I feel like a horse, as swolled up as my bladder is," answered Maimee.

"Where's the little boogerman," asked Maggie Lee.

"Child, I do not know. I ain't his mama," answered Maimee.

"Betcha when he's got a pocket full of money, your happy ass be acting like he's your hugger-mugger baby boy," said Maggie Lee.

"Speak for yourself. You're the one who has kept him confused if Aunt Queenie is his mama or not," said Maimee.

"Aw, be quiet. What the hell do you know? Go on and finish pissing, and let somebody else get some sleep. It's too early in the morning to be arguing with your ignorant ass," yawned Maggie Lee.

"Sleep? That's how the little sucker got away in the first place. Your dumb ass was probably all into dreaming about pissing in a real toilet; and wetted up the whole foot of the mattress," said Maimee.

"And your hinkty ass won't let other people sleep in peace. If you had been minding your own P's and Q's, you would've woke up earlier and caught the little sucker getting away, instead of letting me think I was sitting on the pot, and ended up pissing all over the foot of this bed. No wonder the boy woke up and hauled ass. The piss…"

"That's the most cockeyed excuse I've ever heard. How about if I haul off and smack you upside your head so hard, your lame brain will snap into gear," asked Maimee.

"Now you know, even you ain't that stupid. If you even believed you could do that, you would haul off and smack the shit outta your own self. Besides, you don't want to be marinated with the contents of this slop jar, you crocodile-mouth heifer," said Maggie.

"Aw, shut up. What difference do it make if the boy's ass is gone. What was you gonna do with him anyway? Be glad he's up and gone out of here. He's got to come back...with coins falling out of both drawer legs. I don't know about you, but that young sucker is my meal ticket until Daddy Willie gits home. Far as I'm concerned, that lil' niggah is the second coming of baby Jesus. Your trifling ass ain't adding nothing to the income of this household except matresses soaked with piss. You hurt him, you can kiss your ass good-bye. You be taking food out of my mouth. If you were a little bit smarter, you'd be picking his little ass up and hugging the money out of him instead of yanking him around," said Maimee.

"Bitch, who you think you talking to; a visiting nurse? Ain't that much hongry in the whole wide world."

Finding More Masters

Booker T. was always giggling throughout Hope Newcomb's 'lectures.' "With a name like Booker T., you gots to take care of business, boy. Booker T. Washington stood for industry, thrift, intelligence and property. If you ain't got all of that going for you, everybody who calls they selves black, white, red, yellow or in-between is gonna be putting they feets up your sorry ass; making you their punk; and be taking your earnings for they selves and they chirrens."

Not only did Booker T get lecturing from Hope Newcomb, but he listened to the Irish, the "Jews," the Chinese and the Armenians at the junkyard, grocery store, restaurants, milk trucks, wherever and whomever constantly advised him on how to start making money work for him, instead of him always spending and working for the money. He had to know his junk metal and the money it was worth. He had to know where the empty pop bottles were dumped to get the two cents deposit for each one. He followed the mailman to houses throughout the neighborhood asking the residents for their unwanted coupons, so that he could redeem a penny for every ten coupons from Steve the "Jewish" market owner across the street from Oberlin Park.

After dealing with these kinds of industrious, ingenious people, Booker T learned other ways to hustle up money. He constantly checked under the grand stands at Stanfield Football Field, after the games and carnivals ended, for money dropped accidently by the greedy "white" supremacists while they were sitting in the bleachers buying their kids junk food. They wouldn't let "blacks" attend these performances in that park, so he cut a small hole in the chain link fence by the railroad tracks; and would search the areas under the grandstands after the crowd had left and the management had "secured" the place.

More Hope

So, right away the next morning, young Booker rolled over out of the urine-soaked bed, trying to get to his feet. As his left foot stepped out of the bed, he stepped right into the slop jar...again. Apparently, sometime during the night, one or both of the twins had made good use of the vessel. All he could say was, "Aw, shoot, man! I'm sick of this shit." And that was the major part of what he had actually stepped in.

Booker knew he had better watch his mouth. He didn't have time to waste getting himself slapped around again. He could hear Hope Newcomb's jackass Cecil braying and resisting again, as the old man was hitching him up to his junk wagon. While the girls slept soundly, Booker grabbed his denim cut-off shorts, hobbled out the door; took time to pump the water spigot in the front yard and rinse-off his funky foot. Never mind the piss on his side, his underwear would have to dry from his body heat again as the day went on.

No sooner than Mr. Hope finished hitching up his big old jackass, Booker climbed right up the side of the wagon into the seat to ride shotgun beside the wise old man. Hope smiled down on him in appreciation as they rode off ready to "make a pocket full of jingle-jangles and a whole lot more that don't make no noise."

Hope wasn't much about listening to a crazy kid, so he did most of the talking, strictly reminding Booker T, "Now boy, pay attention. I ain't gonna repeat myself. I tell you something, I'm only gonna say it once. So you best keep your mouth shut, cut out all that snickering and giggling. You hongry, you gots to work for your food. Anything else you want, you got to hustle and scrape for it. That's all there is to it. Early bird gets the worm. God helps those who help themselves."

Booker T took Hope's advice and never said a word, because if he asked the wrong question, the old man already showed he would get an attitude and shut the hell up. So Booker T would just sit there beside the old skin flint, listening to his words of wisdom like he listened to Gramma Sage back in the kitchen. He would just sit there on the junk wagon while watching the curbs of trash in front of each house they passed.

Next to watching "The Three Stooges," he loved to listen to old people talk; especially while looking and digging for scrap metal in trash that could be traded for money. Booker called it "cash for trash." No excuse for anyone who can walk to be broke.

No matter how hard Booker tried, he just couldn't understand why people would even put trash out on the curb. He would ask grownups, "Don't they know it's worth money?" And constantly wondered about those slacker cousins of his, "How come they sit around the house all day, waiting for Uncle Willie to come home from the railroad on Friday nights, and bring them some money for some food, rent, and to pay that racist old 'Jew' insurance man?"

Booker felt that paying for insurance was stupid, also, "It's like tossing your money up into the air and letting the twins git it. That's like betting against yourself; where you only win when you die. Then, you don't get to be the one who spends the money, black fools."

And then, he'd complain about "having to go get Aunt May-May some Garrett's snuff and piss-ass port wine from that Stag Bar Room across from the football field where all those "ku kluxing, chicken-fucking crackers wasted their money, and sat on their funky asses smelling like Fels Naphtha soap and fresh shit in their pants from ripping farts all day; bending their cracker elbows; sucking up that panther piss they called 'Fine' beer."

The junk wagon made its way on down Blake Street and out of the poor black neighborhood to the more lucrative, wasteful white areas. Hope always said, "On this one thang you can rely. The foolish peoples who always make more are the same ones who waste more. If the good Lord could only take a liking to a nigguh, seems like he would save us a whole lot of pain and sorrow, and just give us the shit up front like he do for them crackers. Never mind wastin' shit on them wastrel, greedy bastards. Pretty soon, they gon' be having mo' junkyards and dumps than graveyards. They makes everything a waste that takes up more space."

The July sun rose in the Prairie Cove sky at various times after five o'clock in the morning. After a short time, they came upon a pile of trash sitting out on the curb in front of a mid-century modern, split-level, ranch-style house.

Hope pulled the wagon up to a stop, but wasn't able to climb down so readily. His feet were so swollen with gout that he had to cut out holes in the sides of his shoes so his aching swollen little toes could have room to ease the pain. Booker knew this was the real reason the old man brought him along. It made Booker feel a sense of pride and worth to know that someone really needed him.

"I got it, Mr. Hope. You sit tight," said Booker eagerly seeking an "attaboy" from the old man.

"Nawl, now. You barely can scamper yo' young ass up and down on this wagon. How you gonna heft up something almost as heavy as me? Careful now. Don't mess 'round and git yourself a hernia," would warn Hope as Booker, moaning and grunting for a few seconds, was able to get the old box fan up onto the wagon bed. He would then scamper up the tailgate, over the junk and back into his seat beside the old man.

Hope always asked him, "Ready to go?"

And Booker would nod, "Yessir."

Then Hope would say something like, "Attaboy. You a smart boy. Smart boy. Them old fans and appliances have copper and other precious shit all up in them wires and motors. Not much, but it'll fetch you more than them pop bottles, won't it? 'Tween this dad-gum arthuritis and gout, this sugar diabetes done got my ass jacked up something terrible. I feels like ole Cecil done hauled off and kicked me in the ass and stomped on my feets for extra measure."

Booker, unable to contain himself, would break out in a spasm of hyena giggles.

"Whatchu laughin' at boy? Your time's a-coming. Enjoy it while you can. You keeps eatin' that gobbage yo' Auntie May-May be serving y'all and you'll be shitting razor blades worse than me. First thing you better learn real quick is how to cook for yourself. 'Cause the shit that drunken heifer be shoveling out to y'all young'uns ain't fit for the hogs. Heee-yaaah! Git on up there, Mr. Cecil; gots to be movin' on down the line. Got to beat that trash truck on these sweet streets and meet the sombitches at the dump before everybody else gits to picking over everything they gon' be dumping."

Booker would keep grinning, but he knew the raunchy old man was preaching gospel. Cooking his own food not only sounded like a good idea, but he even asked Hope about growing his own little vegetable garden. Hope told him, there was no chance anything would ever get to grow around May-May's place. "The same little witches that be pissing all over you in the bed each and every night are guaranteed to be beating your ass and raiding your garden, just like they did the first day after you put in a day's work on the junk wagon with me. You may as well go piss into the wind, instead of trying to grow something to eat 'round them hongry heifers. Turn your back and they'll be sucking up the damn seeds outta the dirt."

The Stash

Booker had told Hope of the first time he got back to Aunt May-May's place from the dump, how the twins had grabbed him; tickled him stupid as a distraction; turned him upside down by his ankles and shook all of his money out of his pockets. They took every cent; dropped him on his head on the floor; and ran away, giving his money to their mother May-May who gave them an Atta-girl along with a few pennies to go to the store and get some candy; "And on the way back, stop by the Stag Bar and get me some Garrett's Snuff and a pint of port wine." Two days later, they were still spending his money on themselves. When Booker asked for a piece of the candy, Maggie Lee beat him up real bad and called him, "You sorry-assed black fool. Git yo' randy ass out of my face."

Hope interpreted the situation for him, "Boy, is you deaf, dumb and dufous? You don't never trust nobody, not even your mama, when it comes to your money. You don't never take all of your money home, expecting an "Attaboy" from bitches to sit up there on their lazy, funky asses all day long, waiting to shake your hard-earned cash out of you. You gits you one of them Clabber Girl Baking Powder cans with a resealable top and some waxed paper to stuff inside that resealable lid, and stash away your paper money. Then you take home just enough sucker-bait coins for them hyena bitches and they mama to scuffle over. You needs to train them self-serving heifers, 'cause they think yo' money belongs to them; even before you make it. You don't never let nobody, not even Sweet Lord Jesus know exactly how much money you got or where you keeps it stashed. I mean, don't even keep it in the bank, 'cause them sombitches can be worse than them bitches. Come another depression and those skulking money grubbers won't let you through the front door to withdraw your own cash. That's how and why they 'specially keeps a sharp eye on a nigguh. Everybody, including black bitches and white bastards, thinks they own, and are eternally entitled to yo' money. They see you've got it, the first thing they'll say is, 'What in the hell did I do wrong?' Mothuhfuck that shit. That's when the flag goes up and the monkey dies. The soldier yank that lanyard and slams the pulley through signifying monkey's asshole, as he yanks the flag outta the simple minded sombitch's mouth. Ain't gon' be no more days like that. Not while yo' ass is riding shotgun with me. Boy, you gots to hurry up; pull your head up out of your ass; and mind-fuck all these bitches and bastards to get the hell out of your pockets."

Booker couldn't contain himself. He was giggling like he was watching another episode of "The Three Stooges" and "Amos and Andy." As he always told the twins, "Mr. Hope might be an old grump, but he sure can teach and preach and make it funny."

Yeah, but at least after he got through tickling your funny bone, he didn't rob you. You learned a little more about how to survive the trials and tribulations of life, than how to be somebody's bitch-boy.

"Laugh if you want to lil' nigguh, but each and every word I'm saying is true," chided Hope. "Ain't nothing wrong with telling a lie; especially if it'll save you from gittin' robbed and gittin' a ass-whuppin'. Don't trust them twins or any other man, woman, chicken or child. If one of 'em ask you a question, you tell them bitches the truth like they want to hear it, and they'll be stompin' the shit outta you even more. Tell them a good goddamn lie, and they'll suck it all up; be satisfied, and go away and leave you alone.

Bitches always want all of your money; but the mothuhfuckuhs won't never give you none of theirs. That is unless you they pimp, and be puttin' foot up they asses. Females love money so they can go buy up every god dammed thang in sight. It's like playing cards with them. If you play fair by the rules, they gonna cheat you outta your drawers. Want to keep your money and win? Lie like a poker-faced sombitch, and come home with a bunch of coins, while your paper money, the big bucks, is stashed away in the can."

"Mr. Hope? Are there any good girls that don't try to take your stuff?"

"Aw, yeah. But they too hard to find. You be good, they gon' be good. You be bad, you ain't gonna run into nothing but shit-bitches. You git my drift? The kind of person you are is the kind of woman what comes to you. You just got to be patient, and don't be playing around with no-good bitches. Stay free 'til you run up on a good one. You just got to hurry up and be smart. After all is said and done, it'll all be worth it when you find that sweet one. That's why they call them 'sweetie pies.'"

"Yeah, but no matter how hard I try to leave them alone, Maggie Lee and Maimee try to hurt me. So how can I stay away from them when ain't no place where I can hide from them forever?"

"Listen, boy. Just 'cause they choose to shit on their floors don't mean you have to shit on yours. If you be good to a girl and she shows her ass, look at her like you be looking at that jackass when he cocks his hind leg. Git yo' young ass the hell out of the way from the mothuhfuckuh, or your head's about to git knocked off, and be bouncing down the street."

"When I grow up, I'mo find me a good girlfriend. One that don't have no cards up her sleeves and ain't ashamed to be fair."

"Yeah. Well, you keep using your brain, and give it your best shot. But, all-in-all, don't wind up being no rotten bitch's sucker. If you gotta come home to them, let the no-good ones find a pocket full of jingle-jangle; but, along the way 'fore you git there, stash away the big money…the ones that don't make no noise."

After they split up their money, Hope headed on back toward the house, to elevate his swelling feet. Along the way, he let

Booker off at the "Jewish" market a few blocks away from the weed patch of his stash. After all, the little fellow was anxious to get to his Clabber Girl Baking Powder can, so he could count, gloat, and stash his money away before going back to Aunt May-May's and the twins.

Hope had not only given him the lecture on how to stash his money, but he also explained to Booker why he had to keep it as his "most precious" secret. "Your money is like your life blood: a nigguh man ain't shit, and cain't do nothing but beg without it. The mo' money you stash away, the stronger you become and feel. The place you keep it is called a stash 'cause you hide it before you go home to May-May and them damned twins, and from every other conniving, thieving sombitch in the rest of the world. Booker T., you cain't never trust nobody when it comes to your stash. Don't even let the squirrels and birds know where it's stashed, 'cause no sooner than you walk away, they gon' be diggin' it up for theyselves, too. Come back the next day and you ain't got shit, but scraps of paper and a fucked up tin can. You'll be as sorry as a broke dick dog. A broke-assed nigguh is the most sorry-assed mothuhfuckuh on God's green earth. He quickly comes to realize that ain't nobody got time for his miserable ass when he needs them."

"That's okay. I don't need nobody else's money. You taught me how to hustle for myself, Mr. Hope. I know how to take care of me and my money, now."

"You feels strong, too?"

"Yes sir."

"Always remember, the stash is what makes a man strong. Like your namesake Booker T. Washington once tried to teach black folks in order to survive, they have to git Industry, which is a way to make money; Thrift, which is like to buy something at a cheaper price and save; Intelligence, which is a education; and Property, which is to own your own land and house. Without all four of these, the black man is a weak and no-count dead man walking...like a zombie slave. Never be weak, boy. Three hundred sixty five days of the year, seven days of a week,

24 hours of a day; don't you ever be weak. Long as you got your stash, and yo' pocket full of cash, you are a dangerous man. You can tell the whole world to form two lines behind you; one for each cheek: and they can kiss 'til they eyes pop out of they faces."

"Tee-hee-hee-hee!"

"Go ahead on and laugh if you want to. But your happy young ass will be broke and sorry tomorrow after them bitches git through rummagin' through your pockets."

Booker couldn't stop grinning and giggling. He was amazed at how Hope Newcomb could make everything rhyme and make sense. That's why he loved to listen to Hope as much as he loved listening to Sage. He always said that Hope Newcomb was like a rough granddaddy. He soon forgot about wishing, and started telling everyone that Hope was his other grandpa. The little boy really grew to treasure the old man.

"Kiss the sky. I might not know how to do it, but it sho' don't hurt to try," Booker T. often mumbled to himself as he skipped along the railroad tracks, hefting coins in his right pocket and dollar bills twice-folded in his left pants pocket.

One Weekend Afternoon

One Saturday afternoon, after leaving the Jewish Market, Booker and the twins crossed the street, and headed through the parking lot of Oberlin Park. As they just about reached the other side of the football field sized area, a police cruiser pulled up beside Maggie Lee, and the lone "white" cop called her over to the cruiser. She went over, and the cop opened his door; still remaining seated, and commenced to running his hand up her dress, inside of her thighs.

Booker T lurched toward the cop, but Maimee grabbed him and pulled him back.

The cop said, "Yeah, little nigger. Go on. Git."

Maggie Lee just sobbed a couple of times as Maimee continued to pull Booker T out of the parking lot about twenty yards into the grassy area. Booker couldn't help himself and screamed, "Don't worry Maggie Lee, I'mo tell Uncle Percy."

Hearing this, the cop asked Maggie Lee, "Who's Percy?"

Maggie replied, "You know who he is. You work with him."

The "white" cop said, "Go on, gal. Git."

CHAPTER 11

Contingency Plans

One of the benefits of working with Hope Newcomb was that Booker T's work day was over by the time most people were just getting out of bed. He and Hope Newcomb hit the streets collecting the scrap metals by five o'clock each morning. This was because they had to stay ahead of the other junkers and trash trucks in the neighborhoods, and stay right behind the trash trucks when they arrived at the Prairie Cove city dump, where other early-bird junk pickers were waiting to take their pickings to the junkyards. Yet and still, those who had no mules or other modes of hauling junk were all a part of the crowd waiting to dig for their scrap metal at the dump. After all was said and done, collecting metal from the street was a lot easier than digging through the pile of junk, trash and garbage at the city dump.

On the street, the trash wasn't piled so deep, and there was no bickering with competitors. Things could get pretty nasty at the dump or anywhere two trash picking parties ran into each other, arguing over a tiny piece of copper or brass. A lame old man, a stubborn old jackass, and a randy nine-year-old boy could easily be pushed aside or assaulted and seriously injured.

The worst feeling in the world is when the people you grow to depend on are the very ones to turn on you and do you the most harm.

This was summertime when kids were out of school on summer vacation. After leaving Hope, Booker would stop by Steve's "Jewish" Market, and buy himself a popsicle, some cream filled chocolate cupcakes and milk chocolate covered caramels. About five blocks from his stash, he stopped by Miss Ruby Hargrove's, and got her permission to pick a few big pears from her tree. Then he would skip on down to the end of the street, go up onto the railroad tracks making sure no one followed him down a bit to where he stashed his dollar bills in the tall weed patch. This was his daily routine. Then Booker would cautiously make his way back to Aunt May-May's place by around nine o'clock where the hungry girls would be anxiously waiting for him.

His Aunt May-May was fully aware of the way her teenaged girls preyed on younger Booker, because she was training and encouraging them to do so. At times when the girls were busy in another part of the property, May-May would be waiting and watching for Booker coming down the railroad tracks. She would even call the girls' attention to his approach. If they failed to respond, May-May would beat the girls mercilessly.

As the girls approached him, Booker, being a smart boy, would hold all of the coins in his hands leaving his pockets turned inside out as proof that the only money he had was in his hands. As the girls stealthily came closer to him, he would throw all of the coins out in front of him and run back down the railroad bed, this time pass the stash spot, back in the direction from where he originally came.

On this one occasion, May-May screamed at the twins, "Never mind the damned coins. Bring that little sombitch back here to me. Git him! Git him! He thinks he's so damn smart. I'll show him."

The girls knew that once Booker got a few steps away from them, he was gone. And as he ran away, he yelled back at them saying things like, "You bitches are dragging ass more than your lard-assed mama." Then, once the girls gave up the pursuit, he turned completely around, running backwards, talking more trash to them and insulting their mother May-May, much like the little red fox squirrels do to their pursuers once they felt they were in a safe place, out of reach on a high tree limb.

When the girls returned home with only a few coins, May-May would beat the hell out of them on the front porch with an extension cord or razor strap. On one such occasion, after beating the girls, she heard Booker T giggling off in the distance. She turned in his direction and said, "Booker baby, you know Auntie can hear you sniggling out there. Come on to the house and give Auntie a big hug and some sugar."

Booker replied, "Whatchu think I am, a fool like your chicken-head twins?"

"Now, baby. You know you can't be sass-mouthing Auntie like that. While you're out there, grab Auntie a switch and bring your little mannish ass on to me, Sugar. Be it now or be it later, Auntie's gonna fire it up. So, you may as well come on now, and git it over with."

"Yeah. Like a dumb little kid, I'm supposed to grab a switch, and bring it to you, so you can whup me senseless like you just did with your own stupid-assed kids. Auntie, Mama said you weren't too swift; like the biggest fool in the family. Just because you and your kids are stupid don't mean that everybody else is supposed to be a fool for you."

"By and by, baby, you gots to come home and eat; and go to sleep. Auntie is just gonna have to tighten-up that young smart ass a little bit more now."

Now he was infuriated even more. Aunt May-May had insulted his intelligence by talking to him like he was an ignorant toddler. "You fat fool. I'm sick of you welfare bitches always jumping on me and taking all of my money. The white people are right. All you nigguhs do is sit up on your lazy, fat funky asses all day long with your legs curled up under you like camels, watching soap operas, cartoons, and that he-hank Liberace; waiting for some 'Prince' to come and feed you. You want to whup me, my mama said you got to bring ass to git ass. You're definitely gonna have to git up off your lazy behind and come git me. I'm sick of this shit and you shiftless bitches."

"Sugar, I cain't see how you have much choice in the matter. The more you make Auntie wait, the more she's gonna have to fire that ass up and make it bleed."

"You put your hands on me, I'mo tell my mama, and she said she's gonna come out here and whup-your-ass!"

"Child, ain't nobody scared of your mama but you. Go tell her what I said. I'll whup her ass and yours, too."

That's when Hope Newcomb, stepped out into his yard and said, "Now May-May. You all are going too far. You just cain't keep abusing that boy like that and taking his money. The state will take the boy away from his mama, put him up in a foster home, and lock your ass will up in jail. I'mo bring this shit to a screeching halt right now. I'm going down to the grocery store, and call Queenie to come git him."

Negotiation

The weed patch up by the railroad tracks was not just the place where little Booker stashed his money, but it was the place he found to be most safe and secure for himself. In May-May's house, whenever he was about to receive a beating, he could always duck and dodge and break away out the front or back door or an open window into the open field where none of the females could catch him and hold him. Besides, by now, he had grown almost too big for the girls to restrain for their mother. Booker seemed to know he was just as fast and strong in his thinking as he was in his running.

He relished the game of dodge ball, where he was the one in the center of a circle of kids who were trying to knock his head off with a basketball. He loved matching his wits, speed and deception against May-May and the twins so much so that he would taunt the girls by constantly trash-talking them about their mama and others near and dear to their hearts. Either way, he could fake and outrun his female cousins and their morbidly obese mother.

Yet, once out of the confines of their house, he moved as free as a bird in flight. And once he made it to the weed patch, he and the girls knew he was home free. The girls dared not enter the vastness of his domain for fear of chiggers, spiders, snakes and booby-traps that Booker T would use to assail their ignorance and imaginations. Not only did these myths exist, but the truth existed. The weed patch was the place where he set his booby traps of vengeance. He relished any opportunity to out-smart those older girls and their mother. But he relished even more the infliction of revenge. Yes, he cherished every opportunity to make them pay for hurting and robbing him; like hooking up open diaper pins in their seat cushions or rat traps and nail boards along trails. He also layed down trip wires dangling beer cans as alarms all along the way in the thickets. By him being a high expert with a slingshot; a dead ringer when free-throwing rocks; or being like an incidious Mau-Mau warrior-type blowing narrow nails through a bean shooter or plastic straw, those poor girls were trapped like sitting ducks in a row.

May-May loved to punish Booker as much as he loved inflicting revenge on her and her girls. Poor May-May was even more vulnerable than Booker if she dared to doze off into one of her drunken stupors. Booker T was not above setting off lit fire-crackers between her toes and exposed private parts. Although she would scream like a funk-band singer from the pain, she rarely ever exhibited any outward appearance of excitement. She was the kind of person who was mainly very calm, poised and calculating. She would try to lure Booker by saying things like, "Baby, come here and give Auntie some sugar."

And Booker would reply, "What am I gonna look like letting you put your crocodile lips, smudgin' stankin' brown snuff spit all over my face?"

And the twins would chant in unison, "Oo-o-o-o-o! Mama, did you hear what he said?"

And May-May would calmly reply, "Booker baby being sassmouth with Auntie? Now, Auntie gon' have to tear that smart ass up."

Of course, Booker would always curtly retort something like, "As big as you are, if you start over there with them two dummies of yours, you might git two pieces of ass. But if you start over here with me, you ain't gonna git no ass."

Even May-May would bust-out laughing saying, "Aw, Booker baby boy be a bad nigguh when he be out of reach. Auntie gonna have to tear it up."

"'Neigh-neigh-neigh' said The Lone Ranger's horse silver. Not today; no way; no how," paraphrased Booker. "Auntie just gonna have to go blow it outta her fat ass."

"True dat. But nigguhs gotta come home and go to sleep," his Aunt reminded him.

"I'm just a kid. You're supposed to be the adult. Mama always said, 'If you play with a puppy it'll lick your mouth.'"

"Aw, now he calling Auntie a dog? I'mo lick you, alright. But it won't be with my tongue on your face."

"Once again, mama said if you put your black hands on me, she gonna come out here, and lay waste on your fat ass."

"Baby, I keep-a-tellin' you, ain't nobody scared of yo' mama, but you. And right now, in my house, your mannish ass is all mines. I can wait. By and by. Time will tell. You mine's, smart nigguh."

By that moment, Maggie Lee sneaked upon Booker from behind, grabbing him by the arms, and Maimee grabbed his legs bringing him to their mother, May-May. "Aw, yeah. There my babies with the mighty Booker man. Boy, you gonna always be my little nigguh, even if you git more bigger. But right now, all I want for Christmas is a piece of your little mannish ass. Hold him up here, while I prepare this little piggy."

She gapped her fat legs as the twins pushed his head forward between her knees, like artillery soldiers loading a howitzer shell. And as May-May's knees closed on his head, she held his arms at the wrists, straight up behind his back. "Ow. Ow. You stank. I cain't breathe. I cain't breathe. You're breaking my arms, you fat fool," he screamed at the top of his lungs.

"The more you scream, the more Auntie gon' fire it up. You know, Booker, you've been very nasty to Auntie. You hurt me to my heart. Now, I'mo show you how I feel about you."

"Okay, okay. Auntie, if you let me go, I swear I'll give you more wine and snuff money than you ever, ever dreamed of."

"Whoa, Nellie. Hold this little suckuh up here so I can look him in his eyes. Now what's this shit about wine and snuff?"

"Auntie, you let me go, I can make you very, very happy. And besides that, I can bring you something you like, each and every day. I don't mean nobody no harm. I'm just a silly little boy who likes to always play and have fun. But y'all always be pickin' on me; beating me up and taking my money. How would y'all like it if I always took your money? All I'm asking is you give me a chance to make you happy...without all of this muss and fuss."

Just then, Maimee loosened her grip on his right arm while they had him standing up in front of May-May. Maggie also relaxed her hold on Booker just enough for him to lift his arm and bend his elbow, smashing it into her throat. As she totally lost her grip on him, he commenced to flinging his arms, and broke loose from May-May and Maimee, stumbling out the door right into Hope Newcomb's legs.

"Hold on here, now. What's this mess, I hear you sass-mouthing grown peoples? Boy, you come on outside and let me talk to you." Hope took Booker by the arm and led him out into the yard away from the females. "Have you completely lost each and every one of your senses? 'Til you mama gits here, you gots to watch yo' mouth. You cain't be talking trash to peoples when you is outnumbered; all by yourself; wolfing at three peoples all bigger than you. You're like the only puppy in the pound, 'bout to git your young ass eaten out. For your sake, I already left a message with a Russell lady to have your mama Queenie come here, or git somebody else to come git you quick, fast, and in a hurry: 'cause if I leave you up in this house, these bitches gon' skin your ass alive."

"Mr. Hope? Can I say something?"

"Booker, I knows you got every right to be mad, 'cause they bully and pick at you all the time, and takes your money and stuff. But you can't be talking shit if you ain't got no backup. You gots to learn to hold your tongue; bide your time; and think three steps ahead of them dumb, aggravating heifers."

"Mr. Hope, I ain't scared of Aunt May-May and the twins," Booker T whispered.

"What good's that gon' do you when you're all alone? You too light in the ass to even be thinking 'bout whupping somebody else's ass. You lucky I came in when I did. Boy, you got to learn there's a time and place for everything. Wolf only when you got reinforcements, and another place to go, not when you're the single, solitary little nigguh yapping at three bitches two and three times bigger than you. Who you think you are?? ... Buster Brown? That mothuhfuckuh lives in a shoe...and got a bull dog for backup. All you got is your young crocodile mouth pulling you knee deep into an outhouse pit full of shit."

"Can't none of them catch me once I break loose."

"I caught you, and I'm more fucked up than they is."

"I..."

"Hush now! You too cock-sure and foolhardy. 'Til I hear from your mama, you better stay your ass over there at my place. You go back into May-May's, they gon' be lynchin' you, and eatin' your ass for supper. Gon' over to my house. I'mo go back in here and try to mollify these devils 'til Queenesther gits here."

Within a half hour after Hope had left her a message and notified her of the events, Queenie was in a taxicab heading to her sister May-May's house. By that time, Booker T had downed two bowls of Hope's great northern beans, with a slice of smoked Joel and two pads of his buttered hot water cornbread.

Damn, that man could hook up a pot of beans that was definitely gourmet quality. Even little Booker knew nobody else could make beans with pot liquor smoother than white gravy. He had spent many a hungry day desiring only a bowl of those beans to satiate his craving. He had dreams of downing those beans. Old man Hope seemed to know this, and grew stingier and stingier when he realized that May-May and the twins yearned for a taste, too.

Manipulation

After Booker finished his beans and washed his bowl, Hope gave him a couple of carrots to feed Cecil the jackass out in the yard. As he was feeding the animal, he saw a taxicab pull up out front of the driveway that runs past the front of Hope's house and dead-ends at May-May's little house, where May-May was sitting on the front stoop, swatting blow-flies away from her elephantine legs. As Queenie started walking up the driveway, Booker T started running toward her along the fence line saying, "Mama, Mama, you coming to git me? Can I go home?"

"Yeah. Stay your ass over here with Mr. Hope. Matter of fact, run on back there to your stash and bring it with you. You ain't gon' be coming back here no time soon."

Walking along with Queenie for a few more feet, Booker said, "Mama please, I didn't mean to sassmouth Auntie. But she made Maimee and Maggie Lee beat me up and take my money. Auntie whupped me with my cowboy belt 'cause I wouldn't take them where I hid my stash. All I said was I'mo tell you, and Auntie called me a lil' nigguh and said 'ain't nobody scared of your mammy but you.' That's what she said, Mama. And she... and she said, "Your mammy bring her black a-s-s out here, I'll whup her a-s-s and yours too."

Queenie stopped dead in her tracks and said, "Well is that right? We'll see about that. You go on and do like I told you. I ain't got all day to spend out here."

As Booker T ran off past the twins, he poked out his tongue

at them as he ran past their yard, up onto the railroad bed, and down the tracks toward the weed lot. Queenie continued walking toward the house, yelling to her sister, "Hey, May-May."

"Aw, hey, Queenie. Surprised to be seeing you so soon. I thought you was heading out on the road to sing in Kokomo."

"Naw, I got more pressing matters to tend to here. You better git you a stick or a brick, bitch, 'cause I'm on the road to whup your mothuhfuckin' ass!"

"Then, bring it on sugar mama. You gotta do what you gotta do. Bring it on, with your bad-assed self."

As Queenie stepped upon the stoop, she snatched May-May by digging her nails deep into her sister's matted, nappy hair, and hauled off and slapped her so hard, one of her eyes cocked out of alignment with the other."

May-May screamed, "Aw, you black mothuhfuckuh: you got to bleed behind this shit."

"Um-hmmm. I don't mind giving up the blood as long as I got a piece of your ass in my hands. Bitch, I done told you time-and-time-a-gin', not to be putting your fuckin' hands on my baby. I don't be beatin' on your kids. You don't be beatin' on mine's."

May-May let out a couple of loud farts, and eventually was able to get up to her knees where she drove her head into Queenie's iron hard belly, grunting and squealing, "I'm about to fuck you up, bitch. Is this the best you can do?"

"Naw, you cock-eyed skank. How you like these apples," asked Queenie as she slammed May-May's face into the knob of her screen door. May-May was about two inches shorter in reach, and one-hundred pounds heavier in weight than Queenie who was also slightly taller. So, when Queenie swung her fist, May-May simply ducked low, grabbed Queenie's body, lifted her up and slammed her to the deck.

As the back of Queenie's head hit the wooden floor, May-May straddled her, grabbed her by the hair and commenced to slamming her forearm and elbow into Queenie's face. Needless to say, skirt hems were rising high and only Queenie appeared to be wearing any drawers.

Anyway, Queenie bit May-May on her left breast, forcing her to release her grip on her hair. As Queenie flipped May-May over and assumed the upper position, Maggie Lee screamed, "Aunt Queenie, stop. Please don't kill my mama. She's your sister."

That's when Hope Newcomb stepped in, grabbing Queenie's shoulder, saying, "Here, here now: if y'all don't cut it out, one of you ain't never gon' have the other. Ain't neither one of you got no more sense than to believe the lies and exaggerations of a nine-year-old child? You just fly off the handle and commence to tearing at each other like you some kind of mad-dog baboons?"

"Don't nobody be whuppin' on my child but me," snapped Queenie, as she released May-May and they both came to their feet.

"Well, the best way to make sure of that is to keep your child with you," answered Hope. "And anyway, he don't look as whupped up as either one of you. So what's that tell you? Seems like the little boy made the both of you 'grown-assed' women look more dufous than these damn twins. Come on. You need to straighten yourselves out and act like you got some sense. The whole goddamned neighborhood's standing outside the yard there watching you make bare-assed fools out of yourselves."

May-May being the smaller of the two sisters seemed to have the attitude that the only way to handle her bigger, older sister Queenie was to go crazy on her. Booker knew about his mother's hot temper and love for him. He simply took advantage of it. Everyone knew about Queenie's crazy propensities, so the whole family tended to let her have her way.

"Queenie, you've got the wrong idea. Just because you get mad don't mean the whole wide world's supposed to bow down and let you and your little boy have y'all's way. You run up on the wrong person, and you can get shot or cut. Stop lettin' that boy use you like that. What you think them twins gon' do to his lil' ass while you're gone out there on the road in them little country churches having a ball, singing 'bout the Gospel of a little white boy who wasn't preaching to no nigguhs about nigguhs," asked Hope.

Queenie had no answer. But her silence was testimony enough that she conceded to Hope's sage wisdom.

Determination

A few weeks later, May-May and Queenie mellowed out as sisters again…at least as far as Queenie could see. Yet, the twins still had a bone to pick with little Booker T. "He thinks he's so smart, the two-faced little sissy," claimed Maggie Lee.

"The older he gits, he's still a punk-assed chump. He's dumb as dirt. He wants to be two-faced, let's give him a clinic on 'Two-Faced.' We set him up again; bust his young ass, and show him who's still the boss," offered Maimee.

"You mean be sweet to him; get him to come over; and then whup his ass," added Maggie.

"There you go, Madam Dufous. Aunt Queenie cain't teach him no respect; we will. I bet he still sucks titty with his big baby-assed self," said Maimee.

"When we get through with his ass, I'mo be whupping yours…for calling me dufous, you oaf," promised Maggie Lee.

"Naw. Git me now, bitch. You're gonna be sucking titty through a gap where your two front teeth used to be. And your breath's gonna be smellin' like my feet," said Maimee.

"Yeah, whatever's in your dreams, you fool," said Maggie.

The two girls told their plan to their mother in a quest to get Brownie points and Atta-girls. May-May was really overbearing and obnoxious as a mother; kind of like the president of a motorcycle gang. She was brutal with kids, especially little boys. She thought nothing of teaching a boy with the emphasis of a two-by-four; and girls with a razor strap or extension cord. Her whole existence was based on how she could take advantage of people by stealing their money or through using their identities, and bilking the great state of Illinois out of taxpayer's money. She made Chicago politicians look like Vatican choir boys.

If May-May wasn't beating down males with her weapons and her sex, she was abusing females with her hypocrisy and deceit. "I don't care who it is. Ain't no bitch gonna whup my ass," she always said.

And Booker would always chime in, "That's not what my mama said."

"And what did your mama say, you young tattle-tale sissy," the twins would ask.

"I'm just saying…" would be his answer.

"Well, I'm 'just saying' that punk-assed people who cain't throw no hands shouldn't fat-mouth," would reply one of the twins.

Needless to say, May-May really approved of the twins attempted deception and control of Booker T. Hampton. Yet, he always prevailed and played all three of the females like a virtuoso violinist, running rings around them with his superior intelligence and self-confidence. He practiced and mastered life's lessons; especially as to how women really felt that it was their manifest destiny to be in charge of all things monetary.

Life in 1950's and early 1960's Prairie Cove was pretty bearable for youngsters like Booker T. There was a more solid support system brought on by segregation. Melanated "Afro-American" adults were more concerned with the well-being of each other's children, who were around Booker's age.

Booker T learned not to become too entangled with or expectant of others. Besides having to deal with his mother Queenie's singing career; his Aunt May-May and the twins tried to treat him like he was their "red-headed step child." But, in effect, Booker T grew up hardly enjoying the security of having a full-time mother of his own. He had to make do with whichever aunt would take him in, and how she was willing to care for him.

This young boy was growing fast, and had his own unique outlook and attitude on life. He knew how to spot an opportunity and turn it into a solid resource. He realized early on that learning to take full responsibility for what befell him was akin to having someone or something out there in the universe watching over him. His gut feelings were his surest resources. Whenever he needed teaching, a master of the particular subject would usually appear to teach him.

The one thing he could depend on thus far was the teachings that had been passed down to him by old man Hope Newcomb. He respected this sage's thoughts so much that he missed sitting at his feet while Hope expounded his beliefs, observations and experiences in life.

After Hope Newcomb's passing, Booker eventually learned to soften May-May's heart. Her husband Willie Pickens turned out to be a bigamist. Willie claimed to be overworked by the railroad out in the prairie which he claimed only allowed him to come home to May-May and the twins every other weekend, on Fridays and Saturdays. He would stagger in on Friday nights, drunk, and pass out across the bed after giving May-May some money that was less than what he actually made. That's when May-May and the twins would empty his pockets like they emptied Booker's pockets, only they didn't have to hold Willie upside down to get the money to fall out, since he always left his bib overalls hanging on the bedroom door.

Booker remembered going to Hope Newcomb for advice just before he died. "Mr. Hope, how come when Uncle Willie comes home drunk and falls asleep, and they take his money, he never knows it."

"Boy, that really ain't none of our business. But between you and me, sometimes a man ain't necessarily as dumb as slick-assed women may think he is. Know how you stopped bringing all your money home? You knew them females were dead-set on taking it, and doing what they wanted with it, without necessarily using it all to git something to eat. Part of growing up to be a man is learning how to play dumb, shut your mouth, and cover your ass even while you sleep around women. That not only applies to women, but to each and every other slick sombitch.

Best way to make a fool out of slick peoples is to make 'em think you're a bigger fool than they are. Make 'em eventually kick their own selves in the ass," answered Hope.

"Yeah, and when Uncle Willie and Aunt May-May drink that hooch, they git real stupid. When I grow up, I ain't never gonna drink that stuff."

"Smart boy! You're growing up to be a smart man! Even I git stupid when I drink that hooch. I take out my teeth and git downright cockeyed."

"Ah- Ha-ha. You may git cockeyed, but all of your teeth is for real."

"Drink that hooch and ain't nothing for real. Wake up next morning, don't remember nothing."

"Like the werewolf?"

"Yeah. Like the werewolf. Only with the hairs all over your tongue, instead of just all over your face!"

"God-dog. Now I know I'mo stay sober when I grow up. That stuff is raunchy!"

Charisma Chameleon

As time passed, Booker started noticing his Aunt May-May's tendency to sit alone, whining about being lonely. Booker soon developed the insight and ability to take advantage of these moments by schmoozing his way into her heart. She began calling his newly realized ability "charisma"; but, he innately realized his Aunt May-May's confusion in her understanding of the true purpose in life. He, also, saw this as an opportunity to alleviate May-May's suffering: and later on, the suffering in the lives of other people, regardless of their station in life.

Once, in the past, when Booker and Hope Newcomb were out on the junk wagon, Hope let Booker know he was wise to his newly realized innate ability. Booker told him, "Just because I used to be little, people still think I'm dumber than them. Aunt May-May and the twins just sit on their behinds all day long, whining about being broke and hungry. That's stupid when all they have to do is get up and go make some money for what they need. I keep telling them how to go get it, but they still don't get it."

"Boy, Heaven gave you the ability to shine the light on the shadows so that your people can find hope and go on and do for themselves. But you've got to realize that not everybody's got the same amount of initiative, self-confidence and general spunk as you. Some people just give up, and feel it's easier to be a slacker, and let others carry the brunt of the load. You don't keep giving people a fish just because their asses is hongry. They'll start expecting you to be their provider for all time's sake. After you serve them that first fish, you need to stop feeling so sorry for the slackers and show them how to get their own. Don't let them get used to surviving off of your resources and your efforts. Make the shiftless fools go bust their own asses for their own money. Like Lady Day used to sing, 'Mama may have. Papa may have. But God bless the child who's got his own.' It's only natural that all people git up off their asses and git their own."

By the time Booker T was ten years old, he was a serious, soul-surviving genius. He could master or outsmart whatever situation or person came at him. The one thing he lacked and dreamed of was the court ordered Legal Emancipation of a Child since he was already feeding and nurturing the very people who were supposed to be caring for him.

Hope Newcomb had planted the more advanced idea in his head of, "Don't just look for a job, and make money working for somebody. Train yourself to go to work; do your job; get your paycheck; and go home. Then get to the point where you can put something aside and make the money work for you. One day soon you won't never have to go to work for somebody else. It'll be like they say, 'Let your fingers do the walking through the yellow pages.' You be lifting your fingers to work for yourself."

Hope further said, "They've got colored men down south in hog headed, racist places like Alabama and North Carolina who

111

are multi-millionaires many times over. America was founded on the blood, sweat and free labor of our people. Between these fake-assed religions and jackassed laws, the lies of hypocrites and traitors are still mesmerizing and oppressing ignorant, buck-dancing nigguhs to their dying day. Because of the paradox and fear of sell-out, ignorant nigguhs; and the hypocrisy and deceit of those same lizard-lipped, forked tongued, lying sombitches who call themselves 'white', the good old 'land of the free and home of the brave' is really 'the land of the thief and the home of the knave', in the eyes of the rest of the civilized world. And the damned United States thieves and knaves have been getting away with their crookedness for so long that they can't even see where they are wrong. They expect everybody to keep pledging allegiance to that bullshit along with their dumb asses."

"Well just 'cause they've got everybody else fooled or scared, don't mean I have to be stupid and scared. Don't they ever look in the mirror in the morning," asked Booker.

"Aw, yeah. And just like a baboon looking at its own reflection in the river, they tuck tail and run from the big bad-ass sombitch they see," laughed Hope as Booker T joined in.

Now, Booker really missed Mr. Hope and his honest views about life.

The Spirits of Harmony

While Queenie was on the road singing gospel music with the Spirits of Harmony Quintet, Booker T continued to grow and learn more about life while staying at May-May's place. With so many "negro" church congregations being serviced by competing gospel singers throughout the Prairie Cove vicinity, Queenie's group decided to try more virgin territory like the backwater "negro-popping" towns of Central Indiana. They sang in towns with names like Muncie, Kokomo, Peru and Brazil. In and around these places the "negroes" all talked with a dialect like gobbling turkeys, similar to the inhuman, self-serving "whites" who maintained positions of supremacy over them. And if you closed your eyes, or hung sheets over the heads of both groups, you couldn't tell which was which. If you stood still, you would notice that every other person appeared to be cock-eyed or bowlegged, and constantly spat on the ground. People must have a pretty foul mouth if they can't swallow their own spit.

As Booker grew older, sometimes during the school year the gospel quintet took him along on short trips from their new home in Hallville out to the "colored" cornfield churches in other towns. They rode in a blue 1955 Oldsmobile sedan. The Oldsmobile was nice; but he had to sit in the front seat between the broad shouldered, falsetto singing driver named Walter, and the big-boodied, tenor Ernestine. Her thighs were so big that Booker T had to cross his legs at the ankles to accommodate both people. But Booker swore that sitting in the folding church chairs and solid pews during the sweltering summer heat had to be like sitting in the electric chair up at the State Prison in Michigan City. And when he stood up, he swore it was like somebody had pulled the switch...his legs were so numb it took a while for them to work.

He would bang his head while falling asleep next to one of those big funky melanated sisters who smelled like Ivory Soap mixed with the twins' Saturday night bath water. Once in a while the ladies would "accidently" backhand or elbow him when they declared they were being "struck by the Holy Ghost." Of course, Queenie would pay the particular woman back when she sat down between Booker and his assailant. Queenie's "Holy Ghost seizure" was a bit more violent and precisely directed.

But as soul-stirring as the Spirits of Harmony were, rural melanated people in the late-1950's were more broke than a stray dog. When invited to the libation after services, the group could eat all the southern fried chicken and buttered corn-on-the-cob they wanted: but Gospel groups were lucky if they got enough donations to pay for a tank of gas to get back home.

Finally, after filling their bellies, the group would head back to Hallville. At first Queenie and Booker lived with the group's director Leola Johnson over on Alexander Street. Then, Queenie was finally accepted for a one bedroom apartment in the Oakfield Housing Projects for "colored only." The building complex was segregated because "whites" believed that "Negroes" would rob, rape or eat them alive if they caught them.

CHAPTER 12

The Oakfield Projects

This place was like a small town within the city of Hallville; where the "negroes" were all "contained" and survived by victimizing each other. It was worse than being crabs in a barrel. Anyone who stepped outside of its boundaries was subject to the further oppression of the surrounding, better economically and politically situated "white" residents. Yes, Hallville was a hell hole sitting on the banks of the Wabash River, where nothing was established but the headquarters of the Order of the Ku Klux Klan, a name that sounds like it could only be dreamed up in a chicken's head.

In the projects, Booker T ran into the Stubbs gang's thug and secret homosexual issues; like Jason Willard's bullying. Willard was just another evil-assed ignorant "negro"; much like a Doberman Pincer...born and bred to tear ass. Booker did his very best to avoid all of these cowardly, predatory, bullying, gang boys. At first, he couldn't understand, for the life of him, why these melanated boys couldn't think of anything better to do with themselves than to attack and prey on their own already oppressed people. There just seemed to be no logic to the whole situation, other than the gangs being geneticly encoded nonhumans. If they ever got their heads together "white" people would have been the "new niggers."

One day while walking home from his newly assigned grade school, Booker was making his way through the projects, and ran into Jason Willard who was with three of his boys from his project building, next to Booker's building. "Well, well. Will you look at what we've got here? Mister Goody Two-Shoes himself," said Willard.

"Man, why don't y'all leave me alone. I'm not bothering nobody. I'm just minding my own business," said Booker.

Willard walked up to Booker; tried to stand nose to nose with him. But, the twins had trained him well. Booker T smashed his forehead down into Willard's nose; and as Willard's knees buckled, Booker straight-armed the boy closest to him in the chest, knocking that boy over the second boy who tried to tackle him. Five steps out, Booker looked back to see the bewildered bullies trying to get up on their feet.

"Your ass is mine, suckuh," screamed Willard. "You got to go to school."

"According to you fiends, I had no other choice. Your punk ass best stay with your boys, you no-fighting bitch," shouted Booker.

Instead of running directly into the courtyard of his own building and face mass-disgrace for fleeing a bunch of boodey bandits, Booker ran the long way around the place and went straight to the whorehouse where he worked as a cleanup boy down the alley-like Dudley Street. Out of breath, and furtively looking behind himself, Booker ran head-first into the ample bosom of the First Lady of the house, Miss Lula Reeves. "You can't keep running from those stupid boys forever. Remember... he who fights but runs away must fight again another day," Miss Lula warned him.

"I know it. But Miss Lula, I ain't like no Superman who can just take a deep breath and blow away the whole gang," said Booker.

"Then, you still go on the offensive; git down and dirty...

guerilla warfare. Stake the homos out like the cops do; and deal with the silly boodey boys one-on-one, one-at-a-time. Yeah, you whup the living shit out of them one by one," said Miss Lula. "Nigguhs are ignorant; a disgrace to the African race. Once they start picking at you, and you don't hurry up and go upside their heads, they gits worse and worse on your ass: inside and out. Pretty soon, they'll come lookin' to pick on you just because somebody else in the past went upside their head or kicked them in the ass. Next thing you know, everybody will be callin' you a bitch-boy, sissy, or faggot. Even the little girls won't have any respect for you. I'm a grown woman, and every man, woman, chicken and child knows better than to call me that kind of shit. It's time you start making a respectful name for yourself, before they try to drag it in the dirt. Seems to me they're the ones who are the bitches...can't fight unless they're in a bunch."

"Thanks Miss Lula." As she turned to go back inside, Booker addressed her again, "Miss Lula, please. Before you go...you give me a hug and I'll fight fifty-five gorillas."

"Boy, you are something else. Your mama find out about this, she gonna try to kill me and throw what's left into the jail. Git your big head on over here, and git your young ass on up them steps to Room Six and straighten it up for Miss Bunny. I got to git me some...more...money...aw, SHIT! Aw shit!! Who else been teaching Booker T where 'it's at'," bellowed Lula to the whole house.

When Booker's mother Queenie first moved Booker to Hallville, he couldn't get hired to have a newspaper route because he was less than 12 years of age. But, this didn't stop young Booker T. He got himself the secret job, cleaning up in the whorehouse, a couple blocks away from the projects. All he had to do was change sheets and towels; straighten up the "bedrooms"; and keep fresh water in the pitchers and bowls with a small brown bag of alum on the tables by the door, and sliced lemons in a saucer for the smell in the room.

The pretty women grew to love and look out for Booker.

They would often give him hugs and tips, and teach him hands-on about "the birds and the bees and the flowers and the...." Lord, how that boy loved those gestures of affection, hands-on instruction, and attention. He especially enjoyed it when one sweet young hooker named Vivian would call him up to her room to take a short afternoon nap with her. She would only be wearing a short robe...with nothing underneath it.

When he was with Miss Vivian, he was in a place far better than home: he was in Heaven. For all he cared, his mama Queenie could stay "on the road" and the newspaper route could go with her, while he stayed at home by himself, up until he was twelve years old. He would always say to himself, "When I grow up, I'mo git me a woman who looks like Vivian."

The whorehouse madam, Miss Lula, could have kept the money she paid Booker T. Hampton. He would gladly have kept doing a good job for free, just to keep getting perks like those afternoon "naps," deep grunting hugs, and focused attention from fine Miss Vivian, Miss Ann, Miss Gracie, and Miss Kate.

He loved everything about those women in the whorehouse. Not only was he addicted to the way they felt, but he was mesmerized by the way they sat with their legs crossed in such a way that their thighs flared out wide while pressed against each other. He knew that if his Mama Queenie or Auntie May-May found out about this job, not only would he be in deep dew-dew, but all those sweet ladies at the whorehouse would be up Shit's Creek without a paddle. But Booker was willing to face being locked up and "whupped senseless" just to be able to keep coming back to that whorehouse. He made up his mind that if anybody tried to give him a 'whupping', he would run away and never return home. He planned ahead for this. He determined that he could hide in places like his PC stash site in the weeds; boxcars down near the old PC railroad yard; even hold up in one of the closets in Miss Lula's whorehouse.

Asymetrically Diametrically

Uncle Percy Jarvis would always tell Booker, "Revenge ain't nothing but the start of a vicious circle, like when a dog winds up chasing after his own tail. Regardless of what people say, revenge ain't sweet when it's cold. It's most fulfilling when it's hot, fresh and continued."

At times, the urge for revenge was a sweet temptation causing a battle between Booker's ego and his trust in the laws of nature to handle the fate of his oppressors. To cover that instance, Uncle Percy was unknowingly in agreement with Miss Lula, who reminded Booker that, "Only a fool argues with a crowd: because their ignorance is encouraged by their numbers. You defeat the cowards at their weakest by picking the gang apart, and relating to them one-on-one, one-by-one."

According to Booker's Uncle Percy, "Trained boxers like Nelson Mandela and Rubin 'Hurricane' Carter, who were unjustly imprisoned and pissed on by "the system," are powerful examples of the strongest minds being able to let go of the urge for revenge. The question is, are you ever obligated to respond with force to an oppressor?"

Miss Lula always told Booker T., "He who fights, but runs away, must fight again another day." She also warned him, "Don't forget that you have a duty to nip the situation in the bud so that it doesn't grow up to be too big for you to handle later. In other words, you've got to git it while it sleeps, 'cause when it's 'woke, it's wild."

Booker asked his uncle, "Uncle Percy, why does evil get to keep on growing, while good always has to stop?"

Percy replied, "That's the Way of the world. Maybe facing the hellish situation is the seed for the making of a Heavenly situation. If a sombitch slaps you and you don't smack him right back, he feels he has the eternal right to disrespect you every time he feels like it. We, as fellow humans, are therefore responsible for the fate of others; if we don't clean up our mess ourselves. Evil is like a fungus: left unchecked, it spreads throughout our society. These situations can cause gentle people to have to change into suicidal baboon 'terrorists' who would rather die destroying their oppressors than live another moment under their rule. We all have a right and duty to fight back and make the world a better place for us all."

The problem for the oppressed is to correctly interpret the energy of the oppressor; send it back against the oppressor, and continue on their way unattached and unentangled, the way Mandela and Carter did. Those guys are tough exemplary acts, but not impossible to follow."

Hallville, Indiana was a slightly larger town than Prairie Cove, Illinois. This added to Booker T's problems of isolation and the possibility of death or serious injury. In Prairie Cove, the most danger that Booker faced was when the twins regularly smacked him around and robbed him. But woe betythe anyone else who dared to beat him up. That man, woman, chicken or child would have to deal with the enmity of the twins and any number of other distant "relatives" living in the vicinity. "Revenge" was alive and well in his clan. Around the end of the 1950s, Booker T. Hampton wasn't showing any tendencies of being diminuative in stature: he was rather tall for his age.

Never-the-less, Booker did not have relatives in Hallville so there was no immediate backup for him. He was totally on his own until reinforcements could be activated and brought all the way from PC to Hallville...as if the twins were going to come to his rescue!

The "black" boys in Hallville were not like the "black" boys in PC. The Hallville boys came in groups, empowered by their numbers: fueled by drugs like heroin or Thunderbird fortified wine. Booker T would be minding his own business, walking home from school and out of the weeds would step five boys, five or more years older than him.

The first time he met Booker, the leader of one gang, a little monkey-mouthed thug with a bullet shaped head, named Sporty

Stubbs, backed by five of his lackeys, had the gaul to say to Booker, "Give it up, young nigguh."

Booker burst out laughing at him. All of a sudden, another gang member tried to do the customary push, close-proximity face-off; and Sporty tried to swing a sucker punch to Booker's head. But they failed to realize that Booker had been interpreting and anticipating their energy: responding to their every move. Booker stepped beside Sporty at a forty-five degree angle, stooping down, under, and opposite the incoming fist; and took off running in the general direction he had originally been heading...home.

The ignorant thugs were stymied. They had never seen anyone resist their "authority" and move so fast. Not only did Booker get away from them, but thirty yards out, he turned around, running backwards, and called Sporty's mama "a combat boot-wearing bull-dyker who don't wear no drawers."

"You're a dead dog sucker," screamed Sporty.

"But I always rise like Christ on Easter for your sweet Mama Stubbs."

"This I swear: you can blow it outta your ass now, boy," screamed little Sporty.

"Yad-dah, yah-dah, yah-dah. You're just another little guy turned he-man when he has a gang around him," shouted Booker. "Bring anybody else you want to, except Big Mama Stubbs. And make sure you tell that bitch she still owes me for three weeks of 'quickie-rickeys.'"

It was as if Booker was a suicidal rebel terrorist declaring Jihad on thugs. He seemed to actually get a thrill from living on the edge of impending danger. This boy was a thrill freak who dared to straddle and slide down the edge...of the imaginary giant razor blade.

In the insuing days of 1959, along his route home from school, the other kids watched the whole event unfold from a safe distance. They were amazed and impressed by this new kid named Booker T. Hampton. "God-dog! That cat's got brass balls, man," a voice in the crowd would scream.

One of the girls screamed, "Dag-gone. That dude is the man!"

Another boy yelled, "Gol-l-ly. That dude can kick rocks like Jesse Owens."

"He's got to go down," mumbled Sporty Stubbs. "Bring him to me. He's through."

By the next day, word was all over the junior high school building about the sass-mouthing new dude who could "run like Bambi; punch like a heavyweight; and talk more trash than a Chinese radio." The whole school, especially the girls, couldn't wait until school was out each afternoon to see the outcome of the previous day's runaway foot chase and unmatched mastery of trash talking called playing "The Dozens."

During the morning hours, thugs were usually asleep. They seemed to keep vampire and werewolf hours from around an hour before school let out at four o'clock in the afternoon each weekday, until a couple of hours after midnight when the bars let out.

Once Booker was inside the school building, he realized he was relatively safe. During the day, his stomach churned with anticipation for what awaited him when the final school bell rang, releasing the student body to wander toward their respective neighborhoods and homes.

Know Thyself

But as luck would have it on that day, while at ten o'clock math class, six-foot-tall, collard-green-eating Raymond Jackson took it upon himself to bully the already nervous Booker, teasing him about his impending meeting with Sporty and the Gang. Ray-Ray was just jealous of all the attention Booker was getting from the girls. He wanted to pre-empt Sporty as the bully.

The teacher, Mrs. Viola Randolph stepped out into the hallway to silence some rather vociferous students a few classrooms down the hall from her room. That's when Jackson satisfied his ego as the "King Bully Who Didn't Need No Gang" by smacking

Booker's bald head from behind, trying to sing his version of the Civil War song, "Hickey-coming-two-miles-long. Doo-dah. Doo-dah." Jackson got just that far when the already nervous Booker lost control; swung around a full one-hundred eighty degrees from the waist, smashing his oversized fist with protruding knuckles into Jackson's face; causing crimson red blood to splatter all over his desk and shirt. Jackson's forehead dropped straight to his desk, rendering him momentarily unconscious.

This gave Booker T time to step out of his desk and fully face Jackson, saying, "How you like me now, sucker? Who's got the biggest hickey, now, big boy? Better run and tell your mama and your big brother Horace."

Mrs. Smith heard the outburst of the students in her own classroom and rushed back inside. "Oh, my goodness Raymond Jackson, what in the world happened to you," she asked.

"He picked on the wrong dude," volunteered one of Booker's secret admirers Marva Curry.

Jackson came to, screaming, "Aw, nawl. You gonna pay, Hampton. I swear 'fore God, you're gonna pay, bigtime."

Not visibly shaken, Booker T. stood his ground saying, "By getting paddled by your mama? Anytime you're ready sucker, I ain't scared of you."

What made the situation worse was that Jackson's big, gentle brother Horace went to the Senior High School next door, and their mama was the physical education teacher in Booker's junior high school. The one consolation for Booker that day was that he was sent home early with a suspension, so he would get past the "kill zone" of Sporty Stubbs' ambush before Sporty and the thugs usually set it.

Trust Your Gut: You're All You've Got

For a while that day the gang boys waited in the weeds for Booker. But when all of the other students went home, they withdrew, embarrassed when they finally realized that Booker T had been suspended earlier and thereby evaded their trap. So the next Monday, Sporty had his boys set up an ambush earlier and they waited out of sight for Booker. The rapid gathering of the crowd was a sure sign to Booker of exactly where the bullies' ambush was.

Booker yelled, "I know you ignorant apes are out there. But you're too doped up and stupid to catch me." Booker was so confident of his speed, and excited by the danger of imminent bodily harm in him springing their ambush that he moved out in an open sprint. As the thugs sprang out from the weeds, one thug came close to Booker before he could hit his full stride; and Booker hit him with a left elbow to the middle of his face, breaking his nose. When another boy grabbed Booker's sweater from behind, Booker broke his grasp with a right forearm smash, leaving him screaming, "My arm! My arm! You broke my arm!" Booker got that idea from a film of football highlights where Jim Brown, the full back of the NFL's Cleveland Browns ruthlessly did the same thing to an attempted opposing tackler.

As Booker T broke free of the thugs' "kill zone," and put about a half city block distance between himself and the nearest gangboy, he heard the pitter-patter of foot steps closing in from behind him. At the mere sound of that, he kicked in with more power, running in an attempt to speed up and away from the approaching footsteps. But each time he sped up, the footsteps inched closer to him. In total panic, Booker gave it all he had left, running furiously. But the damned footsteps crept back up to him; only this time, they split and closed in on each side of him, shoulder-to-shoulder. Booker was panting in total fear. He glanced to his right and there was cousin Maggie Lee; and as he glanced to his left, he saw cousin Maimee grinning at him, both looked like that damn Cheshire cat in "Alice and Wonderland."

"Yeah, you big pussy. Look at Aunt Queenie's baby boy running like a scared little bunny rabbit looking for a hole," said Maggie Lee. "Keep up chump. We'll escort your chicken ass home to your mama."

As they ran along, Booker said, "That's easy for y'all to make fun of me. You've got each other and the other cousins back in PC for backup. The both of you are as big as Jim Brown and Jim Kelly, and run like Bambi's mama out-running a turtle. I'm just an out-numbered junior high school kid trying to make my way home in one piece."

As he looked back, he could see that the gang was seriously sucking wind, having fallen back a block and a half farther away. But they had not given up the pursuit. This time they didn't stop and peel off. It must have been the sight of the girls that piqued their curiosity and kept them coming. Booker and the girls finally made it to the projects; up the four flights of stairs to his apartment door. But as he tried to open the door, he realized it was locked and wouldn't even open when Booker inserted his key. He quickly realized that his mother Queenie had gotten home early and was continually locking the door from inside the apartment as he tried to unlock it. In terror, as Booker T heard the hallway door bang open downstairs, and the footsteps of the gang coming up the stairs, he pleaded, "Aw, Mama, please don't do this to me, now. Open the door."

"I ain't raising no silly-assed bitch-boy! Hamptons don't run away; we stand ground and throw hands. You git your punk ass back down them steps and kick some ass or I'mo be putting my foot up yours. Go on back down there and show them punks who's the man," ordered Queenie.

Just then, the door snapped unlocked and out stepped Uncle Percy, Auntie Annie, Aunt May-May and Mama Queenie.

"Aw, shoot. This ain't no fair. How am I supposed to whup a whole gang of ignant nigguhs at the same time, all by myself? I'm just one kid facing six boys older than the twins," whined Booker.

"Boy, age ain't nothing but a number: your ass is just as big as theirs. It's time you start summonsing some pride and start standing up for yourself. Go on back down there and focus on that ring leader. Whup the hell out of his ass and the rest of them no-balls sapsuckers will avoid you like the plague," declared

Uncle Percy. "Don't you see we's your peoples? You that scared? We got your back. All of them low-life sombitches ain't gonna be bothering you at once," swore six-foot-five Percy Jarvis with his .357 Magnum bulging out at his waist, under his shirt. "You just wear that leader's ass out," continued Percy.

"Yeah, chump. We got your back," promised Maimee as she and Maggie Lee started walking back down the the stairs behind Booker T, in front of Percy and the other grownups.

As the clan proceeded down the stairs, the gang met them and preceeded them back out the door into the courtyard. As Booker T stepped back out into the yard behind the adults, he moaned, "Aw, man! Y'all done brought all of the projects here to see me git killed in front of these stupid Hallville nigguhs."

"Yeah, but remember you go crazy like a mad-dog, baboon trapped in a corner when we pick on you. When we do, you fight with all your might like you ain't got nothin' to lose and you're gonna die. Do that now, and whether you win or lose, that sucker's gonna believe he's gonna die with you, instead of walking off in one piece untouched like you was some kind of paralyzed sissy-punk, pushover," promised Uncle Percy.

As the Hamptons and the project residents gathered out in the courtyard, they surrounded Sporty Stubbs and his gang, and the Hampton clan. Booker T finally came face-to-face with Sporty and his boys. Big six-foot-five inch, bowl-legged Percy stepped forward saying, "Y'all looking for a fight? Ain't no whole bunch gonna be beating up on my nephew, today. You there Shorty-Arty or Sporty-Orty Whatcha-muh-call-it, since you're the one who keeps running your mouth, acting like you the leader of the pack, and rip-raring to whup ass, even though my nephew is about six years younger than you, I'mo show you how much faith I have in his ability to whup your ass. I'mo let him surgically disassemble your worsome ass first; then the rest of you can have your turn facing him, one-by-one. We gon' see how bad you nigguhs are now. Booker T have at him. Go on over there and show them what you've got, son."

There in the courtyard stood the six thugs, first staring at the might, height and majesty of the giant Percy Jarvis and his Hampton clan; then at Booker T who, although the smallest Hampton, was at least five inches taller than Sporty Stubbs, the leader of the thugs.

Sporty was somewhat shocked when the giant, bow-legged Percy told Booker T to "Have at him... Show them what you've got. Just whup the hell outta this little runt's ass. Ain't nobody else gon' want to mess with you. We got your back."

"Yeah, Booker. Whup his butt. We've seen you fight before. Look at the little midget: I can whup his behind myself," observed Maggie Lee.

"Woo-oo-oo-oo," roared the crowd. Some started chanting, "Whup-his-ass! Whup-his-ass!"

By this time a large crowd of residents from Willard's building, the next building over, had mixed in with the crowd formed around the Hamptons and the Stubbs gang. Yes, even Willard and his boys were blended in with them. Booker started circling Sporty, sizing him up for his reach and interpreting his energy. After a few circles, he said, "Enough of this mess. I got this sucker. He's all mine."

The crowd moaned, "W-oo-oo-oo!!" when Booker's circling transformed into the direct stalking straight at Sporty.

Sporty obviously wasn't used to being trapped and embarrassed in this type scenario. Being a leader of bullies, he was always used to having his boys see him as their leader with a strong sense of his command presence and superior mind. Now, here he was for the first time in his life, on his own, facing what he always perceived to be a silly, young bitch-boy, transform into a T-Rex physically and mentally superior to him. Age advantage meant nothing now. This boy Booker was now psyched to go crazy on Sporty in front of his boys and the whole wide rest of the projects.

Even though Booker was only twelve-years-old, he was a Hampton; tall for his age at about five-foot-eleven, in comparison with Sporty, about five-foot-six. Yes, they often called Booker "mama's baby" as they chased him; but now his mama, aunties, uncle and cousins were all giants on the scene, psyching him through a series of changes to turn around and whup some serious ass. What his cousins called "a scared little bunny rabbit looking for a hole" now transformed into the likes of a full-blown hybrid T-Rex\King Kong with poisonous fangs: psyched into a suicidal rage, bent on tearing Sporty a new rectum.

As Booker circled Sporty once more, he spotted a familiar face in the crowd. It was Miss Lula and three of the ladies from the cathouse. This really pumped him up and psyched him into saying to Sporty, "Yeah. I got your number now, sucker. You come all the way over here to git me? Well, here-I-is."

The crowd, mostly neighbors whose kids were also victims of the gangs, started encouraging Booker, "Git him Booker. Look at him how he's scared of you."

Suddenly Percy said in his booming basso profundo voice, "Boy, gone and do what you do. Bust his sombitching ass!"

As Booker stepped forward in a fake move, Sporty tried to swing a right hook to his head. Anticipating the hook, Booker lowered his height from his knees in a crouch, twisted his shoulders from the waist, and buried his right fist into Sporty's short ribs above his left pelvis. As Sporty let out a blood-curdling scream, Booker T caught him with a left hook to his forehead, knocking Sporty out cold. Booker's motion plus the motion of Sporty's wild attempted right hook, caused an impact to Sporty's midsection that culminated in a flood of urine in his pants. In the blows, Sporty had accidently bitten his own tongue.

The thugs and crowd moaned in horror as little Sporty fell, gasping and whimpering, desperately sucking wind at the same time. Immediately, Booker shifted his total bodyweight to his rear leg and commenced to kicking Sporty in the face. As Queenie grabbed Booker, pulling her son away from the boy, Sporty curled up in a fetal position, deficating, farting and urinating all on himself like a helpless, sick baby.

"God-dog! Go-d-d Dog," screamed Maggie Lee.

"Da-g-g Gone, Cuz," cried Maimee to Booker. "You must have been playing with us all the time. You ain't no joke."

"That's enough son. You did your job. You the man. The dirty little nigguh's through. Don't look like the rest of 'em want any more parts of you, either. Let's gon' back upstairs before the police come," said Queenie.

Maimee hollered out, "I don't care if my first baby be a boy or a girl, I'mo name 'em Booker T."

"Yeah. And if it's a girl, instead of naming her Booker T., how 'bout naming her Booker May? Or Booker Lee?," teased her sister Maggie. "But, if mine is a boy, I'mo name him Booker Mane; with the nickname 'Boogerman' Hampton," said Maimee with pride.

When the Hamptons all reached Queenie's apartment, they heard the sound of sirens. As they all watched from Queenie's fourth floor apartment window, they saw the police and ambulance crews respond to the courtyard, administering first aid to Sporty. No sooner than the medic broke a small capsule and waived it under his nose, Shorty commenced to kicking and sat bolt-upright screaming, "What—the—fuck! Y'all help me Lord Jesus; Martin Luther King. Help me to my feet. My legs. My legs won't stop wobblin'. What's wrong with me? Git me outta here."

As the police tried to canvass the crowd, seeking information, everyone started walking away back into their respective courtyards and apartments, grinning all over themselves. The ambulance crew hauled away the empty gurney as the police sergeant ordered his men to resume normal patrol. One old lady whispered to her adult daughter, "Lord. Lord. Lord. That big old fella' whupped that poor little boy's ass so bad that Jesus wept."

As Sporty's boys helped him away from the fight scene, word spread throughout the Project and beyond about Booker's decisive knockout victory. Horace Jackson got wind of the Booker/Sporty fight and told his sibling Raymond, "Sucker, you made out. They say that wild assed boy put Sporty in the hospital with a busted kidney. If you know what's good for your ass, you better leave that young boy alone."

Maggie Lee's joking way of renaming Booker spread throughout the Oakfield Projects and the neighborhoods on

Dumas Street, Pissy Creek Parkway and the Humboldt Housing Development clear over to the west side of Hallville. At first, folks called Booker "Booker-the-Man." Then they called him the "Boogermane." Even the older teenaged thugs picked on everyone except him. And when they would see him, all they could say was "Way-to-go young blood. You the Mane."

Even his cousins Maggie Lee and Maimee were treating him with new-found respect. Maggie Lee said, "Dag, boy. We told you to go baboon on a sucker, and you turned into a full blown King Kong. We're proud of you, Booker. When you coming back to PC? You can have the whole bed, while we sleep on a pallet on the floor," offered Maimee.

"Why y'all got to be sleeping on the floor just 'cause I come over? Just put Maggie Lee's ass in a diaper and some rubber drawers, and I'll be fine," said Booker.

"You see me laughing, fool? I stopped pissing years ago; but I can still rumble," said Maggie.

"You still give those good, hard, grunting hugs," asked Booker.

Most people didn't realize it, but Booker T. Hampton's whole life had changed. On one hand, he was astonished that he had such decisive power over older people. But on the other hand, he was angry with himself for not realizing this sooner. He constantly told his cousins of how he was disappointed with himself.

Because of his nature and upbringing, he didn't let his prowess go to his head. He also realized that because of his ability and size, he was in more danger than smaller boys his same age. Uncle Percy always reminded him of the story of David and Goliath.

The Wisdom of the Bigger Man

"Son, most of us people in our clan are kind of like Goliath, in size. But the wise ones try to be like David when facing "impossible" odds. When average-sized people fight each other with their fists, they expect that the most the loser is gonna git is a bad ass-whupping. But when an average-sized person fights one of us, they figure they are not only gonna git a serious big-nigguh-asswhuppin', like you gave that little bastard Sporty Stubbs, but they bet they're gonna die. The wise ones are gonna cover their asses with a weapon or something sneaky to increase their chances of survival. Sometimes you just have to use 'the wisdom of the bigger man.' I don't mean for you to tuck tail; turn your back to them, and run away from a fight. But, if you can sense a man is scared shitless, and ain't about to come at you, try to give him an avenue of escape; keep a sharp eye on him, as you or he walks away. If the fool insists on messing with you, you have no choice but to bust his ass," warned Uncle Percy.

Rely on Yourself Since You're Always the One "With You"

Booker T revered his Grampa Austin like he was a god on Mt. Olympus. And back when Austin was killed in the brickyard "accident," Booker felt as though his whole life had ended. The pallet of bricks that crushed poor Austin may just as well have crushed young Booker T, too.

Mary Alice suffered a nervous breakdown. She had a heart attack and died in her sleep the same night of Austin's death. His death and living life without Austin was just too much for Mary Alice's poor little heart and mind to bear.

It was around that time that Booker received word from Auntie Annie Lee Jarvis that Hope Newcomb had passed away and was buried back in his home town of Smackover, Arkansas.

Overwhelmed by the deaths of so many people he loved and trusted, Booker tried to occupy himself with baseball, in memory of the life and times of Grampa Austin. Booker even tried playing the same position that Austin played...catcher. But it was Booker's misfortune to be accidently struck in the head by the batter. With that, he lost his desire to be a baseball player; but became fascinated with the practice of TaiChi. Each morning during summer vacation, he saw a bunch of older Asian people moving through the Taichi forms in slow-motion in the courtyard of his grandparents' apartment and storefront building.

Eventually he came to realize that Mr. Feng, the owner of the restaurant and laundry, was the Sifu or teacher of this group. After a few more days, Mr. Feng invited Booker to join in the dance. Booker came to realize that the whole Taichi dance, though done slowly, took only about twenty minutes to complete a continuous string of one-hundred eight postures. They were not only meant for the civil practice of relaxing muscles and strengthening joints, but there was a martial aspect, meditation and cultivation of Chi energy resulting from making each move.

After several months, he was able to do the entire TaiChi dance on his own, from memory. From that point on, he was able to speed up the dance and repeat it several times in a row. He also came to realize the subtleties of the movements, like weight distribution, balance, using the mind instead of brute force. With encouragement from Master Feng, he was able to learn things like pressing, folding, ward off, and other principles. Booker even learned teachings like the Tao Te Ching and I Ching. To him, these concepts were The Explanation of The Way of Life he sought. But to others in the community and the Hampton Clan, Booker seemed to be practicing some weird kind of "soft" karate forms.

The day finally came when Booker graduated from junior high school and entered high school. He really missed Grampa Austin, Great Gramma Sage, Mr. Hope and Gramma Mary Alice. He longed for their candor in answering his questions about the weirdness of life and its mysterious people. But no sooner than Austin and Mary Alice made their passage, Uncle Percy and Auntie Annie Lee Jarvis rose up to fill the void left by Booker's grandparents.

Annie Lee especially missed her sister Mary Alice. They had been very close in childhood like each other's best friend. So, even though Annie Lee and Booker's mother Queenie seemed to always end up in a war of words in the early years, in later years Annie Lee became more like a revered step-mother to Queenie.

On Booker's final day of junior high school, after Queenie picked him up for the ride home, she noticed sadness in Booker. "Baby, what's wrong?"

"Aw Mama, it just seems like my whole world is turned upside down. I know it's been almost ten years, but it seems like no sooner than Grampa and Gramma are gone in PC, I got to go to this mostly white high school in Hallville with these uppity middle class negroes and stupid inhuman white teachers who think they know how to get into a kid's head. This pledge of allegiance, national anthem, white Jesus and U.S. Constitution bull crap gives me a migraine headache and makes me want to puke."

"Well, the school won't be all-white no more. There'll be a few more of y'all there to keep each other company."

"Yeah, about a bus load of misplaced, brainwashed, young ghetto kids for the hypocrite three thousand 'whites' to pick on and try to feel superior to. I'm sick of being civil while ignorant, punk-assed honkies constantly try to play stupid mind games on me. I was all set to go to Hallville's all-black A. G. Gaston High School from Gaston Junior High School. Now they've got me going all the way across town to racist, elitist Baldridge High. They always have to play the bully and deny that they know what you're complaining about. If they don't stop, I can see how one day somebody's gonna get a gun and shoot every cracker bully they see."

"Well, don't forget that punk-assed black boys were gunning for your ass until you started whuppin' the shit out of them. No matter who the people are, or where you go in America, you're gonna run into those who are subject to want to have their way with your young ass. Whiteys survive by being two-faced, double-crossing and back-stabbing, and need you to be a stupid inferior-minded person so they can always take advantage. So-called black folks try to fuck you, while calling you their brother. America's not a democracy; it seems more like a paradox and a hypocrisy; a god-damned lie. Don't let other people's devilish perversions get you down no more than a ignorant feral dog will get on your nerves. Just realize that they don't know no better and don't have what it takes to learn any other way."

"Yeah, it really is like y'all always said, 'You can't get mad at the dog for licking its balls.' White people seem to be too stupid to stop messing with you. No matter if it kills them, they still feel they've got to be in charge of you. Yet they always claim that negroes are everywhere, and they're the ones that brought all of us here in the first place. I like things to be segregated and separated. They have theirs, and we have ours. Then we keep dumb colored people in line and stay away from greedy crackers at the same time."

"Yeah, but things don't always work out like that. And like I've told you before, we all didn't come here as slaves on them few little ships," said Queenie. "How you think the Hamptons wound up out in the middle of the Texas panhandle? Them scrub-assed crackers didn't have enough money to buy their own grub: let alone buy and feed a bunch of nigguhs who didn't have nothing to do. You know what I'm saying?"

"No ma'am. Whatchu mean?"

Chapter 13

The Awakening

"I'm saying that our ancestors were already here, before the disease-infested white men showed up on those little ships," said Queenie. "Whose bones do you think are buried in the Cahokia Mounds in Illinois that the white's 'can't seem to find neither hide nor hair' of? We are the original Americans, even before the 'red' people came here over the Bering Straits out of Asia and through Alaska and Canada. The white people mind-fucked all of us, reds, blacks, and browns, by lying through their teeth and changing our names and destroying the history of everything and everybody to be able to get away with stealing and 'legally' hold on to everything else they could get their paws on."

"How can you fool your only son," teased Booker.

"See. That's the problem with your generation. Y'all want to take the easy way out. Whitey feels they have to mess with all melanated folks. They think that since they invented all these bullshit lies and diseases, we are all supposed to be stupid with nothing else to do but fuck with each other; and at the same time, we're supposed to measure up to white folks' standards. Whiteys think they're gonna always have the whole 'cake', and don't want nobody else to have a damned crumb. They fear that if we do get something, we'll get too strong for them to handle and overthrow their supremacy."

"Yeah, they do like to hog it all," said Booker T. "See a nigguh with something and they feel that they did something wrong if they don't already have it, too. I'd just rather stay away from them. I like having all black teachers and principals and schoolmates in our schools. Even the black janitors cheer us on to do things three times better and strive to have our own. I wish my namesake Booker T. Washington was here instead of some of these other so-called black leader preachers telling everybody to turn their cheeks. I'm tired of being bothered with buck-dancing 'coons and their white supreme masters."

"That's not the way the world goes 'round," said Queenie. "You're talking about taking the easy way out. When you didn't have to enter the white world, nigguhs was trying to kill you and fuck you in the ass. This is America. No matter which-a way you turn, the name of the game is 'find a wimp and fuck them over.' That's what some of our ancestors did to each other all around the world until they found some whiteys to sell some of us to. The white men had no machines and their mules didn't have no hands. So they told the African Warlords, 'OK. I'll take all the nigguhs you got.' They couldn't get enough Africans across the Atlantic, so they started grabbing nigguhs who were already here. They turned us into 'beasts-of-burden', house servants, concubines, cotton pickers, and 'cows' for their babies to suck off of," said Queenie.

"Dag, mama. Where'd you learn all of this?"

"From MyDaddy and MaDear."

"How come they didn't tell me?"

"You're too ignorant!"

"Concubine? What's that," asked Booker.

"It's a whore; free pussy at the white man's beck and call. Better and safer than fucking chickens and stump-jumping cows," said Queenie.

"I once heard Grampa say to Grandma that's how I got here."

"Watch your mouth, Mr. Smart-ass: I can still take you out of here. That gooch-eyed, snaggle-tooth, half-breed bastard was my concubine. All men think they be getting the 'snatch.' Truth be told, it's the pussy that snatches them. You men may think this is a man's world, but it's the pussy that y'all must answer to. Each and every one of you git here through the pussy. All throughout your life, you sooner or later, one way or another, all y'all, except the boodey bandits, will give up most of your earnings to the pussy. And most of you gon' die competing with each other over some pussy or a pussy substitute. And the one's that think they don't like pussy, they turn the other man into one. After all is said and done, the men wind up being the concubines and bed-warmers, too. So be grateful you made it this far, Mr. Smartass. I could have flushed your puss-colored ass down the toilet."

"Naw, worse. Gramma and Grampa said y'all didn't have no plumbing back then, down in Booney. All you had was a wooden shed where y'all sat on a board with a hole sawed in it, over a deep hole dug in the ground, full of..."

"Yeah. Say it. You in enough shit up to your big mouth now. It ain't too late for me to turn back the hands of time and warm some ass."

"MaDear. There's no need for you to use such inappropriate language in the expression of your exasperation and frustration with the inevitable world situation. Don't you remember what you promised me?"

"Yeah, you're gonna always be my lil' nigger; even if you git bigger. I know that May-May used to tell you the same thing. But, you know how nigguhs like to lie."

Booker knew this without saying, because he had no siblings and had received all of Queenie's love from his very beginning. The only times he saw her lose her temper were when someone messed with him or falsely accused him of wrong-doing. Anyway, he was bigger than her, now. Yet he knew that once he grew to be too strong for her, she wouldn't hesitate to pick up something and knock the fool out of him.

As the car came to a stop at the traffic light, he wrapped his arm over his mother's shoulder and reminded her, "You always said that I was always gonna be your lil' nigguh, even if I got bigger. And you always used to say, 'Are you mad? Are you sad? Then scratch your ass and git glad.' Well, back atcha, Mama Queenie. Baby Booker is a bigguh nigguh, now: and you is stuck to him like he's your eternal, very own little black Tar Baby. Time is up. 'Lil' Nigguh' is now the Boogerman. You got to git him while he's sleep, 'cause when he's woke, he's wild!"

They both howled with laughter as the cars and trucks behind them blew their angry horns in frustration as they eased on down the road, knowing that no road rage in the world could defeat the two of them together.

Don't Bend

To gain respect in the streets and his school was a notable achievement for Booker. But, to garner the same status at home was a much higher peak to climb.

Mama Queenie had always said, "I have my needs." This was her excuse when she was desirous of getting involved with a man. Just as she behaved out on the lone Texas prairie, she followed suit with the same reasoning with practically every other man she was attracted to. Regardless of their race or hybrid, they all ended up being nothing more than her "concubines." And after a while, she would end up changing them like a street walker changes her worn out boots. If she hadn't marched off and had her "tubes tied" earlier, she would have been a brood mare birthing Booker's siblings.

Other than being around his grandfather Austin Hampton and his uncle Percy Jarvis, Booker T never felt a need for a father figure in his life. He considered himself to be his own father early on, and dealt with whomever Queenie chose as her mate for the time being. Just because she chose to let some of her men live with her, Booker felt he wasn't obligated to obey them and honor their regime as he respected his relatives and great men like Hope Newcomb.

Shortly after the time that Booker T put a beating on Sporty Stubbs, Mama Queenie started declaring that she had her needs again, and began reciting more often to Booker T the phrase, "I'll be so damned glad when your ass gets grown, and you hurry up and get the hell out of here."

Was this because he was starting to become too big for her to handle? Booker never seemed to read into the core meaning of this behavior. He had to stand down each time and accept the fact that he had no choice over who Queenie chose to share their home and her bed with. He was still too young for that level of emancipation and household administration.

This meant that Queenie's man at a particular moment would be granted some authority as the man of the house. All of that stuff came to an end when Booker T finally lost his tolerance at around age fifteen. From that point on, he swore that if the gang boys couldn't disrespect him in the streets, no other person was going to subjugate him that way in his own home. He started reminding Queenie, "Mama, your needs are none of my business. But just because you're scared of some of these suckers doesn't mean that I have to be scared of them and put up with any of their macho mess. I've spent my entire life raising myself to be a standup man like my grandfather and uncle. As much as I love and respect you, I can't stand down as a developing man and put up with the results of your 'needs' for these lesser men and their bull crap."

To that statement, Queenie would always reply, "Then, it's time for your ass to hit the road, Jack."

Booker T started his freshman year at Hallville's Baldridge High School in 1960, with the determination to financially sustain and support himself by getting odd jobs during his first summer in high school. He always said, "I can't be a man unless I'm standing up for myself, on my own two feet." So, he determined to continue working for Miss Lula, and carrying the Hallville Daily newspapers before sunrise every morning of the week. To fend off the dogs, wildlife and druggies, he carried along a wooden club fashioned out of an old table leg while delivering his newspapers.

One night, after about 8pm, a week into the semester, Booker was deep into his homework, when he heard his mother Queenesther wailing softly under her voice as though she was trying to hide being tormented. He grabbed his table leg, walked into the kitchen and saw Queenie's latest "need"-provider, a typical five-foot-six type, named Woody Duggan, choking her with one hand and slapping her upside the head with the other hand. Booker in turn commenced to choking Duggan with one hand and smacking him upside his head with that table leg until Duggan's knees buckled and he collapsed to the floor. Booker, then, grabbed the little man by his long, processed hair and commenced to banging his head into the kitchen cabinet until he felt his mother striking him on his back with her fists. As he turned to face her, Duggan slumped to the floor again like a rag doll.

Booker heard his mother screaming at him as he turned to face her, still pounding on him. As she continued pounding on his chest, he saw her sobbing and scream at him, saying, "I'm sick and tired of you interfering in my business. You have no right to come in here and do this to him. I'll be so damned glad when your ass gets grown, and you get the hell out of here, nigguh."

Booker answered in a basso profundo voice, "What else did you expect me to do? Just stay in my room like a numb-nuts while this fool beats the hell out of you? You're so selfish and needy of this little sawed-off monkey that you've gone and bent over backwards to put up with his shit? You show off for him by attacking your own son who's trying to fight for you? Next time you two want to git drunk, you best do it at his mama's house, 'cause if he comes over here to my mama's house snatching nigguhs, I'mo be issuing out another big nigguh ass whuppin'. And while you're at it, you need to take this lil' suckuh home to his own mama, out of my face. You both stank like smack water jack. Light a match in here, we're all getting blown to Kingdom Come."

By that time, Duggan began to respond to Queenie's slaps and her dashing cold water on his face. He came to and started screaming, "My hair. My hair. Bitch, you're fuckin' up my hair!" He finally opened up his eyes and looked up at Booker T for a moment and said, "Boy, your ass is crazier than your mama's. I'm gittin' the hell out of here, away from both of you crazy mothuhfuckuhs. And Queenie, I ain't coming back here no more."

"That's your best bet, you little knappy-headed runt. If I ever hear of you putting your little monkey hands on my mama again, I'mo be all over you like a gorilla on a football. Then, for extra measure, I'mo go over there on Allen Lane, and put my feet up your mama's ass, too."

With that, Duggan was up and out the door, bounding down the stairs and down the driveway. All the while Queenie was sobbing at Booker, "You have no right to interfere in my affairs. I have my needs!"

If ever Booker T was to grow up into manhood, this was certainly his first sign or omen to take due notice thereof and govern himself accordingly. "Mama, you ought to be ashamed of yourself."

"Ashamed of myself? Aw, you the big man now, Mr. Blowhard Bigguh Nigguh. How you think your ass was born? All based on my needs. Good or bad, out of the bitter came the sweet."

"That liquor ain't made nothing for you no sweeter than a punk trying to give you an ass-whuppin', with total disrespect for you and your son. Queenie..."

"Aw, so now I'm Queenie to you, huh?"

"You always raised me to never take an ass-whuppin' without fighting to the death. Now, I see you taking one, whining like a wimpy little puppy. And you expect me to bow down and just kneel there to this little punk-assed woman-beater like you're doing? You must be drunk out of your mind. I'll get out of your

141

space as soon as I'm able. Never-mind waiting 'til I'm grown, I'm ready to git-to-gittin' now. But, until I can find a place, you need to straighten out your men...or boys. If you can't stand up to them faggots, then bristle up at them the way you be doing to me. I'm the one on your side, but you keep gettin' me confused with one of them. I wish Grampa and Gramma was here to see this mess. Since you've been hittin' that skank gin, you keep losing more and more of your mind and your pride."

Self-Reliance to the Bone

"It's time for you to go, Booker. I cain't take no more of your disrespect. First you whup up on my man. Next, you start callin' me Queenie. And now, you're saying 'shit' while you're talking down at me." Queenie was grabbing for every piece of evidence to prove she'd be justified in getting Booker T out of her house.

"Can you do me one last favor then, MaDear, and call Auntie Annie and Uncle Percy?"

"Gladly," said Queenie.

After she dialed, Auntie Annie Lee Jarvis answered the phone saying, "Hello?"

"Auntie, it's me; Queenie. You got a minute?"

"Like I'mo tell you naw? What you sippin' now, Queenesther? Aqua Velva, Mennen or just some plain old rubbing alcohol?"

"Never mind the bullshit: this is serious. I need a favor. Here: I'll let you speak to him."

"Hi, Auntie. I hate to be bothering you this late. But, can I come stay with you and Uncle Percy for a while," pleaded Booker.

Just then, Booker could hear the screen door slam over the phone as his uncle, Percy, came through his back doorway saying to Annie Lee, "Aw, I thought I heard the phone ring; but I see you got it."

As he turned to go back outside, Annie Lee said to him, "Hold on. I think this one's for you."

As Percy took the phone, he said, "Hello?"

At First, Booker couldn't say anything...he was making choking sounds as he started to sobbing. His Uncle Percy tried to console him.

"I know, I know. She turned on you again, huh? The only person what can make you feel this way is your mama. I don't know why you insist on arguing with her, Booker. You ought to know by now that you cain't win no argument against your mama. She ain't gonna budge an inch on that. She cain't. Bless her heart, she don't know no better, but to have the last word."

"Yes sir. Even with that drunken fool smackin' her upside her drunken head," Booker finally blurted out.

"Say what? She okay," asked Percy.

"Yes sir. She ain't got no visible knots on her head, but that suckuh sure does. And she threatened to put some upside my head for getting in the way of her 'needs.'"

"Aw, yes. Now I see. Queenesther and her 'needs'. Now, even you are in the way. You're lucky she didn't fight you."

"Aw, Uncle Percy. Sometimes she really confuses me. She always raised me not to take no mess without putting up a fight. Now she stands up there like a cry-baby, letting some sawed-off little midget bust her upside the head like she's his red headed stepchild. Then, when I move to jack him up, she jumps on my back, like she's showing off for this suckuh, screaming about how I have no right to beat on him and that she has her 'needs'. Now, she's telling me to get out. I don't need to keep hearing that mess."

"Some things that you don't understand, you have to let them be, for the time being," said his uncle. "The understanding comes later on after you meditate on the principle for a while. Booker, you've got to git ahold of Booker, and don't be gittin' entangled behind other people and their bullshit. You've got to always be the bigger man, and take care of Booker T first, when the very people you trust, start looking like they're working against you. More people have gotten killed and seriously injured by the loved-one they thought was in agreement with them. I don't care if they're gittin' an ass-whuppin' or drowning, people's 'needs' do come first to them, instinctively. That self-preservation instinct kicks in and they will turn on the person who came to save them. Even in the animal kingdom, the animal's 'needs' come first. That's why some bitches even eat their own puppies just to stay alive."

"What kind of mess is that, Uncle Percy?"

"Oh, yeah! It may sound crazy, but that's why you've got to stay your young ass out of Queenesther's business. She gits to acting like a animal, and bites the hand that's trying to save her. She's grown: her house is her kingdom. She rules. Queenie gonna always be the queen. Bless her heart: she-don't-know-no-better. And whether we like it or not, her needs do come first; especially when she be laying up with one of those little sawed-off sombitches. She even got ready to slap her own mama, my wife, and her baby sister May-May, when she was in labor delivering you. For goodness sake, don't get between her and her 'needs'. She feels that if you cain't help her git 'em, you needs to git the hell out of her way when she's trying to get them. That brings the beast out of her more than anything else."

"Yeah. She keeps reminding me that my father was one of them half-breed Mexican white people. I don't care no more. I'm just grateful I was born. Now that I'm here, I'mo make the most out of life and make something out of myself. I'mo always love my mama, but baby Booker is gone. Booker the man is here now. I'mo be a strong man, like you Uncle Percy and Grampa Austin."

"Well, I appreciate that, son. Just don't git yourself caught up in other people's crossfire. Irregardless of who's whuppin' her ass, she still feels she needs their attention…the kind a son cain't give her. And when you step between her and her 'needs', you become the one to blame for the misery. By now, you already know her motto is 'Lead; follow; or get the hell outta the way!' I know it sounds crazy, but some people always hurt the ones they love. You cain't be coming between these people and their 'needs'. 'Self-preservation' and 'self-satisfaction' are two dirty, one way cousins. She's turned on her own ancestors and peers. Now she's twistin' everything around, and gone mad at her only descendant, which is you."

"So I'm just supposed to just stand there like a fool, while some sucker is smacking my mama upside her head," asked Booker.

"Naw, naw: I'm not saying that Booker T. What I'm trying to say is that your best bet is to break camp, and high-tail it outa there before the two of them be turning against your young ass. You just keep your mouth shut; mind your business; bide your time, and haul ass outta Hallville; and hook-up with the rest of us. Don't try to reason things out: just realize that it's time for you to break camp. You've got to be the bigger man: out-think the two of them. Next time they start their shit, make your point with the nigguh away from your mama; and watch your own ass. He's gonna feel justified in saving his own ass and getting his way. He ain't gonna keep standing there, lettin' some big-assed kid put foot up his ass or maul his head. He's gonna try his damnedest to fuck you up worse than he does your mama."

"You know what Uncle Percy? I'mo stay out of it altogether."

"Smart man, Booker. Now, you're thinking. It's her house and her ass; not yours. She wants to bend for a sombitch, that's her perogative; not yours. You can't git mad at the dog for licking his balls or the bitch for licking her ass. They don't know no better. It's theirs; not yours. Stay your nose out of it. You cain't do everything. She thinks she's gonna git what she wants; maybe she's getting what she deserves. She's always been so headstrong, overbearing and obnoxious. She made up her own mind, and started a habit of loving men like that. A lot of women grow big heads and subscribe to the belief in the power of their pussy. But sometimes their 'pussy-power' turns against them: it could turn into a wild weasel. It all boils down to 'power of the mind.' Using pussy power is when a woman bends and starts using something immoral that's easiest to get her way. But when you bend the rules, the joker's wild with no rules to go by; and things invariably can get out of control, and can make her act like a damned fool, and turn on her own people who come to her rescue. And that's also when the son becomes a man, refusing to bend by standing up for her; and can get his ass killed on a bullshit tip. The wise man will watch his own ass: know when and where to bend; and just stay the hell outta a fool's way. Like I said before, if push comes to shove, catch that sombitch away from your mama, in another place and time, and in your own way…like you did them foolish nigguhs back there in Hallville in the school and the projects."

"I hear you, Uncle Percy. I'm good at biding my time. Now, at school and in the gangs, they call me The Phantom Negro."

"Say what?"

"Yeah. I'm The Phantom Negro. They never know when and where I'mo pop up on them outta the weeds in an ambush. That's when it's just me and one of them; payback one at a time, in my time. I always ask 'em, 'Let's see how bad you are now suckuh; now that your boys ain't with you.' That's what I did to this dude named Schooney in the alley behind Mr. Black's house. You and Grampa Austin always taught me to be the bigger man and don't be too big to sidestep a fight if I can. I can be patient. It's not what they call 'running away.' It's what the Marines call a tactical retreat, where you fall back and regroup to destroy a bigger force in your own time, in your own way."

"True dat. True dat. Well, way back when you was born, Annie Lee and me promised your grandparents and your mama that we would always be there in their place for May-May and Queenie, and their kids. But, you don't see none of them bending and calling on us for help. Sure, it hurts my heart. But I always remember what your Auntie here tells me. 'If you find yourself gittin' mad or sad, just scratch your ass and git glad.' We ain't God. Sometimes it's best to mind our own business. Everybody just has to git ahold of their self and don't let the problems get to them. It's like you have to imagine you've got a lightswitch on the side of your head that you flick up and down, off and on. It's really called a 'give-a-fuck' switch. If you see something you cain't do nothing about, you just reach up and flick that sombitch off. And as an extra added measure, ask the person you're supposed to give-a-fuck for to look into your eyes. Then ask them if they can see anyone in there that gives a fuck."

"Ha-Ha-a-a-a! I wish it was that simple, Uncle Percy. Mama gits to sucking that hooch and she starts talking to me like I'm one of those men who try to push her around."

"She's abusing you," asked Percy.

"In the worst sort of way, Uncle Percy." As he cautiously looked around for Queenie, upon seeing her nodding off in the next room, Booker T whispered into the phone, "I think sometimes she's gonna grab her ice pick, and stab me or something. It's like she's trying to build up a case to justify why she should do it. She be calling me all kinds of M-Fs and stuff. I'm not one of her nigguhs that smack her around. I'm her son trying to fight for her. But to her, I'm just another liquor-sucking nigguh that she cain't control."

"Aw, I see. It's done turned to that. Your best bet is to come on back here to Prairie Cove with me and your Auntie Annie. We gonna have to git up there and talk to Niece Queenie tonight. I don't know how she's gonna take this. Especially if she's been hitting that sauce too much."

"Uncle Percy, she respects you and Auntie Annie like she did Grampa and Grandma. I can't keep staying here no longer. Every minute it's gittin' worse and worse with me always being expected to bend low, defend my every move, making way for her boyfriends. A part of me doesn't want to abandon her. But another part of me doesn't want to fight my own mama and git killed."

"Looks like she's trying to take out on you what she should be doing to her men friends," said Percy. On the police department, that's what we call 'transference.' She's gone too far. That's how innocent people gits killed on a bullshit tip. We've got to git you out of there now, son. We got enough shit going on in what's left of this family, without putting up with this perverted mess. Say no more. We're on the way. You just sit still and keep your mouth shut. Now, call your mama back in the room and give her the phone."

Booker went to the doorway, called his mother and gave her the phone. "Hello. Uncle Percy?" asked Queenie. "Aw, naw. Don't tell me; Booker's done gone and dragged y'all deep into my business. Boy, go on in the other room. Me and your uncle got to talk."

"Yes ma'am," said Booker as he left the room.

"Queenie, I know I ain't your daddy; and I cain't be telling no grown-assed woman how to live your life: but Booker's 'bout to go astray. He had enough respect for me and you to 'fess-up on the matter. If it's okay with you, just like with your mama Mary Alice and your daddy Austin, and you and May-May, Booker T is welcome to come stay with us for a while, until things cool down."

"Uncle Percy, I appreciate your offer. I try to carry my own weight and problems; but Booker T has become more than a notion. He's too big for me to be rumblin' and tumbling' with."

"Well Sugar, that's why we've always turned to each other in times of strife as family. It ain't never been no notion or bending to encroachment for us to be there for each other. It's been like the glue where we stick together as one and turn what appeared to be a tough situation into an opportunity to grow into something good," said Percy.

"I appreciate that, Uncle Percy. Don't forget y'all took us in from Texas and helped us git started up here. Besides, Booker T is getting to that age where he constantly needs a man of the family as an example of how to grow and learn. I know y'all have always meant well for my baby. I would truly appreciate you taking him in, but you got to always remember that Booker is mine. No matter how much we may argue or how much he may grow, he's all I ever had."

"Queenesther, you ain't talking to no fool. I know that, and I've always respected that. You have my word as the elder man of this family that I will stand by Booker, for you, as long as I live. Now don't you worry; ain't nobody out to steal him from you. Besides, his ass is too big, now, for anybody to try to be pulling him anywhere against his will. Plus, I bet he eats like a horse. Now you rest easy. Me and Annie Lee are on our way there. Give us a few hours."

No sooner than she got off the phone from Percy, Queenie turned to the suddenly hopeful Booker T nodding for him to come back into the room; standing there beside her, as she asked him, "Boy, who's your mama?"

As he pulled his head back in wonderment, he said, "You're my mama! A man can only git one mama, then that's it."

"Damn skippy. No matter how the world turns, as long as your ass is on it, don't you ever forget that. You're with Uncle Percy for now. Don't make me have to come over there to PC to bust your ass and embarrass you."

"Aw naw, Mama. I would never do that. I love you."

Non-attachment

Percy and Annie Lee Jarvis drove to Hallville that same summer night; gave their niece Queenie a hug, a little conversaton; and headed on back toward PC with Booker T in the back seat of the car.

At about an hour past midnight, while headed west, out the Indiana state highway, Percy was nearly blinded by oncoming high beamed car headlights. As the car passed them, Percy noticed it was a black and white coupe, with a red dome light on the roof. It suddenly made a u-turn back onto the two-lane country road as they continued west at about five miles per hour under the speed limit. Percy noticed the police cruiser speeding up until it was about two car lengths behind them in a tailgating fashion for about a mile.

"Baby, I think we've got some company. Racist police been bird-dogging us for a while since he hooked a u-turn back there by that last billboard," said Percy.

Annie Lee knew the drill. "Oh boy: here we go again. This is how these local yokel sombitchin' crackers in these here one-horse towns pay for their new police cruisers and raise their families' standards of living: just waiting for innocent colored people to come along trying to lawfully make their way to St. Louis or Memphis."

Among the "colored" folks of P.C., the word was out about this stretch of the highway, "Watch out. The police are stopping each and every carload of nigguhs to take their cash along that segment of the state highway."

"If I can just git us to the State Police barracks just up the road, I'll pull us in there to shake this buzzard off our trail before he turns his dome light on. When they're trying to rob money off colored folks, they like to pull you over where they can have you all by yourself with no witnesses."

"There it is up ahead, Uncle Percy... I see the sign for the State Police Barracks."

As Percy pulled the car into the State Police parking lot, the black and white town police car picked up speed and continued on down the road to the intersection; did another U-turn, and drove back by them, heading back east down the two lane highway to its jurisdiction.

"Just to be safe, we should sit tight here for a spell and let that creeping bastard git off our scent. It's a shame that folks cain't travel on the open road, minding their own business within the law, without being terrorized and robbed by the same people who are supposed to be out here protecting them against the outlaws."

"Yeah, well it's mostly our fault for letting them get away with it. And the crooked cops are usually the most fervent 'Christians' and 'patriotic, law-abiding' sombitching 'Americans'...especially them traitors that still wave that stupid-looking confederate battle flag or have sayings like 'Support Our Local Police' on their rear bumper stickers and lawns. They're too ignorant to know anything else besides 'hogging-it-all'," said Annie Lee.

"And the paradox of it all is that down South, you've still got black folks that bend over for that kind of shit. Can you believe they had buck-dancing, traitor Negroes in that rag-tag, piece-of-shit Confederate Army," asked Percy.

"That's because they're inhuman and don't know no better or how to cook. The coward confederate rebels were too scared to give their own colored soldiers rifles to fight the Union troops. The poor colored slaves did like we just did. They out-manuevered the white bastards by biding their time; bullshitting the rebels; and joining the Union for their freedom first chance they got. Some colored folks, today, might call that Uncle Tomming. But "Uncle Tom" was a good black man who stood up for his people. That sombitchin' Sambo was the sell-out, boot-lickin' nigguh who was a disgrace to his race. Those are what they called soul-surviving, quick-thinkin' colored folks," claimed Annie Lee. "They had to be with some two-faced, scared-assed Samboes in their ranks."

"That's why I love and believe in you, baby," Percy said to his wife. "I'm too narrow-minded; but you always think outside of the box. Booker, if you know what's good for your young ass, you'll take your time, and put your name on a good woman, like this one."

"Mama's like that when she ain't drinking," said Booker.

"Yes she is, Booker T. We've got you to remember that she's my big sister Mary Alice's daughter. And Mary Alice is the one who taught me how to think like that," confessed Annie Lee.

"Uncle Percy and Auntie Annie, I just want y'all to know how truly grateful I am to be taken in by y'all."

"That's all because your mama did a good job of teaching you about having gratitude and manners, too. But don't forget the fact that we are family: and we do love, respect, and are just as committed to you as your mama and grandparents. We've known you all of your life, through good times and bad times. So hush little baby; don't you cry," teased Annie Lee. They all broke out laughing as Percy pulled the car back out onto the road continuing west toward the state line into Illinois and on toward Prairie Cove.

"I just feel helpless about Mama. Now that I'm gone, those fools got free will to hurt her."

"Well son. Let me put it this way. I contend that you don't have to worry too much about your mama gittin' too hurt. She's a Hampton. They come in like a lamb and walk out like a lion. What we all have to worry about is the welfare of that poor sombitch when Queenie gets sick of his ass. Way back, when you were barely walking, she cut loose on another lil' sucker named Lester B. Johnson. You probably were too young to remember that: but, Queenesther scared that poor little fella' so bad, he high-tailed it outta his own house, and never came back: never heard from him again. Truth be told, the house y'all was staying in wasn't none of his: it belonged to Miss Mattie Russell, so Queenie had to get a job and pay the back rent herself. That man was so scared, he left all his clothes and tools. And of course, everybody knows we stick together. So you just settle your heart. By and by, everything is gonna be all right."

Leaving his mother Queenesther to her fate was Booker's greatest adult-type decision, thus far. Sure, Queenie was tough on him by other people's standards, but life with his mother was all that he knew. There's an ancient belief that people can live in hell so long that we come to think of it as a rose garden. Booker T was conceived, born and raised by Queenie, and toughened by her and her sister, Booker's Aunt May-May. So the hardest part wasn't living with Queenie. The toughest part was leaving Queenie. He had based his whole life rhythm on co-existing with his mother.

Get On With It, Mr. Hampton. Don't Be a Walley

A few hours later, as the car approached the Prairie Cove city limits, Booker T started expressing what he felt most inside. "You know Uncle Percy and Auntie Annie, I just can't get Mama out of my mind. I feel like I'm ducking out on her. I just don't feel right."

"I know, I know, Booker T. But, you've got to give yourself some time. You're still a growing young man. There are a lot of things you've grown used to, and don't even understand too much beyond that. In time, you'll see how foolish it would be for you to stay in certain places and various situations. There's always a time and place for everything. How many other ways does your mama have to tell you that she needs her space," asked Annie Lee.

"This ain't happening because you're ducking out on her. This is all about human nature…your mama needs her space. How old are you, now," asked Percy.

"Thirteen; going on fourteen in October."

"So that means your mama was only about three or four years older than you are now when she conceived you. She jumped right out of childhood and into motherhood too early. Don't you think it's time to give her a break? I mean, even if it's only for just a little while; like over summer vacation," asked Annie Lee.

"Yes ma'am. But, I just feel like I'm encroaching on y'all. I don't want to be disrespecting and hogging up all of y'all's time and space, too."

"You just wait until we turn this here corner. You'll see how much space we've got," said Annie Lee.

Just as the car rounded the corner and pulled over to the curb, Booker shouted in awe, "Whoa, Nellie! I thought y'all still lived in that little shotgun house over on Blake Street. This is out of sight. How long y'all been living here?"

"We bought this place last year, but couldn't move in until around this summer. It was a boarded-up hot mess, but we got it for practically nothing…the back tax money. It was abandoned with a bunch of racoons nesting in the attic and a big old ground hog living downstairs underneath the back porch. We just gutted and dug out the whole place, top to bottom, front to back, and took our damn sweet time rewiring, plumbing, dressing and painting it right," said Percy. "And we still are holding onto Grandfather Austin and Grandmother Mary Alice's place over at Page and Upton.

"Aw, man. This is nice. It's huge. What's it got; one, two, three floors?"

"The city would only declare it as a two and a half floors with a toilet on each level," said Annie Lee.

"We're pretty much direct back door neighbors with your Aunt May-May and the twins in their new place," scoffed Percy.

"Yeah, and speaking of the twins; they said they cain't wait to shove all four of their feet up your 'back door', as soon as we get through with your ass. Better keep your dukes up, 'cause Maggie Lee done already said she owes you a serious ass whupping," laughed Annie Lee.

"Shoot. She's gonna have to forget about all that. Those days are long gone. They wanted to do all of that, they should have come over to Hallville sooner and got me while I was scared and little. I know myself, now. They know they cain't handle a big nigguh."

"Yeah. Little Archie Farts shot up into a big Godzilla. They hauled off and took a midget to Hallville one day, and he came back to PC a giant the next. Now, you done graduated to whuppin' grown men's asses. What's a little crocodile-mouth gal gone do with you now," asked Annie Lee.

"Especially behind growing up eating Queenie's beans, collard greens and hot water cornbread," laughed Percy. "That woman sure can whup up a mean pot of Great Northern beans and collards; with that creamy rue from them beans; a cup of pot liquor from them greens sprinkled with a couple dashes of that Louisiana hot sauce; and a fist full of hot water corn bread all crumbled up in it; slathered in some butter… Lord have mercy!"

"Yeah. She likes to crumble her cornbread all up in them beans and greens; sprinkle on some apple cider vinegar and salt and that Louisiana hot sauce, too; and sit there crinkling her toes together while she eats it all up with her thumb and first two fingertips," added Annie Lee.

And they all three fell out laughing again.

CHAPTER 14

On-Guard: Challenge

After the passing of Austin and Mary Alice, the Hampton Clan continued on as a matriarchal family. The males acted more like logistics providers and enforcers of the feminine will. Booker T came to realize full well that he had entered the most advanced stage of his life—the high school teenage years. His mother no longer nurtured him. His grandparents were no longer there to see him through to adulthood. His grandmother's sister Annie Lee and her husband Percy Jarvis, along with his mother Queenesther's sister Mayethel "May-May" Pickens became the principal adult relatives, providers and guardians obligated by tradition to see him through to adulthood.

After getting unpacked and reasonably settled in at his aunt and uncle's new home, Booker met up in the backyard with his cousins, the twins Maggie Lee and Maimee, who accepted the responsibility of helping him transfer to and settle in at the Prairie Cove high school. But, prior to that, they had to put him to the "test" in his new size.

"Boy, look at you...all grown up; and starting to grow hairs on your face," teased Maimee. "And is that the beginnings of a moustache I see starting to sprout out above your liver lips?"

"Yeah, and my face ain't the only place I've got hairs sprouting out," fired back Booker.

"You better be glad you're our cousin. We'd be doing everything with your young ass except cooking it," warned Maggie Lee.

"And besides that, you need to be watching your smart mouth, chump. Don't make me have to pluck out each one of those little peach fuzz hairs one-by-one," said cousin Maimee.

"Chump, if you even thought you could do that, you'd apologize out of guilt. How have y'all been doing, anyway? With all those boodeys and titties, the two of you have changed. Who are you; and what have you done with my twins? You look like grown-assed boodey-mamas who stole my cousins' heads," said Booker.

"Shoot. We are grown-assed women now. In this family and this state, nineteen might not mean you can go and buy liquor, but it is over the magic age of emancipation, which means that in this family, we are old enough to do whatever else we please with your young ass," bragged cousin Maggie Lee.

"And we don't have to shut up no more when grown folks be talking, either," added Maimee.

"But you still have to watch your mouth, young boy," teased Maggie. "Op-op-op. Don't you say a mumbling word. That means you still have to shut up when we be talking; and do what we say. Now turn out your pockets and give us some money, Mr. Big Stuff."

"On a cold day in hell. You two shorties may be the oldest, but I'm the bigguh nigguh around here, now. That means you still have to be my body guards; bring me back all the money you stole from others; and last, but not least, hook me up with all of your finest girlfriends. Not like that old gooch-eyed, pigeon-toed, baboon-faced gal over there on Delaware Street y'all keep trying to pair me up with. I ain't coming out of my pockets with no cash to file her teeth down. I likes eye-candy…natural-born, super-fine."

"The only 'eye-candy' you're gonna be meeting around here are gonna be school teachers," warned Maimee.

"Say, hey, now that'll work. I prefer a full-grown, full-blown woman who can fill my hands with patty-cakes, and teach me something I don't already know."

"Which is 'nothing'," shot in Maggie Lee. "Monday is the first day of summer school, fool. Freshmen are allowed to start school early here in PC. And seeing how you're still a child, and we're the grown-ups, we're accompanying Auntie to help get you signed into school. How come you didn't come to our graduation last year?"

"First off: Hallville don't let school out until near the end of June. Second off: didn't nobody warn me that PC would be letting you baboons out so damn early during the month of May. And third off: you suckers didn't even have the decency to give me a heads-up and invite me. Now, what in the hell would I look like showing up all the way over here on my own, while my school was still in session, and you two ig'nant heifers be showing off your black asses in hats and gowns with your he-hanking, monkey-mouth friends?"

"You don't watch your mouth, you're gonna be showing off some snaggle teeth, Junior," warned Maimee with a hug and a pinch. "Your big ass will be favoring a snaggle-tooth refugee from the Planet of the Apes, all about the face in the middle of summertime."

"Ow. Ow. Don't hurt the baby. Don't hurt the baby," feigned Booker.

Maimee grabbed his left arm; draped it over her shoulders as Booker found himself in the double embrace of his two loving cousins. They teased him hard; and took his money when he was little. But they would give a vicious beating to anyone else who dared to assault him.

"Yeah, I missed your graduation, and I missed the hell out of both of you. Now, I'm here, and I'm in charge, I'm in charge. Goddamn, I'm in charge. And woe be-tythe the fool who messes with either one of you. Take me to school, and then, take me to your finest girlfriends," said Booker.

"Boy, what do you think we look like; Booker's nookie bookies or something," asked Maimee.

"We cain't be contributing to the delinquency of a minor. Besides, like we said, all of our friends are grown-assed women like us. Some of them are even single moms," warned Maggie.

"Oh,yeah? That's mo' fo' better. But, if they're anything like the ones back in Hallville, they're nothing more than fast-assed, monkey-minded jitter bugs. They'll be trying to rob me quicker than you two. I like 'em older and growner, but I also prefer they be gainfully employed and fully capable of maintaining a halfway intelligent conversation. Experience makes the best teachers; and welfare pays them for the baby-daddy's free ride."

"No wonder you like older women. You're looking for a second mama," said Maggie Lee.

"Wrong, wrong, wrong. Your chicken-headed girlfriends are already way, way too late. You, Ms. Bigmouth, are my second mama, along with my cousin Auntie Maimee over here."

"Naw. Naw. I'm the 'mama.' I've got something for this big mannish ass," said Maimee.

"It don't make no difference. Just bend your big moose boodey over and let me have first dibs on whupping it," teased Maggie Lee.

A New Teacher

Booker T. Washington High School was for Prairie Cove what A.G. Gaston High School was for Hallville...a hothouse for the development of indomitable, elite black scholars, athletes, artists and businessmen. Booker T. Hampton didn't get to attend Hallville's Gaston historically black high school, but here he was at Prairie Cove's more suitable Booker T. Washington High School.

On his first day of summer school, just minutes after he stepped into the building, Booker T. Hampton knew he was spared from the institutionalized buck-dancing and stagnating white supremacy of Hallville's Baldridge High School. Forced segregation suited him just fine.

The most prominent thing about Washington High was the fact that its student body de-emphasized buck-dancing and hamboning. The "black" educators there consistently stressed and insisted on a higher standard of achievement for their students. This was further stressed in activities like sports, ROTC, drill team, and marching band. Those black teens not only talked-the-talk: they had to walk-the-walk.

Add to this the fact that oligarch "whites" made up less than one percent of PC's Washington High enrollment. The PC black student's main opponents were snooty, upper middle class "blacks" who did their damnedest to hide all vestiges of their family's wealth, to avoid being shunned by their less fortunate peers.

But, credit must be given to the "black" elementary and middle school teachers of the Hallville Public School system. They did a stellar job of preparing Booker T for a PC high school education. He was solid in his Mathematics, English, and Science; and, thanks to Queenie, up-to-date in his more realistic social studies. Yes, young Booker was spared being pumped full of the "white" version of history that awaited the "black" Hallville high students.

At PC's Washington High, on his very first summer school day, Booker T was totally impressed by his freshman algebra teacher Miss Elizabeth Scofield. She was strict, no-nonsense, and absolutely fair. To top it off, she knew her subject inside out and made the study of algebra so much fun, that even an ignorant goof-off was deeply motivated to give her 100 percent attention without her prompting or cajoling him or her.

As soon as the bell rang for class dismissal, as Booker headed for the door to go to English class, a soft voice spoke up from behind him, "You're not from around here, are you?"

He turned to see who was speaking, and caught his breath saying, "Uh-uh, no. Who are you?"

"What's your name?" she immediately fired back.

By that time Booker had gathered himself. "I think you heard me answer Miss Scofield's roll call."

"Booger Hambone," she teased.

"Even with the evidence of morbid illiteracy it sounds better than Rising Mumps," he said.

"Alright. Alright. I apologize Mr. Booker Hampton."

"My name is Booker T. Hampton, Roslyn Mumford: and since this is my first day in this school, I better get away from you before your boyfriend gets the wrong idea and tries to start a fight. If you're this tough, I can imagine the nigguh must be like King Kong or Godzilla."

"For your information and edification, I do not need a boy. I can do bad by myself."

"I heard that on a record by another big mouth sister. But, I'll accept that reply as a 'no'," answered Booker.

"You can take it any way you want. Seeing how we're in the advanced section, you better not be late for classes, because I'm going to be the top gun in every class. I've never made less than an "A.""

"Aw-Haw! We've got us a certified bad-ass here! Okay, then it's on Miss Rozzy. I'll be joining you throughout my whole curriculum. You better double check all of your answers, because you can't let your crocodile mouth be overloading your little hummingbird ass. I'll be setting the pace in Algebra and English, and everything else come the fall. I may not have a perfect record from the past, but I can hang, now."

As she stepped around Booker, she kept her back to him, pulled her pants tighter and asked, "If this is what you call a hummingbird ass, they need to enroll your dumb ass in the remedial biology and physical science classes poste haste."

As his eyes bulged and a smile broke out over his face, Booker conceded, "You win Ms. Mumford...hands down. Please give me a chance to show my sincerity."

"By and by, we shall see. Please realize that they have remedial English for dummies who can't read. Catch you later, alligator."

"In a while, crocodile." Booker was grinning all over himself the rest of the day. As soon as school was out and he got home, he ran straight through the house, out the back door, and over to Aunt May-May's place to confer with the twins. That girl Rozzy had to be somebody known by everyone. Not only was she potential competition as a scholar, but she was already highly respected as a freshman swimming prospect.

On Tuesdays that summer, Miss Scofield's algebra class was Booker's first class of the day. He would always arrive for the class early. Rozzy was right: Scofield was a very serious, impressive person. Judging from her physical appearance, she clearly was some kind of past or present athlete. At about five-feet-ten, she had an easy-going, definite command presence that exuded a sense that she was the type of woman who liked everything she wore to be simple, low maintenance, and wash and wear. She didn't seem to be concerned about appearing to be sexy or revealing. She appeared to be comfortable in just a polo shirt and loose fitting straight khaki pants or skirt. Yet and still, if she wore pants, her back pockets tended to incline more toward a horizontal level. If she wore a skirt, the rear hem tended to ride about an inch or two higher than the front hem. In other words, Scofield had high horizontal back pockets stretched over some serious cheeks. Like cousin Maggie Lee said, "When she walked, Scofield's back pockets looked like two pigs fightin' inside a gunny-sack."

When her next algebra class was over, as the students filed out, Ms. Scofield asked Booker to remain for a moment. After the other students left the room she said, "So your name is Booker T. Hampton. Are you by any chance related to the twins Maimee and Maggie Lee Hampton?"

"Yes ma'am. They're my cousins."

"I see. Booker, I'm going to get right to the point. Your cousins were outstanding athletes throughout their four years at this school. We need more athletes like the Hampton sisters. We need another male on the swim team. If you can perform in the pool like your cousins performed on the track, you're a champion prospect, also. We are a championship team. What do you say Booker?"

"Well, Miss Scofield. I'm sorry to say that I've never been on any organized sports team. And as a swimmer, I'm just a dog-paddler; not even an average swimmer. The most I've ever done in a pool is dare to swim from one side of the shallow end to the other bank."

"Ha-ha! Don't you worry about a thing Booker T. Hampton. We have all summer to get you into shape. Once we get you over your natural fear, I'll have you in the best condition of your life. Are you with me," asked Miss Scofield.

"Yes Ma'am. If you're willing to take a chance with me, I'll give it my all."

"That's all I'm asking for. See you after school."

Pain Is Weakness Telling You To Give In To It

Booker earned a spot on the swim team after getting over his fear of the water, and having increased his level of endurance by persisting at breaking through his "great wall" of pain. On the wall of the pool room, at the deep end of the swimming pool, was a giant banner saying, "Pain is weakness trying to leave the body." It should have had a second line for weaklings reading, "Scofield knows the Way."

No matter where or what kind of building they're in, all indoor swimming pools have one similar feature: echo. Any sound seems to ricochet off the walls, bouncing all over the place, magnifying a person's voice as though each word is like a rendition of a doo-wap singing group, specifically directed toward you.

Street shoes were not allowed around the pool at Washington High. So, on that first day, Booker came in barefoot, trying his best to follow regulations. He left his socks and shoes in the boy's locker room. As soon as he entered the pool area and sat on the bench, the first person he noticed treading in the water was Roslyn Mumford.

Not only was Rozzy an evident star scholar, but she was obviously a potential star athlete in the water. She moved through the water with the grace and speed of a mermaid. This, plus the fact that Booker felt that he was only a novice at the sport, made it even more intimidating for him to consider getting into the water along with the rest of the team. It was more like the most daring thing he had ever done. There stood Miss Scofield in her bathing suit underneath black sweat pants and the whistle hanging from her neck. And in the water was the mermaid-like Rozzy waiting to show Booker T. Hampton who was the boss.

Booker realized, too late, what he had gotten himself into by submitting to Ms. Scofield's encouragement. He couldn't save face by tucking tail and running off like he used to do from Sporty Stubbs, Jason Willard and the "black" thugs back in Hallville. But just like then, he was now trapped in PC by the obligation to return daily to Miss Scofield's and Rozzy's scrutiny of him in the pool, five days a week. It was worse than Aunt May-May and the twins waiting to make minced meat out of him. Yes, Booker T was trapped and vowed to himself to never again agree so readily to other people's requests.

What really made him decide to stay was when Rozzy came out of the water. And an extra added attraction was when Miss Scofield came out of her warm-up pants just before diving into the water. Booker didn't feel trapped anymore. He decided, right then and there, that he would face what comes. The only way he was leaving the swim team was in a body bag.

"Mr. Hampton, do you have a problem adding in logical sequences," asked Miss Scofield.

"No ma'am."

"Well, when I tell someone they are members of the Booker T. Washington swim team, I mean for them to report for practice in swim gear. Will you please excuse yourself to the boy's locker room; see Mr. Shelton for practice gear, and report back here in those trunks; pronto?"

"Yes Ma'am, Miss Scofield, I wasn't..."

"No excuses, please. Hurry along young man. We're waiting," insisted Miss Scofield as the rest of the team guffawed and giggled.

Booker hurried to the boy's locker room; took an empty locker; spoke to Mr. Shelton, and changed into the team practice trunks. There were a few boys still in the locker room from other sports. They went into the shower area, and Booker followed their procedure, washing, rinsing and standing under the cold shower water to close his pores before entering the pool area.

As he approached the poolside near Miss Scofield and Rozzy, who were waiting for him, and patiently treading in the deep water, Rozzy broke out in a sheepish grin while looking straight at Booker's crotch area.

This intimidated Booker so much he looked down only to find that his "outie," which usually hung much lower, had degenerated into an "innie"; more like the button of his navel. It was pressing against his wet Speedo trunks, more like a timid little turtle trying to hide its head. Booker had never been so embarrassed in his whole life. How could "Frankie J. MacPeters" do this to him at such a crucial moment? The most he could do was cup with his hands what was left of his "pride" to block the steady stares of the two females.

"Boy, will you please stop acting like a fraidy cat, busy playing with yourself, and get your behind on into the water? We don't have all day," bellowed Elizabeth Scofield whose voice was magnified by booming off the four walls of the pool house.

The echoes of laughter from the whole team were so deafening that Booker immediately jumped into the deep water, and desperately started dog-paddling the two yard distance back to the bank of the pool.

"Naw, naw, naw, Mr. Hampton! We do not hang on the wall around here, like a piece of meat on a hook. We embrace the water by treading. As long as I'm in the pool, off of the wall, you stay in the pool, off of the wall. You do know how to tread don't you, Mr. Hampton?"

"Yes ma'am...kind of..."

"Mumford, stay with Mr. Hampton. Show him how to maintain position in the water so that he can better condition his body."

"Yes ma'am. Come on Booker. Just move your legs back and forth like you're trying to balance yourself on a slow-racing bike: but instead of pedaling in a full circle, pedal back and forth; staying upright while your arms are raised out at your sides like wings moving in a motion like you're trying to fly," said Rozzy. "Just learn to relax, and don't fight the water. Go ahead, baby Booker. Don't be 'fraid," she whispered. "Mommy Rozzy's got your big punkified ass."

Booker tried his damnedest to do as he was told; trying to imitate Rozzy. For the first time, he noticed others were in the water around them, also. Miss Scofield was out front, facing the team. She was so obviously a very powerful, fearless and calm U.S. Navy trained, frogman-type warrior woman.

Booker once told his grandfather, Austin Hampton, how he admired the way some females were brave enough to admit when they were wrong, and fearlessly honest about their weaknesses. Yet they always strived to improve themselves. He appreciated having been born a Hampton, because boys and girls were raised as equals in that family.

Maybe that was one of the main reasons he took pleasure in meeting and learning from Rozzy and Miss Scofield. They didn't know anything better than the fact that men and women were both weak and strong in their own times and ways. They simply showed that a person didn't need to get over by first lying, and then getting into someone else's head. You earned respect by knowing yourself and never giving up; committing to improvement and sacrificing as each person did their own thing.

Over all, Booker T seemed to have learned that: when he hit the great wall of resistance within himself, he wouldn't stop. He determined to go over, under, around or through it. He would remember, "The wall is nothing more than pain that is weakness trying to make my body stop." He grew to accept the pain as an opposing force the universe has sent to be the seed of his achievement and growth.

Elizabeth Scofield was totally committed when it came to training her swimmers. The girls and boys were all trained together. But due to male influenced state athletic regulations, they were separated by gender when it came time for actual competition. Maybe they were afraid that the girls would prove to be superior to the boys. Anyway, Miss Scofield's swimmers all suffered together in the forty-five minute treading and forty-five minute lap drills: it brought the beast out of them. They knew about the "wall of pain," but stroked right through it in swimming laps. They ferociously swam into their "wall" by repeatedly flipping and spinning in front of the ends of the pool, and pushing off from it into the opposite direction, maintaining the same tempo.

Booker became so avid in doing laps that he developed the habit of occasionally growling on his exhalations during strokes and spins. The more his body seemed to get stressed, the more determined became his strokes. Miss Scofield had to continuously blow her whistle while running beside him when she wanted him to stop. As time passed, she really grew to understand and appreciate Booker's development as a swimmer and as a young man. He seemed to thrive in her intense nurturing and attentiveness.

Friends or Foes

Rozzy had long before noticed Booker's growing affinity for their coach/teacher Miss Scofield. In Algebra I and II class, he was placed in the same group as Rozzy, immediately after the fall semester began. She enjoyed the competition with him for classroom honors. "Boy, you sure have a hard-on for her ass," observed Rozzy.

"Child, please…" feigned Booker.

"Aw, now I've got to be your child, just because you think you can take on a full grown-assed woman? You must be the king of fools. A youngun gunning for a full blown, grown-assed, bull-dyking woman? Didn't the twins teach you anything? Or are you just a natural-born dippy?"

"Dippy": he was not. At Rozzy's mentioning of the twins, Booker's eyebrows shot straight up. Although curious, he asked her no questions, and played it all off by saying, "Listen, Little Miss Fast-ass. Just try to watch your mouth, and be sure to keep your drawers on your own hips and your face in your own books. Children should be seen and not heard," teased Booker.

"You are so ignorant. Don't you follow the latest national news trends? She'll not only lose her job, and be banned from teaching and coaching, but they'll lock her up in prison and register her on a sex offender list way past the time whenever you get finished growing up."

"Not unless I say so. I'll never tell the truth. It won't even hold up in a court of law.

"In spite of your lying-assed testimony, she'll be doing serious time. They won't even tell the world your name or show your pimply face in the newspapers; let alone listen to your lies."

"Only way they can do her in is if they catch us: and I ain't admitting to squat. I'll carry those precious secrets with me to my grave. So, other than that, I guess that just leaves me with only one other alternative…spending more of my time with your young ass."

"Who are you to call somebody else 'young.' You're still sucking your mama's titty, you big punk-assed mama's boy. If I even thought about going with something like you, they would be looking into locking my ass up in jail along with Scofield's. Your best bet is to keep cupping your meager scrotum; smacking water, and growling with those strokes. All you're gonna get here is what's in your little mind," said Rozzy.

"It's not what's in my mind. It's who's getting into your drawers. If she's such a bull-dyker, why do you spend so much time with my kitty-licking cousins? Whatchu getting? Tutoring? You best turn that table back around to yourself. Snakes know the ways of snakes. You're just 'walking the fence'," said Booker T.

Rozzy was visibly surprised. She didn't say another word, but stormed off in a huff, leaving Booker standing there all alone.

Ambiguity

"How come y'all didn't tell me she liked girls," Booker T asked the twins.

"That's not our job. We don't get paid by you," said Cousin Maimee.

"Besides, why are you asking us dufous-assed questions like that," asked Maggie Lee. "Who in the hell do you think you are; J. 'Faggot-Assed' Edgar Hoover or Eliot 'Alcoholic' Ness?"

"What's with you freaky broads, anyway," asked Booker.

"Broads? Sucker I've got your broad at the end of my left arm: and it's about to go upside the right side of your sissy-assed head," warned Maggie.

"Cain't nobody get a straight answer out of either one of you. Besides, when the shit hits the fan, you females all rally the wagons around each other like a bunch of scared-assed hens," said Booker.

"I'mo ask you again. Who in the hell do you think you are? Buster Brown or somebody," asked Maggie.

"Now, if you're my cousins, you won't let me make a fool out of y'all by being left out in the dark by people outside the family. I've been around you heiffers enough to be your baby brother. Stop acting dumb Maggie Lee and Maimee, and tell me about this girl named Rozlyn Mumford."

"Since when did your punk ass start sniffing after young females," asked Maimee.

"After you did. Ain't nobody a punk but you. And you can't have it all," said Booker T.

"You got me there. I must concede: I like pussy. Ain't much more to tell you 'bout that, Cuz. She's just another sass-mouthing young junior flip like you. Just because we're your cousins don't mean we have to be your administrative assistants, setting you up with all of the pussies," said Maimee.

"After all of the life and all of the money I let you heifers rob out of me, you two nigguhs ought to be my nookie bookies emeritus," said Booker.

"First off, real black men do not refer to black women as 'nigguhs.' You trifling-assed, buck-dancing, so-called black males are the nigguhs, because you waste time going to jail behind killing each other instead of the monkey-dick white males who are humping your mamas and sending all of you dumb zombies to prison, where you fuck each other in the ass," advised Maimee. "I could go on and on, but you are already too confused."

"You sound like you two booger-bears are trying to be a reincarnation of Harriet Tubman and Sojourner Truth," said Booker.

"If you had more respect for black women you wouldn't be begging us to help your dumb ass get over on one of us. But, nawl. You've got to be talking that yang shit about women who conceived, birthed and suckled your big cyclopsing ass. As much nurturing as our mother gave you, and the protection we gave you, you should be grateful enough to be selling your own ass to pay us back with interest," said Maimee.

"Then your slacker asses would be standing in welfare lines, mooching for even more government assistance," added Booker. "Even though you ain't even got no babies to feed."

"You keep talking yang, sucker, you're gonna be laying on a gurney with your naked ass poking out of one of those backless johnnie gowns, in the hallway outside of the A.G. Gaston Hospital emergency ward; begging for the doctor to come and pull my foot out of your ass," promised Cousin Maimee.

"You try to do that and even my sweetest cousin Maggie Lee will be heartbroken from her own twin sister accidently kicking her in the back of her head," said Booker.

"A-HA-HA-A-A-A," laughed Maggie Lee. "He got you, Maimee. Aw, you're good Cuz. You ought to be doing standups. You've got a fertile imagination and a quick comeback. No wonder them Hallville boodey bandits were out to put something on your ass."

"Maybe so: but I don't run no more. Years ago, I told them all to form two lines behind me, one for each cheek, and kiss my motherhumping ass. And I stood there and watched them all get mad; scratch their asses; and get glad," declared Booker.

You Can Handle the Truth

"Okay. Okay. Here's the scoop on Rozzy," said Maimee. "Rumor has it, from day one, the young fool thang has just been tribbing, swinging back and forth. But, of course, that's only scuttle-butt," said Maimee. "Of course, unless you catch a person Johnny-on-the-spot, it's only guesstamation. You git my drift?"

"Aw, dag, man. And I really liked her, too," whined Booker.

"Fool. What's your problem? You plan on marrying the silly young thang," asked Maggie Lee. "As young as you are, all you can afford to do is just hit it and quit it. You may as well git your ass in line behind me."

"Aw, hell naw."

"Then have a Coke and a smile and shut the fuck up. Pussy is a trap made for dumb males anyway; because you dumbies knock it all up, and then try to walk away and leave it for some other sucker to pay for it," declared Maimee.

"What the hell; at least we don't have to literally be a 'sucker.' We just lay the pipe; pump the oil; and y'all come mop up the mess behind us," crowed Booker.

"Maggie Lee, you better hold me now, or you'll be holding

your identical twin's hands through prison bars from now on," said Maimee.

"Nawl, now. Look at things this way: you'll be like a bull-dyker in Girls Town; waggling your tongue all through the place," said Booker. "You get my drift?"

"Okay, Mr. Smartass. Just for that, you'll have to figure out the rest of the story for yourself," said Maimee.

"Aw, come on now! I'm a dangerous man when I'm left to draw my own conclusions," warned Booker.

"What more can I say," asked Maimee. "At thirteen-going-on-fourteen-years-of-age, you can't drift too far. You can't even get your feet off the ground; never mind trying to wrap your little childish-assed mind around what some other child is doing with her little narrow behind."

"I cain't be wasting my time running after silly-assed young girls when there are full blown, full grown-assed women willing to teach me how to fly."

"If we tell Aunt Queenie you're sniffing after your school-teacher, your young ass is gonna be flying while it's frying," warned Maggie Lee.

"Aw, man. And I really liked Rozzy, too," Booker kept emphasizing.

"Fool. You must be out of your natural mind. You really do plan on marrying that silly young thing," said Maggie Lee.

"How many ways does a nigguh have to tell you 'hell nawl'," asked Booker T.

"Then quit whining. I keep telling you that pussy is a trap for stupid assed men. Why is it that you fools all keep thinking you're entitled to whatever your dicks point to," asked Maimee. "Cain't you see the best way for ignorant people to become enlightened is to shut the fuck up; use his brain and listen?"

"Then start talking to me in English and stop beating around the bush talking 'Pig-Latin'," shouted Booker.

"That would be our biggest mistake," said Maggie. "You can't even smell the roses when they're being held up in front of your big bassoon nose."

"I may as well be talking to the damn dog. I'm outta here," blurted Booker T as he stormed off.

Training Time

"Why do you insist on messing with the boy's head like that," Maggie Lee asked her sister Maimee, after Booker had headed back over to Annie Lee and Percy's house.

"Because he's always talking that 'bull-dyker' crap. I don't care how big he's getting, he's still just a little punk-assed junior-flip to me. I hope one of them young bitches hooks a ring through his nose; fucks him 'til his nose bleeds; and runs his punk ass around in circles until he can't walk straight."

"Remember the saying... 'You can't get mad at the dog for licking his balls'," Maggie Lee recited. "And why not?"

"'Because the poor sombitch don't know no better'," recited Maimee.

"He's still just a big ole silly-assed kid," said Maggie Lee.

"Then, he should know better. If you don't train them while they're young, they'll grow up trying to bite you in the ass," said Maimee. "That's when they have to learn that if you fuck with the bull, you get the horns."

"'Bull' as in 'bull-dyker'," asked Maggie. "Well, I guess it is about time the young 'stud' starts learning to respect other people; especially us women. He's starting to git too big for his britches."

"Just like some of these other 'men' in Prairie Cove," said Maimee.

"What 'other men'," asked Maggie Lee. "Outside of Uncle Percy and Daddy Willie, the other men of blood kin in our family are all dead and gone," observed Maggie.

"Well, seeing how this young Mr. Booker T. Hampton is the youngest male in our bloodline, it is imperative that he be properly trained. He thinks he's so smart? That's good, because we cain't have us no dumb-punk men in our family. Let's give him a clinic on 'Smart'," said Maimee.

"Naw. All he needs is for us to keep an eye on him. That young Rozzy gal is already into his head. As Mama always says, 'Experience is the best teacher.'"

"I'll give him an 'experience', all right. I'll break his little B-B balls for him," promised Maimee.

"Lighten up, Sis. I've got this one. Let me take the lead this time. I know just how it's going to wind up," said Maggie Lee.

CHAPTER 15

Looking Out for Number One

"How come you didn't tell me you had a hard-on for my cousin," asked Maggie Lee.

"For the same reason you didn't tell me that your cousin had a hard-on for me," replied Rozzy.

"See. There you go again with that smart-alecky little mouth of yours. Answer my question," demanded Maggie Lee.

"First off; just because I speak to a boy doesn't necessarily mean that I like him. I'm competing with Booker T for athletic and academic position; not for personal reasons," snapped Rozzy.

"You know, ever since I first laid eyes on you, you've always thought you were so smart and so slick. You think I'm playing with you?"

"Naw, Maggie Lee. I can't help it if your cousin likes me."

"I find out you messing with any boy, I'mo put your ass in the hospital. Ever been admitted in the hospital, little girl?"

"Naw, Maggie Lee. You know damn well that if you ever do put your fucking hands on me, my brothers will fuck you up, skip the hospital and send your mannish ass straight to the morgue. Who in the hell do you think you're talking to, anyway?

You need to stop wolfing like that. Ain't nobody scared of your ass; and ain't nothing that deep happening here with your big square-assed cousin."

"Well, irregardless: he's running his big mouth, acting like he wants to hook up with you."

"So? The child's uglier than you are. All of you Hamptons don't do nothing but try to bogart people like you own them or something. Ain't none of you nigguhs my momma or my daddy."

"If that's how you feel, from now on you can play with your own self, then," said Maggie Lee.

"Naw, wait Maggie Lee. I was just playing," grinned Rozzy.

"Naw, fool. I don't play that shit," said Maggie Lee.

As she went to stand up from sitting on the arm of the sofa, Rozzy pressed her body forward against Maggie, who grabbed her, as they both tumbled back onto the sofa cushions. Rozzy immediately locked her left leg around Maggie's right leg causing Maggie to suddenly stop resisting. Maggie started pressing against the younger girl.

"Well, la-tee-da. And so it goes," cooed Maggie. "And-so-it-goes."

"No-no-no-no-no, you foolish heifers," said Maimee as she walked into the room. "If mama had walked in here and caught you AC/DC bitches, you both would be getting hauled out of this house in body bags, and shipped down to Chisholm's Funeral Home." Then she looked menacingly at Rozzy while asking her, "Are you itching to die young? My mama doesn't give a flying fuck about your damned brothers."

"Naw, Maimee. I was just…"

"Bitch, just git your little funky ass the hell up out of here before my mother walks in here and we all three commence to be beating the shit out of you," warned Maimee. "Maggie Lee, I'm surprised at how stupid you are. If Mama had caught you…"

"But she didn't catch me. So now, you have a Coke and a smile and shut the fuck up," snapped Maggie Lee as her sister stopped, listened, and then ran upstairs.

Let Things Unfold

Just as Booker T and his Aunt May-May left Auntie Annie Lee Jarvis' backyard and entered Aunt May-May's yard, Rozzy bounded out of May-May's back door and ran into May-May.

"Excuse me young lady, but can't you at least speak to me before you run me over," asked May-May.

"Aw, please excuse me, Mrs. Pickens; I'm sorry. I was just trying to catch the 5:20 bus on time," pleaded Rozzy.

"You're too late. We just got off of it. You were running so hard I thought I got hit by another damned bus," said May-May.

All the while, Booker T was surprised that all three of the women knew Rozzy so well. His mother always told him to use his two eyes and two ears more than his one mouth. He was shrewd enough to keep his mouth shut for an instant, but then he asked Rozzy, "What you doing over here?"

"She's visiting us, chump. You got a problem with that," asked Maggie Lee as she stepped out onto the back porch.

"Y'all cut it out now, and let the child go on her way. Here, Maggie Lee. Instead of wasting energy running your big mouth at Booker T., heft one of these bags. My fingers are damn near numb," declared May-May.

Booker T. said nothing. He just took it all in very calmly and very quietly. After Rozzy ran off, he dropped Aunt May-May's groceries off in her kitchen, and headed back to his Auntie Annie Lee's house.

As he came through her back door, Annie Lee said," Boy if you could see your face; you look like you just ran into some-kind-of-a spook or Spector."

"No ma'am Auntie. I was just surprised to see a classmate of mine over there at Aunt May-May's house. I didn't know she knew the three of them that well, to be coming over to their house."

"Yeah, well, a lot of peoples they don't know 'that well' be showing up in your Aunt May-May's house. Judging from the way you look, you may not need to know how well. All I can say to you is be very, very careful. That young gal, whatever her name is, is very, very shrewd. As young as she is, and fooling around between them damned twins, she's messing with way more than she can handle."

"Auntie, I really appreciate the heads-up; especially coming from someone in our family. Except for you and Uncle Percy, everybody else in this family be acting like everything is a top national secret. They wouldn't tell me if my pants were on fire."

"Smart man, Booker T. Smart man. Just don't ever get entangled. Be like the small bird. Just lay back: fly low, and let things unfold on their own. Then make up your mind about what you want to do."

Train Yourself to Go with Your Gut Feeling

By being the youngest member of the Hampton clan, Booker T was always being accused and automatically assumed to be naïve. Be that as it may, he was not satisfied with being left in the dark by the lack of information coming to him from the Pickens side of the clan. Left in the dark by the family's secrets, he was well-known to think out of the box and form his own conclusions. This is where his Aunt May-May and her twins wound up being the ones who were naïve. They failed to appreciate the power of Booker T. Hampton's ability to size-up situations and reach logical conclusions. Booker had listened well to the lectures from their own elders over the years.

The Hampton clan still had other elders to turn to—the Jarvises, and May-May and Queenie; but the May-May component of this mighty clan was like a ship drifting in a sea of selfishness without a rudder. Everybody was into so many hidden agenda that not only were they somewhat disconnected, but they were, at times, abysmally ignorant. Trying to teach the twins to cooperate with others in the clan was like trying to teach a monkey how to talk.

May-May and her twins were totally ignorant of the fact that they weren't as smart and secretive as they thought they were. Most of all, they didn't realize or appreciate how intelligent Booker T. Hampton was and that they could have included him as a source of direction in navigating the course of their own lives.

Just as it's difficult for people, especially young people, to not show their feeling in their faces; it's even harder for them to get a hold of their hearts and learn to be still.

Booker T. Hampton was very honest and straight-forward; but his feelings ran strong and deep. Add to this the fact that he never had an object of affection that was truly his own. All he ever had were the women in his clan as a relationship. Never had he fallen deep into love with trust in the object of his affection.

By now, even a foolish cherry-boy could see that Booker T. was being strung along by his cousins, the twins and Rozzy. Just like back when the twins tried to sucker him into trusting them when he was three years old. They would snatch the rug out from under him or push him down over the twin kneeling behind him, causing him to bang the back of his head on the floor. Now, ten years later he still felt like his cousins were playing him for a fool.

But the strange thing was that he didn't seem to be mad or disappointed with anyone but himself. "I'm getting sick of this shit," he would sometimes mumble to himself.

Annie Lee Jarvis knew the score, but she wanted the boy to grow up and be able to think and see things for himself. "Booker T, you're more and more becoming a young man. There's a whole lot you need to learn about females. I don't care how sweet and pretty she is, there's a bitch in every woman. Not all of them are going to be fair and square with you," she said.

"Shoot, Auntie. All I can see is they're a lot like snakes; hard to get along with; too slick to handle; and a mystery to understand."

"All you need to remember is that not all women are poisonous snakes. Just you always remember that a snake is always gonna be a snake," said Auntie Annie. "If you find one laying in the middle of the road half dead, just mind your own business and leave the sombitch alone. A female snake will bite you just as fast as a male snake. The wise man respects the true nature of the snake and doesn't trust either one of them. Trust people only as far as you can throw them. Learn to rely on your own inner voice."

"How about if I leave them all alone from the git-go," asked Booker T.

"Now you're cooking with gas. You don't have to wallow with the hogs in order to raise them," said Auntie Annie Lee.

"Like you always say, Auntie, 'Just feed 'em and breed 'em like you're a farmer raising crops, livestock, and chickens.'"

"They ain't your friends: but, you can use the sombitches to get by. We ain't gonna always be here to think for you, Booker. Just try to keep in mind that every brother ain't a brother; and every cousin ain't gonna love you like a true cousin. The twins, bless their hearts, don't know no better. They are the way their mama, your Aunt May-May made them. Let them be. They don't know no better. They ain't got no other way to wash."

"Yeah; cain't blame them for licking somebody else's you-know-what, either," added Booker.

"There you go. That's what they call creative thinking. Keep it to yourself, and they'll call you a sage. Now, come here and give Great Auntie some sugar."

"Tee-hee-HA-HA! Ahem. Moo-oo-ah-ah!"

"Whoa! From alto to basso profundo; you're maturing right before my very eyes. Matter of fact, now, you sound more like your Grampa Austin. Wonders never cease. Next time your mama sees you, she might not even know you!"

"Auntie Annie, Mama don't even know me now; that's how come I'm here hugging on you."

"Give her time. By and by, give her time. Bless your heart..."

Fend for Yourself

More than one smug and conceited person in the Hampton clan often stated or were silently convinced that Booker T was "naïve." But, a lot of times, naiveté is a precaution used by perceptive, highly intelligent people who tend to think out-of-the-box or asymmetric to the matrix. Booker T. Hampton's way of thinking is prima facie evidence of out-of-the-matrix type thinking. This boy, left alone to his own assumptions, would be like Miles Davis being left alone with his trumpet in a jail cell. He would wind up driving the other prisoners coo-coo reaching his own conclusions from another realm.

"Love" is a hard enough subject for most people to wrap their heads around without the added complication of the first party's affection being usurped by the advances of a second party who happens to be the first party's own flesh and blood. The late great comedian Mr. Benny Hill once said, "When you ASSUME, you make an ASS out of U and ME." But Booker T. Hampton had no choice but to arrive at his own conclusions in order to avoid being made an ass of by the "U": in this case his two cousins, the indomitable twins Maimee and Maggie Lee Hampton.

As a high school scholar/athlete Booker had little time to work after-school jobs and even relax. Always short on money, and too proud to ask his Auntie Annie or Uncle Percy Jarvis for money, Booker T developed the capacity to fall into deep rem sleep to get at least 6 hours of sleep per night during the week. This way he could always hold several jobs to earn enough money to have a decent lunch and keep himself dressed in half-way decent clothes for school.

On this one autumn morning, just as he was about to walk past the cemetery, he decided to alter his route slightly to change the scenery on his walk to school. Just about nine blocks from the high school, a female voice said, "Hey, big-head. Wait up." It was the wunderkind, Rozlyn Mumford.

"Say, Rozzy. What's up, girl," said Booker.

"What's up with yourself? I've never imagined you'd be walking to school through my neighborhood. You must be avoiding something," said Rozzy.

"Yeah. Well, it ain't because I'm training my legs for flutter-kicking. I'm short on cash because I spent my last money on these new desert boots. So, it's a case of 'ride the bus and starve' or 'walk to school and still be able to eat a decent lunch.' It sure would be nice if I was old enough to get one job or hustle and make what I get working the paper route and the racist ice cream parlor."

"O'Banion's Market over on Pendleton Pike is looking for a stock boy who's got enough spunk to be able to do whatever else they need done around the place. The old man is getting a little too much inflammation in his back and joints in his later years," said Rozzy. "And my big brothers are too high-priced to even help him: and he's too proud to ask them."

"How do you know all of this?"

"They're my family, ironhead. The old man is my grandma's brother, which makes him my uncle. I'll put in a good word for you after school, Chump. You're gonna be busting your natural black ass, treading and lapping for Scofield, and humping stock for my skin-flint Uncle August O'Banion."

"I don't mind 'smacking water' as you say; but I ain't ready to be nobody's slave. But, thanks the same Rozzy. You know, you're alright as a friend. You hooked me up in school. Now, you're sticking your neck out trying to hook my poor ass up with a job. I wish I had a girlfriend like you," feigned Booker T, schmoozing up to Rozzy.

True. It may appear that Booker partially made an ass out of Rozzy; but this girl had already withheld information from Booker. He had been sulking ever since he ran into her in his Aunt May-May's house, alone with his self-serving twin cousins. One was rumored to swing both ways; and the other was known to prefer only what Booker liked; and we're not talking about food or money.

It seems that the Hampton ancestors had passed on some DNA to Booker, and topped it off with some more advanced training and pre-conditioning. A blind man could see that Booker T was proceeding full speed ahead with schmoozing and using Rozzy. But this was a definite youthful case of "the blind leading the blind." The difference here is that one's blindness is re-active while the other's blindness is pro-active.

On one hand, Booker was clearly resentful and hurt by Rozzy's secret relationship with his cousin Maggie Lee; and, on the other hand, Booker was clearly stringing Rozzy along. She's gonna have a lot to keep her busy, being the center piece in a "Hampton Sandwich." And for a young girl, that would prove to be a tough row to hoe.

"You know, Rozzy, I think I'll enjoy walking to school through your neighborhood instead of walking the old route or riding the bus. Can we be friends? More than anything else in the world, I want to be your deepest friend. Please. I need you, Rozzy," swore Booker.

Bucking her eyes in wonderment, Rozzy said, "Only on one condition, rain or shine, sleet or snow, you must promise to carry my books to the schoolhouse door."

"No problem, partner. I can do that walking on my hands. Besides, if I get hurt, my partner Rozzy will always be here to carry me and our books the rest of the way to school."

"Let's not get too happy," warned Rozzy, as they approached the crosswalk in front of the school building. "You better be getting along to your wall locker. You have to go all the way up to the third floor to Miss Keno's room, clear on the other side of the building."

"I can do that standing on my hands, too," feigned Booker.

"Wow. You are so handy. I'll tell my Uncle Gus at the store that you want to apply for the job. Go by and see him this evening after school. He closes at 6:30pm, but he usually hangs around for an hour or so after he locks the doors."

"Dag-gone, girl. I just got here; and already you're looking out for me better than my own mama. Rozzy, I just want to say thanks for helping me start my new life. I'll never forget this. You're the best girlfriend I've ever dreamed of having. I owe you big-time."

So, he called her his girlfriend and said he owed her. But, how in the hell can a boy who has nothing repay a girl who has everything?

CHAPTER 16

Make the Money Work

Gus O'Banion was a well-respected pillar of his Prairie Cove community. Rumor has it that he had made so much money in his grocery store that, even Wall Street was leery of him, because of his dark melanin skin color. Because of his great good fortune, an awful lot of "white" people were walking around greater PC babbling to themselves, "What the hell did I do wrong?"

It was true that virtually no Prairie Cove "white" nor "jew" wanted to see a "black" man make more money than the average "white" person. But, that's what happens when a man of the "minority" race understands how to make the money he first worked for grow like seeds for a "money" tree that makes money work for him. That's when supremacy-minded "white" folks start asking themselves that same old dumb question.

Old man Gus O'Banion's philosophy was in line with the philosophy of the "mulatto" educator Booker T. Washington's teachings: Industry, Thrift, Intelligence and Property (ITIP). He felt that maintaining these principles was paramount to the survival of all people. Add these qualities to the philosophy of former Urban League President Whitney Young who advised "black" folks to follow the example of the original Irish immigrants of New York City; "Keep your mouth shut: take care of business: and take over." Then, you get some understanding of the depth of August J. O'Banion's zeal and "white supremacy-minded" traitors.

"My niece Rozzy tells me you're from over Hallville way. You're Austin Hampton's grandson. Well, we played ball against each other back in the Negro Leagues. That big man was one heck of a ballplayer. Once he got ahold of that ball, he could throw that sucker to any one of those bases faster than what the pitcher was throwing off of the mound. Yeah, buddy. You've got one hell of a heritage and name to carry on your young shoulders. I can appreciate that, too. Any man carrying the name Booker T. has got to be about something bigger than what the average man strives to accomplish."

"Yes sir. I'm a disciple of Master Young and Master Washington's philosophies. I especially appreciate how no sooner had Master Washington helped Hampton Institute get going, he was down there building Tuskegee Normal Institute from the red Alabama soil that it stands on today. And to top it all off, he recruited Master George Washington Carver out of the University of Iowa to teach at Tuskegee," said O'Banion.

"Mr. O'Banion, sir, if you'll take me into working your store, you won't find a more worthy disciple and employee. I believe in coming to work, doing my job; getting my pay check and going home."

"Well, that ain't all you're going to be doing if you expect to keep working in here. I ain't gonna keep paying people my money if all they're gonna do is spend it. Black folks not only needs to learn about working for money, but they need to know how to make the same money turn around and work for them. Stop spending it all in other peoples' stores: keep it in our own community and make us all strong. And save some and invest it as seed money in securities and investments like land. If you listen and take heed, I'll teach you what I know. If you got a problem with that, you may as well go on and git the hell out of my face."

This old sage sounded like another Hope Newcomb. "Mr. O'Banion, if you'll teach me, I'm eager to learn. But, right now, I've got to spend something on necessities. I can't keep sponging off my Mama, and start to sucking off of my Auntie and Uncle. I like to buy my own clothes and things. Will you give me a chance, sir?"

"Well, since tomorrow's gonna be Saturday and the weekend, you can start tomorrow morning at 6am. We can talk then about your hours and duties."

"Thank you, sir. I'll be back here first thing in the morning."

Booker couldn't wait to get home and tell Auntie Annie and Uncle Percy about his being hired by Augustus O'Banion at the grocery store. He came running up the front porch steps and through the front door. Percy was seated in his favorite easy chair, smoking his pipe full of cherry flavored tobacco. Annie Lee was back in the kitchen listening to the radio, spreading creamed cheese and lemon icing on the freshly baked carrot cake.

"Well. Uncle Percy. I did it. I got myself a real job."

"Where and what for?"

"Over at O'Banion's Market on Pendleton Pike."

"With Gus O'Banion? He's a hell of a good man. You think Hope Newcomb was a sombitch about making money, you better pay strict attention to this old skin flint. He's so tight with money he squeaks when he walks; and he makes each and every penny scream and bleed."

"For real? Maybe I shouldn't work there, then. I can stay on the paper route and keep working in the racist ice cream parlor," teased Booker.

"Doing what? Prairie Cove nigguhs don't read no damned newspapers; especially if it's one that's full of that cracker bullshit that they have to pay for. Ain't nothing in those rags about us colored folks and our concerns. Prairie Cove spooks git their news by word of mouth, fresh off the grapevine. They wipe their asses with them lame cracker newspapers. That damned ice cream parlor don't serve negroes no way."

"Ah-Ha-Haa! Uncle Percy, how about I buy a mule; git a wagon and go junkin' again like I used to do with Mr. Hope?"

"Shoot, man. You want to wind up like Hope? That old nigguh died with money hanging out of both drawer legs, and with feet swolled up too big to pull on his boots without cutting holes to spread his toes outta the sides. Your best bet is to stay your young ass over there with Gus O'Banion. He's a self-educated, hard-grinding old man. He's one of them rich Nigguh Rockefellers like Arthur George Gaston down there in Birmingham, Alabama. White men don't like him; but, the coward sombitches know better than to fuck with him. Like they always say, 'Money talks and bullshit walks.' Each and every time a white man sees ole Gus, the self-serving bastards say to themselves, 'What in the hell did I do wrong?' Gus aint no thug-assed street nigguh like some of his nephews. He's a natural-born teacher who teaches with his back...by example. Just pay strict attention to whatever he says, and keep walking in his footsteps; and them damned twin cousins of yours, and none of them cracker sombitches will ever be able to shake cash out of your ass."

"Thanks Uncle Percy. I'll keep you posted before I make any major moves. Can you tell me more about Mr. O'Banion? He said he used to played baseball against Grampa."

"Yeah, and he played semi-pro football with me, and boxed against Archie Moore. He wasn't the size of Austin, but he was built like a bull and ran that football out of the halfback slot, high-steppin' like a Tennessee Walking Horse," added Percy. "Aw, that man's real talent was running that ball. All the quarterback had to do was hand the ball to him. He would do everything with that football except cook it. One time he ran the bases for Kansas City, the sombitch jumped clean over Austin's big ass and tagged home plate. Aw, Gus O'Banion was one bad little brother in his day. He made most of his money playing three sports—football, baseball, and boxing. He hates spending money so much that most people have no idea of how well-off he is."

After dinner, they sat out on the front porch for almost another hour while Percy ran down the history of the Austin

Hampton and Augustus O'Banion's Negro League rivalry. What was even more fascinating to Booker T was Percy's tale of O'Banion's ingenious accrual and investment of his earnings. "The main problem of the black race is that we don't know how to do nothing but spend money and use credit. That's a nigguh that's broker than broke: a slave to a master that's weaker than he is. Wind up cutting his own brother's throat to get ahead. It's a shame!"

Gratitude and Attitude

It was Springtime, and just as he had promised Gus O'Banion, Booker T first arrived for work early that morning even twenty minutes ahead of Gus. After listening to Percy, he was proud and grateful to be getting hired by the legendary merchant: and looked forward to accomplishing more from that one job than with the others put together.

He was also very grateful that Mr. O'Banion saw fit to teach him. His greatest hope was that Mr. O'Banion would appreciate his efforts and teach him all about making money work for himself. This whole new perspective on finance sounded very intriguing; fraught with the promise of growth and power and the potential toward self-reliance.

Booker always looked at the men and women who taught him as being the great masters of their craft, sent by Heaven to guide him along the Way. His grandfather Austin Hampton always cautioned him to take nothing for granted and to realize that every situation is an opportunity for him to ascend spiritually to better his lot in life.

Booker put his heart and soul into working for Gus O'Banion. Likewise, O'Banion grew to truly appreciate having the young man around. Gus taught him a lot of basics about business and saving and investing his money. "Don't put your money in a bank unless it's to pay your bills and take care of business transactions and costs of living. Banks use your money to invest and make themselves rich. Make your money make you rich by investing it to work for yourself." Booker grew to respect the older man as a role model.

Booker not only became a fixture at the store, but he continued to walk O'Banion's niece, Rozzy, to and from school while carrying her books, He grew to respect her even more although he continually challenged her for supremacy in the classroom and the swimming pool. People along their walk to and from school, and in the school building itself, couldn't help but see their togetherness as a full-blown, serious relationship... like boyfriend/girlfriend...and not as brother and sister.

Word spread rapidly throughout their environments, and soon got back to Booker T's cousins, the Hampton twins.

"Hey, Mag. When's the last time you saw your little young piece-of-thing?"

"Don't start messing with me, Maimee. I don't do you like that."

"Aw. What you mean is that your poor little heart is aching behind the loss of some childish young nookie," mocked Maimee.

"Naw, fool. What I mean is I don't feel like playing with your ignorant ass all up in my business. Like I said before, I don't do you like that," repeated Maggie Lee.

"Aw, dumby why don't you lighten-up. You know I don't mean you no harm. I'm just trying to feel you out about how you really feel about Booker T knocking you out of the saddle with Rozzy."

"Aw, wake up. You know full damn well that all that child is for me is a flash-in-the-pan. You win some: you lose some. In this case, nothing was gained and not a damn thing was lost," said Maggie.

"Yeah. But in your case, you not only scratched your ass, but you were rubbing hers, too. PC has a women's correction unit for grown assed bitches who like to play with young kids. Just make damn sure to stay your big collard-green-eating ass out of trouble, dumby. I can't have nobody looking like me staring out at me from behind bars."

"Fool. The only bars you're gonna be staring through are the ones on the chimpanzee cage at the zoo. You're just mad because your self-serving ugly ass couldn't get your way," said Maggie.

"There you go again, you oaf. We're identical twins, remember? Anything I look like is a reflection on your baboon ass, too."

"Okay. Then, stop embarrassing me by getting those damned mannish-looking buzz-cut haircuts. You could be a really attractive looking female, but nawl, you choose to fuck-up your features up by looking like a dick head detective on a corny-assed TV show," said Maggie Lee.

"Deal…and you stop hopping back-and-forth across the 'fence,' and make up you mind to stick with one man or one woman. You cain't keep hogging them both."

"If you'd let your hair grow long enough, I could yank your head around and look you in your eyes while I'm thumping your forehead, trying to knock some sense into that half-wit brain of yours."

"Dream on, you desperate baboon. Dream on," said Maimee.

"After I was born, Mama should have flushed your ugly ass down the toilet."

"Then you would have grown up to be a bigger chump than you are now," said Maimee.

"Okay, okay, you oaf. You win. Now, have a coke and a smile, and shut the fuck up."

In spite of all of the "bitches" and other derogatory labels they called each other, these two young sisters didn't seem to know how to open their hearts and say "I love you" to each other.

Do Not Form Attachment of the Mind

"Say, Rozzy. What's up," asked Maggie Lee over the phone.

"I'm doing my homework; that's what's up. Whatchu want now, Maggie," asked Rozzy.

"I haven't heard or seen hide nor hair of you in over three weeks, turkey."

"Maggie Lee, I don't want to do that no more."

"Aw, I see. It's like that, huh. You're just gonna kick me to the curb."

"Woman, ain't nobody bothering you. Nobody owns me. Nobody tells me what to do, but my mama," said Rozzy.

"Okay. Well, how 'bout this? I hear about you being around my cousin anymore, I'mo kick you in your little ass and tell him all about you and me. He knows about me, but he ain't so sure about your little fast ass," warned Maggie.

"'Fast'? You're the one who's out here trying to fuck everything that moves. Just because you're stupid, doesn't mean everybody else is as stupid as you need them to be. The boy already knows about me. I don't lie to him about nothing, or take his money like some other people I know. He's my friend; my true friend, and I really appreciate that," confessed Rozzy.

"Next time I see you..."

"Next time you see me, you're going to shit and step back in it. I've already got a mama and a slew of brothers, uncles and cousins who really have taken a liking to Booker T; and who would love to bash in your big head with a baseball bat; then, send what's left of your ass to the county corrections unit for being a pedophile. I'm the child: you're the adult. Remember, Ms. Fast-ass? Only thing keeping them from jacking your shiftless ass right now is because Uncle Gus don't want my brothers to spend the rest of their lives in jail behind fucking you up."

"Well, I guess that's that. I cain't stand your sorry young ass no way, baby girl," said Maggie.

"Once again, I may be young, but I'm not as stupid as you think I am. I've been a foolish child, but society forgives us and feels we're supposed to make mistakes. But, your big country ass is grown, now. You don't get three strikes before you're out. You want to tell everybody about my business, go right ahead on. Like I said, I'm still a kid. Society ain't gonna feel sorry for you or do anything to prosecute me. It's like I've been telling your ignorant ass all along, it won't even hold up in a court of law. The whole wide world will see you for what you really are, a pervert who tried to take advantage of a young girl, but who struck out on the first pitch, and got her creepy ass sent straight to 'JAIL'...without passing 'GO'."

"You haven't seen or heard the last of me yet, Ms. Smartass," said Maggie Lee.

"With your big mouth in this small town? Like I was saying, it's your choice, and your ass. One strike and you're in jail and officially marked for life, Miss Maggie. I'm just another innocent kid. You're famous for preying on other folks' kids. So, why don't you go pick on somebody your own age, and see how bad you are. You ain't no good!"

And with that, Rozzy hung up the phone. She understood the saying that, "[She] who fights, but runs away; must fight again, another day."

Elizabeth Scofield

Elizabeth Scofield led a simple, ordinary life. After graduating from the U.S. Naval Academy at Annapolis, Maryland, she completed her five-year obligation of military service as a commissioned officer in the U.S. Marine Corps; honorably discharged after completing a five year military obligation and attaining the rank of Captain (O-3). Now, two years out of the Corps, she is teaching and coaching high school kids, instead of teaching and coaching Marine recruits. There isn't much difference between the two groups, except that most high school kids are unarmed and three to four years too young to enter the Marine Corps Recruit Depot.

Liz Scofield always said she was forever thankful to the Corps for giving her a head-start in life. The product of a broken home, she pulled herself up out of poverty by her own bootstraps. She survived the Prairie Cove Housing Projects; kept her face in her books; garnered a recommendation from her state's U.S. Congressman; and grinded her way through a free four year college education at Annapolis.

Never married, her main goal has been to have a husband and at least 3 kids. But, at the time, she was too wrapped up in attaining tenureship as a teacher; coaching the PC High swim team; and paying off the mortgage as soon as possible on her recently acquired mid-century modern, single-family home in PC's west end neighborhood.

The four years she spent at Annapolis, and the five years she spent in the Corps had become more a part of her DNA than she realized. Not only had she distinguished herself as the Academy's premier female swimmer, but she also had a reputation for throwing good hands in the boxing ring. Every midshipman in her class was required to study boxing. She could have gone professional, if not for the five year service obligation all midshipmen are required to complete in return for receiving the free college education, plus room and board, medical coverage, and pay while studying at Annapolis.

Everything Liz Scofield did was crisp, simple, and "nose-to-the-grindstone." She accomplished more by six o'clock each morning than most people accomplished after a full working day. She maintained vestiges of what the Marines called "hard Corps/gung-ho/lean, mean and green" now after her military obligation was up. So, one can understand why her physical appearance was especially off-setting in that there was very little evidence of soft feminism in her way and manner. As a matter of fact, the way Liz dressed and wore her hair led most ignorant civilians to prematurely assume that she preferred to mingle with those of her own sex…a grievous mistake on their part.

At twenty-seven, Ms. Scofield was a stone cold virgin who never inserted even a tampon, let alone any other object, sentient or insentient to facilitate her "needs". As can be imagined, Liz had to be hornier than fifty-five gorillas. But her previous Spartan life had trained her to stand down and persevere through any hormonal bombardment. And woe-be-tythe the simple-minded male who intentionally, or unintentionally, melted down her resolve, and rendered her susceptible to grind-it-out in total hormonal surrender to his advantage. Needless to say, she was a very intimidating woman with serious command presence.

Being a red-blooded American male, the Hampton boy, in spite of his inexperience and upbringing, naturally assumed he could handle Scofield's strengths and weaknesses. He was so attracted to her that he had an absolute crush on the woman. Although she was five-feet-ten, weighing in at one-hundred fifty-five pounds, with a solid pear-shaped body, and almost twice Booker's age; these were some of the features that drove Booker to dare dream of pursuing her affections.

"Good morning Ms. Scofield," said Booker T as he almost ran into her when she stepped out of the school's administrative offices.

"Well, good morning to you Mr. Hampton," said Ms. Scofield. This kind of response to him really set his imagination spinning out of control. "Are you ready for the midterm exam?"

"Yes ma'am. Are you gonna be teaching Algebra II next year?"

"I hope to shout. As a matter of fact, I hope to be tutoring Plane and Solid Geometry and teaching the Advanced Placement students. I'm almost certain you will be sitting right up front in all of my classes again." Now what did she have to go and say that for?

"Aw, Miss Scofield, please don't tease me. I hope and I pray what you said is true. I can't imagine studying math under anyone else but you. You make algebra so much fun. After that, I hope you do teach geometry; along with trigonometry, calculus, college algebra..."

"Booker, we need to talk. More specifically, I need to speak with your Aunt, too." Shut the front door!!!! "Do you think you can arrange that for me; to drop by the house this evening? I won't take too long."

"Yes ma'am. I work at O'Banion's Market after swimming practice, but I'll make sure they know you want to meet with them. Ms. Scofield, please don't give them a bad report on me."

"Thanks Booker. See you later in class," said Ms. Scofield.

As she walked away, Booker couldn't take his eyes off of her form as he backed down the hall. All of a sudden a voice said, "Do you like what you see?" As he gathered himself and looked to his right, he saw it was Rozzy. Booker was so busy looking at Ms. Scofield's rear end that he lost his bearings and was wandering onto the wrong side of the hallway, against the crowd. He bumped into another student. "Boy, you are one sick puppy. How many times do I have to tell you to cut the crap, leave that poor woman alone, and get her out of your child mind," asked Rozzy.

"Aw, Rozzy, lighten-up. I'm cool. I'm cool. I was just wondering what she wanted to see my Aunt and Uncle for." •

"Maybe she's tired of you and your little hard-on always pointing at her."

"Naw. Naw. Rozzy, I'm not like you. I wouldn't think of going that far with a grown woman."

"Then stay your ass over on your side of the hallway; cover yourself up; and try to walk down the hallway like you've got some sense. Your little scrotum is trying to show what's on your foolish little mind."

Booker wasn't the least bit embarrassed or deterred by Rozzy's summation of his present situation. As he proceeded to his next class he had flashbacks of seeing Rozzy in his Aunt May-May's house, alone with the twins. He seemed to gloat at having raised her disapproval of his crush on Ms. Scofield. "How you like me now, Ms. Smartass," he mumbled to himself as he headed on down the hallway.

CHAPTER 17

The Scholar/Athlete

That evening, after wrapping up her classes spending about ninety minutes taking the team through swimming practice, Liz Scofield packed her gear into the trunk of her car and headed over to the Jarvis house. As she pulled up in front of the white limestone single-family house with sage green wood trim, she was not sure if this was the correct address. The tall neatly trimmed yew hedges surrounding the front porch blocked the address numbers. As she tentatively started up the walkway and five steps to the porch, she saw Annie Lee and Percy Jarvis already sitting on the porch in the metal, gliding, three-seater that was in the shade behind the bushes.

"Mr. and Mrs. Jarvis?"

Annie Lee and Percy both nodded with Annie Lee saying, "Yes. Good evening, Ms. Scofield. Please have a seat"

"Good evening. I see Booker already told yall about me,"

"You are all he ever seems to talk about. Pleased to see you, Ms. Scofield. Besides Booker's constant bragging about you, we've been hearing of your accomplishments from other parents and students around the neighborhood. We thank the Lord that Booker T is in your hands, now. Not that we want him to follow you into the Marines, but a growing young man can use all the positive influences and examples he can muster into his circle of life."

"Well that's why I asked to speak to you this evening. Booker is a brilliant student, and a very well-mannered young man. With his extra-curricular activities at school and at the grocery store, he certainly has a lot on his plate. However, I also think he can also handle my algebra advanced placement class."

"Oh, we always knew he was exceptional and a good all-around youngster," offered Percy. "You know his grandpa was a professional athlete himself."

"Yes. Mr. Hampton was a trailblazer. And that's how I notice that Booker is not heavy enough into the books, but he truly is on the ball. Mr. and Mrs. Jarvis, I need a little more time with him to help him make sure he is comfortable with the heavier study load throughout his sophomore year. If he can adjust to this time period, he'll definitely be set for junior and senior year. I'm requesting that you give me that permission. I don't need to see him each and every evening, but I do need to be available for him two or three nights a week for 45 minutes to an hour after he gets off from work."

"Well, we don't mind; just so long as he can handle it. I swear, I've never seen anyone at his young age wanting to keep so busy," said Annie Lee.

"I'm convinced that he can continue to handle it. We carried that kind of load at the Academy for four years. Booker is not only a potentially strong scholar/athlete, but he actually has made adjustments to his heavier load so far."

"A scholar/athlete. Boy, will his mama Queenie be proud of him earning a title like that," said Annie. "I know his grandparents would be proud, too."

"Well, Ms. Scofield, looks like he's really in your hands now. God bless you and thank you for your sacrifice in the military. And thank you for committing to our nephew Booker T," said Percy.

"It's my pleasure Mr. and Mrs. Jarvis. And thank you for

your service, also. Well, I promised Booker I wouldn't take up all of your time. So, I'll be on my way."

"Thank you for reaching out to Booker," said Annie Lee.

"You are welcome. Have a good evening," said Ms. Scofield.

After Scofield drove off, Annie Lee said to Percy, "She sure looks a lot like Queenie when she was younger. She's just an inch or two shorter than Queenesther, but she's a lot more level headed."

"Yeah. And she's a lot more eager, too. You may not realize it, but right about now, that fine looking young woman's got that boy's dick harder than Japanese calculus. If he plays his cards right, he's gonna learn a hell of a lot more than some sombitching mathematics, and all that other bullshit put together," said Percy.

"Well Percy, I think he's man enough to handle his life by keeping his mouth shut, taking care of business..."

"...And taking over," they both recited in unison, laughing out loud.

"He better be watching his own ass more than he's watching hers. That young Rozzy gal is hot-to-trot after him, too. If Booker T breaks her heart, she can hang that young school teacher and ruin her career," said Annie Lee.

"Yes, Lord." said Percy. "Like they say at dinner time, 'Don't let your eyes be bigger than your belly. Take all you want, but you got to eat all you take.' Life ain't a bitch; it's the foolish people who are the bitches," said Percy.

Boyfriend and "Girlfriend"

The next day while walking to school, Rozzy didn't say much: Booker did most of the talking. Once in school, Rozzy seemed to be so agitated that she couldn't put her mind into studying at her usual level. For the first time in her young life of fifteen years, she felt the pangs of jealousy so powerful that they totally interfered with her ability to focus on her classwork.

Booker was alert, aware, and knew enough to leave her alone and give her her space. Before she knew it, the final school bell rang, signaling the end of the school day. The swimming practice was cancelled due to an emergency teachers' meeting.

As Rozzy walked out the front door of the school building and down the steps leading to the sidewalk, Booker T came sidling up behind her. "What's wrong with your face?"

"What do you mean what's wrong with my face," she snapped.

"Your face is so long and your mouth is all poked out. Talk to me, partner," asked Booker. "I'm not completely foolish. I can tell that something's eating at you and why."

"Then, there's nothing to talk about. You're so perceptive that you should be back inside waiting on your woman. Aw, my mistake. She can't take no kid to the teachers' meeting."

"Seeing how swimming practice is cancelled for the day, and I've got some down time before work, I figured I'd walk you home. Give me your books. I promised you this for getting me the job at your uncle's grocery store."

"Aw, yeah. I forgot," Rozzy confessed as they crossed N. Main Street and proceeded down 34th street for the mile walk toward her home.

"You know Rozzy, sometimes you can be kind of mean and snappy."

"After all that I did for your ungrateful behind? Boy, your people sure spoiled the hell out of you," she declared.

"No. On the real side: I've been giving you serious play ever since the first day I laid eyes on you. I don't mean to come off as seeming to be ungrateful. I really do appreciate the job at the store, and everything. But why do you think I'm carrying your heavy-assed books?"

"A deal is a deal: you're the one who keeps saying you owe me," said Rozzy.

"Aw, so that's all this is supposed to be to you, is a deal? I suck up to you from sun-up at the beginning of the school day, throughout the classes to the end of the school day, 'til sundown.

How are you able to draw your mouth up to accuse me of having a crush on somebody else when you ain't giving me no feedback on my attention to you? Are you supposed to be jealous or something?"

"Boy, ain't nobody studying your ass! My attitude is for her not losing her jobs and reputation behind you and your childish dreams."

Just as they crossed the street and started walking by the entrance to the cemetery, Booker noticed a green Ford sedan, that belonged to Aunt May-May. The car eased up alongside them, facing in the opposite direction of the on-coming traffic on their side of the street.

Maggie Lee was behind the wheel. "Bitch, get your ass in here," Maggie snapped at Rozzy, "We need to talk."

"Woo-oo-oo! Shit's getting kinda thick around here," bellowed Booker T.

"Maggie Lee if you go down to the next corner and take a right turn, and go all the way down by Page and Upton, you might find a whole bunch of bitches. But if you start from here, you ain't gonna find no bitches," snapped Rozzy.

"So now, sister bad-ass, looks like your best bet is to mosey on home, and park Aunt May-May's new car before she gits home from work and finds out her car is missing," warned Booker.

"Sucker, ain't nobody talking to you. Hey, Rozzy. We need to talk," insisted Maggie Lee.

"People in hell need ice water. That don't necessarily mean they're gonna get it," said Rozzy.

"In other words, Cuz, how about you closing your 'faggot-assed' mouth and moving on down the line," said Booker.

"Boy, in how many ways do I have to tell you to go fuck yourself? This was my bitch long before you slid in here."

"Nawl, fool. It's your jail time. She's still a kid. And besides that, it's your ass, too. As the cops be taking you away, Aunt May-May will be putting her foot all up in your ass, if I tell her about what you're doing out here with her new car. She don't even drive it to work, while you be using it on the wrong side of the street without her authority to chase young pussy," warned Booker.

"M-m-mothuhfuckuh, you've got your mama, and I've got mine. The difference here is that yours gave you up; mine kept me at home, even though I'm grown. Me and Maimee are grown-assed women now: free, black, and emancipated; no more spankings. Mama knows about me and Miss Thang. Why you think she let me use her car," asked Maggie Lee.

"I don't like to get into other folks business, but you, your mama, your sister Maimee and Booker T can all go straight to hell. If either one of you Hampton bitches messes with me, I will kill you," said Rozzy.

"Dammit, Maggie Lee. First you steal my money; now you're aggravating my honey. Like Popeye says, 'I've stands enough; and I can't stands no more.' Aweigh with you, you ugly black bitches. I'mo find me a white girl," teased Booker T.

Just then a yellow Corvette Stingray pulled up in front of Maggie Lee's car and the three of them. "Hey, Roz. What's going on," shouted her older brother Roscoe Mumford.

"'Scoey, take me home. I'm sick of these damned Hampton nigguhs," swore Rozzy.

"Let's go, baby sis," said Roscoe as he walked up to her. "Hey Mag. I catch you or your boy fucking with my little sister again, I'mo stand-in for her, and give you something you won't like. You got my drift," asked Roscoe.

"Roscoe, I ain't got no beef with you Mumfords," said Maggie Lee.

"Then take your shit someplace else. Your best bet is to git your pussy-sucking ass on back over there to your own turf by the railroad tracks, before you wind up getting buried over here," warned Roscoe.

Maggie Lee softly told Booker, "Boy git your ass in this car. That's Roscoe Mumford. Him and his brothers run the vice over here on the eastside of Prairie Cove."

For once Booker T. obeyed Maggie Lee with no sassmouth.

As he closed the car door, Rozzy asked, "Booker T, you gonna walk me to school Monday morning?"

"Rozzy, we need to talk…if it's okay with your bogarting big brothers," answered Booker.

"You ain't getting no beef from us, young brother. Looks like you need to get permission from your ugger-bugger cousin," laughed Roscoe in a high falsetto voice while flashing a gold tooth on the right front side of the center of his mouth.

As Booker and Maggie Lee pulled away from the curb, Rozzy and Roscoe's high-pitched laughter could be heard from a half block away. Booker was in no way embarrassed. To him this was a sign that he had the clearance from Rozzy's entire family to move ahead with her without worrying about interference from his own cousins or Rozzy's brothers, for that matter.

In Too Deep

The next morning, at fifteen minutes before six o'clock, Booker T arrived at O'Banion's Market. This morning, even old Gus O'Banion arrived for work later than Booker. Just as Gus was about to unlock the front door, he turned to Booker and said, "I heard that you and one of your cousins had a run-in with my niece and nephew: I'm talking about Roscoe and Rozlyn. I don't like to butt into young folks business, but Rozzy is family; and she's still a juvenile. She brought you here to me, and I'm sending you back to her. 'Scoey and them ain't mad at you. But you needs to talk to your cousins. I don't want to see nobody git hurt: but, if either one of them gals comes sniffing around Rozzy again, ain't nothing I can do to help your peoples. Go on over there to the car. Somebody wants to talk to you."

With apprehension, Booker looked over at the car parked near the side of the store, and saw a small head in the front passenger side. He took a moment to release a sigh of relief.

"Boy, go ahead on over to the car. That damned gal ain't gonna bite you. I swear, you young men, today, are scared of your own shadows. Just remember when dealing with a female, you can get a hell of a lot more with a teaspoon of sugar than with a pound of salt. Tell that gal I said don't take all day shooting-off at the mouth. I'll be inside."

As soon as Booker walked up to the passenger side of the car, Rozzy said, "Did you tell my uncle about me and Maggie? Booker, I'll do anything you want. Just don't let on to my people about Maggie Lee and me. I know I was stupid. If I had known there would be this much trouble from her I wouldn't have gotten involved."

"Yeah, well it serves you right. You females think you're so smart; always got to have one-up on a sucker by harboring secrets. If I had known you were this freaky and gullible, I probably wouldn't have tried to cozy up to you either."

"Well, you did. So now that you know about my 'freaky' you may as well finish what you started," said Rozzy.

"Not so fast. I may be naïve and inexperienced, but that doesn't mean I'm completely stupid. You've got so many cards up your sleeves that I couldn't care less if you like men, women, or chimpanzees. I just don't know you. And I'm not like you think I am. We can be friends, but after all of this mess, nobody owns me," warned Booker T.

"You think you're so straight and strong. Boy, you are right: you don't know who you're talking to. It would blow your mind if you knew what I could do for you."

"Look, Rozzy. I respect you now, and I always will. But nobody owns me. I don't care what kind of bullshit reasoning you use or what you think you can do for me or to me. I take great pride in the fact that I've always done for myself. You understand?"

"No, you need me in your corner," said Rozzy. "It's hard enough that you got your own cousins sticking it to you every which way but loose."

"So, you think you can be more kin to me than my cousins?" Booker thought for a moment, then said, "Like I said, we can be friends. I didn't get on your case for messing around. Don't you give me no mess for respecting and working with somebody else who's trying to help me make it... I'm talking about Ms. Scofield. She's trying to help me in the same way you say you want to help me. You give me any more lip about her, and we're through, Rozzy. You understand?"

"Okay, for now. Can I have a hug?"

"You get a big hug...'cause you've been a good, good girl. M-m-m. Now bye. I've got to get back inside before Uncle Gus comes back out here to fire me, and be looking to take you home."

She continued to hold on to him saying, "No. I'm not going back home. I'm coming inside to work with y'all today."

"Are you gonna start acting like the Little Black Tar Baby," asked Booker.

"I'll have you to know that I am not black."

"Then what are you?"

"I am a melanated, indigenous, not-from-Africa, original American. My people didn't come here on no damned slave ship; they were already here before the lying, conniving, white people came on their boats and started developing land that wasn't theirs. They feed ignorant original Americans that slave ship bullshit to cheat us out of what's already ours."

"What kind of shit..."

"See. Chump, you need me real bad. You swallowed up all of that African slave ship crap from the thieving traitor Europeans, and we were here all along for tens of thousands of years. Yep. You need me. You're as helpless as a baby sold into slavery."

Booker continued hugging Rozzy for about 10 more seconds, then said, "Okay. That's enough."

Surprised, she said, "Okay Booker. You be that way. Dudes would give anything to hug this. You could have all of this and more. Aw, I forgot; you're still a cherry boy. My fault. You get a pass."

"Yuck, Yuck, Yuck. Come on. Mr. Gus is gonna be cussing and fussing if a customer arrives while we're out here monkeying around like this," said Booker as he coaxed Rozzy away from the car, and up the steps into the store.

Family Betrayal

Even though Booker T did a stellar performance of hiding his true amount of disappointment with Rozzy, it was obvious that she had bruised his ego and confused him about history that his own relatives had never explained to him. All they told him was about "the birds and the bees" and "the flowers in the trees" when he was five or six-years-old. They never took the time to clarify the phrases as he grew older. Even during adolescence they had him believing a girl could be impregnated "from a kiss" instead of "leading up from a kiss." He felt betrayed because they never told him that there were more ways of loving besides a male with a female. He was shocked both by the "truth" and repulsed by the "betrayal" at the same time.

This was more than a family betrayal. It was unacceptable to leave a child to experience this kind of truth on his own, without any forewarning or forearming by the very folks he trusted. No wonder "Afro-Americans" are so misguided by untruths.

And besides the sex thing, there was the "African-American" lie that Rozzy just explained to him. If this turned out to be true, this could be her redeeming grace with Booker. She showed him his vulnerability, of being misinformed by not researching and investigating information for his own good. He grew to appreciate the deeper meaning found in acknowledging and recognizing the signs and symbols, everywhere you look.

Booker T. Hampton may have been misled by the very people he trusted the most; but from this point on, he determined to rely on no one else but himself. After making this realization, while still enrolled at Prairie Cove's Washington High, he was accepted into Mensa, the international genius society. The response by others to this kind of personality could be "out of the box" or "out of the matrix." As has been said, "Genius is next to insanity."

But, if he had learned anything from his relatives, Booker was constantly running into variations of their admonition to "always be nice." Mama Queenie, Grandma Mary Alice, Auntie Annie and all of the other women of his matriarchically ruled clan constantly reminded Booker that, "You can get more with a teaspoon of sugar than with a pound of salt."

True, Booker believed a person could "get more…" but he really wanted nothing more from Rozzy than for her to realize that all males were not meant to service and tolerate her like her brothers and Uncle Gus. As he entered the store, he softly muttered to himself, "And so it goes. And so it goes."

Booker grew up in the full majesty of female, unconditional love. But this meant that just as females in the family loved him up one side, they were subject to smack him down on the other side. This phenomenon was especially true with his mother Queenesther. After Grandma Mary Alice passed on, Auntie Annie came into his life in place of her sister Mary Alice. Maybe this was too late, because after experiencing people like Aunt May-May and her twins, most men would refer to all women as being bitches. But not Booker T. Hampton. He was a living testament of Grandpa Austin's old saying, "Just because one person chooses to dew-dew on their floors doesn't mean that you have to dew-dew on yours."

Other sayings such as, "Be you man, woman, chicken or child, you shall reap what you sow;" and "When you make your bed, you have to sleep in it," proved to be true.

Always Be on Time for the "Train"

Ms. Scofield eventually gave Booker her phone number, not only because she was interested in Booker maximizing his grades, but she was grooming him to become a midshipman at the U.S. Naval Academy.

Inside of four years and his eighteenth birthday, she had Booker swimming like a Navy Seal and Force Recon Marine, even with his sneakers on. Of course, this was only when they were alone in the pool area. Rozzy was about as resentful of Booker spending "special time" with Ms. Scofield as Booker was resentful of Rozzy having spent "special time" with his cousin Maggie Lee.

One day during summer school of his senior year, Booker emerged from underwater, and pulled himself out of the pool. He took a few "staggering" steps and collapsed in Ms. Scofield's arms. As she grabbed him from the front, she pulled him into her. Booker wrapped his arms around her shoulders, pulling her to him, saying, "Oh Miss Scofield. What's wrong with me?"

"Well, Booker. Based on my profound experience, any man with a hard-on isn't so incapacitated that he can't stand up on his own," replied Ms. Scofield as she pulled back from his body, somewhat embarrassed. Words can't explain the surge of energy that was generated in the few seconds he had pressed his body into her body.

"You give me time to graduate, I'm going to marry you," foolishly whispered Booker.

"You want to get knocked down on the ground, try that mess again. I need this job, and I don't need no brash young teenager giving me a bad reputation. You be good; I be good. You be bad; I be bad. You understand me, Booker T. Hampton?"

"Yes ma'am, Ms. Scofield. Please forgive me. I swear I won't ever try that again."

"I know you're embarrassed, Booker. But, your hormones will ruin other peoples' lives. People aren't supposed to carry on like that until they're of legal age to handle the responsibilities that come from that type of behavior."

"I can wait," said Booker.

"I thought you swore you wouldn't try that again? You may already be of legal age, but you're still only a high school senior.

They would fire me and only put you on suspension, setting you back in graduation. Boy, you need to get a hold of yourself. I wonder what the Jarvises would have to say about this."

"Aw, please Ms. Scofield: don't tell my people. They're all I've got. It's not like I committed a crime in the presence of the team. Even though we're alone in the pool area, I'm so embarrassed for going too far."

"Well, it's always the woman's right to draw the line whenever she wants. It's the man's place to be embarrassed and rejected in front of others or not. You need to get a hold of yourself, before other people get a hold of you for being too young to finish what you start. Hurry up and get dressed. I'll get you over to Mr. O'Banion's."

Booker got dressed and met Ms. Scofield in the school parking lot. After a few blocks, he asked her, "You're still mad at me?"

"Booker, I'm not mad at you, but I am disappointed in you. I've always held you in the highest esteem. That doesn't mean that I'm ready to surrender to your young hormones. I'm trying to pass on to you what was given to me by another concerned teacher. Do you understand?"

"Yes ma'am."

"Look at it this way. There's a train coming for you inside of two years to take you to a place I once knew. In order for you to get to where I am, I've got to have you as prepared as I was when I got on board that same train. One day you're going to look back and see that getting on that train was more important than getting into some female's body."

"Promise you won't tell nobody, and I promise to master everything you teach me," swore Booker.

"Booker T. Hampton, I promise not to tell anybody that you tried and almost died; and I promise to teach you what I know. But if you pull that mess again, I'm gonna have to protect myself, and report you to your guardians and the school. This is no light matter."

"Thanks, Ms. Elizabeth."

"You can call me 'Miss Elizabeth' in private."

Booker, smiling, saw her comment as further evidence of how much 'Miss Elizabeth' really appreciated him, and was giving him a way to have direct access to her other than while in school. On one hand, this gesture could be a blessing; and on the other hand, it could be a detriment.

You Blew It, Fool

As the weeks passed, for the most part, things in Prairie Cove went along smoothly. Rozzy, believing she was slick, continued to sneak back and forth across the sexual relationship fence between Booker and other males and females. Booker continued to feign naiveté by schmoozing Rozzy right along while he basked in Elizabeth Scofield's "nurturing" and attentiveness.

In his mind, Rozzy became more and more like a sister. Yet, she continued to maintain the hope that their relationship would grow into a situation that was more than platonic love like siblings.

It was during the summer before their senior year at PC High School that Rozzy posed the question to Booker, "What are you going to do about me, boy?"

"Child, grow up. Like you said, I don't own you; nor am I responsible to you. As a matter of fact, you have, from the start, made it perfectly clear to me that no one owns you. So, whatchu talking about now, Rozzy?"

"You know full damn well what I'm talking about."

"No. I really don't. I only have an idea of what you call yourself doing. You think you're so smart. You want the control, while you walk around as free as a bird in flight, all along hiding your secrets like the cat that swallowed the canary. The way I see it, your life and what you're dealing with is your business. You have a right to jealously guard all that."

"Once again: you know what I'm talking about, Booker."

"Whatever I may 'know' is all in my 'little mind'; drawn from my own conclusions," said Booker T. "One thing you can be sure of is that I feel we are good friends. I can't be allowing you to get into my head or going too deep with someone who chooses to remain ambiguous and private, with secrets like a pig in a poke."

"You calling me a pig," asked Rozzy.

"Naw Rozzy. I'm saying what you're hiding in your trick-bag is like a pig. Anyway, deep in your heart, you need me to be dumb. You keep on with your little game of charades, and I'll keep on being 'dumb.' Any promises I have made to you, I have lived up to. Just because you want more than we agreed to doesn't mean that I am obligated to jump to attention and go along with your change-of-direction. Your best bet is to keep-on-keeping-on with whomever you're doing it with. I don't want to get entangled in no threesome or foursome with you and your secrets."

"For your information and edification, if I was ever involved with someone else, you didn't make things any easier during all that time, by stringing me along," said Rozzy.

"See? There you go again, trying to be so slick with me that you out-smarted your own self. You think you can cover your ass by flipping the script and reversing the table. In the end, you've wound up playing mind-fuck with yourself. I know your game. You screwed up by trying to leave me to draw my own conclusions. I don't owe you anything but the honesty and courtesy of being a good friend from the recent past; and that's as far as this relationship can go. You had your chance. You made your choice. Now, get ahold of yourself," said Booker.

"So, that's how you're gonna be? You've got to..."

"I ain't 'got to' do nothing but stay black and die, Rozzy. I am not bothering anyone. I'm minding my own business. You and no other sucker owns me. And I, for damned sure, don't want to be owning no parts of you after you've kept me in the dark about your secret self from day one."

"Alright, Booker T. We need to talk. Just hear me out, and give me a moment to level with you."

"Naw. Forget about it Rozzy. You're about three years too late. You never should have left me to draw my own conclusions from the git-go. My cousins could have told you that."

"Motherfucker! You don't know who you're talking to. Don't you turn your back on me and walk away," yelled Rozzy. "I'm not through with you yet."

"Aw, poor baby girl Wozzy. She's so spoiled. Whatchu gonna do now, Wozzy; start haunting me? You sound just like cousin Maggie Lee. Your best bet is to keep being satisfied with folks like her. Once a female starts calling a male the M-word, his tour of duty is done. It's time for him to break camp, mount up, and haul ass. Bye-bye." And he was gone.

No Woman Wants to Marry a Weak Man
No Man Wants to Marry a Woman Who Wants a Weak Man

Sure. This all sounds reasonable coming from a young man's mouth. But, any young man worth his salt, would still harbor some feelings about a longtime, good-looking, love interest, no matter how big a man he thought he was.

The only thing helping Booker T 'set the record straight' with Rozzy was his fortunate ability to rebound off of Rozzy, and focus more intensely on whom he now privately called Liz Scofield. Yes, not only did he refocus his mind back on Liz, but he found himself telling her everything but the sexual content about his 'affair' and 'breakup' with Rozzy.

Scofield being the elder and most experienced of the three was no fool. Booker made a stupid mistake. It was one Saturday morning, in the empty classroom, while confessing about Rozzy and his relationship with her, he failed to realize that when it comes to listening to a male's sob-story about other females, female tend to respond in defense of each other. Regardless of race, they empathize with each other. What's more, the male is always prejudged as being like a "typical black" person—guilty and incapable of being completely innocent, as evidenced by the question, "You must have done something to make her do what she did."

"But, I didn't do nothing. I-didn't-do-nothing," Booker whined. To an adult like Liz, this was a definite sign of weakness. Part and parcel of being a "black" male is to be the scapegoat; the opposite of believing justice dictated by the "rule of law" in the American culture.

"Isn't that sort of the same thing you tried to convey to me when you 'innocently' faked illness on the side of the pool? Booker, I thought you told me that your late Grandpa Austin Hampton always told you to be the 'bigger man.'

"Grampa raised me to carry my own weight at all times. He never told me to take any mess."

"What about in the car out front of the grocery store," asked Liz.

"She came on to me. Besides; her Uncle Gus was the one who drove her up there, and told me to go over to her. I didn't expect all of that 'Who-Shot-John' stuff from her."

"Whatever, Booker: no woman wants to hook up with a man who can't carry the weight of responsibility," said Liz.

"That's just it. She's never said she was my woman or asked me to carry anything but her school books. What I'm trying to tell you is that I knew the score, in spite of her thinking she kept me in the dark. She tried to play me; but the real problem has always been that I don't play dumb, as she expects all boys to do."

"Aw, Booker believe me; you are too savvy to be just a 'boy.' Now that you're of age, you know how to think and analogize. But can you keep your mouth shut; hide your brightness; and take care of business?"

"Miss Elizabeth, even though a man may be of legal age; keeping his mouth shut and taking care of business; the poor guy can't do no more about 'taking over' than the woman lets him. I've been in your hands, at your beck and call, all of these years. I made my move and even you shot me down, and put me in my place. Seeing how everybody keeps reminding me that I'm so young, the only way I'mo move on any female is if she's the one who makes the first move in no uncertain terms. It's all a trap; designed so that the woman always comes out smelling like a rose; and the guy is branded as a criminal."

"Am I your favorite teacher," Liz asked as she tickled him.

"Yeah. Yeah. Okay, okay!!"

"Enough grab-ass. Now, git your behind to work," said Liz.

Trouble in Paradise

Now, Booker was in deeper trouble. Not only was his cousin Maggie Lee jealous of his relationship with Rozzy, but Rozzy was mad at him for not letting her have her way with him. That's when the rumors started circling around that section of Prairie Cove that Booker had a crush on his teacher.

If you're born in the right situation, life in this realm can seem like heaven on Earth. Yet, if you're born in this same realm, in the wrong situation, life in this realm can seem like a living hell. But if you only know the hellish aspect of life, it will seem like a rose garden. As far as Booker T. Hampton was concerned, life in his realm grew to be like a rose garden. He reached the conclusion that it wasn't the environment that made the hell: it was mainly the people in a particular environment. People had the power to make a place seem hellish.

Booker concluded that no matter which way he turned, as long as there were people in the vicinity, there was bound to be some dew-dew. He used to say, "Every sentient being has bowels; and is required to stoop to relieve his or her self. So what do you expect? Roses?"

First: there was Aunt May-May and her demon twins Maggie Lee and Maimee.

Second: his own mother Queenie was no archangel, either. Everything seemed to be falling apart when he received the news that his mother Queenie had gotten her drunken self run over by another boyfriend. The car ran over her legs at the ankles.

You see, Queenie had started shacking-up with a little fellow named Horace from some lonesome place in the Cimarron region of the Oklahoma panhandle. This little fellow, behaving like a vicious little cur, wound up being the recipient of a serious Queenesther, big-nigger ass-whupping. He panicked; bit her in the face; broke loose from her grip; jumped into his car; and tried to get away. Now, to show you how stupid Queenie was, she grabbed the door handle of the car to stop her little Shorty-Arty from getting away. But the car was too powerful and she lost her grip when the car was shifted into forward gear. The car's rear tire ran over her ankles. Aw, she was fit to be tied; angrier than a brahma bull that was just branded on the ass with a red hot pitch fork.

Yes, that little man stomped on the gas pedal and ran over both of Queenie's legs. That's when she let out a blood-curdling James Brown-like scream that was heard clear over to the Hallville police headquarters building, in downtown Hallville. It scared the police chief so badly that he thought for sure a giant hole had opened up in the ground and was about to suck that side of Hallville to hell. After all, the whole town was situated on top of abandoned coal mine shafts. The townsfolk thought this was the cause of strange sounds during high winds. But on this day, there was hardly any wind blowing: just Queenie's big mouth.

All the chief could do was tell his officers in roll call, "For God's sake, somebody hurry up and git over there, and cuff up that big old woman. Matter of fact, don't come back here without her ass being hog tied. Last time she pulled this shit, she fucked-up three of my biggest goon cops and tore out the back seat of a brand-new cruiser. And as another matter of fact, when I first met her big gruesome ass, I had about a year in grade as just a grunt street sergeant answering a radio call to her house. Her own boyfriend, I forget his name right now, put in the call for a police wagon to come and haul her big gorilla ass down to City Hospital so they could give her regular dose of Thorazine to her. Only way we could get her into the back of the wagon was to tell her a lie: that we were taking her over to her other nigguh's house. After a short while, she started to whooping and hollering and screaming bloody murder, 'cause she came to realize through the side vents of the wagon that we were going the opposite way, in the direction of the City Hospital. We called ahead for a 6-man backup crew to meet us at the ambulance ramp. You see, it took that many big assed, roebucking nigguh cops to hold that cock-strong heifer down. And the last thing she declared to me was, 'Muh-muh-muhfuckuh, you mines. I'mo be whuppin' on you lil' black ass 'til I gets tired.' After they knocked her out with a horse needle full of some kind of sedative, I'll never forget how she was just laying there, still looking dead at me with that wild-eyed frozen stare; like a dead fish."

Now, many years later, that same five foot six inch tall police sergeant, Luther Ankrum, had been promoted to Hallville police chief. The little Napoleonic-type man personally contacted Booker T by phone, and told him, "Now listen boy, you're gonna have to bring your big happy ass home. Your mama's legs are broken: she's reduced to walking around on her knuckles behind snapping all the metal pins that held her ankles and knees together. It ain't so much because she's too heavy. It's because the first responders are all scared to death, saying she has a grip like Frankenstein trying to caress a daisy. And, anyway, you're the only one who can talk any sense into her. It's getting so that every weekend she be whupping up on one or more of my police officers, and putting them out on injured leave. By now, she's done busted up most of my midnight shift in her precinct: not to forget the jail area and the other prisoners. Boy, I don't want to have to shoot your mama; so your best bet is to come home, pronto."

That was the end of the summer of 1963 before Booker's senior year at Prairie Cove's Booker T. Washington High. This would mean he would have to spend his last year in Hallville taking care of his mother and finish high school at Hallville's majority "white" Baldridge High School. He didn't know how he was going to get by without Prairie Cove, Rozzy, Elizabeth Scofield, Auntie Annie and Uncle Percy; even Aunt May-May and the twins. He realized he would even miss lugging around Rozzy's school books; playing stupid about her "sexual fluidity."

CHAPTER 18

Got to Go

He had grown to be much bigger, now. During the summer after his sophomore year in school, he must have had a six inch growth spurt. He was just over six-feet-three inches in height; already bigger and taller than most kids his age.

Having to return to Hallville was like falling three steps backward as he attempted to take one step forward. When he left Hallville and made it back to Prairie Cove it was like an escape from a poisonous snake infested island to Paradise where there were no snakes. But because Booker was a "bigger man," he didn't consider it much of a burden to move back to Hallville to take care of his mother.

Now in his final year of high school, at Hallville, he oversaw and assisted in the rehabilitation of his mother, Queenie. During that time, he had no extra time for high school athletics. Once again, he was minimally dependent on the ungrateful Queenie's financial assistance; and she made a point of never allowing him to forget this.

During his previous escape to PC, Queenie had become even more bitter than she was originally. So much so that few decent men wanted to couple with her anymore. She lost her pride and strength due to the over-consumption and dependency on fortified wine, just like her sister May-May.

During his absence, Queenie had taken in a stray dog. This dog was another cur...a dyed-in-the-wool feral son-of-a-bitch named Jody. He acted as though he was in charge and wouldn't let anyone pet him but Queenie. Yes, he was a true example of how to "bite the hand that feeds you."

One hot summer day, Queenie ordered Booker to feed Jody. Booker was shirtless, and bent over, blocking the kitchen passageway where he was told to feed and water the dog, Queenie approached, and yelled, "Nigguh, move."

Booker pleaded, "Mama, I can't. The dog is growling." And the dog was not only growling, but he was frozen in position, baring his fangs, while looking sidewise at Booker as he was scooping dog food into the vicious hound's bowl.

Impatiently, Queenie screamed, "I-mean-move-now," as she slammed her open hand onto Booker's sweaty, bare back. That's when the dog sank its fangs deep into Booker's right hand as Booker flinched from the sting of the slap. Poor Booker tried to fend off his mother with his left hand, but she smacked his back a second time. There stood poor Booker T being savagely attacked by his drunken mother and her ignorant hound.

Booker kicked at the dog and his plate of food flew across the floor. As the hound went for the food, Booker turned to his mother saying, "I'm sick of this shit."

"Then hit the road, Jack," screamed Queenie. "You can always join the Army or the Navy, you foolish bastard."

"Aw, so now I'm a foolish bastard. Okay, Mama. Just give me a little time. I'll be back with some good news for you." At that moment, he realized that what Uncle Percy and Auntie Annie had previously told him was finally proven true. This was it. There was no way he could help his mother. The longer he stayed with her, his safety, survival and sanity were in jeopardy. He had to get out of that house as soon as possible.

He went straight downtown to the federal building and saw the U.S. Marine Corps recruiter. The staff sergeant told him that the Corps was forming a Platoon 343 at the Marine Corps Recruit Depot in San Diego, California in four weeks at the end of May.

Queenie aggravated Booker so much that he was more than happy to be signed off into the Marine Corps, now that he was eighteen-years-old. The Marines would ship him out to boot camp as soon as he graduated high school.

"On second thought sir, my final exams aren't until mid-June. If you've got a recruit class going sooner, I'd sure like to be in it."

"We've got a class starting at the beginning of May. That's the next class."

"I think I'll go on into boot camp with that class," said Booker. "I can always finish high school later. I can't afford to stay at home another day."

"She's turning on you that bad, huh," asked the sergeant.

"Yes sir."

"Son, you don't have to sir me. You save that for the drill instructors you'll be meeting at MCRD San Diego as soon as you step off of the bus. You signed the paper, now you can kiss your mama and your young ass good bye. What's your mama's name? Queenesther? If you can hang in there until May 5, the son of the Queen will be the property of the U.S. Marines."

"Don't poke fun at my mama, Sarge."

"Aw, naw, son. The old sarge would never do that. Starting this May, the Marine Corps' gonna be your mama, your daddy, the owner of your sweet young ass. From now on, you just take it easy. Everything's gonna be alright. I'll be in touch with you. You wrap up your business, keep your mouth shut, and don't give your mom no bullshit. The Corps won't take you if the courts and police have something against you. I know this is short notice, but you better make sure your piss is clean, and your hair has no traces of dope in it. We ain't got no place for junkies. You understand me?"

"Yes, Staff Sergeant."

This was a shaky time for Booker. On one hand he knew that joining the Marine Corps was his best option to get away from

Mama Queenie's apron strings and violent outbursts. Yet, it was the uncertainty of moving from her. It was like trying to learn how to ride a bicycle; the awkward feeling of finding your balance so you can move along steadily.

As mean, selfish and distant as his mother was to him, she and the other relatives were the only remaining ones he could turn to when things in life were scary...the unknown. But he knew he had to go out into the world on his own, sooner or later. It might as well be now. He would be twenty-two years old when his enlistment was up. Then he could decide if he should do another enlistment or just take the honorable discharge; use it to get on a police force like Uncle Percy did as a young man, and do four years in college. He had a master plan and an alternate if one path failed.

Prairie Cove was like Heaven; and returning to Hallville was like being summonsed back to hell for an infraction that was out of his control. He had escaped the place only to be dragged back like a dog on a leash, and tied to a tree with his mama Queenie, who still whined, "I have my needs," or "I'll be so damned glad when your ass gets grown, and you get the hell out of here."

As far back as he could remember, he was assailed with these hints of how his Mama felt about him deep down inside. He had grown to realize that he was the one guilty of stealing his mother's childhood. He truly felt that if it had not been for his birth, his mother could have gone on to become a highly educated person of literature or whatever. She read everything in sight; even the cornflake box.

Well, now the time had arrived for him to break away from her, and run loose on his own. All he had to do was lay low for a few weeks and fly out to San Diego on May 5 at 0600 hours, as the staff sergeant ordered.

During this period in his life, so much pressure was placed on Booker that he didn't have time to think very much about Elizabeth Scofield and Rozlyn Mumford. He was too embarrassed and in too much pain and apprehension to talk to them. Rozzy was eager for him to express commitment to her;

yet he couldn't trust her behind her tendency to carry on a secret life outside of their relationship. Liz thought that she was too old and had too much to lose to take him seriously. So, he couldn't express his true feelings for her. She had already served him notice to behave before he got her into trouble. It seemed that both of these ladies had painted themselves into a corner, as far as Booker was concerned. He decided to not contact either one of them until after he graduated boot camp; wearing his Marine Corps olive drab uniform with the red Private First Class stripe and National Defense ribbon on his chest, along with his rifle expert badge. He had it all mapped out.

Come to think of it, these people were pretty much his only friends in PC, other than old Gus O'Banion. Sure, there was Auntie Annie and Uncle Percy. But, they were more than friends; better than parents; on a level more like Grandpa Austin and Grandma Mary.

Life seemed to be full of sudden changes for Booker. Just when he started getting used to someone or something, he or it got removed from the other; as if an invisible mind was up there in the sky, playing with him like he was a chess piece on a board in a chess match or checkers game. At a very early age, he learned not to form attachment of the mind to situations or people or anything else for that matter, since everything constantly changed. He learned that nothing remains the same making an attached mind fertile ground for more suffering. He had to keep stroking against the tide, like Elizabeth Scofield had taught him.

Man, did he like her. It's just that he was born too late to be the right age for her. But, that's how life is: and so it goes.

He'd just have to put his mind into the Corps for now. Those guys taught and fought for each other as a band of brothers. Marines never left their dead or wounded behind. If they couldn't get him out of harm's way, they wouldn't go home without him. They didn't fight for God and Country: they fought for each other, to the last man standing; to the last drop of blood. If your brother was killed, you positioned your team members'

dead bodies in the firing position and held the line; fixed
bayonets on the last round, screaming like a made bull dog, and
taking one last son-of-bitch to hell with you.

Boy, the staff sergeant and the movies really had this kid
pumped up for the drill instructors.

The Long Wait

The month of April must have seemed like the longest month
of Booker's young life. Things got to be more tense for him,
while staying at his mother's house. Eventually he asked an
across-the-street neighbor and friend of his mother, "Please Miss
Wright. I've just signed up for the Marine Corps. I leave for boot
camp at the beginning of next month. Would it be alright if I
gave the staff sergeant your telephone number so he can contact
me when it's time to go?"

"Booker, that ain't no problem. I've known you and your
mother for too many years to be turning my back on y'all when
you ask me for a favor. As long as my name is Johnnie Mae
Wright, you can always turn to me. You don't even have to ask
for that favor. Of course you can use my phone number. As a
matter of fact, I appreciate being the one you turn to in a time of
need. I really have more respect for you for always being
respectful to your mama. No matter what, you've always carried
yourself as a bigger and better man than most. If things get a
little too much for you, you're always welcome to come stay
over here until the Marines come and get you."

Booker was appreciative on one hand; but on the other hand
he told Johnnie Mae, "Miss Wright, it's really hard to ask people
for a favor. It's not that I'm ungrateful or anything like that. But
the whole neighborhood knows about my situation. I feel like
I'm a moocher or something. I'm tired of begging for help. I
appreciate all you've done for me and Mama. Once I get on my
feet, I'mo return the favors."

So, once again he pleaded with the sergeant who said, "Private Hampton, the Corps only has a few Marines. If we started recruit platoons that often, we wouldn't be able to call ourselves 'the few.' We'd be proud, but there would be too many Marines. We'd be as big as the damn Army. You've only got two weeks to go. I'll be by to get you the following Wednesday like I said. You're still at your mother's place?"

"Naw, staff sergeant. I'll be staying across the street at a family friend's house; Miss Johnnie Mae Wright's place. I just don't feel right with the whole world pitying me."

"You'll be okay. Just be patient. In short time, your life will change forever. Enjoy the time off that you have left. We contacted your school, and spoke to your principal Mr. Shultz. He's in your corner and is a former Marine Corps Korean War veteran himself. Seems like he made provisions for you to take all of your final exams ahead of time."

"Yes. I just have two more left. I won't be around to walk with my class; but he said they'll keep my diploma for me. I guess I'm all set with school."

"You're all squared away. You don't need to bring no gear. You'll be issued everything from soup to nuts at the base; so, whatever you bring will only be mailed back home to your mom. You lay low, and stay out of trouble. Give us a call if you need anything else."

"Thanks, staff sergeant."

What a crock. If there is a power higher than the United States federal government and Booker was a half year younger, they should send their law enforcement agency to lock the lying staff sergeant up in Leavenworth for the abuse of an innocent child. Booker is just an inexperienced, eighteen-year-old cherry boy. If he didn't have any teeth, he could still stay home and be sucking on his mama's titty. The Marines like their cherry boys lean and green, so they can make them mean. Maybe they should be called the United States Mean Corps...the best trigger-pullers and team-players in the world. Drop a grenade amongst them, and they'll fight each other to cover it with their bodies.

Wednesday morning, May 5, at 0430 hours, Queenie Hampton rang Johnnie Mae's door bell. Johnnie Mae was already up, ironing clothes. As she opened the door, she said, "Aw, good morning Queenie. Booker T told me the sergeant was coming to pick him up in a grey U.S. Navy Dodge passenger van this morning."

"Morning Johnnie Mae. Yes, the sergeant just called, and said he would be here shortly, after picking up some more recruits. They have to be at the airport early to get all checked in. Is he up?"

"Aw, yeah. He's been up all night. Come on in. He's sitting out back at the kitchen table jaw-jacking with Kate."

As they walked through the house into the kitchen, Johnnie Mae said, "Booker, your mother's here for you. Guess it's getting close to that time you was talking about." As they came into the front room, they realized that no one was there. Queenie had stepped back out on the front porch. As they stepped out onto the front porch, the grey van was parking in front of the house with about six other boyish recruits inside, and Staff Sgt. Willie Hardman sitting behind the wheel.

Booker turned and said, "Thank you very much Miss Wright."

And then, he faced his mother, reached out for a hug and Queenie broke down sobbing, "Aw, my baby. I didn't mean what I said. Come on. Let's go home."

"It's too late Mama Queenie. I already signed the papers and was sworn in. I got to go now. I love you; and I'll write to you."

He had to almost tear himself away from her grip. Johnnie Mae tried to calm Queenie down and pulled her away, saying, "Come on Queenie. I know, I know. He's a grown man on his own, now. You've got to let him go and grow."

Booker climbed into the van's back passenger seat. The van pulled away, leaving the two women and young girl standing on the front porch, and walking out to the curb waving until the van turned the corner and was out of sight.

Staff Sgt. Hardman was right. From the moment Booker T climbed into that dull grey Navy van, and during Booker's four year enlistment in the Corps, his mind was in a constant state of awe.

Welcome to Hell, Mothuhfuckuhs

To begin with, Booker, like most of the other recruits, had never been on an airplane. And of all things and places, the plane flew into the San Diego airport where it seemed like it was trying to land in the San Diego Chargers' football stadium. This seemed like a weird place to put an airport in what seemed like the heart of town, where on the way down, the plane went into a constant coasting spiral past what seemed like a hotel; where Booker swore he saw a naked lady posing in the window. And to top it all off, the boot camp was located right next to one of the airport's takeoff strips. This airport seemed more suitable for helicopters than jets.

The Drill Instructors (DIs) must have been recruited from the jungles of the Congo and Borneo. They snarled, yelped and screamed at the top of their lungs like foaming-at-the-mouth, blue-balled baboons at the confused boy recruits to "Get off the bus... Get off the bus, goddammit"; calling them everything but a child of God. It was totally inappropriate; especially when using words like "dipped-shit," "you fucking turd," "shit-for-brains," "fuck-face," and "you slimmey douche bags." This was intolerably unacceptable for men dressed so crisp and neat and "squared-away." The haircuts sucked, too. They really could have done better using a sheep shearer.

And when they started marching the poor boys, especially in close-order drills, some of the DIs called cadence with voices like Mickey Mouse, Donald Duck, and Popeye; hardly intelligible. And what was even more perverted was Booker's seemingly deep appreciation for this type environment. These DI's were behaving like mad bull dogs; but they fed you good chow, three times a day with all kinds of desserts.

Some of the poor recruits eventually succumbed to the heat, sand and fleas. Others urinated on themselves and in their bunkbeds, because the damned DIs denied them permission to use the restrooms, even after lights-out. One recruit had to go so bad he even deficated, late one night, in the sand between the Quonset huts. The next morning the DIs commenced to screaming like chimpanzees with their rectums on fire. Their responses were totally off-the-chart. They called all of the recruits out of the huts and made them line up in single file and do pushups in the dew-dew until it was all gone from the ground.

To say that Marine boot camp is hard would be an under-statement. Marine Corps boot camp is a surgical destruction of an individual's body, mind, and sense of self; and a precise reconstruction of what is left into a finely-tuned lean, mean and green killing machine; ready to dive onto an enemy grenade bouncing around among the troops.

These kids were trained to think like ants in battle: they got over, under, around, and through each obstacle by using themselves as implements in assisting their brothers' toward the accomplishment of the mission. If one went down, the others thought nothing of staying with him until they could pick him up and carry him back to the platoon area with them. And if they couldn't get his big ass up and back to the end of the run, they stayed there with him doing MCMAP, also known as Marine Corps Martial Arts Program or hand-to-hand combat until he was revived or the others devised a way to get his big ass up off of the ground and back to base camp.

This was total, endless madness: and Booker thrived in this scenario. He came to realize that these recruits really were like the siblings he needed and longed for when he was growing up back in Hallville. This band of brothers was the object of devotion he longed to dedicate his body, mind and soul to.

We Can't Go Home Without Our Dead

He often expressed to his closest Marine brothers that he knew he could never find this kind of commitment in civilian life. This was why so many Marines re-enlisted in the Corps for "life"; why so many Marines could never fully adjust to civilian life once discharged. It was truly what they meant by the saying, "Once a Marine, always a Marine." No matter where one roamed, they could never find this kind of commitment that was instant and unquestioned.

On the battlefield, amongst Marines, there was no red blood; only olive drab blood. Combat made this madness more intense, because that was the ultimate of what all of this crucible/ devotional hype was about. The Marines of the Third Battalion, Fourth Regiment of the First Marine Brigade referred to being in the Marine Corps as being "in the crotch." Here, it was simply a matter of "either you is" or "either you ain't."

Straight out of Infantry Training Regiment at a small settlement called San Onofre, deep inside Camp Pendleton, California, Booker T. Hampton was sent to Mike 3/4 of the 1st Mar. Brig., in a hellhole on the edge of a paradise called Kaneohe Bay Marine Base on the island of Oahu, Hawaii. Young Private First Class Booker T. Hampton never got to see Honolulu, sexy hula girls or any place other than a Jurassic Park looking mountain range called The Pali. It sat in a snake-free jungle called Bellow Woods off of a village called Kailua where they were taught things like search and destroy, ambush; and practicing amphibious landings. They perfected helicopter assaults in the red dirt of an island of lepers and pineapples called Molokai. Here Samoans, other Polynesians and Melanesians; with evil black men from places like Arkansas and Mississippi; and vicious Philippinos. These kids were taught an extension of what Elizabeth Scofield taught Booker; how to come off of ships onto Mike Boats; swim with his boots on, while towing a 70 pound bundle of ammo: how to come out of the water, secure a beach, and move into the underbrush. Yeah, the racist Corps was training him to go to Vietnam in an expeditionary unit, like it did with most of the rest of America's melanated teenagers who dared to join its ranks. His unit never fought in any of the major conventional battles. Day after day, they just aggravated the hell out of the poor communist guerillas and the regular North Vietnamese Army soldiers.

As the hunter\killer force of the First Marine Brigade, they carried out asymmetrical, psychological warfare on the Viet Cong and North Vietnamese communist army's supply lines; constantly ran search and destroy and ambush missions on them; and covered Marine snipers entering and returning from missions deep inside enemy areas. Booker not only survived unscathed, except for snake and insect bites, and leeches; but every man in the squad he led returned home unscathed.

He mastered other things like setting and springing an ambush; penetrating mine fields and booby traps; non-conventional, asymmetric warfare based on the assault strategies of Zulu warriors and army ants; and unbeknownst to him, in preparation for activities in and around vicinities like Hue/Phubai, Chulai and Danang, South Vietnam.

No Thanks for Your Service In Making Us Rich

After all the wild goose chases, and suicide missions, Booker was sent back to Marine Barracks Boston Naval Shipyard, doing burial details and city intersection dedications for as many as three Marines per day in eastern New England.

One day Booker was called over to the Guard Detachment Administration building and grudgingly notified by the two-faced Latino staff sergeant head clerk that his Expeditionary Medal was replaced by the Presidential Unit Citation; the equivalent unit award to the Navy Cross medal that is awarded for individual valor. It's the next highest individual award to the Congressional Medal of Honor.

For the rest of his life, when dealing with his personal Post Traumatic Stress Disorder, PTSD, Booker T would always mutter to himself, "Imagine that shit. We were the 'baddest mothuhfuckuhs in the valley.'" All of those ambush patrols and search and destroy missions were no sweat for Booker T, because his experiences with his mother, the twins and Aunt May-May had taught him to believe that forming attachments of the mind can cause him to lose his mind. Once he allowed someone to build him up, he was granting them the eternal right to tear him down. He never aspired for heroism, so he only wore his medals when ordered to do so. He despised even wearing the foolish ribbons. After honorable discharge from the Corps, his motto was "Never trust even a secret present: it's a two-faced sombitch's set-up for a smackdown." May-May and the twins had taught and conditioned him well.

Poor Booker T. Hampton was a hero, and he really wasn't sure why. Well, that's the Marine Corps for you. When everyone totally commits to each other, even hell becomes like a rose garden, because everybody takes their share of the relentless deluge of shit that eventually develops into a flash flood where they wind up being swept away down Shit's Creek in a zodiac boat without a paddle.

But by now, a dipped-shit would notice that there were a few other inconsistencies which were becoming more obvious with each passing day.

The more dead Marines Booker had to bury, the less tolerant he became of those who desecrated the flag by leaving it up overnight; wearing it as a patch on their persons; or waving it in their hands like at a football jamboree. He and the rest of the Honor Guard respectfully raised it in the morning and lowered it in the evening to music.

The more Gold Star Families he offered the coffin flags to, the more he felt their contempt. They spat, screamed and glowered at him. Some families of the deceased were thankful and cordial, like the "Jews" who invited the whole Honor Guard detachment to places like Kadeema Toras Moshe to eat and party in celebration of the deceased Marine's life. But others would spit in Booker's face, forcing him to backstep with the flag still tucked and folded in a triangle, caressed and shielded against his chest like a precious baby. USMC protocol forbade him from wiping the slime from his face as the deceased's family or loved ones screamed at him at the top of their lungs, "You fucking Nigger! You take that rag and wipe your black ass and your face with it." Or others would bellow," Fuck you, you black hog; and your redneck President LBJ, too."

USMC = Uncle Sam's Misguided Children

Even worse, the "white" Marines weren't as "brotherly" toward the "black" Marines once they all returned stateside from the war zone. So, all of those knit-picking DIs were just whistling Dixie…not full Gospel. Literally. Some "white" Marines returned to displaying their confederate battle flags and nazi broken crosses. To these hypocrite traitors, Semper Fidelis was only valid in the bush along with the proverb,"Yea, though I walk through the valley of the shadow of death, I shall fear no evil, because I'm the baddest motherfucker in the valley." It was all bullcrap, along with LBJ's Presidential Unit Citation, and the eventual salutations like, "Thank you for your service."

In time, Booker's "white" Gunnery Sergeant taught him how to still his spine and clear his mind of all of the racist, supremacist traitors' lies through buddhist meditation and chanting; and realizing truths and verities like "And so it goes," and "Bottom line, whitey will always be whitey, and circle the wagons around their own kind, every time."

Booker wasn't a self-made racist: he was forced to face the reality that a white supremacist, traitor-laden United States was never going to be fair or honest with him or his kind during his lifetime. Despite all of the racism, he appreciated his "white" gunnery sergeant at Camp Lejeune, North Carolina for teaching him buddhist principles like chanting "Nam Myo Ho Renge Kyo"; and he was also thankful to Mr. Feng Cheng Fu who owned the restaurant and laundry in his grandparents' building back in PC; and his navy seal friend from Arkansas for showing him how to practice the civil and martial aspects of Taoist Classical Yang-Style Long Form Tai Chi.

Over time, Booker grew to realize that the true purpose of "racist" Americans patriotism, Christianity, and "respect" for the U.S. Constitution is to mollify the melanated masses into allowing the Caucasians and Khasars the opportunity to figuratively rape them while they dopely wandered through life in a world especially made for super rich "white" American exploitation.

When his four-year enlistment was over, Booker T knew he was no longer any good to the Corps. He told Uncle Percy, "Sir, I've seen the light: I've had enough. I have no more to give." Booker T was honorably discharged from the Marine Corps six months after taking the Prairie Cove police exams.

Now, just twenty-two years old, Booker was hungry for an education and desperately seeking a career path. No sooner than he was back in PC, he landed a job through "Veterans' Preference" as a letter carrier with the U.S. Post Office. At least the government was loyal to its surviving veterans.

A lot can happen in four years. He took his time and after a year, he found out that his old girl friend Rozzy had graduated college and was away in the Boston area, studying at one of its six or more law schools.

His secret love, Elizabeth Scofield, was now an assistant principal and still coaching the swim team at the same school. Only problem was that she had forgotten Booker T, and married an NFL football player; and, she was the mom of a little girl. All Booker could do was sigh and say, "And so it goes" two times. Whoever coined the phrase "You can never go back home" was off point a little bit. In Booker's case he discovered that, "You can go back home; and the house may still be standing there; but most of the people you once loved or knew will be gone or have changed their minds about you."

Chapter 19

Master Young's Advice

Booker knew from experience that love hurts even more when life goes on without you. But, he also knew that pain is even more severe and paradoxical when you have to deal with death. He often recited teachings from his grandparents Austin and Mary Alice Hampton; his great grandmother Sage Hampton; Mr. Hope Newcomb and others who had passed on. "So, as long as you live, you've got to keep on 'keeping-on': Keep your mouth shut; take care of business; and take over; let the other sucker be the one who cries in vain."

Booker T hadn't been working at the post office a good nine months before the police department notified him of a position open to him, if he was still interested, "in the next recruit class, next summer."

"Hell yes," he told Uncle Percy. "I could do that police job standing on my head: especially when it comes to receiving that steady paycheck and a fat pension."

"That's my man. Best way to handle white racism is to get next to them and garner all of their benefits when they try to hog-it-all. Like Whitney Young always said, 'Black folks need to learn how to do like the Irish cops did back in Old New York

City. Keep your mouth shut: take care of business; and take over.'"

That following summer, Booker T traded in his post office grays for the new PC police academy khakis. "The gate is open, and the dog is out," Booker shouted to Auntie Annie and Uncle Percy, in reference to himself the morning he was headed to his first day of police academy classes. Aw, they were so proud of him.

But the lesson that day was about a different kind of police work. Booker and his nineteen fellow classmates spent the entire day doing police work alright...cleaning up the academy building; moving furniture; sweeping and mopping floors; and setting up the classrooms in their khakis, black leather shoes and eight-pointed dark blue caps...no badges or guns...just PC Police patches.

The Prairie Cove Police Department consisted of about four-hundred fulltime officers. So, a class of twenty new police recruits was a really big deal in the small police department and tiny town; especially when it was about three years since the last academy class graduated. By rough estimation, those four-hundred Prairie Cove cops could be spread out between a headquarters unit with specialty branches; four patrol districts with their detective units; and let's not forget the prima donna goof-offs in general that also included superior officers, etc. Divide the remaining three-hundred or so cops between three eight hour shifts and that would come out to be about one hundred cops per shift. Take away around another thirty or forty of them for being on days off, vacations, sick days and injuries, and Prairie Cove would need about a score or more cops for special detectives and plainclothes operations; leaving about fifty or so cops for radio calls and street patrol. And this was a very liberal estimate when you take other situations into consideration.

When Booker T arrived home from the academy that evening, he was mentally tired, and not very impressed. "Uncle Percy, I have never seen so many sandbaggers and no-balls traitors collected together in one place in all my life. If these recruits are an example of the quality of cops they have in the streets, all of us people of color better get some M-14 assault rifles; stock pile 7.62 NATO ammo; and serve and protect our own asses. And while we're at it, set up sandbags with claymore mines set in at the edge of the perimeter, and maintain a twenty-four-hour perimeter watch for the greedy, hog-it-all supremacists on patrol and investigations, on and off-duty, looking for the chance to shoot every nigguh they see in the back of the head while he's lying unarmed under restraint, face-down on the ground."

"Son, it's like this everywhere you work with white males. They have this front/façade they keep up, and then behind it there's their hidden agenda of inhumanity and spreading fear. After all that shit, a poor colored person has got to instinctively be ready for the invisible bullshit coming at them from down the pike," warned Percy.

"Yes, Lord. Like you always say, us black folks must 'learn how to keep our mouths shut: take care of business, and take over'; and keep a wary eye on the back-stabbing bastards all the time. But you know what Uncle Percy? This police job has another wrinkle to it. As a black man not having to work in a factory, and not produce a product, my new-found profession is going to require me to put my life on the line for the general public, and be judged by the same people I serve. This ain't like being in the Marine Corps in the bush, as a soldier of the Navy. Here in PC, my black ass and the scared whitey cops are supposed to be the protectors, not killers, of the people we serve.

There's a big difference between "soldiering" and "policing." Soldiers are outsiders, foreigners who don't give a fat rat's ass about protecting the community they serve. They're there to kill or colonize residents on sight. Police are supposed to come from the community they serve, work with and protect its people on sight. Any coward can stand quivering like a skittish monkey riding shotgun over unarmed people, asserting 'authority' by charging and chanting 'Go-Go-Go' like idiot-assed TV cops do to the people who are expecting the cops to save them. Uncle Percy, these clowns on the PCPD are primed and pumped to kill us, whether we're innocent or guilty. Seems like their parents taught them to talk by chanting, 'I'mo buy me a shotgun and shoot every niggah I see.' These are the same traitors we're expected to pledge allegiance to the flag with. Now I see how hypocrites like Washington and Jefferson could write the U.S. Constitution while they were buying, breeding, and fucking their own hybrid kids as slaves."

"I hear what you're saying, Booker. But, you've got to take into account that those same white cops you're gonna be riding around with all day long, in those stanking police cars, in your community, ain't usually from your community. This is where they've been doing their dirt, like those New York City Irishmen, by keeping their mouths shut; taking care of their own hidden agenda; and long ago these Midwestern crackers have taken over and been shooting damn near every nigguh they see," declared Percy.

"Aw, I hear you talking, Uncle Percy. Add to that the fact that ain't nothing more dangerous and fearful than a scared white boy from lily-white outlying communities, furnished with a badge and gun and the 'authority vested in him as a law enforcer' to murder innocent colored folks trapped in the ghettoes. They do their dirt and cower behind the police unions' thin blue lines, and chicken-hearted judges and jury findings. Worst case scenario, the assassin 'cops' get reassigned to one of those administrative inside desk jobs at full pay with overtime for the rest of their career," said Booker.

"Now you're preaching Gospel, Booker T. Hampton. Take due notice thereof and govern yourself accordingly. The only way to stop a runaway tank is to get inside the sombitch."

"Aw, I realize that I'm in it, Uncle Percy. And I ain't getting out of it until I drive it all the way home in their neighborhoods. I've already seen them hypocrite white boys turn traitor on us once we left the combat zone. Bottom line, whitey will always be whitey. In their minds, it's always gonna be 'I'mo buy me a shotgun and shoot every nigguh I see.' They're scared to death of black men taking charge of them and paying them back like they did to us. Their worst nightmare is to be outnumbered and bossed by us. They feel they've got to stay in charge no matter if the whole damned world blows up."

"And so it goes. AND SO IT GOES."

It's Good to Have Friends in High Places

After Marine Corps boot camp, and finishing four years as a combat Marine grunt, and completing his enlistment at Marine Barracks on burial details dedications, sixteen weeks of training at the Prairie Cove Police Academy was like training for a security guard position in Disneyland.

As a matter of fact, the police academy's Director, Captain Angus O'Sullivan, pulled Booker aside into his office one day to say, "Listen kid. I've been reviewing your record here, and I can see that you scored the highest on all three phases of the Department Entrance Exams. Add to that, you've got the highest marks in your academy class. In my honest opinion, you shouldn't be wasting your talents trying to make it on a job like this. You've got the makings of a top notch law enforcement professional. The state police are seeking minority applicants for their open exams. You might want to consider taking it. You've got no wife and kids pulling on you. Barracks life would be no problem for a single guy like you. All of the training troopers are former Marine DI's. You would ace any problem they threw at you."

"Captain, I truly appreciate you looking out for me. But, after having lived through Marine Barracks, I feel more committed to the welfare of my community. State troopers seem to work mostly on the outskirts of cities. Besides, I don't want to spend my career chasing pigs and chickens."

"Ah-hah-ha-ha. Now, that's what I call sound reasoning

enough to stay on this god forsaken job, and put up with Mickey Mouse bullshit. You're a true Jarhead Hampton. Semper Fi, Marine," said O'Sullivan. "Just promise me you'll keep what I told you under your hat. We don't need the other recruits accusing me of favoritism around here. And for Heaven's sake don't go giving that excuse to any troopers. They'll murderize you."

"I promise, sir. And thank you very much. Will that be all, sir?"

"Yes. Yes. Carry on."

As Booker left the captain's office, he could still hear him mumbling and laughing to himself about Booker's answer to his suggestion. Booker knew that this meant that someone in high places was in his corner and would be a great resource for advice and direction in the future.

And as soon as he got home, he went straight to Uncle Percy to get his advice. "Well Booker, I've only had the pleasure of meeting Captain O'Sullivan occasionally in the past: but he sounds like a pretty righteous fellow if he leveled with you like that. You know, some of them Irishmen are pretty decent people. Just because a fellow ain't the same color as you doesn't necessarily mean he's your enemy. Thurgood Marshall once said, 'A black snake will bite you just as fast as a white snake.' Every once in a while, you should run a critical situation past Captain O'Sullivan before making a decision. Yeah. I think you might have a friend there. Just be careful though. A lot of them whiteys always like a big nigguh who doesn't frown, bare his teeth or snarl at them. Don't befriend the sombitches by cooning like a Sambo The Monkey eating shit out of a light socket, either. It's like you said, 'If push comes to shove, whitey will always be whitey.' And like all smart people, when shit hits the fan, they circle the wagons to cover each other's asses. A negro will only do that for you if you're from the same church, or lodge, or family. When the shit gets too thick, a jacklegged nigguh will leave you standing alone or sell you out to a cracker. But, who in the hell am I talking to? You didn't get this far by being nobody's dumb coon."

And just as Booker had predicted, going through the PC Police Academy was just like taking a walk in the park. Those four months went by so fast that for a while Booker couldn't believe he no longer had to sit through eight-hour days of instruction with his silly, two-faced classmates. Deep down inside, he just knew which ones were going to show their true natures once they received their precinct assignments. Already he could see vestiges of the diminutive Sporty Stubbs in a diminutive "white" classmate's efforts to get inside of the heads of the few classmates who still had little faith in themselves. No matter how noble the intent, all you need is one bad apple to spoil the whole bunch. PC's citizens were about to be subjugated to as many as nineteen more idiots practicing their new-found "authority" by violating the constitutional rights of the PC citizens with the mindset of "I know".

After he qualified as high expert at the revolver range, Booker was finally issued his blues, badge and permanent, brand-spanking new service revolver. Oh, this was enough to make any person feel some new-found sense of responsibility: but not so much as to cause Booker T to start losing his mind and feeling that he had to go and kill every "whitey" he saw. When decent-minded people start seeing the frailties of other human beings, they should also be able to notice the frailties within themselves. Booker was learning the frailties within himself which drew out of him compassion for others.

After the graduation ceremony, Booker T swore to Capt. O'Sullivan and Uncle Percy, "If I have to put up with being around any of my old classmates while on duty, I will go running down the turnpike to the state police academy like my bald head is on fire."

Uncle Percy and Capt. O'Sullivan both burst out horse-laughing with the captain telling Booker, "You ain't seen shit yet, Hampton. The veterans aren't as childish as the rookies, but they have a higher and more lethal level of bullshit that has landed more than a few bad cops in jail, and ruined their family's good name. Learn early how to tell a rotten son-of-a-bitch to kiss your ass, and stand there and watch him get mad. Don't trust anybody trying to linger behind you. Never sit with your back to the door, and be careful of whose hand you shake. In other words, don't grip the bastard's hand so hard that you can't let go of what he's palming and trying to give you all rolled up in a tight little wad. Oh, yeah. It's an insidious world out there," said O'Sullivan.

After Percy and Booker were headed home, Percy told Booker, "Book, I'mo say it again: it's rare when you can get someone to give you good life-saving advice like the captain just gave you. You will do well to turn that man into a friend. He put a good word out on me. I've got a feeling that as long as he's on the job, he's got your back, too."

I Didn't Come onto This Job to Avoid the Work

"Delta-two-one-three."

"Come in 213."

"I'm in foot pursuit, past 17 Holcombe Parkway, of a Hispanic male, Ramone De Jesus; a black male, six-feet tall; wearing blue jeans and a red, white and blue Nautica jacket; wanted for a home invasion."

"Standby 213. I'll get you some backup."

"212 enroute."

"210 enroute."

"Delta 101 on scene, heading west on Holcombe. Where you at 213," inquired Booker T.

"I'm in the backyard; about four doors down from 904."

"Freeze, nigger!"

"McManus. Are you for real?"

"Oops. Sorry Hampton. I didn't recognize you."

"Let's see if you can recognize this, bitch!!"

"Naw, Book. Hold up partner. He ain't worth the Departmental Hearing or your job."

"Mothuhfuckuh, you and me were in the academy together. I guess all nigguhs look the same, huh."

"Naw, Booker T. I swear man, I'm sorry," swore McManus.

"Sorry my ass mothuhfuckuh: if you ever pull a gun on me again, you better shoot me."

Tradition

Traditionally, all PCPD rookies begin their patrol careers working with a training officer on the day shift for at least 6 weeks. After that, most of them would return from days off to work four tours of duty on, and two days off duty, all on the night shift called first and last half of the night.

But when Booker T's "black" partner, Craig "Big Daddy" Wright, was suddenly promoted to Detective, for the rest of Booker's training period, Booker was assigned to patrol wagon duty with an older veteran named Daniel Perry. Their job, mainly, when not transporting prisoners, was sector patrol of a precinct area. The problem here was that Officer Perry was a drunk who was intent on never "allowing" trainee Officer Hampton to drive the wagon. As soon as they left eight o'clock roll call and hit the streets, Perry would drive the wagon straight to the parking lot in back of Ye Olde Irish Pub; park it and say, "I'll be just a few minutes, kid. Honk the horn if we get a radio call."

After a couple of days of this selfishness, Booker finally spoke up for himself by saying to Perry, "Man, I can't take no more of this shit."

"What's your problem kid," asked Perry.

"Mothuhfuckuh you're my problem. It's bad enough you keep hogging the wheel, but you won't let us get no real action. And what's even worse, you bring your sorry ass back from the bar, all shit-faced, wanting to make punk-assed motor vehicle stops, locking other mothuhfuckuhs up for moving violations when you're already driving drunker than the mothuhfuckuh you're pulling over. The bosses find out about this cockeyed bullshit, I'll be the one who gets fucked out of a good paying job, because I'm still a rookie on probation. You, being a police union protected sombitching Irish veteran cop, just get a slap on the wrist and a nice quiet inside job until you turn in your gear. Your ass needs to get some kind of professional help, 'cause I ain't gonna keep sitting out here with my thumbs up my ass, waiting on no drunk-assed hypocrite cop no more."

"Aw, kid. Come on. Give me a break. You let the cat out of the bag on this, I may as well kiss my pension goodbye. I've just got another five months to go and I'm home-free for life. Work with me on this. I'll try anything."

"Seriously? Okay. Back in the Corps, in Marine Barracks, I knew a dude who tried using chocolate bars and coffee until he got off-duty Liberty time," offered Booker.

"Aw, come on now. You shitting me, kid?"

"Naw, man. Straight scoop. The mothuhfuckuh swole all up, but it helped him temporarily control the hooch. Tell you what, Perry. Either way, I've got to see me some action or I'mo go bug-fuck. I didn't come on this job to babysit your little narrow ass. What if you go tell the boss that you don't want to ride with the nigguh. He's a fucking Irish alchy like you: he'll understand. What you think?"

"Well, it won't be like the first time a randy-assed rookie showed up craving for some action. I'll run it by him as soon as he comes in to work this morning."

True to his word, Perry ran it by the captain who, hung over from the Irish wake the night before said, "No problem, Danny Boy, send the lad in here." After Booker came in, the captain said, "Close the door lad. I saw your mentor Captain Angus O'Sullivan last night, and he speaks rather highly of you. We don't normally put rookies on nights so soon. Henceforth, you better keep your nose clean or you'll be issuing ass-wipes up in the men's room of the District Attorney's office. If I hear that you so much as cut a fart, then you'll be wiping ass. You get my drift, boy?"

"Captain, sir, with all due respect, I'm not even my mama's 'boy.' She and the rest of my kin folks call me their 'main man.'"

"You trying to be a cute prick," asked the captain.

"Once again, sir, with all due respect to your rank, and seeing how it's just you and me and no witnesses, I'll knock an old mothuhfuckuh out faster than a young one. See, I've already heard that you're an ex-pug. But, you've got them little bitty monkey hands with them short baby arms and bat wings of fat already flapping out of the back of your biceps. Plus, a lil' fifty or sixty-year-old dude like you with that tire wrapped around your gut is only about a welterweight. I'm a cruiserweight, at least three times a week knocking dicks into the dirt. I'll knock a old mothuhfuckuh out before he gets within ten feet of me."

"Aye, laddy. Me cousin Angus said you've got big brass balls, and to take good care of you. I think I kinda like you too, Hampton. You make me laugh. Just don't let your crocodile mouth overload your young hummingbird ass. You come sass-mouthing me like that again and I'll run your young ass up the flag pole, and bring charges against you. Your best bet is to do like that black fellow Whitney Young once said, 'Keep your mouth shut; take care of business; and take over.' You understand me?"

"Yes sir, Captain. By your leave, sir," respectfully asked Booker.

"Your new mate is Torio. Dismissed." replied the captain. And in a whisper, out of the side of his mouth, the captain mumbled, "Jeez. Louise. What-the-Fuck," as Booker left the office.

Out of the Frying Pan; Into the Fire

At midnight of his third day off, Booker reported for duty and was assigned to a two-man cruiser with a self-absorbed veteran officer named Joe Torio. Al Capone would have stabbed this character in the neck. He was rather snotty to Booker, with an attitude of entitlement and supremacy. But, Booker did not relent to any of his foolishness.

As to be expected, the self-righteous little cop finally derived the gall to say to Booker, "I'll do the driving; and don't you touch the radio."

Calmly, Booker looked at him and asked, "Mothuhfuckuh, who do you think you're talking to; your fucking wife or your mama?"

"Hey. Hey. I'm talking to you, soul brother," replied Torio.

"From this sitting position, I can still break your jaw and knock out all of your teeth on this side of your head; thereby causing you to continue talking out of the other side of your face. But, on second thought, I'mo let you drive this mothuhfuckuh for now, only because I don't know the crime turf around the sector, like you do. So, rather than waste any more time trying to see how far you can yang-talk me before I go off on your little monkey ass, your best bet is to go on and be my bitch-assed chauffer."

"Why I got to be all that? Did I call you a…"

"Easy, now: watch your mouth. You're well within my reach; and there ain't a mothuhfuckuh close enough to stop me from going upside your head at least four times."

"Look, Hampton. I've already been warned about you. I ain't looking for no trouble with youse."

"Didn't your people teach you no manners? Nigguhs be looking for shit reasons to go off on little midgets like you. So show some respect, and don't be talking no shit to big nigguhs that you cain't get away from. Now, you want to drive; then go ahead on and drive this mothufuckuh, while I handle this radio," said Booker.

Torio's whole play for supremacy had just back-fired in his face. Instead of coming in like a lamb and walking out like a lion, he came in like a lion and walked out like a lamb; grievous mistake. This didn't seem to bode well for a veteran cop, being severely reprimanded by a new-age "black" rookie.

After a few minor radio calls, and the police radio began to settle down with the sun that evening, Torio tried to make a last ditch effort at salvaging his manhood. He swung the cruiser onto the red light district's main street, and a few moments later turned down a side street with his headlights off. He eased the cruiser ever so slowly down the street, and into a dark parking lot that was empty; except for one car with its lights out and engine still running.

Suddenly the head of a white male occupant popped up from the back seat area, and Torio quickly put the cruiser in park; jumped out with his service revolver in one hand and flashlight in the other, and crept over to the driver side of the car while Booker covered him likewise from the right passenger side of the parked car.

"Let me see your hands, and slowly back your ass out of the car," said Torio to the "white" male.

"Okay, okay officer, I'm unarmed. Please, don't shoot. I can't walk with my pants down."

"Then you shouldn't have pulled them down back here in the first place. Take baby steps and drop to your knees," said Torio. As the man finally backed out of the car and lowered himself to his knees, Torio noticed his collar and exclaimed, "Aw-w-w, holy shit. You a fucking priest or something?"

"Yes officer. Please. I don't mean no harm."

"Aw, for Christ's sake, Father. Pull your fucking pants up," cried Torio as he holstered his weapon.

While the priest was fumbling with his pants and pleading with Torio, Booker saw another figure lying in the back seat, with her legs still gapped open, and starring him directly in the face. "Aw, shit. Sister, git your nasty ass up out of the car," ordered Booker. "Don't tell me you're a nun."

"Naw, baby; not even sanctified."

"Yeah. Well, caught you rolling with that priest. So, I know for damned sure you ain't no holy roller, either."

"Baby, you're the one called the 'Roller.' You're a new cop? You're so funny, and kind of cute for a big daddy. They call me

Carmen. And I think I like you. What's your name, baby?"

"What's this: soul mates in love at first sight," asked Torio as he came around the car with the priest still stumbling and fumbling with his pants.

The hooker faced Torio saying, "Officer Joe, please. I cain't take this pinch. Cain't you show just a little mercy this time?"

"Bitch, shut the fuck up," Torio bellowed as he turned to the priest, finished getting his personal info and told him, "How would you like the archdiocese to know what you're doing before you confess to it?"

"Please, officer. If you give me a break, I promise I won't ever do this again."

"Then go on. Git the hell out of here. I see you creeping around here again, your whole church, all the way to Rome, will know you buy black pussy."

After the priest's car was gone, Torio turned to the female. Booker, being silent and wisely observant all the while, patted her down and stepped back to further see what Torio was going to do.

"Bitch, I'm hauling your black... Never mind. You're going..."

"Aw, please Officer Joe. I cain't take this pinch. I'm already tied up in municipal court. My man's gonna stomp the living shit out of me."

After patting and frisking her for weapons, Torio said, "Just git in the cruiser, and shut the fuck up."

Booker looked at Torio suspiciously, but checked Carmen out for razor blades in her wig and around her collar; opened the cruiser back door, and closed it once she sat down and pulled her feet inside. He climbed back into the passenger side front seat, and Torio headed the cruiser back toward the police station. But at the next intersection, he swung the cruiser into an empty parking garage and drove up to the top fourth floor.

There, he parked the cruiser, got out and started unbuckling his gun belt.

Upon seeing this, Booker asked, "Man, what the hell is your problem? You got the screaming shits or something? You've been cutting rot-gut farts all night long. Now you're about to squat here, like some kinda dog?"

Immediately the female said, "Brother you want some of this, too?"

Booker was bewildered for a second and immediately replied, "Aw. I get it. You two are acquainted with each other. Sister, just because he chooses to shit on his floors doesn't mean I have to shit on mine."

"Then, will you please mind your own business? I keep telling y'all I cain't be taking this pinch."

"Locking your ass up is my business. Ain't you got no pride in yourself," asked Booker.

"If I did, I wouldn't be out here selling pussy," reasoned the whore.

"Aw, give me a break. And you, you little racist guinea; get your little monkey dick back in your pants and your little narrow ass back in this cruiser before I haul off and slap the shit out of both of you nasty-assed mothuhfuckuhs. How would you like it if I grabbed an Italian bitch and tried to get some snatch or a blow job off of her rancid ass, right in front of your greasy stanking ass?"

"Aw, come on kid. Enough is enough," cried Torio.

"Yeah, fool. You got that right. So, either you go on and lock this whore up, or you let her go. Ain't nobody fucking or sucking in front of me. You stopped the priest; now, I'm stopping you," declared Booker T.

Torio opened the back door and said, "Carmen, go on; git." As she jumped out of the back door, and ran down the ramp, Torio said to Booker, "This ain't gonna bode well for you, kid."

"Yeah. Like I give a flying fuck. I'm really scared that I'mo git a whupping."

"Whatever you git, I just want you to git the hell away from me," said Torio.

"I'mo tell you like you told that hypocrite priest back there. How would your wife feel about you raping skank black whore pussy? You git your little weasel ass back to the station house, and tell that Italian lieutenant that you can't ride with me. And then, we never even speak to each other again, you little turd. Now, git this mothuhfuckuh back on the road. I've had enough of you and your slime for the rest of my career."

"No problem. Have it your way, pal. You gonna rat on me?"

"You ain't never been my pal. I don't owe you no loyalty, bitch. You're just a fake cop I was forced to ride with for the shift. The academy staff all are right. You're no colleague of mine: you're a self-serving, low-life scavenger who feeds off of people like me. And naw, I ain't no rat. I'm a rat snake who kills traitors like you. You never were on my side; and I ain't on yours, even if a gang is kicking the shit out of you. I just pity your poor wife for having to put up with your nasty degenerate ass squirting your jism all up inside her, and jeopardizing her immune system."

"Hey, hey. Leave my family out of this."

"Yeah. That's just like you pigs. You disgrace the uniform by being a fuck-off; then try to hide behind your holy hypocrite family, and the thin blue line of the racist police union. Bad white people love to support you racist white cops. So, why don't you patrol your own white communities and fuck your own skank white bitches?"

"Look, man. I ain't got no beef with youse."

"Then have a coke and a smile, and shut the fuck up until we get back to the station."

Torio drove back and parallel parked the cruiser in front of the station house, and Booker said, "It's your call. You go in first. I'll speak for myself after you've had your say: ratting on yourself, bitch."

Torio jumped out of the cruiser, slammed the door, and ran up the stairs straight into the duty supervisor's office where the duty lieutenant and patrol sergeant were having a discussion. After a short while, he came back out to the cruiser and told Booker, "They want to see you. Happy trails to you, Lone Ranger."

Booker replied, "It's Kee-Mo-Sah-Bey to you, bitch,"

249

R-E-S-P-E-C-T

After Booker got out of the car, Torio slammed the cruiser into reverse, spinning tires, and screeched off down the street. Booker walked up the stairs, into the building and into the duty supervisor's office where the Italian lieutenant sat behind the desk and the "Jewish" sergeant stood to the right of the desk, facing Booker as he entered.

"I haven't even had the chance to introduce myself to you, and already you're knee deep in shit. What's your problem, Sunshine," asked the sergeant.

"Sergeant, with all due respect, I know your name is Goldblum from roll call. And when you called my name at that time, you didn't call me no 'Sunshine'," said Booker.

"Well, be that as it may, I'm Lieutenant Ruggiero. Now what's your problem with Officer Torio?"

"Sir, I can get along with anybody as long as there is mutual respect and consideration in the situation. Officer Torio obviously had his say and is gone on his way. I won't refute whatever he said. I instantly and unquestionably follow the orders of my superiors, and go where ever I am ordered."

"Seeing how you can't seem to get along with partners, I'm putting you down on a foot beat in the red light district 'til the captain makes the final decision," said Lt. Ruggiero.

"That's where you'll walk the beat alone, until the captain figures out what to do with you," said Sgt. Goldblum.

"Will that be all Lieutenant," asked Booker.

"Yeah. It's a little too late to head down to the foot beat, now. You go on home and come back tomorrow evening at 1800 hours."

"Yes sir. Thank you very much, sir," said Booker as he took one step backwards and did an about-face, and walked over to the sergeant who had since moved over by the door, and he whispered, "Sarge. You got a moment," as they both walked from the office, out of the building and onto the front sidewalk. As they both came to the curb, Booker stepped down into the street and turned still looking down on the sergeant saying in a soft voice, "Sarge. With all due respect to your rank and grade, I don't play that 'Sunshine' shit. I don't be fucking with so-called Jews about their true Zionist names and ancestry or question the legitimacy of so-called Israel. I especially don't take no shit about being called out of my name. As a matter of fact, I'd rather be dead than to be another man's 'sunshine.' You get my drift?"

"Oh, no, Officer Hampton. I meant you no disrespect. I'm here if you need me. We minorities gotta stick together."

"Yeah, well, 'we' ain't 'together' on the same page, if you're gonna be showing off on me in front of the fucking Romans. You get my drift?"

"Loud and clear, Officer. Excuse me, but I got to be getting back inside."

"Yeah. That's your best bet."

CHAPTER 20

Booker T. Meets Will T.

Just as Booker was about to step back onto the curb, a long green Cadillac Fleetwood Brougham eased up behind him with a well-dressed, lightly melanated gentleman sitting behind the wheel. "Evening officer. I'm Will Thompson. Folks call me Will T. My associate, Carmen, told me how you came to her rescue from that racist Officer Torio," said Will T.

Booker sized him up for a moment; then said, "So?"

"Well, uh-ruh, I don't mean no disrespect. I know you didn't have to do what you did. I just wanted you to know how much I appreciate what you did," said Will T.

"Well. You're entirely welcome. I was just doing my job not only as a cop, but as a brother. My name's Booker... Booker T. Hampton. The 'Officer' title ain't nothing but a pay check."

"Aw yeah, I know you. You're Uncle Percy's other nephew from Auntie Annie's side of the family. We got your back...you good to go. Word went out on the streets even before you came outta the academy. You be careful though. These white cops are about as human as iguana lizards. They're no more about policing than I am...yeah. I'm a ladies' man. But, I takes care of my peoples. Them white cocksuckers will leave you standing alone; set you up to get you outta the way. And these Uncle Tom assed, so-called black cops will play right along with them… especially that one with some half-ass detective rank. You know who I'm talking about."

"Yeah, Cuz. Who don't," asked Booker T. "I really appreciate the heads-up. You and me need to rap some more. Why don't I catch you when I come back on duty and get assigned to the beat tomorrow evening."

"Damn. You made the assignment happen even before they made it official and permanent. We all knew about you coming to the beat before you even got assigned with Torio. See you tomorrow night?"

"Dead up," promised Booker T.

"Peace. Out, Cuz," said Will T."

"And one more thang, Cuz," said Booker looking over his shoulder. "We keeps the family connection under wraps like the guineas, kikes and harps do with their shit. Savvy?"

"Gotcha," agreed Will T, as he pulled the big Caddy away from the curb and eased on down the street.

Booker intuitively sensed that Will T. would be a powerful resource. Uncle Percy and Auntie Annie Lee had also told him of how they took Will T. and some other kids in from time to time as foster children when Will T. was in his teens.

Booker already knew he himself was in a bad way with most of the "white" cops, including the two-faced, elitist "Jews" who all wore the very same uniform and swore allegiance to the same flag. But regardless of the clothes, smiles, and words, he knew he and the "white" cops could never work together unless he made the "white" cops believe they were in charge. Since leaving the Corps, Booker T. Hampton always knew that he would never fully trust the Europeans in any way. He dismissed them as people born cold-blooded the same way as snakes; from an egg yolk inside of a shell. He always said, "They have no respect for anyone with color in their skin. They can only operate when every result is in their favor: like if they see a melanated person with something special that they don't possess, they usually blurt out or think, 'What in the hell did I do wrong?'"

But as Uncle Percy had told him, "Being black on this police job is like being the only puppy in the pound, sucking on a sweet tit. You better go lockjaw, because Whitey's gonna always try to force you out of the job by you letting that tit go. But, you must not ever, never let go of that tit until you either retire or drop dead. A black mothuhfuckin' ex-cop is worse off than a black ex-con…a pariah; especially to his own black people."

While riding home, he decided that in the future he would utilize his police academy training and patrol experience by combining it with his life knowledge; Uncle Percy's thirty-three years on the force, and seventeen years in grade as a sergeant, culminating in his uncle being the senior sergeant on the entire police department. This is how Percy came to know so many superior officers who seemed to watch over Booker T. Cousin Will T would be very useful as a resource and asset. Thus, Booker T realized that Will T had already proven he could be more reliable as a comrade than any of those self-serving traitor "white" cops.

Natural Police

Two tours of duty later, Booker T could have sworn that fate had been eavesdropping on his earlier conversation with Will T.

At about 1:30am on a Friday morning, while standing on the corner of South Haven and Jefferson Streets beside Benny's Lounge on the South Haven Street side, Booker T heard the sound of a gunshot just around the corner next to the same building, no more than fifteen yards on the Jefferson Street side.

As Booker eased up to the corner of the building, with his revolver hidden behind his right thigh, he peered around the building and observed what he found to be the biggest, most muscular human being he had ever seen. This guy had to be a Nigerian or Ghanaian, somebody from the deep forest, like a sasquatch, because he seemed to be at least five inches taller, and two feet wider than Booker. The big man was tucking a silver revolver into the waistband of his trousers while walking into the recessed doorway of the unit next door with his back still toward Booker. He appeared to be drunk, rocking back and forth from heel to toes.

Booker had the presence of mind to step back a bit and call over his walkie talkie for backup from the police dispatcher. He then re-holstered his revolver, held his cap in his hand, and crept up to the man without him noticing his approach. As he stepped in front of the man, Booker dropped his cap, and grabbed his wrists, saying, "I'm sorry big brother, but I've got to take you in."

The big man said to Booker, laughing in an even deeper basso profundo voice than Booker, "I no go no place. Take your baby hands off of me or I will kill you." At the same time the big man started to raise his hands and spread his arms in resistance like Booker was a toddler hanging from a jungle-gym.

All of a sudden, in the same instant, the man's body lurched up about 6 inches off of the ground as he was slammed back against the door. The two biggest pimps that side of the Mississippi River, Will T and Mule, were each holding one of the African's arms as Will T. said in his rich falsetto, "Mothuhfuckuh are you deaf, dumb, and stupid? The officer said you're going in. Now, behave King Kong: and show some support for your local brother police."

Whereupon, Mule and Will T. spun the poor man around while a third pimp, Youngblood, removed the revolver from the African's waist band and handed it to Booker T, saying, "Go 'head officer and put the cuffs on him. This sucker better not even breathe hard. We'll stay here with you 'til your backup comes."

The wagon and cruisers never came from Delta precinct. The 911 dispatcher had the presence of mind to anticipate the lack of Delta unit responses and after realizing a non-response from them, had switched channels and sent a wagon and cruisers from neighboring Bravo precinct. No backup ever responded from Delta.

After the prisoner was taken to the Delta precinct house, Booker T. turned to the three men saying, "I owe y'all big time. Y'all saved my ass. And I ain't never gonna be ashamed of telling the world that my cousin Will T and his main men Mule and Youngblood are my foster brothers."

"Ah-ha-ha," laughed Will T. "And we're gonna keep watchin' over you like bitches watching over their last puppy. We ain't never met a cop like you. We got your back."

"I appreciate that. I appreciate it from the bottom of my heart," said Booker. That very moment, something clicked inside of Booker T. Hampton. As he later conveyed that evening's events to Uncle Percy, he came to realize the true meaning of the title "Natural Police." It means that a real cop realizes he's not a soldier who relies solely on his weapon, badge and uniform to carry out the authority vested in him by the government he represents, to perform his duty. That kind of cop eventually catches a beating or a bullet. "Natural Police" work with the people as one of the people.

With every fiber of his being, Booker T. Hampton determined to be a "natural police": someone who works intimately in cooperation and coordination with the people he swore to serve and protect. The uniform belonged to the people: but, the city paycheck belonged to Booker T. Hampton.

If You Want to Respect Something, First Respect Yourself

In time, Booker T. moved into his own apartment: the basement apartment of Grandpa Austin's storefront building around the corner from Uncle Percy's place. By now, Uncle Percy was really his main man. After each tour of duty, Booker couldn't wait to go by Uncle Percy's the next morning, and sit with him at breakfast, letting out all of what had transpired the previous evening, for the "old school" police sergeant to peruse. No sooner than Percy started to sit down in his chair, Booker took a deep breath and released all of the current events from his foot beat.

"Aw, yeah! Talk to me. Let it all out, son," Percy would say.

"You know, Uncle Percy. I thought I had seen it all in the war; but the Viet Cong ain't got nothing on these PC cops. It's one thing when a person gets killed by one of these racist bastards; but it's a whole 'nother thing when a woman is forced into sex or a man is murdered by one of these cops. It just better not happen on my beat," he would declare as an example.

"How can you police somebody else's pussy, and their livelihood when it's not even yours," asked Percy.

"Naw. It's our Sacred Gate to and from Heaven, called the 'Lips of Saint Mary'," joked Booker.

"Shi-i-i-i-it!! That's a bunch of Pie-In-The-Sky, noble-sounding bullshit, man, that some bitch wove together for the power to bend you and all of the rest of mankind to the will of her pussy. And therein lies your suffering. This realm ain't meant to be no damn Heaven. Her pussy ain't only none of yours, but it ain't no portal to a goddamn place or thing a man will ever fully understand. Pussy is one of Nature's, and women's, main instruments to having their Way… culminating in reproducing our kind. Every man, woman, chicken, and child must learn to understand and respect the true purpose and the power of pussy. When you were a little boy, one of your first jobs after old man Hope died, was to work as a water boy in that whorehouse over there in Hallville," declared Percy.

"Uncle Percy, what kind of shit…?"

"Oh-ho yeah. You thought you was just about one slick little nigguh: but Annie Lee and me peeped your hole card by way of your grandma and grandpa. When it comes to evaluating pussy, Booker, always remember that whorehouse. It's like your grandmama used to tell your mama and Aunt May-May, 'Ain't no social security in pussy: but, don't get caught in its way, because there's a bitch in every woman.' With all of that in mind, who in the hell do you think you are to be putting stock or honor on somebody else's stank hole," asked Percy Jarvis. "Even the 'pretty-boy' pimps ain't nothing but moneyholders, there to bail the bitch out of jail so she can be right back out there in the streets, working that ass like ain't no man got the power to ignore it."

"It's a matter of respect," blurted Booker T.

"My young nigguh, have you completely lost your cotton-picking mind? Pussy is the most indestructible thing in the world. Mule dick roebucks and water melon-headed babies have stretched that snatch every which-a-way but loose, inside and out; and it still snaps back to grabbing dick as tight as the woman wants it to be. Back on Okinawa, you were there too, they had a whore named Gripper. They say she took a rubber ball with a string run through it; gave one end to a Jarhead and stuck the ball up her ass. I'll be damned if the sombitch could yank it out. It was like the bitch had lockjaw in her pussy. Sombitches live and die, and go to hell and jail, and while they're doing time, that stankin' pussy hole is still free, moving around society in rotation, fucking everything that moves. Pussy don't give a fuck about you or your plans, honor or respect: it fends for itself, because every man, woman, and child had to pass through it; and is subject to run in to it before they take their last breath. You want to respect something, learn how to respect yourself. That bitch wanted to drop drawers for that pig. You shouldn't have given a fat rat's ass about wasting your time trying to recognize any honor in her thang."

"I'm sorry Uncle Percy, but ain't no cracker or other sombitch gonna fuck no black woman, bitch, whore or otherwise, in front of my face. I've got to look at myself in the mirror each and every day."

"I agree with that, Nephew. Amen to that. I bet you look at that mug every time you pass a mirror or a puddle of water. Ha-HAAAAA! But on the real side, the point I'm trying to make is for you to just remember, like when you was in the Marine

Corps, in that war. There is always gonna be some collateral damage. Just make sure don't nothing be zappin' or splashin' on your ass."

"I hear you knocking, Unc. But yet and still, that's all a bitter pill to swallow."

"If you keep your mouth shut and take care of business, you don't have to be swallowin' shit. You made up your mind to become a police officer; you're gonna have to deal with shit nobody else wants to bother with. Whether you're here or not, after all is said and done, crime marches on: pussy will continue to be bought and sold and given away for free. Police deal with all kinds of society's shit and garbage that normal people don't want to handle. Just because you walk upon a turd don't mean you have to handle it. Just keep your mouth shut; step over or around it without missin' a beat; and keep on moving down the line. Besides, society pays you big bucks to come to work; and do your job. Just pick up your paycheck and go the fuck home...leave shit laying where you find it. Almost like a doctor doing triage. Take care of the worst first and don't take nothing home to your peoples."

"I hear you, Uncle Percy. You should still be wearing this monkey suit with some stars and bars on your shoulders."

"Naw, naw. It takes a special kind of man of today to keep at what you're doing today. My time is up, they put me out to pasture. As far back as I can remember, you were always telling people you wanted to be a policeman. You're honest, smart, resourceful and care about more than just your own ass. You go ahead on with your bad self. Keep illuminating the shadows, helping blind people to see."

"Thanks Uncle Percy. After talking with you, I think I've got a couple of other people to talk to tomorrow."

As he walked back around the block to his apartment, Booker T felt like a combat Marine veteran feels after finally getting rid of an angry old ghost that had been haunting him from the past; releasing all traces of his PTSD immediately after leaving the battlefield. He realized his great good fortune in having Uncle

Percy to run his dilemmas by. He decided right then and there that he would, also, bring Capt. O'Sullivan up to snuff on his situation.

Last night was a pretty eventful tour of duty for Booker; dealing with "King Kong" and those "no-show" racist "fellow" cops and all. Booker never was one to run from a problem, but deep down inside, especially after talking things over with Uncle Percy, he could see that he had not made stupid decisions and that it was best for him to be prepared to handle his own problems.

People of the life condition of a lot of the traitor cops don't change from the way they are. It's a pathological, cultural infection with them. They're low-lifes who don't know any better than to have a weaker person to oppress. At some point the oppression gets out of control and turns into more perverted sociopathic/psychopathic acts, forcing the oppressed and the oppressor to resort to the commission of a crime, and the meeting of their fate.

Same Old Booker T.

Anyway, when you walk a beat, closure isn't always reached in one tour of duty: it goes with the territory. Booker knew he had to live with himself, and had no choice but to move on and face what comes. Once the tour of duty is over, you have to learn to leave the job and its problems in the wall locker.

One evening, just as he neared his neighborhood, he decided to stop by Father John's, the local liquor market for a nice bottle of fine Japanese Sake. As he entered the store, he joked with his friend the store owner, Mr. Singh. After chatting a few minutes, Booker went to the back wall of the store, reaching up to the top shelf for the quality Asian wines. No sooner than he grabbed the Sake of his choice, he felt a small hand gently caress his right bicep. Flexed for action, he slowly turned and moved his body into the person, only to realize that it was a woman.

"Sucker, you've gotten rusty in your old age," she said.

Instantly, Booker T recognized the timbre of the voice saying, "Rozzy. Where you been, girl?"

"Don't be acting dumb. You know where I've been. Quinn and Roscoe told me you've been asking everybody around town about me. Yeah fool, I'm still single. I just finished law school. Now I'm home, studying for the bar exam in July. And I better not be hearing of your ass messing around with no other bitches, Mr. Rookie-Assed Policeman. Let me get you in court, I'mo run rings around your ass."

"Aw. Now, you're back to being my second mama. You're gonna wind up making me follow you into law school like I followed you into the pool."

"Yeah. Whatever! Hang with me, you won't be needing no lonesome-assed Japanese rice wine. Rozzy will help you grow some hair on your tongue; we be sipping 'Jack.'"

"Just listen to your wild self. Where are you staying, now? You still at home sucking off of your mama," teased Booker.

"Like I said. I be sipping Jack… JD…straight out of Lynchburg, Tennessee. I moved upstairs above the store. When Uncle Gus retired, he left me the building and apartment space, and moved out to the farm over in Millstadt. Once my brothers Quinn and Roscoe went legit, he gave them the business, and started farming fulltime."

"Damn, Rozzy. It looks like you're pretty much all set."

"As Miss Scofield used to say, 'I hope to shout.'"

"Ha-ha. How's she been doing, anyway?"

"Well, you know she got married to that womanizing football player, and wound up having a kid by him. She's still over at the high school; but now she's assistant principal and still coaching nigguhs sucking water," said Rozzy.

"Yeah. I guess that's what happens when you've got a kid to feed. You've got to keep pulling that wagon and humping that hill. But, enough of my yapping about other people's business.

Tell me more about you," said Booker.

"You already know enough about my business. What are you into besides being a nosey policeman, bogarting everybody else around? Did you go back to school and graduate?"

"I graduated high school on time with my class in Hallville, just before shipping out for boot camp. I just didn't get to walk with my class, because I had to go to boot camp ahead of time. Remember, back in those days, Hallville graduated in June; instead of in May as they do here. The Corps' earliest recruit class started in May, so they let me jump in early."

"Okay. So, whatchu doing about education now," asked Rozzy.

"I ain't got time for that yet. I'm finishing my probationary period on the department; waiting for classes to startup over at Hobart College, after probation this January. I can still start back carrying your books between now and then."

"Cut the shit, Booker T: I'm serious."

"Whatchu think I'm doing; whistling Dixie? Why you think I'm standing here, talking to you with your new muscled quads and hamstrings popping out all over the place. What you been doing, drinking more milk?"

"You're just trying to set up another one of your one-night stands."

"Naw, Rozzy. You know dog-gone well, from way back when we were kids, I was the one who tried to hold on, and get it going. You were the one who had to always fiddle-fart around, hem and haw, and roam. Remember?"

"Sucker, don't you start playing mind games with me again."

"Rozzy, I'm as serious as a heart attack, even more than before. Just be still and think back. I tried everything in my power to hook-up with you back then. And as God is my witness, I'm standing here with you right now, trying to reconnect with you. And even up to now, you ain't never given me nothing but some work. The closest we ever got to 'it' was while wrestling, and acting a fool."

"That's because you never tried. You can't go for the gusto, shooting blanks with a short-arm."

"Rozzy, I was just a kid, scared, stupid…and inexperienced. And what's more, I still have my cherry."

"Man, you must think I'm a damn fool; don't you be playing with me. I don't have time to be pacifying your big ass."

"Give me a chance to make it up to you, and prove myself, Rozzy. Take me with you up to your crib. I'll even settle for some pacifying pussy. We're both free, black and grown now. I'll even cook for you while you hit the books, tomorrow, for the bar exams. You can even invite Quinn and Roscoe over for dinner."

"I don't need my brothers riding shotgun over me. Besides, even though they're legit, they're still nervous about cops. It's like combat PTSD. And your black ass is still on probation. One screw-up and you're summarily dismissed," reminded Rozzy.

"Yes ma'am, Miss Rozzy. I promise to behave."

"Any other man talking those old nursery rhymes would be picking his ass up off the ground by now. But, bless your heart: you don't know no better. Aunt May-May and Mama Queenie can't help you now, June Bug. It's time for your big ass to finish growing up. Come on. Follow.

"Aw, I get it. You want a King Kong Indy car racer," concluded Booker T.

Just like the usual spirit of Booker T. Hampton, he came in like a lamb, but here, he ran into a lioness. After telling this woman a damn lie, he's going to have a long way to go to be able to walk out of this like the King-of-Beasts. Or maybe she's the one who will have a long way to go to be able to walk out of this like a lioness. She fell for the lion trap by overestimating her power and falling for Booker T. Hampton's charismatic trap. By now, he was a grandmaster of letting a woman have her way, in order to get his way. She was the same old Rozzy who didn't know the real Booker.

You Asked for It; You Got It

"I could have sworn I heard you say something corny, like 'I still have my cherry'," said Rozzy.

"I do," said Booker as he proceeded to let his fingers disprove what his mouth was saying.

"Man, you're lying. Aw. Booker T. Hampton, whoever those women were, they made you such a liar: you're lying so. Cain't no...cain't no cherry boy find his way around like this. Whatchu...whatchu doing?"

"No matter where I roam, there's no place like home."

"Aw, Booker T. I'm so wet. I've got to go take a shower."

"You ain't got to do nothing 'but stay black and die.' Remember? Until then, we still have got a long way to go; and many rivers to cross. There ain't gonna be no pain or sorrow on this journey, 'cause Booker T. gonna swim with Miss Rozzy until she reaches the Kingdom 'Cum' again and again."

"Aw, I don't know if I can swim with you Booker. Now you behave. You're such a bad, bad man to be the police."

"I need a shrewd, smart lawyer like you to show me the way," said Booker as he pulled away from her, and they simmered down.

"You may say that you like me, but beyond that, you're just whistling Dixie," said Rozzy.

"How's that when you've always been the one to leave me dangling on a string," asked Booker.

"You called me 'Liz' two times while trying to lay it down to me."

"You can't hang a man based on his dreams, Rozzy."

"How'd you like it if I called you Maggie Lee?"

"I know I'm no Adonis, but, good Lord, please don't mistake me for being that ugly," begged Booker.

"I wouldn't do that to you. And I'm not doing anything with her. But, I do still have my 'needs'," said Rozzy.

"Rozzy. I grew up and left home behind those very same words. I won't get in your way or hold that against you. You're going to always be my girl. We are what we do: and keep on doing what we like the most."

"Booker, I feel the same way about you. But, you've got to remember what you always used to say; 'You can't get mad at the dog for licking his balls…'"

"'…Or the bitch for licking her ass.'," finished Booker.

"I can't reach my ass," said Rozzy.

"And if I could lick my own balls, I'd have to have a broken back, and be hauling my balls around in a wheel barrel," said Booker. "Rozzy, we are what we are. Let's always just keep on loving and liking each other. I trust and respect you. I want to always be putting my money in your pocket."

"I'm a dangerous woman with some money in my pockets. Didn't your Aunties teach you nothing," asked Rozzy.

"I can always make some more money. I've always trusted in you since you got me the job in your Uncle Gus' store. I ain't scared of you Rozzy. I'll always owe you. But, as hard as we may try to be loyal, ain't no body obligated to the other. Enough talk. Now, where were we?"

Consulting a Friend

The first thing that following Monday morning, Booker dropped by the police academy to see Capt. O'Sullivan.

"Morning Booker. Come on in and have a seat. Close the door behind you," said O'Sullivan. As Booker closed the door and sat down across the desk from the captain in the crowded little nine-foot-by-twelve-foot office, O'Sullivan said, "So I heard you knocked heads with the foolish bastard Joseph Torio."

"Yes sir."

"You watch out with that fucker. He's not about policing. He's a useless piece of shit; always up to no-good shootings, and no honest police work. He's dragged down more than one good cop behind his foolishness."

"Wow, Skipper, I guessed it, but I didn't know all of that about him for sure."

"You did the best thing a cop with any kind of brains could do…you got the fuck away from the bastard by his own request…not yours. But, you still watch your back. You never know when or where it's gonna come from with a no good son-of-a-bitch like him. They all think everyone else is a rat who doesn't let their shit slide by. Don't quote me, but you need to make yourself an expert on something. Do like Hoover did on the FBI. Keep a record of what goes down on each and every son of a bitch you have to deal with or even think about. Later on, when you add all of that shit together, you've got a lot to slap them in the face with, and stop them from fucking with you. That's the best way to stop a shithead cop dead in their tracks. Don't waste time kicking their ass, you'll be jeopardizing your job and your life. We've all got guns. Stroke them back with the shit they try to pull on you. Hell. Who am I to be telling you. You're a jarhead. What's that saying? 'If you fuck with the bull, you get the horns?'"

"I hear you, Skipper. Like you told us all in the academy, I keep my little blue notebook full of info time, date, place and what went down and was said," recited Booker.

"You know, Booker, it's a shame that the public has to be the ones who are trained in how to behave when stopped by these kind of cops. It's not natural for a coward cop to be stopping people anyway. Not only should the cop not be allowed on the streets, but if his ass can't be recycled and retrained, he or she should be terminated from the service or locked up. All of law enforcement shouldn't have to be reformed behind the shit of these few creeps. Police supervisors, police chiefs, prosecutors and judges need to get up off of their asses and do their jobs by firing and locking these fuckers up. What good is millions of dollars being spent on civil settlements, and whatever, if the judges, legislators, governors and police leaders refuse to do their goddamned jobs and hang these foolish bastards. They'll hang a black fellow for smiling at a white woman, but they won't do shit to a white cop for murdering a black person. It's a pretty sorry-assed system of justice we have here in America. Next thing you know, these traitors will be building a bridge to Russia."

"I agree with you Skipper."

"So your boss is gonna keep you on that foot beat. All cops should spend some time on a foot beat. That's a safe place, if you keep your guard up and be natural police. Pimp the pimps and let them keep things under control. And stay the fuck out of other people's pockets. The only pay you take is a City of Prairie Cove paycheck with the son-of-a-bitching mayor's signature on it. Once you start accepting gratuities from these outside bastards, the fuckers own you like you're their whore. I know your Uncle Percy already schooled you on all this shit; but, I'm just sayin'...."

"Yes sir."

"If you do anything, you do everything in the line of duty for free, without signing your name or grabbing for shit. Always earn respect for your name. Let the other fuckers be the ones to say they owe you a favor. That's what they call goodwill. It's better than money...has the force of the heart, honor and credibility behind it. Makes the most heartless villain speak well of you and swear allegiance to you as a professional police officer and a true friend. Now, you head on over to the station and talk to your boss. He's good people; so don't be too hard on him. And tell that no-balls, so-called 'Jew', Zionist sergeant I said to stand up like a man; stop 'eating cheese,' and running around sucking up to all of the fucking Irish, while putting down the blacks."

"Well now, captain. I don't think that's..."

"Just kidding lad. You just keep standing your ground with that no-balls little prick. He may kiss your ass up and down, but he ain't your friend. The only thing he respects is a man who stands tall. If you bend, he's gonna try to do one or both of two things; ride your back or fuck you. Tell my old pal Sgt. Percy Jarvis that I've got a few things to run by him."

"Yes sir," said Booker as he backed out of the office and left the building.

Be Nice – But Set Things Straight

No matter how hard he tried, Booker just couldn't figure it out. Just when he felt that he had every right under the sun to label and catalog all white males as "reptilian," he would always come across true professionals like Capt. O'Sullivan or regular "white" dudes like his good friend Bobby Bradshaw. These guys had no prejudice or no fear; faced whatever came at them; and called the cards of life the way they fell.

Yes, it was surprising when his white friends would call out his white enemies by the way they behaved. But, Booker was determined to judge all men the same way; by their character. It was kind-of like the way Booker could call no-good blacks "nigguhs"; but his friends Baxter and O'Sullivan couldn't call them "niggers" in public. There were two different meanings and two different intentions in uttering the same word. And for someone who's not "black" to say "nigger," turns it from a term of endearment to a weapon of last resort. The one who uses it is the one who is it.

Regardless, after a year or so, Booker's watch commander started assigning him a beat-up old marked police cruiser to park in his beat area as he made his rounds. This was not usual. Beat cops usually got nothing extra, but a call box key or a big old vintage walking talkie to call for help, and be checked up on when the duty supervisor wanted to make sure the cop wasn't goofing off. The old cruiser gave Booker the chance to warm up in the winter; rest his feet; take breaks and study for his college classes. He would park the cruiser in the supermarket parking lot with its rear backed into a two-story brick wall of an adjacent building while studying or when he needed a rest break. Even the usually amiable Booker T. Hampton needs to be alone at times.

Once he got situated on the beat, after a few tours of duty, he finally ran into his cousin Will T, as he came walking out of the supermarket parking lot. Will T walked along with Booker T. as they slowly came to a stop at the corner of the 4-way intersection.

"Will, how you been, man?"

"Not bad, Officer…"

"Naw, Will. Uncle Percy straightened me out. You and me are family: two foundlings taken in by a loving couple. You don't have to keep calling me 'Officer' like I'm some kind of alien. You're my cousin Will T., and I'm you're your cousin Booker T. We're kin folk."

"Just trying to show respect, Booker."

"Well, I appreciate that, but I don't need my ego stroked by subjugating my own people. That craps for little men who really ain't about nothing but trying to be bigger than themselves by getting super strength from inhuman soldier authority they don't even know how to handle."

"I'm with you on that call, Cuz."

"'Man, I didn't ask for this assignment. They made me walk this beat as punishment. Just 'cause I've got to do that doesn't mean I'm God's head nigguh in charge of everybody I see. My spin on it is that I'm entitled to receive a pay check from a cut of y'all's taxes in a promise to 'serve and protect' y'all. You all have been down here making your living thousands of years before I was even born. I ain't out to get in the way of merchants secretly buying and selling stuff or even pussy. Those are victimless crimes whose commissions lead to the personal satisfaction of the parties involved. I'm not a cock-blocker, looking to be no sneaking undercover agent of these two-faced, crooked cops and their bosses, either. But since I've got to be down here, and you've got to be down here, let's respect each other and work hand-in-hand. I don't want no money from nobody. I just want you to keep on being in charge of your people and we respect each other's business. I walk the beat: y'all sell the pussy, and so on and so forth. When I'm on duty in the vicinity, you don't let your people disrespect me by doing their shit anywhere around me. When I'm out of sight, you're still in charge. You police your people and don't let shit happen that's gonna make us both look bad."

"I read you loud and clear, cousin. You're the Man. I'm the Man. We keeps everythang cool and make each other look good. I can understand and respect that. But what we gonna do about them assholes like Torio and their house nigguh Officer Jack Russell on the day shift down here before you come on duty?"

"The day shift ain't my time. I'm just a grunt-assed rookie patrolman. But, if they want to come fucking around on our shift, Will T and Booker T will put their heads together and put something on their asses. I don't claim to know it all. I can't do it all. My probation is over, but these suckers keep thinking I'm still just a green-assed rookie, nigguh cop. They don't need to know that we're cousins; that we put our heads together."

"I can dig it. Just beware that there's a lot of money being made down here; a lot of shit going on. Seriously. You can call the shots. How much you want," asked Will T.

"Like I told you before, this is your turf, and all proceeds and credit from it go to you and the captain or that lieutenant in Vice. I only accept paychecks from the city with the Prairie Cove mayor or city manager's signature on it, after taxes are withheld. We have an understanding that as long as Will T is in charge, Booker T don't go to jail behind no bullshit or to the hospital behind being shot or stabbed or whupped. We make each other be safe and look good, because we're people."

"I read you loud and clear, and I can dig it again. I'll keep you posted, Booker. But, don't forget what I told you. That little guinea bastard Torio thinks he's the head nigguh in charge down here. Watch your back. Word out, he's got a hard-on for you being black and for messing up his regular blow-jobs and grab-assing from Carmen and Lewis," warned Will T.

"Regular blow-jobs," asked Booker.

"Aw, Cuz: he sucks and fucks the bitch and our other cousin more than he does his own wife. Word is, they all went through high school together," said Will.

"Well, ain't that a real mother-for-you. No wonder some whiteys have the kind of mentality that excuses white cops who murder unarmed blacks," declared Booker T. "Good looking out, Cuz. I went easy on them both: gave them some respect. Mothuhfuckuhs keep me in the dark damn sure ain't on my side."

"Just remember. This whole area and the police station have a very close secret relationship, more than Torio and Carmen. That police station is sucking more money out of here and, before you popped up, ain't sent nothing down here but Torio-types in return," said Will.

"Man, that shit pisses me off," replied Booker.

"It's all low-life. Don't let it get to you. Like you already said, this shit's been going on long before we came along. All of these players are full of shit. Like Uncle Percy always said, think of everybody as being like an undercover baboon. Sooner or later, they're gonna get fucked up or eat each other up. We're just the zookeepers; stay out of the way and let shit keep on keeping on," added Will.

"I appreciate the heads-up. I'll keep you posted," said Booker T.

"Bet," said Will.

As time went on, Booker T with the backing of Will T and his lieutenants, Mule and Youngblood, settled into being a pretty savvy beat cop. As a matter of fact, the veteran cops across the whole town of Prairie Cove began to label him "natural police." A title that is rarely bestowed upon the cop whose charisma and intuitiveness connected him so closely with the people in his sector that crime statistics there diminished in great numbers.

When a cop attains this status, the district commander cherishes him as one of his most valuable assets; even if the cop is an honest cop. After a few years, the beat-up old police cruisers, occasionally used by Booker, were replaced by a brand new state of the art, air conditioned, marked cruiser permanently assigned to, and used only by P.O. Booker T. Hampton. Just the very sight of the thing being parked in front of the supermarket was a sign to all businesses, whores, druggies, crooks and cops that Police Officer Booker T. Hampton was on duty.

On that tour of duty, the Bravo precinct radio activity and the crime statistics would plummet as the beat went on.

Hands Are Tied

Booker's return to tours of duty from days off started at the police station at six o'clock in the evening, and ended at two o'clock in the morning, four days on duty and two days off duty. No sooner than he climbed into his cruiser, logged on the police radio, and headed out Martin Luther King Boulevard towards his beat, he heard an arrest in progress being made over his police radio. It was taking place at the Bennie's Lounge on his beat, involving a handbag having been snatched by a "light complexioned black male, about six feet tall; very slim build; in his early to mid twenties."

Booker stepped on the gas after turning on his blue lights and siren. He arrived at the scene in front of the Lounge just in time to see P.O.Torio leading forty-five-year-old, dark complexioned, obese, and very openly gay Lewis Ingram out of the bar room with his hands cuffed behind his back.

As Torio was roughly pushing Lewis' head down while pushing the submissive, genteel man into the back seat of his police cruiser, Booker asked Torio, "Aw, come on man, where do you think you are; in South Africa, Rhodesia, or someplace? What do you think you're doing?"

Torio replied, "What does it look like I'm doing, soul brother? I'm locking the faggot-assed bitch up."

"For what," asked Booker.

"For snapping a handbag. Ain't you got your radio on?"

"Aw, my radio is on. What about your brain? Man, you, me,

the police department, and the whole goddamn free world know this is a crock of shit. I know this guy. The heels on his shoes are so high, and his pants are so tight, he can't even get away after snapping his own handbag; let alone try to run away with somebody else's. The kid you want is damned near two feet taller, and half this guy's age. The palms of his hands ain't even light complexioned. It takes him 3 minutes to climb down off his bar stool just to go take a leak. He just hangs around the bar all day, with his hands on his hips, trying to make eye-contact, popping his chewing gum, and pulling tricks. He's got more money in his bossom than you have in your pocket."

"You trying to interfere with my pinch?"

"I'm trying to tell your pervert racist ass that this is a bullshit pinch," said Booker. "And sucker, you know you're wrong. Dead wrong. Why you got to be fucking with him? He refused to give your faggot ass another free blow job? Or did he refuse to let you give him one? If I have to, I'll testify against you in court, in front of your family, the newspapers and TV, and at your Departmental disciplinary hearing. You don't come on my turf and pull your crap. You better talk to somebody. I don't think Mrs. Torio and the rest of the Italian community needs to hear about this kind of chicken shit," warned Booker.

"Hey. Do what you gotta do. You got a complaint? Take it up with the bosses. As far as I'm concerned, this is the mothuhfuckuh holding the bag," insisted Torio.

"Okay then. Where's the fucking handbag at? Where's the victim? Only in your pervert mind," said Booker.

"Like I said. Do what you gotta do. Talk to the bosses. Even they can't tell me not to make a pinch," said Torio.

"They can take your fuckin' badge and gun, and kick your stinking racist behind out of the police station without pay. Until then, just give me the chance to whup your little narrow ass."

"Listen Hampton. You put your fucking hands on me, I'll be having them kick your buffalo butt out of the station; be suing your sweet ass. And the next time you call me a guinea, I'm gonna call you a you-know-what," threatened Torio.

"Oh yeah, bitch? Well, why wait. Go ahead: say it: spit it out and I'll serve you your warty little weenie on a toothpick."

At that moment, Booker heard a soft voice come from the back seat of Torio's police cruiser. It was Lewis saying, "Don't do it Officer Booker. Whitey banks on us gittin' mad and actin' like a baboon. They'll take an ass whuppin' just to git your job. He just mad 'cause he be saying that I burned his down-low ass. He ain't worth it. I got friends down at the police house. I can beat this shit by myself."

Just then, Youngblood and Mule stepped from around the corner as Torio jumped into his cruiser to head to the police station with his prisoner. "Take care of Lewis, if you can, Officer," said Mule.

"I'm already on it," said Booker as he jumped into his cruiser and followed Torio; just to make sure no detours were taken, and that Lewis arrived at the station in one piece.

Hands Are Free

At the booking desk sat Lt. Louis Mancini. A tough, hard-nosed man, short in height, but known department-wide to be big in heart, and not too ashamed to call a "spade" a "spade."

As Torio approached the booking desk with his prisoner Lewis Ingram, the lieutenant looked up from his log book and asked, "Oh boy. What kind of bullshit are you bringing for me to babysit tonight?" Before Torio could get a word out of his mouth, the lieutenant said, "Never mind, numb-nuts. Just hook your prisoner up to the wall. Go grind out your incident report and I'll deal with you then."

As the booking officer searched and questioned Lewis as to his medical condition, Torio grabbed an incident report form and headed for the guard room to write his report. The lieutenant told Booker, "Hampton, go git my friend Lewis, here, a chair."

As Booker headed to the lieutenant's office, Mancini began

conversing with Lewis. By the time Booker came back with the chair, Lt. Mancini muttered to him, "This is a crock of shit."

Booker immediately replied, "Lieut', he grabbed this guy off of my beat. I tried to tell him this shit wouldn't hold up, but he outright told me to go fuck myself and mind my own business."

"Uncuff this man," ordered the lieutenant. "Lewis, have a seat over here beside my desk. I'll be right back. Hampton, go tell Shit-For-Brains his presence is requested post-haste, in my office which is really the captain's office in the daytime."

CHAPTER 21

Bum Pinch – Bum Cop

Booker smiled like when he was a little boy about to tell the twins to go to Aunt May-May so she could whip them. After advising Torio of the lieutenant's wishes, Booker followed him to the lieutenant's office door where he heard the lieutenant say, "Torio, get in here. Hampton, close the door and stay with Lewis."

Torio took great pleasure in slamming the door closed in Booker's face. Even though the door was closed, Booker T, Lewis, and everyone else outside the office could hear Mancini's booming voice yelling at Torio. "What kind of cock-a-maimee shit is this, Torio," asked the lieutenant.

"Well, sir..."

"Well my ass. Don't you realize that you just locked up Sergeant Percy Jarvis' son on bullshit charges? The whole goddamned town and suburbs listen to all of our shit go down on their fuckin' police scanners. The real perp was arrested while you chose to bust this poor bastard's balls. As a matter of fact, they just cuffed the real felon's young ass to the booking desk wall."

"Well, uh-ruh..."

"'Uh-ruh' my ass, you foolish bastard. You must be snorting cocaine up your fucking wazoo to even think I'm stupid enough to sign my name to your lying-assed incident report, and babysit the wrong fucking prisoner on your trumped up charges. It's true, I can't tell you not to arrest the motherfucker, but I don't have to accept his ass in my jail, on my shift, by signing my good name to your bogus-assed goddamned paper work. And if you try to book him at another station, I'm gonna call ahead and break you balls from here on in. I'm writing out an IAD Form 911 right now to cover my ass and everybody else on this shift. This is a matter for you and the Internal Affairs Division. You aren't dragging me into your shit. Now you go get your cuffs and bring me your overtime slip. I'll grant you the four-hour minimum this time, but you make god-damned sure you take your sweet ass home for the remainder of these four hours, and stay the hell off my tours of duty. You're a useless piece of shit, and couldn't amount to a pimple on a good cop's ass," snapped the Italian lieutenant.

I Just Want to Testify

"Lieutenant, sir..." began Torio.

"If you ever get hauled in and sued, you better hope to Christ I'm not called to give testimony," cut in Lt. Mancini. "Now, run tell that to your asshole union rep. And while you're at it, tell that son of a bitch I said you both can go take a flying fuck. I'm not losing my pension behind you and your high and mighty greaser bullshit. Now, hurry up and git the hell out of my police station."

Torio left the office and went straight to the booking desk; got his cuffs, filled out and left his overtime slip for signing. All the while, Booker just stood there with Lewis with a smile on his face.

Torio looked over at the two of them and said between his teeth, "It ain't over. It's on."

"Aw, Lord. We is so scared of you, little Mr. Bad-ass. What in the world is we gonna do," asked Booker.

"Both of youse can go fuck yourselves," said Torio as he stormed out the door.

"Yeah. Like you just did to yourself," yelled Booker, as Torio jumped into his raggedy old Plymouth coupe; and peeled off down the street, squealing his tires.

"Come on, Lewis. Let's go see the lieutenant and get the hell out of this place," said Booker T. "I'm starting to go stir-crazy up in here."

Watch Your Back

After the lieutenant released Lewis, Booker and Lewis got into Booker's cruiser and headed back to the bar. Lewis said, "Officer, I think you better watch your back with this Torio fool. You made him look like a fool by springing me. He knows we only have so long to live: he ain't got nothing to lose."

Booker missed the "point," and answered, "Aw, I've been holding his number for quite some time, Cousin Lewis. When he makes his move, I'll have justification to squash his ass like the blow-fly that he is," said Booker T.

"Yes. But a blow-fly is full of maggots. Just don't let none git on you," warned Lewis.

"I don't worry about no maggot: we used them to stop gangrene infections in Vietnam. Anyway, you're the one who needs to worry. I've got the gun and the right to shoot in the city, if he makes his move. You ain't got shit, but your wits. You've got to bend over and let him fuck with you until another cop comes along and makes him let you go. You're just lucky this time that the cop was another brother," said Booker.

"I know. I know. And I thank you for your standing up for me. But, in the end, we both are gonna die. Honey, I'm just gonna bide my time and bend and be flexible. Every time he touches me, he guarantees his fate. I've got something for his smart ass. You can drop me off at the house over on Tudor Street by the bridge."

After dropping Lewis off, Booker sat there for a few minutes wondering what Lewis had for Torio's "ass." Finally he put the car in gear and drove the police cruiser back to his beat, parking it in front of the supermarket. As he was getting out, Will T drove up beside him. "Everything go okay, Book?"

"Oh yeah; everything's copasetic. It just seems strange how we all are related and stuck making a living down here," said Booker.

"It beats the hell out of digging ditches while some dumb-assed, white mothuhfuckuh is standing over you with his thumbs up his ass," replied Will T.

"Yeah, I just couldn't let that little racist piece of shit frame a completely innocent man. I don't care what part he's playing in all of this mess, Lewis don't deserve that," offered Booker T.

"Well, for what it's worth, Cousin Lewis ain't no paragon of virtue, either. He knows what he's doing. He's been bending over, servicing that greasy sombitch more than Carmen."

"Like they say in the Corps, 'If you fuck with the bull, you get the horns'," added Booker.

"Well, Torio may be thinking he's the bull in that threesome, but he ain't necessarily the one wearing the horns. He thinks he's so damn smart. Lewis and her are working a 'round-robin' on his dumb ass," said Will.

"No shit? I hope it's with the Feds."

"Worse. This shit's been going on for a while. And now, that greasy bastard even looks like it's starting to get to him; serves him right. I hope he burns in hell. He used to be one of them cock-sure Green Berets. I bet my bottom dollar that sucker's met his match; gonna git more than he bargained for," said Will T.

"Well, I'll be blessed. So, he's out to fuck over Lewis and every other nigguh no matter what. I knew something stank about that suckuh. Payback is a mothuhfuckuh. It's a small world; too small for anybody to get away with his stupid kind of shit. I hope he gets what he deserves: help in getting the hell outta here sooner rather than later. And so should the rest of the traitor cops that behave like him. What goes around comes around," said Booker.

"And what a wonderful world it would be. In his case, the shoe fits: he's got to wear it. One never knows what kind of shit human beings is up to. Just by our very nature, we're all in this thing together. That silly-assed white cop comes down here to wallow with the nigguhs, he's gonna go down by the nigguhs. Yeah, buddy; with blue flames blowin' outta his asshole," said Will T.

"Ha-ha-a-a-a-a," shouted Booker. "I cain't wait. Fucking Torio not only fucked with the bull and got the horns; he fucked with the bull and got his head stomped. This kinda shit sends a lot of cops up the river without a paddle. You'd be surprised who all is involved in that shit. I know one thing. I cain't wait 'til Torio gets what's coming to him," declared Booker T.

"Just 'cause a man's got to work with the hogs don't mean he's got to act like one of them. Like in the dope business, it's a dead dealer who uses his own shit," said Will T.

"Aw, man it's a shame. This is why I keep my nose clean; not because I'm a goody-two-shoes. I just don't want no Karma bullshit coming back to haunt me," said Booker T.

"What about when you can be paid in free pussy," asked Will T.

"Pussy is a trap. Behind every sweet piece is a fucking asshole. I ain't scared. I just don't need no shit," said Booker T.

"Ah—ha-ha-a-a-a!! Word is out that you ain't necessarily scared of pussy, because of what it can do to you: you're scared of pussy because you ain't sure of what you can do with it," teased Will T.

"Shi-i-i-i-t!! Check with the whores on Okinawa...down in the Koza Four Corners region. They called me Big Daddy Meat Packer," swore Booker T.

"Ah-Ha-Ha-a-a-a. Go ahead on Cuz. Preach. Ah-ha-ha."

"I laid pipe from the halls of Montezuma to the shores of the Ryukyu Islands. Marines and police both wear uniforms, but are on two different kinds of missions. I get my way with charisma, like a natural policeman, working with the people. These white cops get their way like a natural soldier, relying on a uniform and pointing a gun. The curse of the slick cop leads to nothing but doom and gloom coupled with the disgrace of the police department and the family name. Now, I just be patient; he's already set to get his," said Booker T.

"Cuz, just be careful. Keep an eye on that sucker and his boys. Word is, he's out to get you back," warned Will T as he climbed into his Caddy.

"In the movies, John Wayne called them, '...fearless men who jump and die.' Marines jump and kick ass," said Booker T.

"Why you think my Broughham and Fedorah hat are green," said Will T., as he eased the big green Caddy on out of the parking lot.

As the two o'clock hour started to approach, the sound of blues music started to swell and fade from Bennie's Lounge. It was Friday night and folks started drifting from the area in their finest clothes, after spending their paychecks, living for the weekend.

And Booker T turned his cruiser into the station; changed into his civies; got into his old white pickup truck and headed home.

Support Your Local Hypocracy

For some people, there's something about receiving a badge, gun and police uniform that brings out another facet of their being. When their society endows them with the authority to enforce its laws: this authority goes to some of their heads, only proving that human beings aren't fit for authority or the right to play God.

A lot of people complain about bullies, yet they foolishly

turn to them in times of "threats" by employing them on police departments all across America to "serve and protect" their interests. But no sooner than the perverted cops get out into the streets on "patrol," the self-serving, traitor communities give these "cops" positive reinforcement to continue their oppression by fostering the idea of "Support Your Local Police." This is like what happens when you give a baboon a loaded gun: the slogan becomes "Support Your Local Baboons."

Booker T. Hampton's heart was into establishing peace in his area of responsibility or beat. He seemed, by his actions, to respect all people of his community, melanated or otherwise. Whether the person was "good" or "bad," Booker tried to accord every man, woman, and child the same respect they accorded him; especially during times of strife.

Now, after eight years on the force, what seems most difficult for young Booker to understand is how a police officer could be a murderer, a mafiosa or even a heroin addict. And at the same time, ignorant, selfish members of the community express their condoning of this injustice by saying "Support Your Local Police." It would seem that civilized, loyal, patriotic Americans would protest the violation of the U.S. Constitution with its threat to our Democracy, and scream for the accountability of the traitor/coward cops, and the reform of the law enforcement agency, and the termination of its incompetent leadership.

Booker finished his tour of duty, went home and went to bed. But, he couldn't sleep that night. And first thing the next morning, he was sitting on retired sergeant Percy Jarvis' front porch steps.

Don't Jump to Conclusions

"Well looka here, looka here. The sky broke open, and look what the Heavens dropped down here. Is that my nephew Booker T. Hampton," teased Annie Lee.

"Oh yeah, that's who it show 'nuff is. Look at how his face is all long and his mouth is all poked out," teased Percy. "Talk to me. Don't just sit there like May-May just gave you a whupping."

"Good morning Uncle Percy. Morning Auntie Annie. How is your day starting?"

"Same as usual. You know Percy and me ain't too extra sensory when it comes to perception. We're the last people you want to leave in the dark to draw their own conclusions," teased Annie Lee.

"I met this sweet man down by the Corner Lounge last night who declares we are cousins. I know me and Mama are from the Texas prairie, but why can't the family bring us up to date about who's our relatives. Sometimes I could swear, nobody in this family would tell me if my behind was on fire," said Booker.

"Now, you know full dog-gone well that ain't so, Booker T. We are all grown-up, intelligent peoples, even though ain't none of us graduated from no kind of college. We respectfully allow a negro to figure out shit for himself...especially if it's a relative who is one of them self-serving, no-count sombitches," said Percy. "No reflection on you and Queenie or your grandparents. I mean people like that slick-assed Lewis Ingram boy," said Percy.

"For a while back before you was born, we took in the ungrateful little booger from Percy's foot beat as a foster child. When we stuck out our necks and took him in, we got by for a while. The state paid us a little stipend every month," said Annie Lee.

"Well, I'll be..."

"Naw. This ain't no reflection on you. We had to move fast. He was a little booger. His mama died of birthing him, and his 'believed-to-be' daddy was trying to raise him up by himself," said Percy.

"Yeah. His daddy not only was raising him, but he was diddlin' with the poor child. You cain't be doing that to nobody, and whup the shit out of him like he's a dog tied up to a tree," said Annie Lee. "Hell, a dog might git over it, but a person, especially a child, will be scarred for life."

"Of course, this was before you was born. He got grown 'round the time when you was a little stump-daddy riding shotgun on Hope Newcomb's junk wagon," teased Percy.

"So…"

"Now hold on. Let me finish. You accused us of hiding shit from you. So here it is from the horse's mouth…or shall I say from the horse's ass," said Percy. "Like I was saying, his step-daddy messed him up. He disrespected and horribly abused the poor boy as a small child. So Lewis started acting out, and finally snapped and stuck the rotten sombitch through the heart with a screwdriver. And all while he was locked up in that stanking juvenile hall, them big old jail house faggots was all over him like monkeys on a football. They say them lousy bastards didn't give the poor boy no rest. He come outta that place a full-blown screaming he-hank."

"Well even though that made him do bad, it doesn't necessarily mean he's a bad person. I couldn't let that sadistic racist trump up charges on him and put him in the pretrial lockup like that," confessed Booker.

"We know. My old partner Lou Mancini called and told us what you did on Lewis' behalf. We appreciate you sticking up for him, Booker. He won't listen to us, now that he's grown. It only goes to show the kind of good man that you are. Not just this family, but this whole damned community is blessed with you being on patrol down around there," added Annie.

Some Things Best Be Left Undone

"Son, there's a whole lot about this mess that you don't know about, and best not know about. But, just because you don't know about it don't mean you're being disregarded or disrespected," said Percy.

"Oh, yeah? Then why did y'all talk in pig Latin whenever I came around as a kid?"

"This ain't about you. This is about all the shit in other people's lives. Tell me the truth. Would you want each and every Tom, Dick and Harry in our family and elsewhere to know everything about your ass," asked Percy.

"I found out everything about y'all's inside of two days of listening to y'all trying to speak that dumb pig Latin around me. All you do is take the first letter and put it at the end of the word and add an 'A.' When y'all was saying 'Isska yma assa', I knew you were saying 'Kiss my ass.' Seriously, though, I wouldn't want everybody to know everything about me; just the salient things that y'all needed to know," confessed Booker T.

"That's a crock of shit, and you know it. For real, how would you like it if all of your aunties, cousins, grandparents and parents and foster cousins knew all about the shit you was into…even about the sombitches you had to kill," asked Percy.

"Well, naw. They don't need to know everything," answered Booker T.

"So you say. That's your opinion. Now, who in the hell am I to get mad at you for not telling me all about your business? Queenie might have busted your ass for it, but…"

"Okay. I see. I just don't like being left in the dark; wind up looking like a fool," admitted Booker.

"Better you look like a fool for not knowing all of my business than for me to look like one for spilling my guts out to you about me or anybody else for that matter. And anyway, Lewis told you and showed you about his business himself," declared Percy.

"So now; straighten up your ugly face and go on in the kitchen and git yourself something to eat before it gets cold. I whupped up a batch of grits and rind bacon with some white gravy… Aw, boy; gone in there and help yourself," said Annie.

"Come to think of it, I think I'll render you some backup. I'm about ready for my second helping," said Percy.

"Now, you know you don't need to be making no hog outta yourself," said Annie Lee.

"You can't get mad at the hog for..." started Percy.

"Licking his plate," finished Annie.

They all fell out laughing as they headed back to the kitchen.

CHAPTER 22

Surprise; Surprise; I've Got You in My Eyes

After finishing breakfast and helping Auntie Annie wash the dishes, Booker T said good day; went back around to his apartment; changed clothes, and went for a jog through the neighborhood. In spite of the white flight, the homes hadn't changed for the worst. As a matter of fact, the whole neighborhood changed for the better. Most of the homes that formerly were rented were now single-family, totally owner occupied; thanks to folks like Annie Lee and Percy Jarvis, and Austin and Mary Alice Hampton who realized nice investment returns by buying abandoned buildings cheap for few hundreds of dollars; rehabbing with a little TLC; and occasionally selling them to other single family owners seeking to occupy them for tens of thousands of dollars.

The widow Mattie Russell made a small fortune flipping houses that way after Lester B. Johnson ran off and didn't come back to Mattie's garage that he had converted into a home. She went on to buy abandoned homes, renovating them by hiring crews of local out-of-work handy men; and using recycled materials from salvage yards as much as possible.

Just as Booker was jogging past Mrs. Russell's house, a big Chevy station wagon pulled up alongside him and came to a halt as he stopped. As he started to bend over to make eye contact with the driver, he realized right away by the hands on the steering wheel and the limbs under the steering wheel that it was a leggy melanated female.

"What do you think you're looking at mister," the sassy lady asked Booker T. "Do you want to get knocked out?"

"What kind of..." he started to say. "You and your husband can even beat me, kick me, or shoot me. You toyed with my heart as a kid, and ran off and married yourself a grown man; a football hero," said Booker. "Now I..."

"Now, Booker T, let's get this smack straight, right here and right now. I never gave up on you. You ran out of here, back to your mama in Hallville. And the next thing I knew was that you had run off and enlisted in the Marine Corps. And that so-called guy you called 'a grown man, football hero'washed out as a husband and father still chasing 'cheerleaders.' He turned out to be more of a kid than the one he left behind with me. I've seen you from a distance around town occasionally in your policeman's uniform and your spiffy little police car. Looks like the Corps did a good job of teaching you how to correctly wear your clothes and gear...all the way down to the dimple in your policeman's uniform necktie."

"Ms. Elizabeth, the only thing that's probably changed about you is your last name."

"Wrong again, young man. First and last names are still the same; Elizabeth Scofield. But now that you're a grown man, you are herewith and henceforth given a battle field permission to call me Liz."

"You mean, you're willing to give this poor grunt non-com a chance," asked Booker.

"I'm here, aren't I? My Lord, how you have changed. You've even grown a moustache and a few more inches taller in your adulthood. How old are you, now; twenty-eight or twenty-nine-years old?"

As she climbed out of the car, and walked around to his side of the vehicle, he could see that child birth had not done any damage to her physique. "Wow, Liz. You don't look any worse for the wear, either. As a matter of fact, you look like you've been pumping iron, girl."

"Oh, hush. I didn't come this far to start up a pissing contest with you, Booker T. How about a little grab-ass? Get over here and give your old teacher a hug. You've been a bad boy running away, and not bothering to get in touch and... U-u-ummmm. They don't teach you how to hug like this in the Corps. You've been practicing a lot overseas, making a lot more love than war."

"Naw. You did all of that by running off and marrying a knucklehead, and hiding from me in plain sight. We need to talk."

"Well, as you can see, I've got a passenger in the back seat." Sure enough as Booker peaked into the back seat of the car, he could see the sleepy little eyes of a little girl. "How's your schedule tomorrow?"

"I'm free all day. Give me a call when you're free," offered Booker. They exchanged numbers, kissed, and parted ways.

Whatchu Gon' Do?

The very next day right after twelve noon, while deep in his studies at his desk, his phone nearly jumped off the hook. Liz came by soon after offering to pick him up. As soon as he climbed into the station wagon, she indulged him by saying, "I was so surprised to run into you last evening that I forgot about one important commitment I had today. Remember the sleepy little girl I had in the back seat last night? Well, today is her birthday. I'm on my way to pick up her and my mom. We rented the Pizza Place so some of her little friends can celebrate with her. Want to come along?"

"I'd more than appreciate it, Liz. I hope what I'm wearing is appropriate. I can run back up stairs and put on a sport jacket and tie."

"You're more than appropriate. Get in. Ms. Scofield is gonna take big Booker to meet her family."

Even a fool could see by the same boyish grin on Booker's face that he still had strong feelings and deep respect for Liz. The only difference was that now he appeared to be more relaxed; more confident; and grown.

As Liz pulled the car away from the curb, she started the deeper conversation. "Booker, a lot has happened since you went away. It's been what, ten or more years? You know, a lifetime can occur in that time."

"Yeah, like growing into adulthood. But my heart still beats the same for you, Elizabeth. And I ain't scared of no child. I know she's a great person, 'cause she has you for a mom. I mean, look at what you did raising me. It's a Rembrandt."

"Aw, stop," she giggled. "Your mom did a fantastic job of raising you. Sofie's a good girl; loves her some school. She's a first grader; and just like most little girls without a father, she craves attention. So, give her a chance to snap to."

"I'll do my best in spite of her possibly being spoiled rotten by mom and grandma. So, do you miss him," asked Booker.

"I said that Sophie misses him. I don't miss a damn thing about him. The breakup was all my fault, because I did a lousy job of selecting a mate in the first place. His main problem was when he tried to use his hands on me, when he couldn't get his way by using his brain. The very first time he went to raise his hand, I cold-cocked his ass. Yes, I gave his behind two black eyes when the second punch in the combination broke his nose. He doesn't know how to do anything but tackle a poor man that's not looking at him while trying to catch a pass. Sofie could have knocked him out."

"Ha-ha-a-a-a! That's right. You said they made all midshipmen box at the Naval Academy: and you were the champion during your last year there. I know you opened up a 55 gallon barrel of whup-ass on him. Well, I'm just glad you didn't get hurt. Some guys really need to check themselves out. So, what about Sofie?"

"She's getting over him. It's been a couple of years now; and she makes a definite point to let everyone know that she's not a baby anymore. He's too ashamed to come around. I guess his ego is too big to accept getting whipped by a woman. You know what that comes from?"

"What," asked Booker.

"His mama was too democratic with him. She failed to show him her baboon side, and didn't bother to spank his ass. That's why they always tell mothers to warm their sons' asses while they're young; that way when the boys grow up to be giant men, they still feel their mama is bigger, and subject to transform into a mad dog baboon, and knock the living shit out of them."

"Oo-oo-oo, Miss Scofield. You said 'shit.'"

"School's over and out for you, Junior. You're a big boy, now. And besides, we're both jarheads. And I, for damn sure, am not a nun."

"Yeah, that's right. You were a Marine captain at that!"

"How about you. What rank did you reach," asked Liz.

"Sergeant. E-5. All battlefield promotions by the time I was nineteen years old."

"Well, go 'head on with yo' bad self. And thank you for your service, Sarge."

"Don't thank me, ma'am. Thank the Marine Corps."

"Oh my goodness. How many times did we all use to recite that phrase? That's when you knew you were hopelessly gung-ho," added Liz.

"Semper Fi, captain. But, on the real side, Liz. All I'm really gung-ho for, now, is you. I must confess that every woman I have seen since I first met you when I was a kid, I expected those women to measure up to your standards. Even though you never took advantage of me, you did affect me in a most profound way. I know you've been hurt and disappointed in the past. But, you and I go way back. You're in me in more ways than one. It was your principles that kept me strong during the most stressful and demoralizing time of my life, and helped me survive the war. I know you're older than me, but we're both adults now. Besides, guys marry older women all the time, now-a-days.

"Whoa, whoa big guy. Lean back and settle down, now. I'm not going anywhere. You're the one who broke camp, and hauled ass. I've been right here in little old Prairie Cove from day one. Let's just take one step at a time," advised Liz.

"Just like when you taught me how to swim and tread water. I still can hang. I can endure. I'm just glad to be back in your presence again," said Booker.

"Speaking of 'presence', I've got to pick up Miss Lady and her grandma. That party we're giving her is a surprise birthday party. So, don't let the cat out of the bag when she gets into the car."

"If you, Miss Lady and Mrs. Scofield don't mind, I'll climb in the back seat and let your mom sit up here with you. That way I won't get too intimidated by being surrounded by all of these powerful sisters sitting behind me, staring a hole into the back of my head."

"You're a policeman. Remember? They'll be totally impressed."

It's Showtime!

Days off were usually boring times for Booker. Outside of Auntie Annie and Uncle Percy, Booker's family life was pretty near a zero. Oh, he had the twins Maimee and Maggie Lee, and Aunt May-May, but of course they were like horses of a different breed...more like jackasses, to be specific. Self-serving, self-righteous, they simply refused to band together in the traditional family sense. So more and more they grew in their own selfishness. Finally, Booker chose to give them a wide berth.

This present situation was a new and rather frightful situation for Booker; going to a little kid's birthday party, and meeting her and her grandma for the first time; while trying to "get on the good foot" with little Sophie, her mother and grandma, all at the same time.

Booker naturally was somewhat phobic with little kids. Whenever he was around them, he always sensed that within two days he would come down with a fever and the flu. To Booker, this was a nasty setup. He wished the kids would go their way and he would go his way; like snakes stay to themselves and people stay to themselves. To Booker, kids were like disease farms. If their hands weren't in their mouths, they were everywhere else on themselves, into toilets, trash, and back into someone else's face.

And they were the most aggravating/inquisitive little people. They demanded so much attention. Oh, the things a man would have to put up with, just to get next to their moms.

Liz's mother, Mrs. Ruth Ann Scofield, was like an older version of Liz. She was a god-send for keeping little brats in their place. But even she couldn't keep total restraint on little Sofie Scofield. She was like an impetuous genie out of a bottle. And that first time she met Booker, all Sophie needed was a split second to slide up onto Booker's lap, look him dead in his eyes; giggle, and cut a fart.

"Aw, man," cried Booker as he immediately lifted her up from his lap and placed her onto the seat next to him. "There. You sit there in your seat, and I sit here in my seat," posited Booker T.

While Ms. and Mrs. Scofield were deep in conversation in the front seat, without any warning, in a flash, Booker felt Sofie's little monkey hand slap him on the left side of his face as he was turning away from her. "Aw naw, you didn't, little girl," whispered Booker.

"Yes, I did Mr. Man."

"Now Sophie. You behave yourself back there," said Ruth Ann, unaware of the fact that Sophie had already misbehaved.

As Ruth and Liz continued their conversation, Booker whispered to Sophie, "Yeah. Do like your grandma says or I'll…"

"Well, Officer Hampton. I see you've already introduced yourself to my daughter Sofie. She doesn't normally take to strangers. I see you two are getting along famously," said Liz. As they all piled out of the car and headed for the front door of the Pizza Place, Liz said, "Excuse me for a minute. I have to get the sodas passed out."

"I can…" started Booker.

"Surprise," shouted the crowd as Sophie entered the crowded pizza parlor.

"Oh, no-no-no, Booker. You are a guest. You, Mom and Sophie don't mind me, and find us a table. I'll be right back," said Liz as she hurried back to the rear of her station wagon.

"Now Sofie, you be nice to Mr. Hampton and all of your friends. He came all the way over here to meet you and wish you a happy birthday," added grandma Ruth as she also walked away leaving Booker alone in Sophie's hands.

As he and Sophie found a table and sat watching the two women disappear, Booker T felt an insistent tug at his sleeve.

"I know you like my mama," said Sophie.

"Smart girl, Sophie. Smart girl," said Booker. "I truly respect your mom from a long time before you were born. She changed my life, and helped me grow up. Now, why don't you run and play with your friends and other guests?"

"You're not my daddy. You can't tell me what to do."

"Smart girl again, Sophie. You are right. I am not your daddy. I'm not even trying to be your daddy. But, you don't ever put your hands on me. I'll wear your little behind out, and embarrass you in front of your mama, your grandma and all of your little friends."

"You put your hands on me and my mama will beat you up."

"Ain't nobody scared of your mama but you, Sophie. By the time your mama gets over here, your little behind will be on fire. Now, go and thank your friends before I give a bad report about you to your mama and your grandma."

"Go ahead, and tattle on me. They won't believe you," whispered Sophie. "You're the adult. I'm just a little kid. It won't even hold up in a court of law."

"Wow. Sophie, you are so smart. With such a sass mouth, and a sharp mind, I'll just have to spank you in front of them and shoot all of y'all with my gun."

"'All of y'all'? You're ignorant," declared Sophie.

"And you're getting on my last nerve. Either you behave yourself or I'm going to leave."

"It's my party. You're all my guests. You have to do as I say," insisted Sofie.

"Right-O, kid. It is your party: and we are all your guests. But you have to be nice and show us respect like we try to show you respect by coming here to celebrate your birthday. Now apologize to me for being such a bad little kid."

"Hee-hee. OK. I apologize. Don't leave. I'll go get you some pizza. What kind of soda?"

"Grape. And just plain cheese pizza. And take your time, and say hello to your guests."

"Okay. Stay here. Don't leave. I'll be right back," said Sophie as she ran off.

There's an old saying, just where you think you've found the most Heaven is where you'll find the most hell. Booker was overjoyed to have run into Liz again. It had been years since he last saw her. His feelings for her were even more intense now than ever. But in his absence, Elizabeth Scofield had moved on in life and become the mother of a frightening, prematurely shrewd little girl named Sophie. This child was a royal pain, but Booker was determined to be with Liz in spite of the aggravation.

He quickly figured out that little Sophie was a child of extraordinary intelligence who craved extraordinary attention. Somehow she must have sensed that Booker or any man for that matter was going to be diverting some of her mom's time and attention away from her. Grandma, alone, wasn't enough. Sophie wanted it all. And this new man, Booker, could be an interference if he wasn't willing to go along with the "program," and give Sophie a massive amount of his time and attention, also.

Booker also surmised that once Sophie perceived the possibility of this conflict, he, the man, would have three alternatives: bend to her rule, pass the test or go away. Booker determined to handle the situation, but he missed the point: little Sophie had the experience and the advantage. She had been the partial cause of three other men being sent packing from Liz. Booker had no experience or success in this type situation. He had a problem.

Clemency

After the party, much to Booker's surprise, Ruth Ann Scofield talked her granddaughter Sophie into coming home with her and spending the night. Sophie jumped at this opportunity. Grandma was her staunchest supporter and constantly submitted to her game... Sofie could do no wrong with Ruth Ann. Booker T was so happy he almost blurted out, "Glory, Halleluiah! Thank you Sweet Saint Jesus." This was his sign that grandma had faith in him, and was cutting him some slack by giving him the opportunity to share some quality time, alone, with her lonesome, only child Elizabeth.

Booker T relished this chance. As soon as Ruth Ann and Sophie walked away and into Ruth's house, leaving Booker and Liz alone, Liz said to Booker, "Get your young ass up here in the front seat. You're coming home with Miss Scofield, tonight. I mean, of course, you don't have to, if you're scared and can't hang beyond your curfew."

"Ah-ha-ha. Like I had to tell Miss Sophie, 'Ain't nobody scared of your mama but you.'"

"Man, you wait until I get your young salty behind home. I'm not only gonna knock you out, but first, I'm going to give you a serious spanking."

"Miss Scofield, I've been keeping myself in check, dying for some more attention from you, since I was a kid. Now, here I am all of a sudden realizing that I'm a grown-assed man; no more 'Miss Scofield': from now on it's 'Liz': and I get to come over to your house; and you said…"

Liz drove the short distance from her mother's home to her own little house in the westend of Prairie Cove. No sooner than they got out of the car in the garage, Booker was all hands, and Liz was all giggles all the way from inside of the garage; through the kitchen; and on to in front of the great room sofa.

"It feels so strange being allowed to do so freely what was taboo for so much of my life,"admitted Booker. "I can't be suspended and you can't be fired and jailed."

"Well, let's be patient just a little longer until I unload the car, before it starts smelling like yesterday's pizza trash," said Liz.

"Sorry, you feel so good I got carried back in time," swore Booker. "This is the first time you allowed me to touch you. Your ex must have been the King of Fools to take you for granted, and go chasing after someone else."

"It's mostly my fault. He needed so much attention. I just couldn't fill the bill getting pregnant so soon. It was a case of either bending to him or the newborn child. I failed to see the child in him, and administer to it. So he went looking for someone else to fill the bill." As they finished unloading the car and reached the kitchen counter area, Liz dropped the last bag of leftover pizza and sodas; turned around facing Booker, pushing his arms above her shoulders saying, "Yeah. I guess that makes you the lucky man. I must admit, I've been wondering about this for a long time, also."

He pulled her body closer, gently caressed her waist with his giant hands, and commenced tasting her lips, then lowering his hands as he kneaded and massaged her thighs.

"Umm. Booker, you could easily qualify as a masseuse," she said softly.

"Woman, I just made a quantum leap all the way from

adolescence to now. You can't imagine how many times I dreamed of being your private masseuse. Now that I'm here, I will cherish connecting to each and everyone of your pleasure points, lymph nodes, and strive to keep you addicted to my every touch," promised Booker T.

"You mean pressure points."

"No-no-no-no-no Liz. This is my dream. Other people have mere 'pressure points': but you are a joy to behold, and a pleasure to touch."

"I hope to shout, my soul is awaken," said Liz. "Never mind the grab-ass. Let's 'get on with it'."

"You used to yell those same words at me when I was a slacker kid in your pool," said Booker. "Let's take our time. This is the high point of my life."

"You can say that again. As a matter of fact, at first, you had me worried if you grew up from your first day in the pool. "Frankie J." was just stunted from the cold water," teased Liz. "But now I see that 'Frankie J. McPeters' is just the nickname for Frankenstein Jones McFearsome. Marine Corps was right. I done fucked with the bull and now I'mo get the horn. Go easy on your teacher, darling. I'm getting so wet I'm ashamed of myself."

"This is what a woman is supposed to do if a man is doing his job. Go ahead. Git nasty. Let loose all over me. I missed you real bad."

He was truly, finally getting to live his dream. She was literally showing her appreciation for his attention. And he was so appreciative he wouldn't allow her to lay down.

He started peeling of her clothes and commenced to peeling of hers until they both were embracing and caressing each other in their shirts, socks, and shoes.

He lifted her up by her cheeks with one of his big hands hefting her up by her tail bone and his other hand caressing her waist. As he entered her about a quarter of an inch, she started whimpering and twitching spasmodically. "Am I hurting you? Shall I stop?"

298

"You're going to hurt me, if you stop," she insisted. "When I get my 'needs', I'mo tear your ass up. Get on with it Officer Hampton!"

Speak Now or Forever Hold Your Piece

After his two days off, Booker returned to work. After standing a small, less formal roll call, he and the other four beat cops were witnesses to a new formal union. Joe Torio and Carlos Diaz were permanently assigned as partners in a rapid response unit.

Diaz was a new transfer from Bravo precinct that had a large Hispanic population. He had a reputation around the Department for victimizing his own countrymen in the same way that "African-American" "Uncle Toms" disrespected and sold-out their own people to their oppressors. He was transferred to Delta precinct because none of the cops in Bravo precinct wanted to ride with either of them.

Booker sized the little cop Diaz up to be almost a narcissistic clone of Torio. Not only did he behave and talk like Torio, but he sucked up to Torio; literally looking at him with adoration. It was sickening. This meant much more trouble for all of the melanated Hispanic and "black" residents of the Delta community.

As roll call was turned out and the cops all headed to their beats, Diaz sidled up to Torio saying, "Hey. What's up boss?"

Torio looked around furtively, and when he saw no other cops near him, he whispered, "Nigguhs is up. I can see all of them now, hanging from the trees like old, abandoned sneakers," as the two of them headed down the front stairs of the station house.

By the time they reached their cruiser, as Diaz headed to the passenger side and Torio approached the driver's side, a deep voice from the adjacent cruiser softy said, "Did anyone ever tell you that you two fairies favor each other in more ways than one? Two little runts that have wings and that melanated, swarthy complexion kind of like mine. Yet, I bet you fashion yourselves to be 'white' boys. Or shall I be more specific and say that you wannabee white supremacist boys."

"Oh yeah? Well what do you wannabee, Mr. Mulatto Pinto," asked Diaz.

"I wannabee like Jack Johnson and break you in by whupping the living shit out of your little monkey ass," said Booker as he stepped out of his cruiser.

"Well, that wouldn't be a smart move to make, seeing how we all are packing Glocks," said Torio.

"Wow. What is this? Love at first sight? I can drop both of you little bitches with one shot from the front," warned Booker T.

Chapter 23

Bully and Addict Must See Role to Rehab

Human beings can be so naïve, shallow and superficial in their thinking, expectations and discriminations. On one hand, we are put through many years of medical study and apprenticeship to be allowed to perform surgery on living human bodies. But on the other hand, the same society takes the same type of people through a mere several months of class instruction and pistol range firing exercises, and then gives them the authority to take peoples' lives and freedom, all based on this "officer's"own mood, discretion and interpretation of "THE LAW." In each of these paradigms, we hapless "citizens" would be dealing with various perverted versions of bullying and tribelism.

In the case of the Delta 101 car, we have an instance of two such cops having been authorized by the local government to behave as aforementioned to its farthest extreme.

After the two partners climbed into their cruiser and headed toward their patrol sector, Diaz asked Torio, "Where we headed this tour of duty, boss."

"It's your call, partner. Nigguhs is just gettin' up off of their slacker asses, anyway," volunteered Torio.

"Latinos have been 'up and at it' all day long, and will still be hustling all night. So that leaves only the nigguhs and chucks to be hunted," said Diaz.

"Now, how am I supposed to know what the fuck a damn 'Chuck' is supposed to be," asked Torio.

"'Chuck', my dear old chap, is the nickname for Charlie. As in Mr. Charlie…like you gringoes," said Diaz. "It's a Marine Corps, Vietnam War era term."

"Aw. I see. You're supposed to be another Jarhead like that Hampton baboon, huh."

"Yeah. Only that motherfucker's got issues. I sometimes wonder if his ass wasn't so big, would he be so bad. And then, I realize he could be worse. Ain't nothing worse than a giant nigguh walking around in a police uniform with a gun on his hip and a chip on his shoulder, out to kill every honkey he sees."

"Ain't that called a Bigger Nigger Complex," asked Torio.

"Nah. That big motherfucker is half ya'll, partner," said Diaz.

"Well, forget about it. Big galoot-assed Hampton getting smaller will never happen. He's just gonna be a big old armadilla niggah gorilla nightmare that's gonna haunt us 'til we leave this job. Once they send you here to Delta Rapid Response, no other precinct wants to be bothered with your ass. Especially a little Chihuahua mothuhfuckuh like you. You've sent more Puerto Ricans up the river, doing more time than I've got left to live. I don't fuck with nobody until they fuck up. You? You make a mothuhfuckuh fuck up, then go lock him up. Kind of like entrapment," said Torio.

"Hey. Way I see it, if the shoe fits, you gotta wear it. It all breaks down to court time and overtime rates on days off and mucho pesos. My kids need food, housing and shoes. Your kids need the same basic shit. Who else gives a flying fuck, Mr. Chuck? I've gotta maintain my monthly overtime average. They garnish my paycheck every payday, and give it all to my ex: leave me the pay stub to pay the taxes. And if I'm lucky, I can scrape up some court time and overtime pay to live off of," said Diaz.

"Yeah. Like they say on that nigguh record, 'It's cheaper to keep her.' Now, they've reduced you to robbing Peter to pay Paul. In your case, it's more like robbing Pedro to pay Paulo," teased Torio.

"Fuck you, Torio. You're just mad 'cause you're too brown; and they say you can see the mountains of Africa from Sicily. Lest we forget: didn't that black dude Hannibal lay big black cock all over your little island after he conquered the Romans," asked Diaz.

"And what about the black part of your little midget ass, fuck-face? I can't see no Arawak in your knappy hair," countered Torio.

"I'm what they call 'natural police'," replied Diaz.

"You're a little bald headed 'natural nigguh.' You can't even grow enough hair to have a natural; let alone be big enough to qualify as a pimple on a real natural cop's ass," said Torio.

"Damn, Joey. Why you got to be hating, man?"

"No hate. I just call a spade a spade, mothuhfuckuh."

"That's not what your mama calls me," mumbled Diaz.

This sort of ignorant banter would continue throughout the evening; never ending in a physical fist fight. Both morons were too ignorant to converse or relate on any deeper level. "Aggressive" patrol was underway.

CHAPTER 24

Asymetrical; Down and Dirty Again

It was really disgusting and frustrating for Booker, by now a seasoned veteran of eight years on the force, to have to watch the various prima donna beneficiaries of the good ole boy network get promoted and garner all of the job privileges with no problems or obstacles at all. And it really was insulting to see them get promoted not only to detective, but to sergeant, lieutenant and captain with only an average of at least three years service on the job.

Booker T. Hampton had put up with a lot of racist supremacy of individual cops for the sake of Prairie Cove and the Prairie Cove Police Department. Just to make sergeant, he had to deal with the examiners cheating him and other "blacks" on their scores on five successive Sergeants Promotional Exams. And once he finally attained the rank by suing the racist supremacists, they still cheated him three more times on the lieutenant's exams before he transferred those efforts and study times to obtaining his Juris Doctorate degree from night classes at West Central Illinois Law School.

Nevertheless, once Booker received his new sergeant's stripes, the good ole boy network proceeded to wait for him to set up his own demotion and "execution." There, Retired Sergeant Percival V. Jarvis warned his nephew Booker that, "These kinds of insidious people have learned over the years that they don't have to go after a "colored" man anymore to bring him down. Their style now is to set him up, and give him enough rope to hang himself on the slightest procedural violation where they could decide whether to hang him or let him go. This was all a part of the hidden agenda," said Percy. "You just do everything by the book: go to work; do your job; get your pay check; and go the fuck home. Don't play no cute games with these no-good sons-of-bitches. The sergeant who masters the departmental rules and regulations, and criminal law and criminal procedure is the crooked cop's worst King Kong nightmare. Especially if the sombitch is black."

One day Booker T was returning from a weekend in Chicago when he found himself stuck in a massive traffic jam on while trying to get back to Prairie Cove for a tour of duty that same night. It was about five hours before his midnight shift started. Booker had the presence of mind to call ahead to his precinct to let the on-duty lieutenant know that he was stuck in traffic up north around Chicagoland and would most likely be a little late arriving at the precinct for his tour of duty. It was the same respect all sergeants accorded the lieutenants when anticipating being late before a tour of duty. Once the sergeant arrived for duty, the lieutenant would get to go home about four hours early...unauthorized by his superior, a captain or above.

Young Lt. Francis Hagler answered the phone; listened to and conversed with Sgt. Hampton, saying, "No problem Booker. Take your time. I've got you covered."

Booker eventually made it through the traffic and arrived at his precinct. By the time he got dressed in his uniform, he was only about five minutes late getting down the stairs to the duty desk. Lieutenants always covered for sergeants because it is the sergeants who always cover for the lieutenants, allowing them to get the early-go.

Yet, as Booker walked behind the duty supervisor's desk to

look at the new duty roster for his tour as patrol supervisor, his duty supervisor, Lt. Patrick Hamm said, "Oh, Sgt. Hampton. Give me a written report explaining why you were late for your tour of duty and missed roll call."

This was unheard of prior to this time. Sergeants and lieutenants historically worked together as an inseparable team. Booker calmly looked at the young lieutenant and his seven "white" patrol officers and clerks standing and sitting around his desk, smiling at the lieutenant's apparent under-handedness in "breaking the new 'nigger' sergeant's balls." They all, including the lieutenant, were sipping a gold-colored, frothy liquid from sixteen ounce red plastic cups. Booker respectfully replied, "No problem lieutenant," and as he walked out of the area, he glanced into the hallway trash can, and observed a large number of empty beer cans inside the trash bag lined 45-gallon trash can.

Judging from the fact that the evidence room door was still open, he also could see other cops opening cans of the skunk beer from cases confiscated as evidence in raids on unlicensed after-hours drinking establishments months ago. Seeing how beer only has a shelf life of about six weeks, this is why it's called "skunk beer"; it's flat and also called "panther piss," and other derogatory names.

Booker wasted no time in writing the foolish report and handed it to the buzzed-drunk lieutenant while he and his ignorant errant officers in full uniform and on duty, were still standing around the duty desk, snickering and sipping the alcoholic beers.

Wanna Play Mind Games; It's on Bitch!

Booker calmly walked out to his patrol supervisor's cruiser, drove to a pay phone in the parking lot of the supermarket on his old foot beat, and made a call to the duty deputy chief who had, on a previous occasion, given Booker his home phone number to keep him abreast of all activities ahead of the police chief. When the deputy chief answered, Booker calmly said, "I'm sorry to bother you, sir, at this time of the evening. Per your request, I'm just keeping you informed that our Bravo duty supervisor, Lt. Pat Hamm, along with the four walking beat officers on the evening tour, is drinking evidence beer at the duty desk and in the evidence locker as we speak."

"Good work, Sgt. Hampton. Do not say a word to them or anyone else. I'm on my way there. You proceed on with your duties as patrol supervisor. That way I can catch them red-handed for my own edification without involving you," advised the deputy chief.

Fifteen minutes later, the deputy chief arrived at the Bravo precinct house; went straight to the trash bins and retrieved a 45-gallon trash bag half full of empty beer cans having fingerprints and DNA all over them.

Lt. Hamm and the four drunken officers of the 6pm to 2am shift were relieved of duty and replaced with spare units from the other surrounding PCPD precincts. The next morning the deputy chief in charge of patrols met Lt. Hamm and Sgt. Hampton in the Bravo captain's office. "Close the door, Booker. Pat, let me put this shit in a nutshell before we proceed, seeing how you're still having a hangover. You brought this chicken shit about because you're pissed off because Sgt. Hampton here, won't let you have his overtime at the community meetings. So, per your well-known vindictive nature, you called yourself stroking him last night for not going along with your game plan. Well, for your information and edification, I specifically and specially ordered the good sergeant to attend those meetings because both he and I have to answer up each and every week downtown at police headquarters to the police chief, command staff, community leaders, preachers and their respective residential constituents as to what kinds of problems and solutions we had been aware of and addressed in Bravo precinct. Who in the hell are you to undermine my direct orders and interfere in my efforts?"

"Deputy, sir, I... I don't know what you mean?"

"Lieutenant, don't try to play mind-fuck with me. You know full goddamn well what the hell I mean. You're trying to pull the same cockeyed chicken shit here that got you kicked out of your last precinct and dumped over here. You want to pull rank and hog all of the fucking overtime. This is why you've been fucking with all of my sergeants. A goddamn lieutenant drinking fucking skunk booze on duty, in one of my precinct houses with four uniformed, on-duty foot beat cops getting blitzed? You must be out of your freaking gourd. If this shit had reached headquarters or the news outlets, my ass would have been fried and fired. I'm not losing my rank, my job or my goddamned pension behind you and your self-serving fucking asshole bullshit. You're dismissed until I can find something else to do with your foolish ass and take this damned report and rip it up right now."

After Lt. Hamm left the office, the deputy chief turned to the sergeant saying, "Booker, I apologize for making you a witness to all this shit; but what the fuck: you called me: I didn't call you. You're a damn good cop: but that sombitch is about as useful as balls-on-the-pope. As a sergeant, everywhere you go, you make me and the rest of the department look good. But, you know the protocol of the rules and regs. When there's two superior officers in a beef, the junior rank has to take a hike. I pre-emptively spoke to Captain Danny Murphy over at Echo Base about this incident. He says you were one of his training officers when he first came on the job, and that you helped his dad Ron get elected Patrolman's Union President by swinging him the black vote on Bravo. It's time you start winding down in the action department and start studying for Lieutenant. Matty wants you over there with him. Whattaya say?"

"Well, Deputy, with all due respect, I am kind of sick and tired of being disrespected and mistreated by these foolish, young superior officers. Not only do they disrespect me and try to disgrace me, but they do it in front of these rookie troops. I hate to leave this base, sir, but I'd be a fool for refusing to accept this offer."

"Just watch your ass. As they say in the Corps, 'Shit rolls downhill.' This prick's own brother, a sergeant down at headquarters hates his guts. I don't know what he did to his brother, but don't let it happen to you."

"Thanks for the heads-up, sir. If he feels friskey, I've got something special for him and his boys."

"Oh-ho! I do believe! But, if a man is fool enough to fuck his own brother, who the hell are you and I. I've got something special for his ass, too. See ya' around Book."

Booker was transferred the next tour of duty to Echo precinct, the easiest precinct on the PCPD where respected veterans finished their studies to further their police careers and retire.

CHAPTER 25

If You Don't Bend, a Sombitch Can't Ride You

By now, Booker T felt he had just about seen a lot in life. It was one thing for the citizenry to respond like a stupid, submissive, sub-specie when a couple of cops stoop to go criminal. But all hope is lost when other citizenry turn coward and make a complete ass of the law and judicial system to support this sort of betrayal.

To the ordinary person, the sight of a police cruiser swinging down their street would give them some semblance of security. But in reality, this unit was not functioning as 'police.' This unit was prowling in the 'hood looking to victimize the residents and visitors. This unit's only concern was to accumulate a certain level of money that would provide these two miscreant cops with an easy source of income and bragging rights that they could take back to their communities and meet the personal financial needs of themselves and their families.

"Whoa. Don't that look like your boy Lewis Sheffield," asked Diaz.

"Whoop: there he is. What's he doing up this early in the morning? He must really be hard-up. Let's check this faggot 'coon out," said Torio.

The cruiser eased over to the curb beside the lone "black" man who was just walking down the street, minding his own business. "Yo. Lewis. Hold up my man, I want to holler at you," ordered Diaz.

As Lewis slowed down, Diaz and Torio got out of the cruiser and walked over to him, patting him down. "What you doing up this time of the morning," asked Torio.

"Aw, come on now, Joseph. I ain't no damned kid bothering nobody. I'm minding my own business, walking down the street in my own neighborhood," answered Lewis.

"Nigguh, just answer the man's question," ordered Diaz.

"Like you ain't no nigguh, neither," answered Lewis. "Just 'cause you got a badge and a gun, and run with the half-assed white boys don't mean you one of them. Git your fucking hands off me, you little Latino Uncle Tom bitch."

"Aw, we got us a bigguh nigguh boodey-bandit here," said Torio as he drew his Glock.

"Yeah, you coward bitches. Smile for the cameras. We got your asses on film for the lawsuit. Come on. Smile for the deep pockets of the city and your family's money," said an unknown, unseen voice from a window in the apartment building next to them.

"Git off me mothuhfuckuh. This ain't no South Africa. I know my rights," claimed Lewis.

"That's cool," whispered Torio as he holstered his weapon leaning toward Lewis' ear to speak.

"Nigguh, git yo' funky breath outta my face," snapped Lewis to Torio.

"Another time. Another place. You're mine, sweetie pie. Now git," whispered Torio.

"Not 'cause you say so; but, because it's my right," snapped Lewis.

The two little cops slowly backed off and got back into their cruiser.

Lewis Sheffield, still standing on the sidewalk recouping his dignity; brushing himself off from the touch of the filthy cops; wolfing and threatening to seek legal counsel.

This type of field interrogation of melanated people would continue throughout the day as the police car manned by soldier-minded oppressors ran free-will throughout the "black" and "Latino" communities.

Later that day, around noon, Torio grew tired of driving and said to Diaz, "Man I need a break. You feel like taking the wheel?"

"Not really, Bwana," said Diaz.

"What the fuck is your problem? What's with all of this "Bwanana" shit," growled Torio.

"Bwana! You know; like in the old 1950s African TV flicks like 'Ramar of the Jungle' where all of the 'coons are on safari in loin clothes, humping the white man's load on their heads moaning spiritual songs, with that one little punk-assed white motherfucker with his hands empty, always calling the shots. Like you, when you always feel it's your manifest destiny to be in charge 'cause you think you're a white man," quipped Diaz.

"Suckuh, I didn't ask you for all of that shit. I asked you did you want to take the wheel. If you can't hack it, mothuhfuck it: I'll just keep on driving," said Torio.

"Yeah. You'll keep on all right: keep on driving this same old block in circle, after circle, after boring-assed mothuhfuckin' circle. Give me the wheel." After they got out and swapped places, Diaz said, "God Damn! You shit your pants or something? Or you just don't bother wiping your funky ass? Where's today's newspaper," asked Diaz as he reached back feeling behind the seat.

He got out and pulled the Sunday morning newspaper from the back seat; put it on the driver's seat and sat on it.

After going around and sitting in the passenger seat, Torio said, "Let's take a cruise over around Hadley and Jefferson. I've still got a bone to pick with Lewis...gotta keep my nigguhs in line,"

As the cruiser turned onto Hadley under the overpass, Torio said, "Well speak of the devil: here he is."

"Where?"

As Diaz stopped the cruiser, Torio said, "You just passed the bastard. He's in the walkway between the liquor store and the railroad bed."

Lewis Sheffield had spotted the cops and struck out running toward the back of the liquor store.

Torio bolted from the cruiser on foot in pursuit. As he rounded the corner at the end of the lone building, he saw Lewis trying to climb up the six foot tall chain link fence.

Torio grabbed Lewis from behind, around the waist line; pulled him down from behind, while applying a choke hold on his neck. Lewis struggled for a moment but his body began to thrash deperately, then wane in movement as Torio continued to increase pressure to his neck. Gagging and gasping, the man's arms dropped as he commence to twitching; then ceased all movement. Yet, Torio continued increasing the pressure on the hold.

Diaz ran up, pulling Torio off Lewis' limp body; grabbing the man's wrist, saying, "Aw, shit, partner. This motherfucker's dead as a door nail." After frisking the body, Diaz further said, "He ain't got no weapon, and you choked the life out of him. What the fuck are you; a part-boa constrictor or something?"

Torio began to get excited, shouting, "Fuck! Fuck! The nigguh made me do it."

Diaz said, "Well, you best start thinking about how he made you do it, before the first responders get here." He reached down, pulled a small .25 caliber Beretta from his ankle holster. "Always carry a throw away, my man. Only in this case, we call it the give-away." He pressed the little pistol all in Lewis' limp hand, getting Lewis' fingerprints all over it. He then let the piece drop to the ground without touching it.

By this time, neighbors who had been looking out the windows of the apartments in the rear buildings and above the liquor store began to shouting. "There you coward motherfuckuhs go again. Done murdered yourself another black man," yelled an unseen female voice.

"You better get your stories together, you little no-balls

Puerto Rican bitches. Your little wannabee white asses is gonna pay for this one," yelled a male voice.

"We've already got back-up on the way. I called for the duty sergeant, too. This is a crime scene. Keep your eyes open. No telling where a round can come from back here," whispered Diaz.

The Fickle Finger of Fate

Off in the distance began the woeful wail of sirens accompanied by the yelping and howling of neighborhood dogs.

"The fuckuh went for his pocket...his coat pocket, "swore Torio.

"Man, shut the fuck up. Stay cool and save that shit for the patrol sergeant and the plainclothes guys. Don't talk to no one deep until you see the union rep and lawyer. Stick to the same story. The motherfucker had a piece and resisted you. You found yourself in danger and applied the pressure, and that's that. I'm calling the union rep now."

Police cruisers and an ambulance began arriving one after another. In all of this activity came Echo Patrol Supervisor, Sgt. Booker T. Hampton; the senior officer on the scene at that point, because the Bravo P.S. was tied up on another shooting at that time. "You two okay," Sgt. Hampton inquired. At the same time, Booker immediately recognized the body on the ground was his foster cousin Lewis Sheffield.

"Yeah Sarge," said Diaz apprehensively. He had to expect from experience that Sgt. Hampton was going to call the cards the way they fell. As Hampton went about perusing the scene in silence, Diaz whispered to Torio, "Partner. You is in deep dew-dew. Better watch your mouth; watch your step, and cover your ass 'til you speak to the union rep."

"Okay, now. What was the ETA of the EMTs," Sgt. Hampton inquired as he approached the two cops again.

"Sarge, I'll ascertain that right away," said Diaz trying to hide the fact that he had totally neglected taking that tally. But, unbeknownst to them, and due to the nature of the call, the 911 police dispatcher had already recorded that time.

"We've got one body face down. A gun is laying on the ground at the bottom of the fence," began Sgt. Hampton.

"And witnesses in the windows," yelled an unknown voice from a window. "We know you pigs always cover up for each other after doing a brother."

"Go ahead and git your lying-assed stories together. You mothuhfuckuhs better be right, 'cause a motion picture with sound don't lie," warned another anonymous male voice from a window.

By this time, other cruisers and an unmarked unit arrived with two plainclothes officers walking up to Sgt. Hampton. "Detective Beacham, besides this shit, it looks like we've got anonymous witnesses all up in these two buildings around the upper floors. Can you and your partner start canvassing the immediate area? Help yourself to as many uniformed officers as you need."

"No problem, Sarge. Det. Lieut. King is enroute from his home," said the detective.

"Thanks, Billy," said Sgt. Hampton.

Torio and Diaz each were relieved of their service weapons and removed from the scene while it was being processed by specialists. They and their cruiser were taken back to their precinct house prior to the removal of the body.

From the outset, Booker T chose not to take statements from either of the men, but based his preliminary report strictly on what was observed and said at the scene by all parties present.

The Det. Lt. Jeffrey King arrived and took over the scene of the shooting. This arrival made King the senior officer in charge, relieving Sgt. Hampton. "Something stinks here. We've got to call the cards the way they fell, Book. These two dirt bags ain't worth you, me and the rest of the Department's reputation being sullied any more than they've already done."

"Who you telling," said Booker as he climbed into his cruiser. "There's eyewitnesses and possible camera imageries all over this place in practically every window. Tell your guys not to forget to check for CCTV recordings from the stores also, Jeff. I'm like you. Knowing the two assholes involved, I could smell this was a bunch of shit from the moment I saw the poor bastard was choked to death, with the Beretta laying on the ground beside him."

"10-4, big guy. Stay cool," said King. He always emphasized that he was a hybrid Italian-Irish man, whose mother was from the Genoa region of Italy. Lt. Det. King always bragged about this when a Sicilian cop committed a disgraceful act. Even on occasions when someone mistook him to be Sicilian, King was quick to correct them to the fact that he was "Genovese"; his mom's hometown was Genoa on the Italian mainland and not on "a shit-hole little island named Sicily down at the toe of the Italian boot.

What's the Scoop?

As a few days went by, Sgt. Booker T. Hampton and Lt. Det. Jeff King and his crew of precinct detectives; along with the Ballistics Unit, Homicide Unit, Identification Unit, Coroner's Office, etc. all brought together their evidence and presented it to the State's Attorney.

"Paulie. The word's out that Matthews up in Homicide and that new State's Attorney Roberson are putting the Torio matter before the courts for a trial mainly for manslaughter," said Booker.

"Are you shitting me? With all of that film of the excessive way that scum bag choked that poor helpless guy, they have enough evidence to skip a murder trial and summarily execute Torio's greasy ass by sundown. Even a blind man can see this was pure cowardly murder. What are these fucking prosecutors trying to do; foment another American Revolution or Civil War," asked Lt. Det. King.

"This is the first sign of a cover-up; meaning that the system is going to protect a murderer cop by trying him for the lesser charge of Manslaughter thereby allowing the murderer cop to avoid the possibility of facing capital punishment, life imprisonment, or a prolonged sentence for the openly cowardly assassination. You and me both know that the all-white jury or even a judge is gonna let that creep go on the technicality that he only applied pressure as he was trained to restrain the suspect. They feel they need his racist ass back out on the streets to protect their supremacist asses by violating melanated people's rights," offered Sgt. Hampton.

"Of course, you know the cowardly little bastard has already started going around the department saying that the fault for his being brought up even for a Manslaughter conviction was 'that nigger sergeant and hybrid-assed Genovese lieutenant detective are out to get me.' He constantly harped this shit to his partner Diaz and the police union who all are starting to avoid his moronic ass. They're sick of Torio's whining. Even that corrupt little Hispanic uncle tom Diaz is ratting how Torio got himself into trouble and now is liable to suck Diaz into the morass along with himself," said King.

The police union, as with all coward killer cops, stood with Torio all the way, taking on his legal expenses with their own in-house lawyer, Attorney Maurice "Buster" Piccolo who had a reputation among intelligent, informed cops as being a whore and sellout, when offered a sweet bargain. But even they refused to go along with Torio's misinformation relative to the one black superior officer on the Department being "out to get" him.

It was supposed to be an unwritten code within the ranks of the police department that as long as a fellow police officer was lawfully performing his duty according to Department Rules and Regulations, but was the victim of human error, the troops would form a "blue line" around him. This was a fallacy. As long as the killer cop was a "white," the rank and file wouldn't let him hang.

The line around Torio was fading to very thin by his incessant whining, "For crying out loud! What the fuck am I; a nigguh? What I gotta do; suck up to the Irish to keep from getting warehoused away for the rest of my fuckin' life," asked Torio.

A year later, after time had defused the situation, and Torio's hair turned snow white, his case went before an all-white jury and he was found not guilty of even Manslaughter and all other counts. He was free to return to duty in the streets of Prairie Cove, and awarded all of his back pay, sickdays, and vacation days with interest. And the "black" community had a shit fit, and began to forgive and forget.

One week later, Torio was back on duty, in lily-white Alpha precinct doing an off-duty assignment called a "paid police detail"; parked outside of a closed liquor store at 3 a.m. in the morning. It had been regularly burglarized. All was secure, but the dumb little cop appeared to have made the mistake of dozing off asleep while sitting out front of the store in his new yellow and tan Chevy Camaro convertible. Whatever else may have happened, the effects of a copper-jacketed hollow point, .357 magnum projectile entered his mouth; blew out his pineal gland, and the back of his head. Unfortunately, the cowardly killer cop never felt any pain.

"You know, Uncle Percy, when the store manager came to unlock the doors the next morning, she found that sucker just sitting there in his car with the remnant of his head tilted back against the head rest, with his mouth gapped open, and parts of his brains and dried blood splattered all over the car interior behind him. The poor woman was retching and horrified out of her wits," said Booker.

"Yeah, and I heard the funeral was in a storefront, little old funeral parlor over in Little Italy. Way I heard it, hardly anybody attended but the family; local hoodlums; a couple members of surrounding small town police departments and security guards; a handful of Sicilian Prairie Cove cops and of course the PCPD command staff. I know they say he was a rotten son of a bitch, but not even his partner had the decency or respect to attend his 'sending away'," said Percy. "The undertaker may as well have displayed the corpse like they did back in the old days: propped the coffin up in the front window so mothuhfuckuhs could just drive by, sneak a peak, and keep on trucking."

"Dogs run together in a pack, but sooner or later, they turn around and start biting each other in the back," said Booker. "Most of the major religions of the world encourage prayer, forgiveness, and a slew of other responses humans should express during times when harm befalls one while walking 'through the valley of the shadow of death', while being trapped in this crucible called 'life'," offered Booker T.

"Yeah, well since that O.J. murder trial decision, our damned county court system has been dead set on coming to Judgments. The judges show their fear of not supporting their local rogue cops who commit the cowardly, inhuman act of hunting down an innocent black man, and taking his life as a trophy. The big question is why the judges and juries who swear to be patriotic Americans allow these kind of cops to go unpunished," said Percy.

"It's all because black people just don't get it...at the end of the day, whitey will always be whitey," answered Booker. "Since the beginning of time, before they had domesticated beasts of burden and machines, they've always had nigguhs. Since slavery was abolished, the dirty bastards have had it in for nigguhs in a perverted kind of way. But, like you said, 'This old-time shit has been boiling up since the O.J. decision.' And Lord have mercy if they ever elect a black President of anything. Now, these racist, supremacist sombitches feel that the cops are their last line of defense against a bunch of angry, vengeful nigguhs turning into savage beasts bent on revenge for what these whites have been doing to us for the past five hundred years."

"These cops haven't the slightest idea or intent on acting as 'police.' They think and act as soldiers fighting a common 'black' eternal enemy in a war on their own homeland," said Percy. "They're just pissed-off because they cain't hog-it-all. If the late great five-star General Dwight David Eisenhower had been even-handed with all of his troops serving in his army during World War II, he would have had more reason to summarily hang whiteys the same way he had lynched his own black troops. And he didn't even bother to ship their bodies home. The racist traitor white rank and file buried them all in Normandy, rather than bring them home for interment in the United States. And many of these black American soldiers were only alleged to have raped foreign white females," added Percy. "Imagine that? Hanging a man on a white woman's claim that he stole some pussy? You'd think it was the white men who got raped instead of the white women."

"Wow, Uncle Percy. Police in the United States are supposed to be trained to work with and for the community that pays them a salary for their professional service that culminates mostly three decades later into really nice lifelong, guaranteed pensions. These two cowardly assholes in little old Prairie Cove were behaving like marauding soldiers on a search and destroy mission; no different than the U.S. Army, Vietnam atrocity at My Lai where that white lieutenant and his boys butchered unarmed Vietnamese citizens trying to escape from their American "liberators" premeditated intent to butcher and bury them."

"And you know that," answered Percy. "Yet, the sad part of this mess in PC is that there is a certain segment of its citizenry sitting in judgment, who finds security and solace in finding this same kind of shit is fitting and proper in an American town today. Or maybe they just fear the loss of white cop protection from marauding 'niggers' if they call the cards the way they fall."

"But, what's even more confusing and perverted is that no cop within the entire Prairie Cove Police Department had the courage to isolate the culprits and speak in defense of the citizens they swore to serve and protect. The most they did was take the assassins off of street patrol and bury them in the police dispatcher's unit and other districts until dumb-assed, forgiving nigguhs forgot about poor Lewis Sheffield," said Booker.

"In the meantime, now as in my time, the generally accepted police procedure is for all patrol units, especially on the midnight shift, to lay low on cruising the black neighborhoods and not get caught like that asshole Torio, sleeping on the job. This shit will last for about one month before the forgiveness of the brainwashed black Christians takes full effect in "defusing" the whole situation. By that time, hardly anyone will remember the victim negro or how that slime-ball Torio died," said Percy.

"Uncle Percy, all I know is that every time I run into a person with their lips dripping with hate toward someone they've never met before, I'll realize I've met another person who is bending to the cowardice in his heart; has lost his soul and humanity. America seems to be full of these illegitimate traitors who feel it their divine right to hide behind bum cops and to have America all for themselves. I can feel my heart beating in my ears like the pounding of war drums. To keep from losing my soul, I always try to remember what Gramma Mary Alice and Grampa Austin used to tell me to repeat: 'Bless their hearts. They don't know no better.' Don't bend to their endless cycle of revenge. Just keep my mouth shut; take care of business; and take over."

"Yeah. Don't you be the executioner. Nobody gets away with anything after living in this realm," said Percy.

– THE END –

ABOUT THE AUTHOR

E.S. Louis is the pen name of a veteran Police Officer who served for 33 years (17 years in-grade as a Sergeant) in the Police Department of a major city in the USA. Louis worked out of Precincts in high crime sections of the city. His experiences helped develop the main character (Booker T. Hampton) for his first book "Don't Bend" in his "Prairie Cove" series. Booker T. learns how to deal with racial prejudice and the realities of life and love in the fictitious towns of Prairie Cove and Hallville, somewhere along the Mississippi, where the Mississippi and Illinois Rivers converge.

CPSIA information can be obtained
at www.ICGtesting.com
Printed in the USA
BVHW041323150819
555787BV00014BB/464/P